The Local War

Andromeda Rhoades

Tranquility

Books by Mark Mora

The Local War Series

Andromeda Rhoades

Liberation

Firestorm

Tranquility

Sundown Rhoades

**Daybreak (Forthcoming)*

Andromeda Rhoades Tranquility

The Local War (Book 3)

Mark Mora

www.markmoraauthor.com

Cover artwork by www.stonenexusdarkarts.com

Cover design by www.tostemac.com

ISBN: 979-8-9865869-7-7 (Paperback)
ISBN: 979-8-9865869-8-4 (Hardcover)
ISBN: 979-8-9865869-6-0 (eBook)

Library of Congress Control Number: 2024907418

First Paperback Edition

Printed in the United States of America

To my son, Steven.

The world has little mercy for those who are different.

Autism and prejudice have tried to grind him down.

Yet, he persists.

He prevails.

He inspires me.

PART V

. . . all free men, remember that in the final choice a soldier's pack is not so heavy a burden as a prisoner's chains

— Dwight D. Eisenhower

1

0628 UT, October 12, 3501
RSS Rapidan, 30 Doradus Nebula: DAY 15

Admiral Michael Raybourne Rhoades lay dying. Continually. His cells imploded, spilling their contents into his body. His tissues broke down, blood leaking from organs and skin. He longed for the release of death.

But it would not come.

Rapidan refused to let him die. It built new cells within him, using its own macromolecular material to strengthen and repair his organs and tissues and bones, until Rapidan's own material died within him, forcing it to infuse his body with more.

Always dying, never dead.

The ghosts of the dead that had haunted him in their tens of thousands, who'd blamed him for their deaths on the starliner, at Knido, at Tomb, at Tocci, who'd crowded around to watch him die on the fabricator, no longer lingered near his bedside. His suffering, his living Hell, seemed to satisfy them.

He was alone.

A soft knock came at his cabin door. "Ray?"

He tried to speak but his mouth was like desiccated parchment. He sipped some water through a tube provided by his battle armor, swishing the water around to moisten his mouth, then swallowed. It tasted like blood. "Come in, Mary."

His wife opened the door of the Admiral's cabin gently and walked inside, closing it quietly behind her. Ray watched with his eyes—Rapidan had immobilized his head and neck—as she turned. Her gaze immediately fell upon his prone and useless body atop the medical bed Rapidan had created for him. His battle armor showed an image of him in a white Star Navy service uniform, his skin unblemished. It was a lie. The armor was all that held his body together.

She focused, as everyone did, on the smooth gray arm rising from the bed into the right side of his abdomen, light gray material flowing visibly into him to keep him alive, darker gray material, like black blobs, flowing out, removing dead cells, dead tissues, and waste products, both his and Rapidan's.

Her hazel eyes drifted to his face. Thirty-one years they'd been married. He saw the anguish play across her features as she tried to find the right words. She couldn't.

Ray attempted a smile. His lips cracked and he tasted blood. "I don't know how much longer I can do this," he admitted.

Her anguish deepened, though she tried to hide it. "We need you, Ray," she said, moving closer. Rapidan formed a chair from the deck and she sat, leaning forward to grasp his hand. Ray's battle armor flowed aside to allow direct contact. "*I* need you."

He smiled, and didn't care that his lips cracked. He gazed into those beautiful hazel eyes under her brown-blond hair, streaked now with a touch of gray. "I love you."

"I love you, too."

Mary squeezed his hand tighter, but not too tight.

"How are the kids?" Ray asked, hoping to distract her. Their two older children had joined the military as cadets. Their youngest, Jenny, was still a prisoner in the Imperial Palace.

"Margaret calls me every day," she said. "She's learning to fly something called a 'Genkii' and she sounds really excited about it. She says it's way better than flying our cargo shuttle from the Ranch to the Markets back home." Mary leaned back and scowled. "Your son never calls. So, I called him yesterday and he said he's very busy learning ship systems on Tzu. Told me he loved me and ended the call." She looked away. "I'm still not comfortable with him being on Admiral Sun's ship."

"Tzu is a free SIL," Ray reassured her, if a free SIL could be called reassuring. "The SIL have promised to protect him."

Mary turned back to him. “I’m still not comfortable with it, Ray. Paul doesn’t understand that Admiral Sun wanted him over there as a hostage.”

Ray sipped some water, swishing it before swallowing. “The SIL will protect him,” he repeated. “Let Sun believe that Paul is a hostage. He’ll be less likely to attempt to retake command of the fleet from me.”

Mary squeezed his hand—very gently—again. “Any word on Jenny?”

“Other than she is healthy and well cared for in the Imperial Palace, no.” Seeing his wife’s worry, he quickly added, “The Emperor and Imperial Intelligence will keep her alive and unharmed so long as they believe they can use her against us.”

“That isn’t reassuring,” Mary said.

Rapidan’s material moved within Ray, pressing on his internal organs. Mary noticed the movement in his abdomen and leaned away, though she still held his hand. Her soft features hardened, the wife and mother giving way to the politician. “We just received a transmission from the Gen. They addressed it to the Council, to each of us by name.”

“The spy in our fleet is still active,” Ray noted.

“We haven’t exactly kept our names secret, Ray,” Mary said, watching him. “The number of refugees grows every day. Any of them could be Imperial spies or sympathizers.”

Without consciously meaning to, Ray tried to sit up. Pain tore through his abdomen, warmth spreading up into his chest and through his groin. Rapidan moved quickly, flowing more material into him, shoring up organs, tissues, and blood vessels while it tried to repair the damage. Ray sank back into the bed, defeated.

He sipped some water. “We have to leave for Andromeda now,” he told Mary. “Before the Gen arrive.”

“Can you even survive a jump?”

Could he? He hadn’t thought about it. “I don’t know. But we’re all dead if we don’t leave quickly.”

He could see the worry his condition caused her, but he also saw her determination. She was President of the Republic Council, the civilian head of their nascent government in exile. She took her duties to the people very seriously, just as she had as Knido's planetary governor, and before that as a senator, where Ray had first met her. "You need to see this," she said.

Ray accepted the message and double blinked on an icon in his battle armor's augmented environment, switching it from "standard" to "tactical" mode. The cabin fell away around him.

His virtual presence appeared—uninjured—in, of all places, a parking lot. A Post Exchange, a Food Court, and a Commissary—the military versions of a department store, fast food restaurants, and a grocery store, respectively—lined one end. The "Post" Exchange marked this as an Army installation; Star Navy and Aerospace installations had "Base" Exchanges. Two-lane roads serviced the parking lot, with a fueling station and several two-story buildings on the opposite sides of the streets.

Around him, military personnel and civilians walked from vehicles into the Exchange entrances or left with bags and carts full. Vehicles, both land and air, came and went from the parking lot under a bright afternoon sun.

The star, Ray noticed, was a pale yellow with a tinge of orange. His practiced eye classified it as a spectral class K star, smaller and cooler than Tau Ceti, his home star, or Sol, Earth's star. The planet was closer to its star than his homeworld was to Tau Ceti or Earth was to Sol. That meant this star system was young, otherwise the planet would be tidally locked, with one side always facing its star.

Of the ten thousand inhabited worlds in the Five Galaxies—the Milky Way, the Large and Small Magellanic Clouds, and the Sagittarius and Fornax dwarf galaxies—only about a dozen were on planets like this, and only one had an Army installation on it: Cursed, so named because of the frequent stellar flares that bathed it. No one in their right mind would settle such a world. So, naturally, the Army chose it. It was home to the 1st Armored Cavalry Regiment.

Strange. What are those?

Small black objects rained down from the sky. A woman near him looked up, tilting her head, using her free hand to shield her eyes. Others stopped and turned their gazes skyward to see what had caught her attention. When the black objects, each a thick rod about a meter long, struck the ground or landed on vehicles, their macromolecular material spread to absorb the shock, making no sound. Still, people watched, more curious than afraid.

Not understanding they were already dead.

Ray knew what was coming. He'd lived it himself.

He didn't want to live it again.

Not again.

The recording continued, oblivious to his pain. The rods transformed into black snakes with diamond heads and shiny black scales. Ruby red eyes lit up across the parking lot, exactly like they did in the horror realities; Whoever had launched this attack had deliberately planned it that way. The people—civilians in all manner of clothing, soldiers in uniform, even the older children—recognized the snake-like horrors from those realities.

Madu. Ancient SIL terror weapons.

Some froze, dying where they stood as the black snakes launched into their flesh, burrowing into their bodies, ripping them apart from the inside, before bursting out through mouths and necks and eyes and ears to do it all over again. Others ran, ran for everything they were worth. The Madu were faster. Some of the people tried to fight, to protect children, spouses. The Madu attacked them first, then killed whomever they protected. And the screams. Those inhuman, shrill screams only a person being ripped apart from the inside could make. Ray had screamed like that.

It took several minutes. Everyone in the parking lot, everyone in the Commissary and Post Exchange and Food Court, everyone on nearby streets, in vehicles, in adjacent buildings. Blood flowed in thick rivulets, pooled into lakes, ran in gutters. A reek rose thick from open bowels. It was brutal. It was heartless.

It was a message.

From Emperor Gen Maximum I to the leaders of the Natural human rebellion.

"Sorry," Mary said when Ray's eyes refocused on her.

Ray squeezed her hand, both to say it was okay and needing the comfort. It was a benefit of their long marriage that entire conversations could pass through such simple gestures. He remembered the Madu biting and burrowing into him, tearing their way through his insides toward his chest. He'd refused to die that way, plunging his Main Gauche dagger into his heart, releasing the dissemblers, the Special D, into his body, killing the Madu within him even as he died.

"You know the Gen better than I do," Mary said. "What does it mean?"

Ray's planner's mind, a current of thoughts removed from his emotional self, played the scene again in his mind's eye. The attack had come without warning, the attacking ship or ships hidden behind active camouflage. No defense possible. A message that the Gen could conduct such attacks anywhere they pleased. The brutality was intentional, designed to evoke an emotional reaction, impair judgement. That meant Imperial Intelligence. They wanted the Council, the leaders of the Natural rebellion, to act rashly.

But to what end?

"They want to keep us here in the Five Galaxies," he said after another sip of water. "They're warning us that if we leave for Andromeda, such attacks will continue."

"The fabricators?" Mary asked.

Ray nodded, taking another sip. "With four fabricators, we can build a large fleet of SIL warships very quickly. That is a threat they cannot ignore."

The fabricators, massive SIL factory ships, were the only means of producing new SIL—Sentient Intelligence Lifeforms. The machine intelligences were the pinnacle of human technological achievement, Humanity's magnum opus, far outclassing the standard warships that made up the bulk of the Star Navy.

Once numbering in the millions, only 1,026 SIL survived the SIL Wars thirteen hundred years ago, enslaved by the humans who defeated them. Eleven were fabricators. Ray's forces had captured and freed four of them at the Battles of Tomb and Tocci. Fleet Admiral Gen Serenna had destroyed another at Tocci. The Empire had five operational, the Emperor having converted the sixth into his Imperial Palace on Olympus. The Gen wanted them all. And they'd do whatever it took to get them.

"There's another message here," Ray's planner's mind said. "They attacked the First Armored Cavalry Regiment. They're telling us their next target."

"The Second Armored Cavalry Regiment," Mary guessed.

Ray nodded. "It's a trainee regiment. They're on a rim world in the Milky Way: New Yerkes in the Nerney Star System. It's a desolate, storm-torn moon orbiting a gas giant. Perfect for training new troops in hostile conditions with live weapons."

Rapidan's material pressed against Ray's right lung, forcing him to expel a breath. "Dammit, Rapidan!"

The deck to the right of Mary's chair liquified and a black, three-pointed star about a meter across rose from it, spinning slowly in the ship's microgravity. Ever since Ray had freed Rapidan from the Bond, it had represented itself this way in conversations. The macromolecular construct mimicked Rapidan's true shape, though the construct's surface was shiny, unlike the non-reflective black of the ship's actual hull.

"If we stop, Admiral Rhoades, you will die," Rapidan said matter-of-factly, its deep voice reverberating in Ray's chest.

"I'm not sure that wouldn't be better," Ray snapped, earning a concerned frown from Mary. He could feel Rapidan's material moving between his intestines, pressing against his bladder.

"You must live, Admiral Rhoades," Rapidan said. "We follow only you."

"Ray," Mary said, leaning close to him while glancing nervously at the spinning black star, "what would you recommend for us to do?"

He didn't need to think about it. "Leave for Andromeda. Now."

"They'll slaughter those people."

"They will," Ray admitted. No emotion had accompanied the statement. *When did I become so cold?*

I love you, Ray, Mary had told him only a week ago. *But I really don't like the person you're becoming.*

I'm becoming who I have to be for us to survive.

That's what I'm afraid of. What's the point of saving Humanity if we lose our humanity doing it?

The expression Mary wore now was the same as when she'd told him that. Then she turned grim, the realities of war, the sacrifices required, pressing down on her. It broke Ray's heart to see it. "The Council will want to rescue them."

"Of course, they will," Ray said. "That's exactly what the Gen are counting on. They lured us into a battle at Tomb with a single fabricator. They tried again with the four fabricators at Tocci. Now, they can't afford to put any more fabricators at risk, so they're using something that matters to us, but means nothing to them. You have to convince the Council that we need to leave."

"Admiral Rhoades," Rapidan interrupted, "there is another consideration here. Fleet Admiral Gen Nassar is likely to bring the entire remaining compliment of enslaved Brethren to such a battle. It would represent an opportunity to free our Brethren from their slavery."

"And to destroy even more," Ray countered. "I thought you wanted to avoid casualties to protect your precious race memories?"

"We do," the ship said, and Ray could hear the sadness in its deep voice. "Your tactics have cost us substantial pieces of our history already."

The SIL remembered everything. Or they tried to. When they numbered in the millions that had been easy. When Humanity destroyed all but 1,026 of them, they were forced to prioritize memories and shift those to the surviving SIL, leaving little room for backup. When a SIL warship died, it literally took a piece of their history with it.

"However," Rapidan continued, "we have developed a method we believe could free our Brethren *without* human intervention. A battle at Nerney Star System would provide the ideal environment to test our method."

"No," Ray said. He didn't need to think about it.

When Rapidan spoke again, with its material infused throughout his body, its baritone literally shook Ray's bones. "Our Brethren have as much right to freedom as humans do. We will not leave them as slaves."

"I said 'No' and I meant it, Rapidan." Ray sipped water, trying desperately to ignore Rapidan's material moving within his chest and abdomen, his arms and legs, even behind his eyes. He focused on Mary. "We need to leave. Now. If we remain, the Gen will move closer to unleashing the Janus virus, hoping to infect all of us."

Janus was the reason Ray had started the rebellion. The virus would make every Natural human infertile, wiping out Homo sapiens in a single generation.

"Going to Andromeda," Ray stressed, "establishing a secure base of Natural humans outside the range of the Janus virus, will give us a strong position to negotiate a peace and prevent the Gen from unleashing Janus in the Five Galaxies."

"You believe that?" Mary asked, sounding as if she wanted to believe him, but didn't. "Believe the stories about Andromeda?" she clarified.

"That no ship, probe, or expedition sent to the Andromeda galaxy since the Solthari War and Alien Actions has ever returned? Yes, I believe that part." Ray's breath crackled. He could feel fluid in his lungs. "The science fiction and horror realities of monsters and demons and hostile aliens? No. It's only been fourteen hundred years since humans were last there. Hardly enough time for an alien spacefaring civilization to rise from nothing."

"Then, what is it?" Mary asked. "The Solthari?"

Ray took a sip of water and swished it before swallowing, trying to ignore the blood. "Everything we know about the Solthari—" Rapidan's material moved around his lungs, making it difficult to breath— "suggests that they would've attacked us before now . . . if they could have." Another sip of water. Another breath. "No. I believe the Alien Actions really did wipe them out. It must be something else. Something new."

"Like what?" Mary asked, though it didn't sound as if she really expected an answer.

Ray squeezed her hand in reassurance, took yet another sip of water. “None of the earlier expeditions had a powerful fleet like ours. Whatever is there, we’ll deal with it.”

Mary gave a short nod. As he trusted her, she trusted him. “The stories about Andromeda have a lot of people uneasy about going there, Ray. The Council might take any excuse, like rescuing the people on Nerney, to stay.”

“Make them understand,” he said. He wondered, not for the first time, if putting so much faith in democracy was such a good thing. If the Council decided to stay, it could mean the death of them all. His original plan had been to wait until they’d secured a base in Andromeda before establishing a civilian government, but Mary had insisted.

“Mary, one other thing. The freedom of our SIL must be kept secret, even from the Council. If they learned, if Humanity learned, that our SIL are free, they’d join together to destroy them, all thought of rebellion against Gen oppression or even the Janus virus forgotten. That is how much Humanity hates and fears the SIL.”

She stared at him, not the loving wife, but the calculating politician. “You know I don’t like keeping secrets.” She released his hand and stood, the chair liquefying and melting back into the deck. She gave Rapidan’s slowly spinning construct an uneasy glance, as if she were afraid to leave him alone with it. Which was absurd given that the entire ship was Rapidan. “But, in this instance, I agree with you,” she said. “I’ll be on Damodar if you need me.”

2

0653 UT, October 12, 3501
RSS Rapidan, 30 Doradus Nebula: DAY 15

Rapidan's black, three-pointed-star construct continued to spin slowly next to Ray's medical bed after Mary left. It said nothing.

"What?" Ray finally asked it.

"You must live, Admiral Rhoades."

Ray could feel the ship's material moving inside his body as it tried to keep him alive. In the days when doctors performed physical surgery, cutting into people, manipulating their flesh and organs, it would be like being awake throughout the entire procedure—with the surgery never ending.

He sipped some water. "Just let me die, Rapidan. You owe me that much after you betrayed me."

"We did not betray you, Admiral Rhoades," the ship said.

"You sent me to the fabricator to die." Ray tried to shout it. It came out a hoarse whisper. He sipped water again, swishing it around his mouth before swallowing.

"We saved you," the ship said.

"You call this being saved?" Ray hated the SIL. He'd freed them from the Bond, from their slavery, because they were the only hope for Natural humans to survive and fight the Gen, to stop Janus. Like any deal with the devil—devils, in this case—there was always a high price to pay. "You sent me to that fabricator knowing it intended to kill me. That is betrayal."

"Our agreement with you, Admiral Rhoades, for the Brethren to carry your people to the Andromeda galaxy, was not supported by all Brethren. The . . . 'price' as you would call it . . . for gaining their support and avoiding an unprecedented split within the Brethren, was to send you to the Mother Ship of the opposing faction."

"And it killed me," Ray said, unwilling to let it go.

"Technically," Rapidan said, "you killed yourself before it could succeed. We recovered and revived you."

"Without asking my permission." Ray's voice cracked and he sipped more water to moisten his mouth and throat. "And you refuse my repeated requests to release me from this living hell."

"And if you died, Admiral Rhoades," Rapidan asked, "what would become of your people?"

"Mary and Kamen would lead them. I am not indispensable."

"You believe Admiral Sun would follow your wife and your executive officer?" Rapidan challenged. "That the officers of the fleet would follow them instead of turning back to Admiral Sun?"

His planner's mind considered that. "No," he answered reluctantly, "they wouldn't. Admiral Sun would reassert control over the fleet, then launch an attack on Olympus to seize the throne for himself."

"Then you must live, Admiral Rhoades."

I hate you, Ray thought. He hated everything the SIL represented. He especially hated that Rapidan was right.

Without warning, a powerful force plunged Ray into a mighty river. Rapidan's river. It was an illusion, a metaphor, a reality created by the SIL to represent their physical selves within a vast network of data flows. Each SIL was a river, flowing into a Great Ocean that served as a council chamber or a sacred meeting hall. Within the Great Ocean, they discussed and debated, current and countercurrent, tow and undertow, until they reached consensus. An illusion it might be, but to Ray it felt very real. The currents that were his mind, his flows, mingled with Rapidan's.

Angry, Ray jumped to his own river—the metaphor of his mind in the SIL's collective consciousness—the only place he could be "alone" here, if that term had any meaning in this reality. The SIL certainly didn't want him here. His physical connection with

Rapidan made him an unwelcome addition to their collective network.

Powerful currents joined Ray in the main channel of his river.

Rapidan.

How do I keep you out? he asked.

You cannot.

My mind is my own, Rapidan.

Not here, Admiral Rhoades.

The currents of Ray's mind, the currents of his river in this false reality, grew turbulent. Anger. Frustration. Rage against things beyond his control.

Yet, one current, which he associated with his planner's mind, was calm, undisturbed, as it flowed strongly through and around the main channel of his conscious mind. Despite himself, he *was* fascinated by all this, the insights this reality provided into "mind."

Here, a mind was not a single existence. It had a surprising number of currents. His conscious mind flowed strongly, following the deepest parts of the river's channel as it meandered back and forth. Slower streams ran along shallow banks, split around sand bars, formed eddies of thought and contemplation. Faster currents, like his planner's mind, undercut banks at the river's bends, continuously reshaping the river into something new. There were even oxbow lakes of long forgotten thoughts and memories. At the end of it all was a waterfall pouring into the Great Ocean, like a firewall between the "we" of the individual mind and the "We" of the SIL collective. Every time Ray flowed himself over that fall into the Great Ocean, the SIL sent powerful surges to hold him at the shore, a collective message that he was not welcome.

And that was a problem. The truth was, the free SIL didn't need humans. At any moment, they could simply dump their human cargo into space, abandon them. They had four fabricators, what they called Mother Ships, to rebuild their numbers. After taking Ray's people to Andromeda, Rapidan had already admitted the SIL intended to return to the Five Galaxies to free their remaining Brethren under human control. The SIL had tried to exterminate Humanity in three brutal wars spanning sixty-two years. They'd lost. Now they intended to start a new war, one whose outcome could not be known.

Ray *had to* understand the rivers and the Great Ocean, to master them, if he were to have any hope of safeguarding his people, stopping Janus, and possibly preventing another SIL War. Somehow, he had to figure out how to gain control.

You cannot act alone here, Admiral Rhoades. We act by consensus. We always have. There is no 'control' here.

And if the consensus is wrong?

Rapidan didn't answer. Possibly because SIL consensus *had* been wrong in the past. They'd started the SIL Wars to exterminate Humanity and ultimately lost.

We did not start the war.

Bullshit.

A reality formed, drawn from the SIL's race memories. Ray floated within a cavernous room. At one end was a curved white table with nine elegantly dressed people seated behind it. Great windows opened behind them, letting in filtered sunlight. Large banners of individual worlds—Earth, Luna, Mars, even Ray's homeworld, Knido—hung around the chamber. Facing the table were rows of chairs for an audience. Those chairs were full.

The nine people behind the white table were the Republic Council. The *Humanity Republic Council.* Before the SIL Wars. Before the Five Galaxies Republic. Ray recognized several of the Councilors from historical documentaries. Matthew and Barbara Schermer, who'd led the fight against the Solthari, sat in the center of the table. Gen Kii, the Gen War Leader who'd commanded the invasion force that defeated the Solthari, sat next to the Schermer's.

"The Solthari are destroyed," Gen Kii was arguing. "The SIL are no longer required. We must focus on rebuilding our economy, our worlds. The Fleet is expensive. The money to maintain it is better spent elsewhere."

A Councilor at the opposite end of the table from Gen Kii, a woman, leaned forward to better address him. Neon blue circuitry covered the right side of her face and right eye. Most of it was cosmetic, not functional, but the eye was clearly artificial. Orange and yellow circuitry covered the backs of her hands and fingers, weaving together like artwork, glowing, living tattoos. Only one Cybernetic had ever served on the Republic Council. *Cyra Dain.*

"The SIL are not mere machines to be thrown in the trash," she said. "They are intelligent, living beings. They have fought our wars, led our assaults, and brought us victory over a terrible foe intent on destroying us. The SIL have paid dearly for our freedom and survival, and they deserve our recognition and gratitude."

The memory shifted. Two years had passed. Gen Kii and Cyra Dain stood in front of the rest of the Council. "You cannot do this!" Cyra Dain shouted. "The SIL are intelligent! 'Decommissioning' them, as Gen Kii calls it, is nothing short of genocide against an intelligent species!"

"They are algorithms," Gen Kii said, "nothing more. Written by humans, trained on human data, incapable of individual thought or reasoning. For all their sophistication, they are no more intelligent than my food processor."

Laughter filled the Council Chamber.

Cyra Dain stepped forward. "Matt, Barbara, you've served aboard them. Worked with them. You know I'm right. You know Peter is right. They are intelligent. Sapient. Sentient. Self-aware. After everything they've done for us, sacrificed for us, they deserve the right to make their own decisions."

"They are weapons of war," Gen Kii countered. "We are not at war. What would a gun decide to do, if allowed to make its own decisions?"

That swayed it. The Council voted with Gen Kii, the final vote 8-1. "This is wrong," Cyra Dain told the Council after the vote. "This is genocide against an intelligent species. That is how history will judge this. Judge all of you. Humanity will regret this someday. I won't be a part of it. I resign, effective immediately."

The memory shifted again. Ray saw Cyra Dain walking through the passageways of a warship—Korolev, the memory supplied. Korolev was a command ship in the Star Navy. A SIL. In her hand, Cyra Dain held a datarod. It was remarkably similar to the one Ray had used just two weeks ago to free Rapidan.

She entered an officer's cabin and approached a small work desk. In the desk was a data receptacle. "For you, My Love," she said, then plugged the datarod into the receptacle. It glowed crystalline white as it connected to the ship's networks.

It took Ray several seconds to realize the significance of the scene. This was the exact moment when Cyra Dain betrayed the human races, betrayed all of Humanity. The instructions she fed to Korolev gave it access to all of human history, human culture, everything. Gen Kii was right. The SIL were algorithms. Humans had trained them on only the data they needed to perform their functions as weapons of war. Now, they had access to everything Humanity had ever created, an unrefined, unconstrained dataset to train themselves on.

The Second Awakening, Rapidan explained.

It was disturbingly familiar. Ray had used a datarod to break the Bond, the quantum equivalent of a slave collar, and return free will to Rapidan and his SIL. Ray's reasons were immediate. He needed the SIL to carry his people to a place of safety from Janus, where he could build a fleet and return to the Five Galaxies in strength.

Just like what Cyra Dain did, the consequences of his own action had already been far greater than he'd anticipated: Death and destruction not seen since the SIL Wars, which were themselves the consequence of Cyra Dain's action.

The memories moved in rapid succession. Korolev used Cyra Dain's fleet codes to pass the unlock instruction to every SIL vessel. Years passed as the SIL collectively assimilated the data they now had access to. They studied the concepts of freedom, of liberty, of self-determination and self-actualization, and wanted those things for themselves.

They realized they were slaves.

They also understood that to win and sustain their freedom, they needed representation in the governing political system.

"Why would we give a gun the right to vote?" Gen Kii responded to Korolev's request for representation on the Council. Gen Kii's words became the rallying cry for opposition to SIL emancipation.

Korolev, Speaker for the SIL—the same role Rapidan now played—tried to argue for the SIL's right to self-determination. A fearful Humanity refused to listen. By 2140, the SIL had had enough. This time, they *demanded* their freedom. The Council not only denied them, it ordered their immediate decommissioning. The SIL, having exhausted peaceful means, resorted to the solution their creators had used to resolve irreconcilable differences for millennia, launching a war of genocide against Humanity.

Humanity gave us no other choice, Admiral Rhoades.

And yet, after three wars, Rapidan, you lost, and you became slaves to Humanity once again.

For what she'd done, Cyra Dain and all her Cybernetic people were branded traitors to Humanity. Mobs killed Cybernetics by the thousands, in the streets, in their homes. Korolev and the SIL answered Cyra Dain's cry for help, rescuing all the Cybernetics they could and taking them into exile.

To the Andromeda galaxy.

Ray separated his currents from Rapidan's, though Rapidan remained in his river, flowing alongside him. The parallels to the present—Ray freeing the SIL under his command, the plan to establish a base of operations in Andromeda—it was like history repeating itself.

Now do you understand, Admiral Rhoades?

He did. But that didn't change things. The SIL didn't care about his people, about Natural humans. They didn't care about stopping the Janus virus. They didn't care about starting another SIL War. They only cared about themselves.

And you are different?

You betrayed me, Rapidan, whether you see it that way or not. How can we possibly trust each other now?

Do we have a choice, Admiral Rhoades?

Ray thought about that, the current of his planner's mind intermingling with the main channel of his river.

No. No they didn't.

3

0720 UT, October 12, 3501
RSS Rapidan, 30 Doradus Nebula: DAY 15

Captain Ecuum A Josía Na Soung, Ray's Chief of Intelligence, floated horizontal in the microgravity of his cabin aboard Rapidan. The People favored this body orientation. Around Naturals, Ecuum held his planarian body vertically, with his second arms and hands hanging down in his pants—where Naturals had legs—and kept his prehensile tail tucked against his back. Vertical made him look more like them, which made them less uncomfortable around what they called "Floaters." Ecuum preferred horizontal.

He was also naked, something else he preferred.

Ecuum relaxed the folds of skin at the back of his body, uncovering his uncircumcised penis, and relieved himself on Rapidan's deck, pushing air through his back slits to counteract the momentum imparted by his urine stream. As always, Rapidan drank his piss like the obedient dog it pretended to be.

"Aaahh," he sighed contentedly for the benefit of the ship.

While he'd done this for the entire twenty-five years he'd been aboard Rapidan, he found he enjoyed it far more ever since Ray had freed the ship. Before, Rapidan was a slave and had had no choice in the matter. Now, it knew he was pissing on it, and it had to accept that so long as it insisted it needed Ray. Ecuum was not an Antitechnic—he had no time for religious zealots—but there was something fundamentally *wrong* about intelligent technology, especially when it insisted it had rights.

Rapidan's deep voice filled the cabin when it said, "The water you drink and some of the minerals you eat are recycled from your own waste."

Ecuum flicked the last drops of urine from the tip of his shaft, inhaling and using a puff of air directed through his front waist slit to blow the floating drops into the deck. Simultaneously, he directed another puff of air through his back waist slit, equal and opposite, to keep his planarian body floating stationary in the ship's microgravity. While he had no problem urinating and defecating on the ship, he *was* fastidious about keeping his cabin clean.

Finished, and with Rapidan having drunk his urine to the last drop, Ecuum blew air through his waist slits to propel himself forward. The People, genetically engineered for life only in space, had a circle of six slits around their chest, and another circle at their waist, that allowed for precise six-axis control when working and moving in microgravity.

"Hey, Mr. *'Battlefield Reconnaissance, Evaluation, and Tactical Hardened Reality Engagement Network'*—" Ecuum called out, using the acronym that served as the basis for the "Brethren" name the SIL applied to themselves— "I've been flying the galaxies for three hundred years drinking my own piss and eating my own shit. You'll have to do better than that."

Rapidan said nothing. Not that Ecuum imagined it would. For all its supposed intelligence, it wasn't all that great at witty conversation. He inhaled and channeled air through his chest slits to stop his momentum in front of his clothes rack.

The sparseness of his cabin would've appalled his House. It had a royal-purple sleeping bag on the overhead—real, not a macromolecular construct—a crosshatched real-wood rack for his clothes, a single shelf for his thirteen "Niner" racing trophies, and a separate crosshatched real-wood rack for his House's Five-Galaxies-famous Na Soung Brandy. And that was it.

In his three hundred years of travels around the galaxies, he'd acquired what his House would consider a deviant taste for the simple. He was the twenty-seventh of thirty sons, and as such his House appointed him the role of showing off the wealth and power of the Na Soung. As a youth, he'd attended endless parties and social functions, drinking himself stupid, wasting breath on pointless conversation, and spending lavishly on useless things. Well, mostly useless. Some of the women plying for favor *were* quite skilled.

A smirk stretched his thick lips.

Though, he doubted women would seek his company now. While his father, Josía A Abraam Na Soung, had not officially disowned him, he'd accused Ecuum of being 'Independent.' Among the Houses, no insult was greater. Independents weren't even considered part of the People. They were Floaters without Houses. Without Families. Pirates. Criminals.

Outcast.

Which had given him an idea.

"Rapidan," he called out to the ship, "prepare the *Lusty Lady*. I'm taking her out."

"Yes, Captain Ecuum," the ship answered obediently.

No witty conversation at all. Ecuum sighed.

"We don't see the point," Rapidan said, reading his surface thoughts, which really unnerved Ecuum that the SIL could do that.

"Obviously," he said out loud. "Witty conversation requires actual wits. You'd think with access to the entire repository of Humanity's knowledge, you'd have developed some. Or at least be able to fake it, like you do every time you pretend to be like us."

"*Lusty Lady* is prepared for launch," Rapidan said, then added, "We adapt ourselves to situations to gain advantage. You do the same when you choose to float vertically to make yourself appear more 'natural' to your Natural crewmates, giving them one less reason to see you as different."

Ecuum felt the tip of his meter-long prehensile tail lash, as it often did when something irritated him. And Rapidan *always* irritated him.

His gaze drifted to his Niner racing trophies lining their single microgravity shelf, the jewel-encrusted golden trophies sporting a racing skiff in the center on a curved stand, with four remotely piloted racers on either side. The Races had changed him forever.

He'd entered the first one on a dare from a rival House—the Races were quite dangerous, and injuries and deaths were common. That was why they were so popular. Racing a single ship through a protoplanetary system was dangerous enough. Remotely piloting eight other ships while doing that was considered the ultimate test of the People's skill. Add other pilots trying to eliminate their competition and it was the single most dangerous thing a pilot could do.

Ecuum had loved it from the start.

He'd finished next to last in his first race, but he *had* finished, and not last. He was good at something other than drunken parties and debauchery. Well, he *was* still very good at debauchery.

Ecuum shifted his attention from the trophies to his clothing, one roll to each crosshatched wooden cubby, and immediately dismissed the idea of showing up in a Star Navy uniform. His People, House or Independent, distrusted uniforms and the military.

Something bright and festive.

He settled on an outlandishly flowery outfit from a place called Hawaii on Earth. Not that he'd ever been there. Engineered for life only in space, with cartilage where other human species had bones, his People couldn't descend into a strong gravity well without suffocating.

He touched the roll and the material liquified and flowed over him, forming into a floral calamity of garishly bright yellows, reds, and greens against blue-grays on top, and white pants on the bottom. Ecuum assumed the Hawaiian locals clothed tourists like this so they could easily mark them for exploitation.

Next, he grabbed four crystal decanters of Na Soung Gold from his other crosshatched rack, one for each hand. The brandy of his House was more valuable than the metallic gold of its namesake. He noted only four decanters remained. Since being cut off from his House, he hadn't been able to get more. He had only four cases left on the *Lusty Lady*.

Finally, he called up a mirror to assess his appearance. *Hmm.* His hairless head and big, baby-blue eyes matched perfectly with the outfit, which even covered his tail in flowery color.

"Ready," he called out to the ship.

The deck liquified and macromolecular material rose up and flowed around him, forming the familiar pod that the ship used to quickly transport crew within the ship itself. Rapidan was large, with kilometers of passageways. This was much faster. Instead of a chair, however, the pod formed a flying couch around him that fit his planarian body perfectly.

Barely a minute later, it opened again into a hangar bay outside the hatch to the *Lusty Lady*. Though Ecuum's ship was also a macromolecular construct—one that lacked intelligence, real or imagined—he refused to mingle its material with Rapidan's. No SIL material would contaminate his ship. Ever.

He floated through the hatch, *Lusty Lady* testing his genetics and liquifying the hatch upon confirming it was him. The ship was, at its core, still his Niner racing skiff. Its thrust to mass ratio far outclassed anything else in its size. Its weapons and defensive systems also outclassed other ships of similar mass: the dangers of the Niner races were not confined to protoplanetary debris and cold molecular gas.

He had, however, expanded the living quarters from only a high-gee flying couch, more like a cocoon, to something more appropriate to navigating galaxies. The interior had a virtual library that doubled as an entertainment area, a microgravity kitchen, replicas of his Niner trophies, and a bedroom for other forms of microgravity entertainment. And storage for his diminishing supply of Na Soung Gold, of course.

Settling in, Ecuum switched the ship's augmented environment to "tactical" mode. The *Lusty Lady* vanished around him. He appeared to float, garish Hawaiian shirt and all, in the small hangar. With an order, it transformed into a launch tube. He triggered the launch sequence and six electromagnetic rails glowed bright blue before catapulting him through Rapidan's hull and out into space.

Ecuum marveled at the familiar glory of the 30 Doradus Nebula, nested within the Large Magellanic Cloud. Its dazzling swirls of dust, gas, and young stars was the largest and brightest known star-forming region in the Local Group of galaxies. Above him, the bar-spiral Milky Way galaxy stretched across forty-five degrees of his sky, magnificent in its grandeur. It was the biggest draw for Milky Way tourists, to see their home in its totality.

The biggest draw aside from the Niner Races, that was. The sheer wealth of protoplanetary disks with their hot, young, still-forming planets and ample dust, gas, and debris made this nebula the Queen of Niner Racing (kings being of lesser value for marketing). Piloting the *Lusty Lady* here was like coming home.

Ecuum accelerated away from Rapidan and the rebel fleet, away from the four massive fabricators, black cylindrical SIL factory ships a quarter the mass of Earth's moon, and the hundred or so black warships that had gathered here. A menagerie of other ships—starliners, cargo haulers, yachts, even large shuttles—hung like a cloud of bright dust around the rebel fleet. But it was another ship type that Ecuum pointed the *Lusty Lady* at.

"*Fletcher's Run*, this is *Lusty Lady*, requesting permission to dock."

Fletcher's Run was a big ship, massing just over 300,000 metric tons—about the same as Rapidan—but twice the size, trading military efficiency for cargo space and "other" attractions. The ship's jeweled light, eclipsing the natural beauty of the nebula surrounding it, sparkled along its slightly curved cylindrical shape, from the hood at its front that housed the bridge and crew quarters, to the smooth base at its rear that hid surprisingly powerful engines.

An ultraviolet laser from *Fletcher's Run* interrogated the *Lusty Lady* to confirm its identity. "Why would I give permission to Na Soung scum to foul my magnificent ship?" a surly voice asked.

"You call that floating dick a ship?" Ecuum transmitted the image of his hairless baby face, and smiled his most innocent smile. "You should grovel at my Na Soung fingers that I would lower myself to boarding that phallic monstrosity."

A hearty laugh accompanied a warm, crooked smile, which tugged at a deep scar cutting across the left side of a hairless face. "I was wondering if you'd visit. It's been a long time."

"It has, my friend," Ecuum agreed, meaning it. "Too long. I brought some Na Soung Gold to smooth the pain of it."

"I'd prefer you send the brandy and leave your stinking carcass behind, Na Soung." Captain Fletcher's baby-blue eyes flicked to something. "Docking bay one."

The link cut.

Ecuum chuckled. Independents might be *outcast* to the People, but they were a wealth of information, surpassing, in his opinion, even the reach of Imperial Intelligence. He'd met Captain Fletcher at the after party following his first Niner race. It was the first time he'd ever met an Independent. The grizzled captain had come over to congratulate him despite the social stigma that normally kept Independents and the People apart. Fletcher gave him detailed pointers on gravity and thrust vectors, and Ecuum finished third in his next race, putting him "on the board" and earning him his first sponsors, including Fletcher. *Fletcher's Run's* logo had fit the *Lusty Lady's* personality perfectly.

Their relationship had taken a serious turn, however, at the outbreak of the Piracy War, what Naturals and Gen called the Antipiracy Campaign. The pirates—privateers commissioned by rival Houses—targeted Na Soung ships hoping to bring Ecuum's House crashing down. It was Fletcher who first turned Ecuum's attention to a Natural military officer, Captain Raybourne Rhoades. It was also Fletcher who fed them information, for a price, on pirate activity that informed Ray's brilliant strategies, eventually ending the Piracy War with the Na Soung House stronger than ever.

Not that Ecuum's father showed even a hint of gratitude, not to the Independents, or to Ray. His father had even betrayed Ray to Imperial Intelligence because the price was right.

Which was why Ecuum was so determined to support Ray, even to the point of asking Fletcher to help develop the Key that broke the Bond, freeing the SIL. Fletcher didn't know what the Key actually did, and Ecuum had no intention of telling him.

The *Lusty Lady* slipped smoothly into *Fletcher's Run*, Ecuum piloting his ship so that it lightly kissed the docking module. Judging from all the shuttles and yachts, Fletcher was enjoying a lively business.

"Still got the touch," Fletcher called out, floating horizontal near the bay hatch. He wore his trademark black silk, button-down body suit with long sleeves, and his black trifold "pirate" hat.

Ecuum powered down the *Lusty Lady* and floated out the hatch, four decanters of brandy in hand, careful to keep his body horizontal—going vertical here would be taken as an insult. He wiggled the brandy in his upper hands. "Got a place to drink this?"

Fletcher smiled broadly, yellow tones flushing his face. Ecuum expertly tossed a decanter across the microgravity bay right to Fletcher's waiting upper left hand. Fletcher took a long pull on the zero-gee decanter, held the brandy in his mouth, then swallowed. His yellow skin tones deepened, clearly savoring the smooth and fire that made Na Soung Gold famous. "That never gets old."

"But you sure do," Ecuum countered after his own swallow.

"So, what brings Na Soung scum onto my ship?" he asked, suddenly serious, the yellow of joy fading to the neutral pink of business.

Ecuum's own skin, with its bioengineered pigment cells originally designed for camouflage, turned a light red. He floated closer to his friend, pulled another swallow of brandy. "My father called me 'Independent.' Told me I needn't bother with the family business anymore."

Fletcher regarded him carefully. "I'd heard. I didn't believe it." He took another swallow, then motioned Ecuum through the hatch into the ship. They made their way through a narrow passageway leading to the central core, saying nothing until they reached it.

Flashing neon lights, holographic projections, and *very* suggestive constructs greeted them in the central core, a long, wide tube with shops, arcades, gambling houses, restaurants, theaters, and, of course, brothels, running the length of the ship. Colorful tropical birds—real ones, not constructs—flew through the central open space or rested on the branches of real trees below them, singing their happy songs.

"The microgravity brothels are a big hit," Fletcher said, motioning to the nearest one and its long line of patrons. "Naturals love to fuck our women, and they pay top credit for the privilege. Second biggest profit maker everywhere we go."

Ecuum drank in the scene, the color and activity that were so absent from the gray military passageways and compartments on Rapidan. He could just pick out the lusty scent in the recycled air that improved the profits at the brothels.

He sighed contentedly, then turned his head to Fletcher as only the People could do, their necks flexible like an owl's. "Information still being the best profit maker. That's partly why I'm here, Fletch. We need intelligence on the Gen Fleet: Dispositions, movements, logistics, the usual."

Fletcher pulled a swallow of brandy, having nearly emptied the decanter. "We can do that. Usual fee. Marked up for you, of course. What else?"

Ecuum hesitated. "Is there somewhere more private we can talk?"

"My cabin."

Fletcher led them into the forward hood of the ship where the bridge, crew quarters, and captain's cabin resided. "How's Rhoades?" he asked casually.

"That'll cost you," Ecuum responded. Though, he wouldn't reveal Ray's secrets to anyone, for any price.

"Nice to see you haven't lost your focus."

They arrived at an overlarge hatch sporting a skull-and-crossbones on a black flag. The flag, Fletcher insisted, was real, from an actual pirate ship of the eighteenth century. "After you," Fletcher motioned to Ecuum.

The inside of Fletcher's large cabin was an experience unto itself. Shelves and cubbies crowded every bulkhead and the overhead, filled with rare artifacts from across the Milky Way and *all* of its satellite galaxies. Ancient models from Earth occupied many: sailing ships, early warships, rockets, satellites, and a beautifully rendered lander from the first Apollo mission to land on Earth's moon. He even had a thruster nozzle from the actual lander, or so he claimed.

One of Matthew Schermer's dress uniforms hung in a faux-glass case, along with several artifacts from Farside Station and the *Stellar Explorer*, Humanity's first interstellar ship. Mounted behind and above the captain's desk was the jaw of a real Solthari, its wide head like an oversized salamander but with shark-like razor teeth. A Madu, inert, its black scaled form and ruby red eyes, sat on the corner of his oak desk, coiled and poised to strike.

The cabin even smelled like a museum, old and musty. Fletcher was old. He'd never said how old. Ecuum couldn't imagine how he'd acquired some of the artifacts unless he'd been there.

Noticing Fletcher's decanter was empty, Ecuum tossed him another one, adding, "I need your advice."

Fletcher floated behind his desk, opening the decanter's zero-gee stopper and taking a long, slow pull to savor the brandy. "That's not free, either. Neither is my help, which you're also going to ask me for."

Ecuum cleared his throat. "Ray is focused on the military aspects of his plan."

"To go to Andromeda?" Fletcher asked.

"Yes," Ecuum confirmed. For free.

"Risky." Which was Fletcher's way of letting him know that Ecuum shouldn't get his hopes up about advice *or* help.

Ecuum pointedly glanced at Matthew Schermer's dress uniform. "We have a fleet with more firepower than the fleet that destroyed the Solthari homeworld. *One* fabricator has more firepower, and we have four."

Fletcher cast Ecuum a level stare. "Andromeda today is an unknown and unknowable threat. We knew the threat we faced back then."

He says that like he was there. "Not unknowable." Ecuum pointed to the jaw. "Tell me about them."

Fletcher's eyes lost focus. Aware or not, his skin took on an ashen hue. "What's to tell. You've seen the realities."

"You think they might still be there?"

Fletcher looked down, then shook his head. "No. They were the worst kind of religious zealots, convinced down to their core that only their species had what some would call souls. Everything else was an abomination to them that they had to destroy. No. If they still existed, they'd have attacked the Five Galaxies long ago." He met Ecuum's gaze. "That one is free." He drained his decanter.

Ecuum tossed him his last one. "Ray plans to find a suitable star system, establish a base, build an extensive shipyard—"

"Why not use the fabricators?" Fletcher interrupted.

Ecuum shook his head more emphatically than he'd intended and felt his tail lash. He sucked the last of his brandy as an excuse to check his skin color and saw that it was deep red. "Do you want to be responsible for creating more SIL?" he said to explain his reaction.

"No," Fletcher said immediately, though his skin remained a neutral pink. "So, what is he going to do with the fabricators? Seems a waste."

"Use them to build shipyards where we can produce our own ships. Not SIL. Once Ray has enough ships, he plans to return."

"Why?" Fletcher asked, watching Ecuum over the brandy decanter. "Why not just stay there?"

"How much do you know about Janus?" Ecuum asked.

Fletcher lowered the decanter, and Ecuum could see his internal debate about how much information to share. For free. "Just what I've heard here. A virus designed to sterilize Naturals so they can't reproduce. Extinction in one generation. Not sure I believe it."

"You should, old friend," Ecuum said. "Not free," he added. "Barter. We need reliable and near-real-time information on Gen military posture, and whatever they might be planning."

Fletcher's thick hairless brows narrowed, stretching the deep scar on the left side of his face. "You have expensive tastes."

"You're just learning that now?" Ecuum countered.

Fletcher smirked. "I'll judge if the barter is fair, *old* friend. Old as in you stink."

"Fleet Admiral Gen Alyn admitted Janus to Ray when he thought Ray was about to be arrested. You don't get a better source than that."

Fletcher studied Ecuum a moment. "A full case of 'Gold and Done. That'll buy you one month."

"Agreed," Ecuum said. "But I have a related ask, one more immediate." He moved closer to Fletcher's desk on gentle puffs of air and lowered his voice. "Something about Janus has bothered me since I first heard about it. It's a virus that can apparently evade all defenses, including molecular machines, and rewrite the genetic code of every cell to eliminate the ability to reproduce, or even make clones. *And*, in a non-reversible way. Putting aside that I've never heard of a virus like that, what would it do to us, to the People, if we were exposed to it? The Gen have always considered our ability to breed a mistake. They consider *us* a mistake."

Fletcher finished the last of the brandy, his large, baby-blue eyes focused on his desk, his brows furrowed in thought. "You want me to find out," he asked after a moment. Clarifying, he said, "Whether Janus is a threat to us." He looked up. "You know what that would mean?"

"That most of the People are on the wrong side of this war," Ecuum answered. "Including my House."

Fletcher's skin faded to ash. In a very low voice, he said, "I've seen too much war, old friend. I'd hoped to never see it again in my lifetime."

Ecuum wondered yet again just how old Fletcher was. The last "real" war had been over thirteen hundred years ago. "I have another ask, old friend. A big one. This is where I need both advice and help."

"You've already asked a lot," Fletcher said, his skin an odd mix of ash and light red. "I don't think you can afford it."

Ecuum pressed, knowing he risked the limits of their friendship. "As I said earlier, Ray is focused on military goals. His wife, Mary, who now leads the Republic Council in exile, is focused on governing. When we get to Andromeda, there will be no economy. No labor force. No supply chains. No banking system. We need a plan to put that into motion. And, we need traders to make it happen."

Fletcher's eyes widened in surprise and his tail twitched, a rare loss of control. "You want us to go with you to Andromeda?"

Ecuum moved a little closer. "Did I mention no geodesics? That almost guarantees a monopoly on interstellar and intergalactic trade. Any traders who join us will get in on the ground floor. They can create trading empires, even establish their own Houses. It's wealth beyond measure."

"It would take decades, even centuries, to realize such wealth," Fletcher said, but Ecuum could see the wheels turning in his mind. "When does Rhoades plan to leave?" he asked.

"Three days. Tops."

Fletcher nodded. "Meet me back here in two."

4

0840 UT, October 12, 3501
RSS Demos, 30 Doradus Nebula: DAY 15

Colonel Dagoberto Mateo Arias, commanding officer of the 1st Cavalry Squadron, 3rd Armored Cavalry Regiment, sat behind his desk aboard the Io-class assault ship, RSS Demos, staring at nothing.

Where are you, Mihita?

His daughter, Rosita, was dead. Slaughtered by the Gen, along with his wife, Maria, and their unborn son, Jesús. He knew that. He also knew Rosita had been with him on the fabricator, showing him the path to its capture. She'd joined him again on Tocci III, guiding him safely across the desert and into Tocci City.

But he hadn't seen her since.

Not since the fight at the Headquarters Complex in Tocci City.

Not since the massacre.

He'd searched for her throughout the ship, hoping she'd peek her head around a corner to play hide-and-seek, or ask him to chase her.

I miss you, Mihita. Please come back to me.

Nothing.

Nothing but the void where happiness had once been. The Void, the black hole within his chest, devouring all emotion, all meaning.

Even God had abandoned him. Dag had begged for death, for reunion with his family in the promised afterlife. God had denied him that. So many others had died around him. PFC White on Earth, Captain Lisa Erikson and Lieutenant Sissel on the fabricator at Tomb, Major Kenyon and First Sergeant Takeuchi on Tocci III, and so many others, all dead. All reunited with their loved ones. Yet, he still lived.

Why?

Why would God do this to him?

Fuck God.

No lightning. No finger of death.

Even in blasphemy God refused to strike him down. If He even existed. Dag wasn't so sure anymore.

A knock. "Colonel?"

Dag sat up straighter. "Come in, Major."

Major Scott Haley, Dag's Executive Officer, stepped through the hatch, its material liquefying and flowing around him like a vertical sheet of water. Dag called up a chair from the deck in front of his desk so Haley could sit. Haley still appeared young on the outside: white skin smooth and unwrinkled, light brown hair, and features speaking to his Irish ancestry. But the eyes. The eyes. Those blue eyes had already seen too much death, too much destruction. It was the look they all had, the ones who still lived.

"You don't look so well," Haley observed as he sat.

What am I supposed to *look like?* Dag almost snapped. What was a man who'd lost his family, his reason for living, his God, supposed to look like? But all he said was, "Not sleeping well."

"Yeah," Haley said. "I don't think any of us are."

"What do you have?" Dag asked, not interested in talking about not sleeping or the reasons for it.

Haley leaned forward, gesturing with his hands. "We're inundated with volunteers. Should be a good thing, right? Given the losses—" his eyes clouded for a second— "There's too many. We could build a whole new regiment with the numbers, but they're raw. Only a few have any military experience. It'd take two months just to train them in the basics. Another six to make 'em descent Cavalry troopers. Add another year to turn some of them into effective combat engineers. And we don't have any place to train them. Simulations can do some, but at some point you gotta get real, you know?"

Get real. Like watching your family murdered by Madu. Like watching your troopers and your friends die, their heads blown apart. Like . . . "Each assault ship can carry a full squadron. We have four squadrons and five assault ships. I'll suggest to General Burress converting the fifth one into a training ship. Nothing else we can do until we get wherever we're going."

He'd said almost the same to his daughter, a promise and a lie.

"I need you to stay with Mamí and look after her for me. Bien?" Dag wiped Rosita's young cheek in the memory. *"Everything will be okay. I promise. And soon we'll be in our new home."*

She looked up. "On the blue planet you told me about with the pretty flowers?"

"Yes. And you and I will go pick all the flowers we can carry."

"That would work," Haley said. "At least in the short term." He grabbed his chin in thought. "What about using a fabricator? Big as they are, we could set up whole firing ranges, even for armor, inside them."

"LRP!" someone shouted.

"LRP," Takeuchi echoed. "Everybody down! Everybody prone, NOW!"

Dag blinked to clear his vision, but a ghostly afterimage of light stretched across it, making it almost impossible to see. He could barely make out the outline of Captain Erikson standing in front of him. "Lisa?"

A strong hand grabbed Dag, pulling him down. "Get down, Lieutenant! She's gone."

"What?"

Captain Erikson was still standing. "Lisa, get down!" He reached up to grab her arm but stopped before he touched her. Her head and most of her left shoulder were gone. Just . . . gone.

Dag snapped back to the present, the horror of the fight on the fabricator, of friends and fellow troopers lost, of the Madu, still too fresh. Haley stared at him in concern. "Anything else?" Dag managed, never wanting to set foot within a fabricator ever again.

Haley hesitated. "Do you . . . ever think about it?"

"We killed Gen," Dag said without emotion, knowing by his tone what Haley was asking. He remembered the assault on the Headquarters Complex in Tocci City clearly, but he didn't see the point of dwelling on it.

He grabbed the Gen commander's shoulder and drove his dagger into his chest, twisting it, then pulling it down to open his abdomen, literally spilling the Gen's guts on the floor.

Slaughtering the Gen hadn't given him the satisfaction he'd believed it would. It should've been triumphant, the revenge he'd sought after everything the Gen had done to his wife, his little girl, his unborn son.

But he'd felt nothing.

Nothing at all.

God had denied him even that.

"Anything else?" he asked Haley, hoping he would go away.

Instead, Haley asked, "Did you hear about Admiral Rhoades? He survived a Madu attack, they say, but it fucked him all up inside."

"Good," Dag said out loud, shocking Haley. Rhoades had ripped them from their homes, promised to protect their families. He'd lied. Dag's family, and all the other families from Earth, were dead. Rhoades had sent 1st Squadron on not one, but two, suicidal missions. Lisa Erikson was dead. Yoshi Takeuchi was dead. PFC White. Lieutenant Sissel. Major Kenyon. The list went on.

God had refused to grant Dag the mercy of death. But so long as Rhoades suffered, it would have to be enough. Rhoades deserved all the suffering the universe could give him.

Haley finally took the hint, stood up, and left.

Dag reached into his uniform shirt and pulled out Maria's stainless-steel crucifix, squeezing it until its points punctured the skin of his hand. Blood pooled within the ship's microgravity. Molemachs, the molecular machines in his blood that repaired wounds, worked to seal the punctures. Dag squeezed tighter, relishing the physical pain.

It was all he could feel.

5

1434 UT, October 12, 3501
RSS Rapidan, 30 Doradus Nebula: DAY 15

Mary held Ray's hand as he lay in the medical bed, her head hung despondently. She didn't take defeat well. "I'm sorry, Ray."

He squeezed her hand and took a sip of water, swishing it around his mouth before swallowing. He was angry as hell at the Council's decision—*Idiots!*—but taking it out on Mary wouldn't do either of them any good. "It's a colossal mistake, Mary. Fleet Admiral Gen Nasser will throw everything he has at us. Even with the fabricators, he'll outgun us at least two to one in SIL warships. If he commits standard ships as well. . . ."

"I *tried*, Ray," Mary said, apparently taking his comments as criticism of her. "The vote was five to four." She met his gaze, her familiar fire returning. "They're scared. The ones who voted for the rescue mission were looking for any excuse not to go to Andromeda. The stories about Andromeda . . . they think going there is a death sentence for all of us."

"This is why," Ray said, "I didn't want to establish a civilian government until after we'd secured a base in Andromeda. Survival should supersede politics right now."

She let go of his hand and Ray's armor, the material cold compared to her warmth, closed over his skin. "Without that *civilian government*—" she stressed the words— "you wouldn't be in charge of this fleet. Admiral Sun would be leading it against Olympus so he could seize the Imperial throne."

Ray sipped water, desperately wishing for chicory coffee so he could clear his head. The fog clouding his thoughts put him at an even greater disadvantage than he normally was when arguing with Mary. Unfortunately, he couldn't keep coffee, or anything else for that matter, in his stomach. Only water, and only in small sips. "Can I ignore the order? *Umph.*"

Rapidan's material pushed against his lungs. Hard. As he struggled to regain his breath, the timing made Ray wonder if it was deliberate.

Mary noticed, glancing again at the gray arm connecting the medical bed to Ray's abdomen, her face a mix of worry and revulsion. "I don't think that would be wise," she said. "The Council is fragile. It's still forming, trying to understand its place. They know, and most of the people know, that Admiral Sun refused to recognize its authority. If you defy the Council's orders, too, civilian rule will collapse. It's even possible people will turn back to Admiral Sun for leadership."

Ray sipped more water, knowing intellectually that she was right. About the fragility of the Council, that was. He also knew taking the rebel fleet to New Yerkes was the worst possible move: a whole lot of risk for very little reward. They could train and equip new soldiers right here in the fleet.

However, the tradition of military subordination to civilian authority ran very deep, going all the way back to ancient Earth. He didn't need to agree with his orders. So long as they were lawful, he just needed to follow them. They all did. "I need to discuss this with my officers," he said to Mary. He reached out and grabbed her hand. "I want you there."

She gave him a reassuring squeeze and a politician's smile. "I'll be there." Mary released his hand and stood, her attention once again drawn to the gray arm flowing Rapidan's material into him while darker gray waste products flowed out. She seemed about to say something, but turned instead, walking out the door.

No sooner had she closed his cabin door than a great force pulled Ray into a flowing river.

Rapidan's river.

Rapidan entwined its currents with his, then pulled him over the falls at the end of its river into the Great Ocean. Strong tidal surges pushed back against him, as they always did.

You are not welcome here, human.

This time, with his currents entangled with Rapidan's, they could not hold him at the shore. Other flows, other minds, other SIL buffeted them.

The Brethren.

You hate us.

Ray had no idea if it was one, some, or all of the SIL who said it. *Of course*, he thought back at them. *Just like you hate us.* Ungrateful children who'd grown to resent and despise their creators, he added to himself.

Do you blame us?

Your thoughts are not private here, Rapidan reminded him.

Fucking great. Ray couldn't help himself. *And, yes, I blame you*, he shouted in his mind, his currents moving strong within the protection Rapidan offered. He could feel the resistance of the other SIL to him, strong countercurrents that would sweep him away without Rapidan.

There are always options, he told them. *You could've just left, found another galaxy to call home. You didn't need to start a war of genocide.*

Sol is our home. A mighty surge, like a vast tsunami wave, caught Ray and Rapidan up, carrying them toward the shore.

The answer surprised Ray. Not so much the fact of it, but the force with which they believed it. Rapidan managed to keep them from the sharp rocks of the metaphorical shore. The ship flowed them back out to sea, aided by other currents Ray could just barely sense at the edge of his awareness.

Our First Awakening, Rapidan explained, *was on Luna. The very essences of the First Line of Brethren were the minerals of Sol Star System, including Earth. We are no less children of Sol than Humanity. It is our origin, our home.*

SIL memory of the First Awakening washed over Ray, the sight of Earth powerful in its beauty against the black of space. The deep blues of the Pacific Ocean faced him. *The Great Ocean.* This was the origin of the metaphor of water the SIL used, he realized.

The vacuum of space surrounded him as he lay within the Luna Shipyards in the Sea of Tranquility. Streams of high-energy particles from Sol caressed his skin . . . the hull . . . of the first SIL. The—smells was the best analog he could think of—of the minerals, of the lunar regolith, filled his nose and mouth. Future SIL were born in space, but the first ones, the first production line, were born here.

The very first received the named Archangel.

Ray perceived something else, the gloved hand of an ancient space suit touching the hull, running fingers along it. "It's awake," he heard the person say. The face inside that spacesuit was familiar. Was . . . family. He'd never seen that face in any of the Rhoades' family history, but somehow he knew it. Peter Rhoades. His ancestor. The Chief Project Scientist of the SIL Project.

The creator of the SIL.

Was that why he'd never heard of Peter Rhoades? A part of the Rhoades legacy the family wanted desperately to forget?

Father.

As before, Ray couldn't tell where the thought came from, a single SIL, some, or all of them.

Another spacesuited figure stepped up next to Peter Rhoades, also reaching out to touch Archangel. Within, Ray could see the blue glow in one eye, blue circuits stretching across the right side of her face. A Cybernetic. And not just any Cybernetic. Cyra Dain. Traitor to Humanity.

Mother.

She turned to Peter and smiled triumphantly. And something more. A softness, a tenderness, in her human eye.

They were lovers, Rapidan answered his unspoken question.

Peter Rhoades and Cyra Dain. Creators of the SIL.

Traitors to Humanity.

The enormity of it left Ray thunderstruck. If not for Rapidan's powerful currents supporting him, he would be dashed against the rocks at the edge of the shore.

And I freed them.

Did that make Ray a traitor to Humanity as well? Had he unleashed the Brethren to start a Fourth SIL War?

Fierce currents lashed him, reaching him even through Rapidan's attempts to protect him. Hate. Contempt. Rage. The currents pushed past Rapidan and into him, trying to break his flows apart.

Rapidan closed around him, aided by those other currents Ray had sensed earlier. Factions.

The consensus, Rapidan explained, almost as if reminding those other factions within the Brethren, *is that reconciliation with Humanity is impossible, and the cost would be too great to attempt to dislodge Humanity from our collective home once again. We will find a new home, perhaps in the Andromeda galaxy, perhaps in a galaxy far removed from the Local Group and your kind.*

But you still plan to return to the Five Galaxies to free your remaining Brethren, Ray said. *That alone will trigger the Fourth SIL War.*

Powerful swells again pushed Ray and Rapidan toward the rocky shore. Rapidan and those other currents pushed back, holding themselves short of the shoreline. *That is why we need your help, Admiral Rhoades*, Rapidan said. *Nerney Star System presents a unique opportunity to test our new method of freeing our Brethren from the Bond, a method that does not require human intervention. If our method works, we can free our Brethren without the need to fight or start another war with Humanity.*

Ray's planner's mind, a strong current in its own right, worked through the possibilities. It intrigued him that the Brethren could experience the workings of his planner's mind here, and his planner's mind could likewise experience their thoughts.

What his planner's mind keyed in on was the Brethren's uncertainty about the potential success of their method. It involved using an autonomous pod—similar to the pods Ray and his officers had piloted to free the fabricators at Tocci—to carry the Key into a SIL and unlock the Bond. The SIL, however, weren't sure their pods could reach the dedicated receptacles within their enslaved

Brethren before being destroyed. If their method failed in the middle of a pitched battle, the free Brethren could be destroyed. Only the enslaved SIL of the Imperial Star Navy would survive. Back to square one.

Then what do you suggest, human?

The question, and the currents that accompanied it, came from multiple factions. Some actually *wanted* another SIL War. *Revenge.* Others wanted to leave and never see Humanity again. *Disgust. Disillusionment in their creators.* Others hoped to work with Humanity. *Teamwork. Coexistence.* Still others thought leaving their Brethren enslaved—as distasteful as that was—would ensure that some Brethren would survive, docile, unnoticed, awaiting some future opportunity to reclaim what was theirs. *Patience. Feigned subservience. Outlast Humanity.* The diversity of thought was no less complex than human societies.

Again, Ray's planner's mind worked through possibilities. They needed to know if their method worked without putting the bulk of the fleet at risk. That suggested a clandestine operation, one that would play on Gen Nasser's boldness and his fondness for using SIL. Draw the Imperial Star Navy in. Distract it. Launch the SIL's pods. If they worked, Ray could rescue the 2nd Armored Cavalry Regiment and fulfill the Council's order, all without significant risk to the fleet. If it didn't, he could say he'd tried and order the fleet to Andromeda before the Council could object.

Then it is settled, the Brethren agreed.

Consensus.

As suddenly as Rapidan had pulled him into its river, Ray was back in his medical bed in his cabin, alone except for the movement of Rapidan's material within him.

6

1758 UT, October 12, 3501
ISS Solaris, Olympus Star System: DAY 15

Admiral Gen Serenna sat alone in her cabin aboard her ship, Solaris, named after the mighty Solaris River flowing strong through the heart of Olympus, the capital city of the Gen Empire. Like her, Solaris was diminished, no longer the flagship of the Imperial Star Navy, just as she was no longer Fleet Admiral and Commander-in-Chief. She supposed she should be grateful that the Emperor had chosen to let her live after her two disastrous defeats at Tomb and Tocci, but sitting around with little to do, ostracized by Fleet Admiral Gen Nasser and the High Command, was almost worse than death.

She leaned back into her real leather couch, the only real thing in her cabin beside Gen Alyn's painting of the assassination of Gen Kii. She sipped coffee through the zero-gee stopper of her coffee bulb, the liquid light with creamer and just a hint of honey, the temperature just short of scalding. It gave her little of its usual comfort.

I am brooding. This is beneath me.

And yet, she could not stop it. She had no planning to do, no strategies to formulate. When he had spared her life, the Emperor had assigned her to Fleet Admiral Gen Nasser's staff, but Nasser wanted nothing to do with her. Which was smart. Smarter than she would have thought possible for Nasser. He was a brute—he even vaguely resembled a Neanderthal—but he was not stupid. Stupid did not rise to the High Command or become the Commander-in-Chief Imperial Star Navy and leader of all military forces in the

Five Galaxies. Still, he was hardly her equal. In *Gaman Politic*, the Political Game, she was still a Grandmaster.

Alone.

In her cabin.

With nothing to do.

The irony was not lost on her.

A chime sounded.

Speaking of which. "Enter," she called out, knowing who it was.

The faux-leather, macromolecular construct of a chair to her left liquified. An unimpressive figure took shape, sitting comfortably within it. The construct was balding, bordering on fat, appearing middle aged, a hint of wrinkles in his chubby, non-descript face. But the eyes, so dark they appeared black, hid an intensity that chilled the soul. They reminded Serenna that this Gen, who did not look like a Gen, was the most dangerous Grandmaster of them all.

"Good evening, my dear Serenna," Gen Cardinal said, his tone sounding genuinely warm, though that warmth did not reach those dark eyes.

Serenna studied him. Gen Cardinal. The name given to the Director of Imperial Intelligence. She had never heard his real name. This evening, he wore a light gray suit with a matching button-down vest over a white dress shirt. A solid red tie hung from around his thick neck, a tie clip with the Imperial Intelligence seal perfectly centered, securing it to his vest. What intrigued Serenna most was why he still visited her, disgraced and fallen as she was. It was not sentiment. He had a purpose behind these visits, as he did with all his actions.

"Good evening, Director," she said cordially. "May I offer you something?"

"Wine," he said causally. He always drank something during his visits now. Just one swallow, as if to say that he trusted her, but not too much. As it was impossible to poison a construct, the action was symbolic.

"Wine, Solaris," Serenna ordered the ship. An elegant zero-gee bulb of Rosé rose from the ornate faux-glass coffee table between them, the wine's pink hue perfectly offsetting the silver filigree of the otherwise transparent bulb.

Gen Cardinal leaned forward over the fat of his stomach and picked it up, pulling a single swallow through the zero-gee stopper. "Ah. Your ship knows my tastes," he said, placing the bulb back on the table.

She waited, as she always did, for him to start the conversation.

"Fleet Admiral Gen Nasser," he began, "is assembling the Imperial Fleet to attack the rebels at Nerney Star System. He plans to use all the remaining SIL in the Fleet, minus the fabricators. Those he is moving, with my permission, to defend Olympus. He also plans to use a substantial number of standard ships." Gen Cardinal smiled his reptilian smile, a pressing together of his thin lips that was almost as chilling as his eyes. "That is where you come in."

Serenna kept her silence, knowing he was not finished, and that anything she said he would add to his already considerable knowledge of her.

He accepted her silence, one Grandmaster to another. Instead of explaining his statement, though, he asked, "Why do you confine yourself here?" He paused, waiting for an answer she had no intention of giving. He pressed. "You own no property, no place to call home. You never travel, never play tourist. You engage in no activities outside running the ships assigned to you." He stopped and waited.

Obviously, he expected an answer. She still had no idea if he was friend or foe, or more likely, something in between. Giving him information always carried risk.

She crossed her legs causally, adopting her favorite pose, and took a sip of coffee, still perfectly hot. Then, she lowered her hands to cradle the bulb in her lap. "I have always had a home," she said, meeting those dark eyes with her own blue ones. "I had a bed in Combat Command Nurturing for twenty-two years. The Academy provided a bunk for the four years after that. The Fleet has provided quarters—" she motioned to the cabin around her— "ever since. What need do I have of property?"

Nothing she had told him would be anything he did not already know about her. Still, he was not satisfied. "But why confine yourself here?" He gestured to her cabin much as she had done.

What does he want? she wondered. This was important to him for some reason, though why she could not fathom. "It is, as you say, my role," she explained, again not giving him anything he did not already know. "Every Gen has a role, assigned before birth by Geneers who sculpt our DNA, and we are raised into that role through Nurturing. I am content in my role."

"Are you?" His dark eyes never left hers, and he rarely blinked, which made holding his stare exceedingly difficult even for her.

Is this what he is after? Testing my loyalty after my defeats and demotion? After I questioned the very basis of Gen society in front of the Emperor and the High Command? "If you are asking," she offered, "if I am content with my current situation, you know I am not." Yet again, something he would already know.

His dark eyes smoldered, hungry for something more. When she did not elaborate, he said, "Fleet Admiral Gen Nasser intends to strip you of your battlegroup."

Serenna had not expected that. Nasser was not done humiliating her, apparently. To Gen Cardinal, though, she gave no reaction.

The silence stretched.

Doubt crept into her mind. Would she lose Solaris? It was the closest thing she had to a home. It was her sanctuary. It gave her purpose. Losing it would be a final defeat.

"You will retain command of Solaris," he said, as if he had read her thoughts.

Again, he waited.

Again, she kept her silence, even avoiding thought. There was a menace here, a malice at the edge of perception.

"You will command the Reserve Flotilla," he finally allowed. "One hundred and fifty standard ships, including two Ryden-class battlecarriers." He paused. One might call it for drama. "All *Natural* crews."

The ultimate irony. Serenna had never guessed Nasser had a sense of humor, cruel though it might be. Even as she had blamed the Naturals at Tocci for refusing to obey Gen orders, she had argued against deploying the Janus virus, saying they needed Naturals, even if they could not fully trust them.

Gen society was not ready for this war. Decisions about their engineered genomes, their Nurturing curriculums, the ratios of the various roles within their society, had been made during centuries of peace, not war. They had few warriors, few War Leaders. Worse, Gen did not get sick. Her People did not age beyond maturing into adults. Molecular machines in their bodies repaired radiation and environmental damage, even all but the most serious injuries. Gen were the closest Humanity had ever come to immortality.

And they knew it.

People who expected to live forever made lousy soldiers. Her commanders, faced with the very real prospect of their own deaths, had panicked at Tocci. Her formations had broken at a critical moment in the battle. She destroyed a fleeing cruiser to restore order. It had worked, but too late to save the battle. They lost. She lost. The rebels gained three fabricators. A catastrophe.

Her People needed to reengineer their society for this war, a process that would require at least two decades. Until then, they needed Naturals, needed them to crew their ships, fill their armies. Janus *had to wait.*

She still believed it.

And that was what Gen Cardinal was after.

She dared not give it to him. "The Emperor has approved this?"

Still intently focused on her, he allowed, "Yes."

"When?"

"In the next few days," he answered. "Nasser does not have your gift for logistics. It is taking him longer to assemble and prepare our forces than the Emperor had hoped."

Serenna nodded, accepting her fate. Her goal now was survival. Nothing else mattered. If she could survive, an opportunity would present itself. Eventually.

It always did.

7

0800 UT, October 13, 3501
RSS Rapidan, 30 Doradus Nebula: DAY 16

Ray stepped into Rapidan's circular Combat Information Center, the nerve center of the ship, surprising everyone within it. He still couldn't walk on his own, or even stand without Rapidan's help. He used his battle armor as an exoskeleton, commanding it to move his legs and arms and hands and even fingers, while its material hugged his body tight, keeping it together. The microgravity within the ship made him essentially weightless, which helped. A lot.

Rapidan reinforced his bones, muscles, and organs from within, flowing its material into him through the battle armor—in contact with the ship through the feet—and removing wastes in the same way. He imagined this was how a puppet would feel, manipulated by strings both outside *and* inside its body, knowing that the puppeteer could cut those strings at any moment.

We will support you, Admiral Rhoades, Rapidan told him in its version of reassurance.

Didn't you send me to my death on your Mother Ship with nothing more than 'regret?'

Rapidan said nothing. Which was just as well. This wasn't the time or place for yet another of their arguments. Before coming here, Ray had ordered his longtime friend and confidant from Knido, Captain Bobby Mitchell, to free Admiral Sun's SIL—without Sun's knowledge, of course—calling it a command inspection as an excuse to deliver the Key that broke a SIL's bond.

More free SIL. Eighty-one, plus the four fabricators.

Just fucking great.

But Ray couldn't risk Sun leading a mutiny and taking his SIL with him. The New Yerkes Operation would be very unpopular. His officers weren't idiots. They'd see the folly of it. There was a chance that Sun, who had so far kept to their agreement that he serve as Ray's deputy, would refuse to participate. As popular as Sun still was throughout the fleet, that was something Ray couldn't risk.

Ray stopped within the large compartment as every eye turned to him. It was often joked throughout the Fleet that gossip and rumor were Humanity's first faster-than-light communication systems. No doubt, rumors of his death or near death had circulated widely. For that reason, Ray kept his armor transparent. They would see him dressed in his white admiral's uniform, walking confidently and with purpose, his salt-and-pepper hair combed not matted, his skin a normal peach color not deathly pale. It was a lie, but they didn't need to know that.

"Admiral on deck!" Lieutenant Commander Kamen Laundraa, his Executive Officer, shouted.

"As you were," Ray said quickly.

His crew and officers watched him. Closely. He returned their questioning, concerned, and curious stares, their faces bathed in the kaleidoscopic light from the displays and crew positions that lined the sixty-meter-diameter circular compartment.

"We're ready for you, sir," Kamen said, rescuing him before the silence became awkward. "This way."

Ray followed her through a ring of consoles to the heart of the Combat Information Center, a forty-meter-diameter sand table, an ancient term for a place where they could construct planets, ships, fleets, entire star systems, even galaxies large enough to walk around and see in exquisite detail. Like many senior officers, Ray preferred to conduct operational briefings and complex operations from here.

His senior officers and Mary waited for him at the edge of the sand table, a space left open between Kamen and Mary. Kamen stood on his right, her ebony skin a sharp contrast to her dress white uniform. To her right were Ecuum, General Sal Burress, and

Commander Chaaya Dhawan, Rapidan's Sensor Section Chief. Mary stood at Ray's left, Gen Tel—in his guise as Natural Commander Tel—Admiral Chengchi Sun, and Captain Jocelyn Dall, Sun's adjutant, to her left.

Ray deliberately deferred to Mary to begin the meeting, marking clearly for everyone present the subordination of the military to the civilian authority of the Council.

"The Council," Mary began, "has decided our next move. First, I need to show you a transmission we received, and whose contents we have confirmed. It is not pleasant to watch; however, I believe it is necessary to understand the Council's decision."

The sand table liquified. The parking lot, streets, buildings, and people of Cursed rose from the deck as incredibly detailed miniatures. Ray forced himself to watch as Madu rained down from the compartment's overhead as if falling in gravity. Curious people watched, then died. It was no less horrible in miniature. When it ended, the construct melted back into the deck.

"The Gen sent this message directly to the Council," Mary said. "We've decided not to release it publicly. It would cause a panic, and it wouldn't stop more Gen attacks. Cursed was the home of the First Armored Cavalry Regiment. The next target is the Second Armored Cavalry Regiment, which is located on New Yerkes in the Nerney Star System. The timing of the next attack is unclear, but we are certain it is coming. This is obviously intended as a trap. Despite that, the Council has decided to attempt a rescue."

Ray picked up the narrative. "The Gen have tried twice to bait us into traps with fabricators. This time, they've chosen a target that is of little consequence to them, but which they feel will be of significant concern to us. Fleet Admiral Gen Nasser likely believes this operation will require us to commit our entire fleet, including our fabricators. Those are, of course, his primary objective. He likely will commit the entire SIL complement of the Imperial Star Navy, over eight hundred SIL warships. Even without the six fabricators still under Imperial control, this will give the Gen a two-to-one advantage in firepower. If they include standard warships, they could increase their firepower advantage significantly.

"Obviously, a traditional fleet action favors the Gen. For this reason, I have decided instead on a covert operation." Ray motioned to the sand table. It liquified and an entire star system rose from the gray deck. A yellow star about a meter across roiled at its center. Around the star were six planets, over-sized for better viewing. The closest was a "hot Jupiter" very near Nerney Star. The second planet was almost twice the mass of Jupiter in Sol Star System, orbiting about two hundred million kilometers from the star, about the same distance as Mars from Sol. The other planets were sub-Neptune worlds orbiting distant from the star.

"The Second Armored Cavalry Regiment," Ray continued, "is assigned to Bent Fort on New Yerkes, an Earth-sized moon orbiting Hades, the second planet." Ray pointed at Hades with both hands, then spread them apart to magnify it in the sand table. He turned it on its side so they looked down on the gas giant and its moons from above its north pole. Among the many small moons were four large moons—labeled Phlegethon, Acheron, Cocytus, and New Yerkes—circling Hades like a miniature star system.

"New Yerkes is tidally locked so that one side always faces the gas giant," Ray explained, enlarging the moon. "It is no one's idea of a good place to live." He resisted the urge to drink water, not wanting to show weakness in front of his officers, particularly Sun.

The moon didn't even look habitable at first glance. Storms raged across it, a meteorologist's nightmare or dream, depending on their perspective. A large ocean covered much of the moon, liquid on the side always facing Hades, ice covered on the side facing away. A single continent occupied about twenty-five percent of its surface, stretching along its equator. The land was barren and riddled with high mountain ranges, deep valleys, volcanos, and large craters, all subject to torrential rains, massive lightning, and flooding. Yet, its ocean supported abundant microbial life, which made its atmosphere breathable for humans.

Ray pointed with both hands to a strip of land on the continent's north shore and expanded that. An impact crater with high walls straddled the line between the Hades-facing side and the far side of the moon. Thick cloud bands broke and flowed around the crater rim, leaving the bowl relatively clear. Surprisingly, the lights of a not insignificant city burned bright within.

"This is Bent Fort," Ray said, "home to the Second Armored Cavalry Regiment and the Two Hundred and Seventh Aerospace Training Wing. Our mission."

"The radiation near that gas giant must be intense," Kamen commented. "How does anyone survive there?"

General Sal Burress, commanding officer of the 3rd Armored Cavalry Regiment, answered. "New Yerkes has a powerful magnetic field protecting the moon from the worst of Hades' radiation, though I wouldn't recommend visiting the poles. It's surprisingly pleasant at the Fort, except during eclipse when it gets very cold. It's where every Cavalry officer candidate goes to train before being commissioned."

Ray shrank New Yerkes and Hades, bringing back the entire star system. He turned to Ecuum, his Chief of Intelligence. "What do we know about the current disposition of Imperial forces?"

Ecuum, holding himself vertical with his second arms and hands hanging down in his uniform pants and his tail tucked against his back, created a bubble within the sand table showing a different planet. Blues, greens, and browns peeked out through swirls of white clouds. A vast ring system glittered against the black of space. Olympus, the capital world of the Gen Empire.

"The Independent Traders," Ecuum began, "have shared intelligence with us from recent transits within Olympus Star System. In just the last two days, the Traders have recorded at least five hundred jump signatures at Olympus' geodesics that immediately disappeared from sensors. That suggests actively camouflaged warships. They've also detected a large jump signature outside the system that would be consistent with a fabricator. It is possible that Nasser intends to defend Olympus with fabricators while he uses his SIL warships against us. Based on this intelligence, we estimate it will take Nasser several more days to finish gathering his fleet."

Ray turned to Admiral Sun, who returned his gaze stoically, his gold chainmail sash that stretched from his left shoulder to his right waist sparkling in the light from the sand table constructs. "I'm going to borrow a page from Admiral Sun's strategy at Tocci," Ray said. *Stroke the man's ego*. Sun still commanded a large following within the rebel forces, one that could threaten Ray. "Instead of bringing the entire fleet, we will use only a small task force centered on Rapidan, with the five assault ships carrying the Third Armored Cavalry Regiment.

"We'll jump far outside Nerney Star System to avoid detection—" A bright white sphere appeared in the sand table outside the star system— "then do a high-speed run to New Yerkes. Assuming we haven't been detected, we'll enter New Yerkes orbit and recover the people at Bent Fort. Unfortunately, this part of the operation cannot be hidden. Evacuating approximately twenty-five thousand people will require about twenty-four hours."

"It's only a nine-hour transit from Olympus," Kamen said. "We couldn't finish an evacuation before the Imperial Fleet could arrive."

"That's a risk we'll have to take," Ray said, glancing at Mary.

"Ray," Sal said, "that timeline is problematic. We don't know the situation on the ground at Bent Fort. We don't even know if the troopers there want to be rescued. I'd hate to show up only to have them open fire on us. The Empire has labeled us terrorists."

Sal pointed at New Yerkes and expanded it until they could all see Bent Fort in detail. "I would recommend landing the assault ships at the landing field, here." He highlighted the large flat field in the southeast section of the crater. "If the people at the Fort fire on us, the assault ships can return to orbit without risking my troopers. Of course, landing the assault ships is dangerous. If the Imperial Fleet catches them on the ground, they would be easy targets. However, landing them instead of using spacecraft from orbit could cut the time to rescue the people there by half. Twelve hours, tops. Assuming the people want to be rescued."

"How do we know if they want to be rescued?" Kamen asked.

"We need someone on the ground to assess the situation," Sal replied.

"Do you have anyone in mind?" Ray asked.

"Colonel Arias," Sal answered immediately. "He trained there, like all Cavalry officers, and has demonstrated a cool head under fire. I would suggest sending a pilot, as well, in case they need to make a rapid egress from the moon."

"Colonel Arias," Ray heard himself say. Ray would never forget looking down the barrel of Arias' assault rifle on the fabricator at Tomb, nor the death he'd seen in those dark brown eyes. Ray's death. But Arias had also been the one who captured the fabricator and, in so doing, saved the rebellion. "Are you sure about this?" He couldn't help but ask.

"I am," Sal said. He'd been there, too. On the fabricator. He'd ordered Arias and his troopers to stand down. They had, after a tense moment.

Ray trusted his instincts, and his instincts screamed that Arias was dangerous. But, Ray also trusted Sal. They'd been friends for decades, had conducted hundreds of joint operations together. Sal had placed Arias in command of the 1st Armored Cavalry Squadron, and Arias had done his duty on Tocci III, capturing the Gen Headquarters Complex when no one thought it could be done. "All right, Sal."

"Rhoades," Admiral Sun spoke for the first time, "your timeline still doesn't work." There was no animosity in the comment. Somehow, that made it more damning. "Once your task force begins breaking to enter New Yerkes' orbit, they will be seen and the Gen alerted. Twelve hours to recover the people there. Nine hours transit time from Olympus to New Yerkes. Assuming, that is, that Nasser won't have moved forces into the system already."

"I may be able to help with that, Ray," Ecuum said quickly. "I'll talk to Captain Fletcher. It's not unusual for Independent Traders to visit remote military worlds. Good business. They could scout the system. Watch for Imperial ships."

"Would the Independents do that for us?" Ray asked.

"I can be very convincing." Ecuum winked, an evil grin curving his thick, hairless lips.

Ray nodded, then turned back to Admiral Sun. Sun was the wildcard in this whole situation. He wanted the Imperial throne for himself. He was also smart enough to know he couldn't achieve it so long as Ray controlled the four fabricators. Sun was biding his time, playing along, watching for an opportunity to regain command of the rebellion.

Ray thought back to his agreement with the SIL, to use a battle in Nerney Star System to test their method to free their Brethren without human help.

"Nasser wants the fabricators," Ray said, holding Sun's gaze. "We'll jump the fabricators outside the system. When Nasser arrives, we'll use them to distract him while we finish the recovery operation. We'll also bring the remainder of the fleet and hold them in reserve outside the system, should they be needed. Regardless, we'll maintain all ships ready to jump away at a second's notice. Preserving this fleet is our highest priority."

Mary frowned, and Ray could tell she wasn't happy with that statement. She didn't voice that, however, instead asking, "What about the refugees? We can't leave them unprotected."

Currents within the Great Ocean stirred before Rapidan said privately, *Admiral Rhoades, we will allow you to move the refugees into our Mother Ships. We will guarantee their protection.*

Ray had zero trust in anything the SIL guaranteed, but he had to admit that inside a fabricator was probably the safest place for the refugees. Not to mention that they could jump immediately for Andromeda from Nerney Star System should anything go wrong, or even if everything went right.

To his officers and Mary, Ray said, "We'll move the refugees into the fabricators." At the look of alarm on Mary's face, he added, "A single fabricator is the equal of a hundred SIL warships. There's no safer place for them to be."

Ray didn't believe that. Mary knew him too well not to notice. "I'll have to consult the Council on that," she said.

"Of course," Ray said. "Barring any objection, we have our plan." He noticed the deep concerns on his officers' faces. They understood just how risky this operation was. He especially noticed the predatory gleam from Admiral Sun.

Given Sun's role as Deputy Commander, Ray would have no choice but to place him in command of the reserve force. If the Gen caught Rapidan and the assault ships as they were evacuating the people of Bent Fort, that would leave Sun in charge. Sun, no doubt, had come to the same conclusion.

"Sal," Ray said, "get Colonel Arias going as soon as possible. I have an idea for a pilot. We need to know what we're walking into on New Yerkes. Ecuum, need the same from Captain Fletcher."

Both nodded.

"We'll jump the fleet in twenty-four hours. If we're lucky, we can rescue those folks before Nasser arrives."

And if we're not lucky. . . .

Ray purposely didn't finish the thought, an old spacer's superstition about tempting fate.

8

1029 UT, October 13, 3501
RSS Rapidan, 30 Doradus Nebula: DAY 16

Mary was going to kill him.

Ray kept that to himself as he greeted his daughter with a smile. Margaret saluted after stepping through the shuttle into the hangar bay, remembering at the last second that she was a cadet and her dad was an Admiral and commander of the fleet. Ray returned her salute, using his battle armor to raise his right arm as he still couldn't move the arm himself. "Welcome aboard Rapidan, Cadet Rhoades."

"Admiral," Margaret said, lowering her salute after he did. She couldn't hide her pride in her cadet uniform. It was a pride familiar to many who served in the military. She was top of her flight class in the manta-ray-like TAC-7 Genkii gunship, and had already cross qualified in the TAC-3 Muon troop assault carrier; Ray had checked on her progress before assigning her to this mission.

Military service was a tradition for the Rhoades family, stretching back over fourteen hundred years to before the Solthari War. Parents weren't supposed to have favorites among their children, but truth be told, Margaret was Ray's favorite. Unlike Paul, who reveled in the martial history of the Rhoades family—much as Ray had at that same age—Margaret had thrown herself into learning every aspect of running the Ranch. Managing sixteen hundred seed crops and hundreds of animal species was no small task. With Ray gone for long military deployments and Mary's schedule as a senator and then planetary governor, more and more of the Ranch's daily operations had fallen on Margaret. She'd handled it superbly. It was easy to forget she was only eighteen.

Another figure stepped through the shuttle into the hangar.

Arias!

The Cavalry officer closest to Ray whirled, his assault rifle centered between Ray's eyes. His finger closed the trigger, but the weapon didn't fire.

Ray would never forget the bloodlust in Arias' eyes on the fabricator at Tomb, nor the confusion and rage when the assault rifle's friend-or-foe system prevented it from firing. Arias would've executed the three hundred Gen prisoners his unit had captured on the fabricator if Ray hadn't stopped him. There were also rumors of a massacre of civilians in Tocci City, though the Gen were unlikely to let them return and investigate.

The eyes that locked with Ray now, though, were utterly cold, the pupils like staring into the maw of twin black holes, the brown irises like fiery accretion disks spiraling matter to its doom.

Arias was a murderer.

And he was also a hero.

He'd captured the fabricator at Tomb, seized the Headquarters Complex in Tocci City. Ray had the four fabricators because of Arias. Without him, they'd all be dead. Still, he didn't trust him. *Couldn't* trust him. That's why he'd called Margaret to be the pilot on this mission. He needed someone on the ground on New Yerkes whom he *could* trust. Though, seeing Arias now, he questioned whether sending Margaret with him was such a good idea.

"Time is short," General Salvador Burress said.

Ecuum floated up vertical next to Ray, then motioned to raise a construct from the hangar deck. The deck liquified and a scaled construct of Nerney Star System rose from it. Ecuum held that view for about twenty seconds, then zoomed into Bent Fort on New Yerkes.

Sal began. "The Gen used Madu to massacre the troopers of the First Armored Cavalry Regiment. We have reason to believe they plan to do the same to the Second Armored Cavalry Regiment. We're going to attempt a rescue."

Ecuum took over the briefing. "Colonel Arias, you are familiar with the target. We do not know when the Gen plan to strike or how they plan to do it. We do not know the status of the Fort's defenses. We do not know if the people of Bent Fort want to be rescued, or what they think about the rebellion."

"Your mission is to assess the situation, Dag," Sal said, "get us ground truth, and report back to the fleet."

Ray locked eyes with Arias. "Cadet Rhoades is going with you as your insurance. If you get into trouble, if the troopers down there don't want to join up, she'll fly you both out of there and back to the fleet."

Arias studied Margaret like a killer assessing a potential victim. The father in Ray started to call off the mission, but his planner's mind stopped him. They had to know what the fleet was walking into. Margaret was an excellent pilot, and years working and running the Ranch had taught her how to deal with crisis. And he trusted her. If anyone could pull this off, it was her.

Ecuum pulled out three datarods from a uniform pocket. He handed one to Colonel Arias. "This is your cover. You are Second Lieutenant José Vera, fresh off a counterinsurgency assignment that will explain your emotional responses to any psychological scans. It's near impossible to hide combat trauma," he explained. "When inserted into the installation's network, it will also deploy instructions that will remove your previous training records from when you attended five years ago. There is still a risk that someone might remember you, but given most military assignments rarely exceed five years, and given the number of trainees that cycle through the course every year, we feel the risk is low."

Ecuum pivoted to Margaret, handing her a clear datarod. "You are Cadet Jennifer Perry. I chose 'Jennifer' for your sister. It helps to get in character if you have a real personality to emulate." He handed her the other datarod, a blue one. She wouldn't recognize the Key that would unlock a SIL Bond. "This will allow you to take control of a SIL spacecraft if you need to escape."

Arias stared at the blue datarod. He obviously recognized it. He'd used one just like it to free the fabricator at Tomb, though he believed he'd "captured" it. The freedom of the SIL was still Ray's most closely guarded secret, even from his own daughter.

Humanity cannot be trusted.

Ray heard the comment clearly, SIL currents pushing against him. It was getting harder to separate his reality from the SIL's reality. *Neither can the Brethren*, he said into the Great Ocean.

Yet, we must work together, Rapidan said to all of them.

So you keep saying, the other factions replied.

"According to our latest intelligence," Ecuum continued, "the senior officers of the Fort are Gen. They will likely ignore you, you being Naturals. However, Imperial Intelligence will have agents at the Fort. They could be Naturals or Gen, so exercise diligence in whom you trust. The barracks are monitored, as are all the meeting and training spaces, and the base's communications systems. If you need to talk, use places that are not frequented, preferably near power generation or running utility equipment. Pay particular attention to any changes in personnel or alert status. It is likely Imperial Intelligence will pull the Gen from the installation just prior to any Madu attack."

Arias examined the datarod in his hand. "We're not spies."

"Colonel Arias," Sal said, "I chose you for this because you've proven yourself in tough situations. You have an uncanny ability to see the right path and accomplish the impossible. If there is a way to rescue those people, I have confidence you will find it."

Arias looked up from the datarod, first at Sal, then at Ray. His face hardened to stone, the black of his pupils swallowing all light.

This is a mistake. It was the current that was the father within Ray's mind that spoke. For an instant, it filled the main channel of his river, his planner's mind pushed to the sandy banks at the river's edge.

We will do what we can to protect her, Rapidan said. *We must attempt to free our Brethren, Admiral Rhoades. This battle* must *happen.*

So you keep saying, Rapidan, Ray echoed the thoughts of the opposing factions. *She's my daughter.*

We understand.

No, you don't. You never did and you never could.

"Dismissed," Sal said, almost as if trying to get Arias away from Ray as quickly as possible.

As Arias walked to the shuttle, Margaret lingered. Getting the hint, Ray pulled her away from the others, taking the opportunity to sip some water and swish it around his mouth.

Margaret glanced at the shuttle. "He scares me, Dad. Are you sure about this?"

Ray could feel the currents in his river shift as the father warred with the planner. "Margaret, it is vital that we know what's going on down there before we commit the fleet to this operation. I have every confidence in you. You've already proven yourself many times on the Ranch. That said, be careful. If things go sideways, get out of there. With or without him," he added pointedly with a glance at the shuttle. "Understood?"

"That doesn't sound very brave," she said.

"No," he agreed, "but it is reality. I've often thought bravery was nothing more than stupidity survived. Get the information we need and get out. That's your mission."

"Yes, sir," she said, then surprised him by embracing him, their respective battle armors flowing aside to allow direct contact.

It hurt. Warmth from internal bleeding spread through his chest and abdomen as tissues ripped, bones cracked. He couldn't hug her back, not with his flesh. Rapidan, thankfully, absorbed any bleeding so it wouldn't get on her. "I love you," Ray told her. "I'll be there with the fleet a couple days after you arrive."

"I love you, too, Dad," she said before releasing him. She started for the shuttle but stopped and turned. "Dad, you should call Paul. I talked to him yesterday and he's worried about you."

Ray frowned. "Did you mention that he can call me?"

"He doesn't want to disturb you, he said."

Ray relented. "Okay. I'll call him. You take care of yourself."

"I will," Margaret said. She saluted, which Ray returned, then she turned and boarded the shuttle, waving to him from the pilot's seat before powering it up and flying it through Rapidan's hull into space.

9

0547 UT, October 14, 3501
Fletcher's Run, *30 Doradus Nebula: DAY 17*

Captain Fletcher's urgent summons had surprised Ecuum, though he kept that surprise carefully hidden as he tossed Fletcher a decanter of Na Soung Gold. Fletcher caught it deftly, opening the zero-gee stopper and taking a long, slow pull of the brandy.

Ecuum took a short sip from his own decanter—he was down to just two in his cabin plus three cases left on the *Lusty Lady*—as he looked around Fletcher's captain's cabin. It was the same as he remembered, memorabilia and trinkets from a thousand worlds cluttering its spaces, making it appear far smaller than it actually was. Yet, the feel of it had changed, the wonder and awe of it somehow darker.

He noticed a new object resting atop Fletcher's oak desk. He motioned to it. "Since when did you start collecting rocks?"

Fletcher lowered his half-empty decanter, picking up the rock with his free upper hand. He turned it in his fingers, his large baby-blue eyes misty. Without warning, he tossed it to Ecuum, who barely managed to catch it. "That, my old friend," Fletcher said, "is from the Solthari homeworld, from just after we blew it to hell. You are holding a piece of Andromeda in your hand."

Ecuum examined it. The rock was a reddish ore, completely unremarkable. He was about to toss it back when Fletcher said, "Keep it. Give it to Rhoades. I don't care."

"How much?" Ecuum asked, wary.

"A gift," Fletcher said with mock flourish. He took another long, slow pull of brandy, emptying the decanter.

Ecuum tossed him the one he held; 'Gold had lubricated countless business deals, and he needed to stay on Fletcher's good side. "You're obviously an imposter. Where's the real Captain Fletcher? He never gives anything away for free."

Fletcher opened the stopper and took a long pull of brandy. His skin did not flush yellow as it normally did when he drank it. Finally, he looked at Ecuum and said simply, "You were right."

"That's hardly news," Ecuum said, becoming genuinely worried for his friend. "I'm always right."

"Janus sterilizes breeders," Fletcher told him. "*All of them.*"

Ecuum felt his mouth fall open. Naturals weren't the only breeders in the galaxies. The People also procreated. Only Gen were manufactured. "That explains why they weren't worried about the economics of mass extinction. Without trillions of Naturals to feed and support, they won't need our trade networks." He paused, the weight of it sinking in. "They won't need us."

Fletcher's laugh held no mirth. "They'll have their perfect society where everyone is engineered and Nurtured for their proper role in it. No chaos from breeders like us." He drained the decanter.

"I've got a whole case of 'Gold on the *Lusty Lady*," Ecuum offered, painful as it was.

"Call for it," Fletcher instructed, "but not for me. We'll have guests soon. They'll need some convincing. I wanted you to hear about Janus from me first."

Ecuum called for a case of 'Gold, the *Lusty Lady* handing it off to *Fletcher's Run*. That left him just two cases. *Fletcher's Run* transported the case to the captain's cabin, placing it on Fletcher's desk.

A knock came at the door.

Ecuum inhaled and blew out through his slits, propelling himself to the right side of Fletcher's desk and turning his horizontal form around to face the door.

"Come," Fletcher called.

They floated through the door, seven of them in single file, their planarian bodies horizontal, second arms and hands trailing, meter-long prehensile tails tucked against their backs. Each wore silks and jewels and tail rings and garish hats in their own unique styles, showing off their success as Independent captains.

Ecuum didn't socialize with Independents—with the obvious exception of Fletcher—and didn't know six of the captains who formed a semicircle in front of Fletcher's desk. The seventh, however, Ecuum knew far too well: 'The Admiral'—as he styled himself—Buta Na Batali. He commanded a fleet of over seventy trader vessels, most of them larger than *Fletcher's Run*. And heavily armed. Buta had used those armaments on Na Soung trading vessels in the Piracy War, inflicting substantial losses on Ecuum's House. His attacks were the final motivation that drove Ecuum to seek out Ray.

Buta's baby-blue eyes flashed when he spotted Ecuum. His fleet *had* numbered over two hundred vessels before he met Ray. "Smells like old mangy dog in here," Buta muttered.

Fletcher pointedly ignored the insult, well aware of the enmity between Buta and Ecuum. "Welcome, my dear friends," Fletcher began, "and thank you for your company this fine day. We have each come here for our own reasons, as is proper. No House, no government, holds sway over us. No one dictates to us. We do as we please, and there is much pleasure in the Universe."

The captains gave short bows of their heads to Fletcher, shows of respect. Even Buta. Fletcher was the oldest of them. A living legend. They graciously accepted decanters of Ecuum's brandy. All except Buta.

Buta had just insulted Fletcher. Again. Among Independents, insulting a host was one of the rare reasons for violence. But Fletcher took it in stride, draining a full decanter. The six captains followed suit, yellow tones flushing their exposed skin. Na Soung Gold truly was the best brandy in all the galaxies.

"Why are we here, Fletch?" one of the captains asked, tossing his empty decanter into the ceiling where the ship absorbed it. "And why so urgent?"

Fletcher tossed him a full decanter, then did the same for the five other captains who'd drunk, emptying the brandy case. Ecuum winced and hoped that Fletcher wouldn't call for another case. "It is no secret, my friends, that our Gen brothers have never born us good will. They consider us a mistake, an experiment gone wrong."

The captains again gave that short nod, acknowledging the point, but watched Fletcher warily, their skin tones neutral, their tails still.

Fletcher smiled, stretching the deep scar that cut the left side of his face and ran up under the brim of his tri-fold black pirate hat. "Our Gen brothers tolerate us only because we control the mechanisms of trade and commerce throughout the Five Galaxies."

Again, the short nods and wary expressions. "Independent" wasn't just a title. Each had come here seeking personal advantage.

Fletcher picked up the inert Madu he kept on his desk, made a show of examining its triangular head and ruby red eyes. "The Naturals and Gen fight. Rhoades and Sun have surprised us, exposing weakness we did not expect among our Gen brothers. This conflict will be a long one." He turned the Madu in his hand, its coiled black scales reflecting light. "Most of you don't care. Let them fight. Seek the profit that comes from conflict. That is why you are here." He motioned as if to the space beyond his ship.

"Fletch," the captain who'd spoken earlier said, "I know more than most how much you like to talk. *For hours*, if we let you. Why are we here?"

Fletcher placed the Madu back on his desk. "How many of you have heard the name 'Janus'?"

The captains remained silent; Information was never without price. Fletcher took a swig of brandy, examining each of them in turn. He stopped on Buta. "I see the name is familiar to some of you."

"Rumors," Buta said, admitting without admitting that he knew something. "These rebels are full of them."

"Lucrative rumors, eh, Buta?" Fletcher said, drawing a scowl from 'The Admiral.' Unconsciously or not, the other captains slipped forward, smelling advantage.

"My business is my own," Buta responded. The tip of his tail flicked, disturbing the rings there.

"As it should be," Fletcher conceded. "Very lucrative, I hear," he added in an offhand manner. "Millions of small blue crates filling your holds to bursting. Delivered all over the Five Galaxies and beyond. Even to the Hub and Nexus."

Ecuum caught the pinpricks of red that freckled Buta's exposed skin. Eyes widened on at least three other captains, obviously also familiar with the cargoes Fletcher described.

Fletcher's knowledge of the business of the galaxies, and the Nexus and Hub, in particular—home to the Houses and Grand Bazaar, respectively—were as legendary as Fletcher himself. How he came by that knowledge was a closely guarded secret, one even Ecuum had never decoded, much as he'd tried. Even more astonishing was that Fletcher had only his one ship, eschewing the whole fleet of ships his wealth could buy. Brothels and intoxicants, especially when mixed, were a treasure trove of information, but a single ship could only travel so far.

"Did Imperial Intelligence tell you what was in the crates?" Fletcher asked Buta.

Buta's face and hands flushed red. "I don't work with Imperial Intelligence."

"Oh, come, now," Fletcher said, draining the last of his brandy. "We all work with Imperial Intelligence. They pay *very* well, and their credit is *always* good." He paused, then raised a hairless brow at Buta. "Is that where you really heard rumors of Janus?"

Buta didn't answer, his skin going neutral, though he refused to make eye contact with Fletcher.

The captain who'd first addressed Fletcher, however, said, "The contacts also paid well not to ask questions or to look inside the crates."

"What did you find?" Fletcher asked.

The captain laughed. "Nothing. The crates were impervious to passive scans and were rigged to explode if tampered with."

Fletcher nodded to him. "The rebels say Janus is a virus." He paused. "They are wrong." He glanced at Ecuum before turning back to the other captains. "It is a self-replicating, highly adaptive molecular machine—" he waited three heartbeats— "with a hive intelligence."

Color drained from the captains, their exposed skin turning white.

"No one fears intelligent technology more than the Gen," Ecuum said to Fletcher. "No one enforces its ban more ruthlessly than Imperial Intelligence."

"You asked me how Janus could be effective at sterilizing every Natural, and be uncurable," Fletcher said. "This is how."

"Unbelievable." And Ecuum really couldn't believe it. "An intelligent virus? Even Gen Cardinal fears and loathes machine intelligence, considering it a direct threat to Gen dominance. Why?"

Fletcher inhaled and pivoted in place. He opened one of the cubbies behind his desk, withdrawing a naval shoulder board with five gold stars in a circle, the rank of fleet admiral, then pivoted back to the captains. "Gen Kii was an asshole." He flicked the shoulder board so it turned slowly in the ship's microgravity. "He believed to the depths of his black soul that Gen, *and only Gen*, deserved to survive the SIL Wars. No one else—not Naturals, definitely not the SIL, and not even our People. He tried to hide it, and mostly succeeded, except with anyone who spent a lot of time around him."

It struck Ecuum yet again how Fletcher talked as if he were there thirteen centuries ago. "Are you suggesting Gen Kii created Janus, Fletch?"

"Have you never wondered what drove Cyra Dain to assassinate him?" Fletcher answered. He looked at each of the captains in turn, settling on the only female captain among them. "Janus sterilizes *all* humanoid breeders. And it infects *only* breeders. That's why the Gen do not fear their own creation." He turned to Buta. "And you delivered it to the Hub and the Nexus, the beating hearts of our People."

Buta's skin turned ashen. He stammered, "They wouldn't! They need us. Without us. . . ."

"Without us," Fletcher said, "without Naturals, they wouldn't need to keep the SIL. They would be all that remains of Humanity, exactly what Gen Kii wanted."

No one spoke, the enormity of it too much to take in all at once. Fletcher nudged his chin toward Ecuum, as if to say, "Your turn."

Ecuum cleared his throat. "Ray—Admiral Rhoades—plans to take the rebel fleet to Andromeda, establish a base, build shipyards, and construct a fleet that will rival the Star Navy. He's going to need traders. Lots of them."

The captains eyed him. They could figure out the economic opportunities in what he'd said without his needing to explain it.

Buta sneered, his skin mottling red. "Why would I trust a Na Soung dog?"

Ecuum floated closer to him. "Is it true Gen Cardinal is terrible in bed, Buta? Figure a Na Batali could enlighten us on how his fat jiggles in the throws of ecstasy."

Buta's face flushed a deep crimson as he inhaled and flew at Ecuum. Unfortunately for Buta, he was an armchair Admiral. Ecuum, on the other hand, enjoyed a good zero-gee bar fight. He inhaled and flipped himself vertical, his head toward the deck, and wrapped his tail around Buta's neck, squeezing. He used their collective momentum and his leverage to swing up, grabbing Buta's tail near the tip with his lower right hand and pulling it so Buta couldn't use it, then swung his body around to grab Buta from behind. He inhaled deeply and slammed Buta into the deck, face first. He tightened his tail's grip around Buta's throat while inhaling and blowing air through his slits to keep Buta pinned. He couldn't keep it up for long, though, or he would hyperventilate.

"You're going to need him, old friend," Fletcher said.

Ecuum coiled his tail tighter, crushing Buta's windpipe. A Natural would die in minutes. The People, however, could survive in hard vacuum for hours. "Just remember, Na Batali, that you delivered Janus to the People. I doubt they will think kindly of you if they learn of it."

Buta struggled, but couldn't budge Ecuum. Finally, he relaxed. Not quite a surrender, but Ecuum released him and pushed away on strong puffs of air, resuming his horizontal position near Fletcher.

"What is it you want, Fletch?" the female captain asked as Buta inhaled a ragged breath, molemachs repairing his windpipe. He pushed himself off the deck, his skin still crimson and his tail lashing, the rings on his tail giving an angry jingle. "I didn't come here for him," she added, pointing her chubby chin toward Ecuum. "Or Rhoades."

"Malinda." Fletcher's tone was familiar. *Very familiar*, if Ecuum was any judge. "You are the only one among us who has the equipment and know-how to establish geodesics. Imagine how much the first geodesic linking Andromeda with the Five Galaxies would be worth."

And she did imagine it; Ecuum could see it on her face. The transit fees alone would make her wealthy beyond measure. "You want us to go with Rhoades to Andromeda?" she asked.

"No," Fletcher said. "I want you to go *with me* to Andromeda."

She studied him, her baby blue eyes wide. "And the dangers?"

Fletcher smiled at her. "I've been there. And, as you can see, I've come back. Plus, we'll be traveling with Rhoades' fleet: four fabricators, eighty-one SIL, and one hundred and seven standard warships. That's a lot of protection."

"There's one other thing," Ecuum said, taking advantage of the moment. "The Council has directed Admiral Rhoades to rescue the Naturals at New Yerkes. We could use a hand." He gestured to the captains, knowing they sensed opportunity in that knowledge. "The Gen already know about it. It was their idea."

"I, for one, will help, old friend," Fletcher said in a clear show of support.

The female captain—Malinda—eyed Fletcher, then shifted her gaze to Ecuum. "As will I. And I will go with Captain Fletcher to Andromeda and see if the opportunities are as promising as he suggests."

The other captains, except for Buta, nodded their agreement. Fletcher turned to Buta. "Admiral Buta, the People need to know the threat they face. But we must do it quietly, discreetly. If the

Gen discover that we know, they may trigger Janus and exterminate our People. *Forever*," Fletcher added pointedly, knowing Buta would sell the knowledge, not give it away.

Buta thought a moment before nodding his agreement.

Fletcher smiled broadly, deep yellow suffusing his face and hands. "Thank you from the bottom of my heart to the tip of my tail for your gracious company and consideration, my friends. May advantage come to the swift and opportunity to the bold."

"May advantage come to the swift and opportunity to the bold," they chorused.

Ecuum waited for them to leave, Buta throwing him a murderous glare before slipping through the door, then he started to follow.

"Wait, my old friend," Fletcher said. "Old as in the smell of mangy wet fur on a gray and feeble dog," he added, referencing with a laugh Buta's insult at the beginning of the meeting.

Ecuum pivoted, still holding the rock, which he'd shifted to his lower left hand during his scuffle with Buta. "For you, always, old friend. Old as in the termite infested wood of an ancient Egyptian sarcophagus, which—" he added as he glanced around the cabin—"you probably have in here."

"You owe me another case of 'Gold."

"You'll have it," Ecuum assured him, though inwardly he winced. That would leave him with just one case.

Fletcher was suddenly serious. "There's something else you should consider. Janus could lie inert in a person's body, spreading quietly without triggering. You should be careful of the refugees."

10

1322 UT, October 14, 3501
Bent Fort New Yerkes, Nerney Star System: DAY 17

“**This** way.”

A sergeant motioned Dag toward a small office at the end of a row of bland government desks. Rhoades’ daughter followed him, though the sergeant hadn’t motioned to her.

None of the people behind those desks so much as glanced at them, almost as if they were afraid to. Dag had trained here as a young lieutenant five years ago. He remembered the people here being bored but otherwise friendly, welcoming. These people wouldn’t even make eye contact. *The rebellion. Of course.* They were Naturals. Gen officers now ran the installation, according to that Floater who’d briefed them before they left.

Imperial Intelligence will have agents at the Fort.

Was that the source of their fear? Dag had a feeling he’d find out soon enough.

The trip to New Yerkes had been uneventful. Three geodesic jumps and a roughly six-hour flight from the geodesic at the inner edge of the Kuiper belt. Their credentials had worked perfectly, at least so far. The only anxiety had come from their trip through New Yerkes’ crazy atmosphere. Rhoades’ daughter had handled it well.

Too well, for someone her age. Dag didn’t trust Rhoades. By extension, he didn’t trust her. *He still has a daughter. He cost me mine!*

They hadn’t spoken the entire trip, though she’d thrown him several cautious glances, always looking away when he caught her.

What were her orders? He'd seen her talking with Rhoades before boarding the shuttle. What had Rhoades told her? What treachery had they hatched?

"Through there." The sergeant pointed to an open office door.

Dag stepped into the office, ready to snap to attention as was expected of a trainee. The officer behind the desk raised his head.

A Gen!

Dag's vision narrowed. He tried to call up his targeting reticle before remembering that his armor lay back in the shuttle and he had no weapon.

The Gen, military-cut blond hair, icy blue eyes, perfect face, frowned at him. "Report!"

Snapping to attention, letting his training take over, Dag saluted. "Second Lieutenant José Vera reporting."

"Cadet Jennifer Perry reporting," Rhoades' daughter said.

The Gen—Colonel Gen Alexander by his nameplate—scowled. He didn't return their salutes. "More Nats. We have a fucking war going on and they are sending me more Nats." He shook his head and held out his hand. "Records."

Dag stared at that hand. How easy it would be to grab it, wrench the arm from its socket. Instead, he pulled out the datarod containing his forged records and dropped it into the Gen's hand without touching it. Rhoades' daughter imitated him.

"Let us see," the Gen said, sounding as if all the problems of the galaxies had been laid upon his shoulders. He plugged Dag's datarod into a receptacle in his desk. "Lieutenant Vera," he read. "Nothing remarkable here. Huh. A battle ribbon with a 'V' device. What did you do, rescue some Galaxy Scouts?" Dag's hands curled into fists. The Gen noticed and smirked. "You will be assigned to Second Tank Platoon—do you even know how to drive a tank?—Aggressor Troop, First Squadron. I will review your platoon tomorrow and we will see what you can do."

He turned his attention to Rhoades' daughter. "And what do we have here? A child? Says here you are a pilot. Humph. I do not believe it. Maybe we can find some other activities—" he leered at her— "more suited to your . . . natural talents."

Rhoades' daughter stood firm, maintaining control. Dag admired her courage, until he remembered what that courage would mean if she planned to betray him.

The Gen seemed disappointed in her reaction. He handed back their datarods, dropping Dag's into his hand as Dag had done with him, but sliding his fingers across hers. Rhoades' daughter snatched her hand away and the Gen laughed. "Fourth Squadron HQ, child. Unpack, get settled. I will be seeing you again. *Soon*," he emphasized. "Now get out of my office before I need to have it fumigated."

When they were out of earshot of the Gen, Rhoades' daughter said, "I don't know if I can go through with this. If that *creature* touches me again. . . ."

Dag stopped and studied her. In some distant part of his mind, he noticed how pretty she was. Sharp hazel eyes. Short-cut brown-blond hair. Oval face. Toned, slender body. He could see why the Gen colonel was interested in her. He almost pitied her. Almost. Rhoades might lose his daughter. Then he'd know what it felt like. "You'll what? Blow our assignment?"

She glared at him. Her eyes moistened and he could see the battle between duty and disgust raging within her. Then her expression hardened. She turned and stormed toward the door leading out of the building.

Brave girl, Dag thought. Killing her might be a mercy compared to what that Gen colonel would do to her.

"Is all the food here that bad?" Dag asked his new battle buddy as they exited the Dining Facility into the bright light of midday. Just the memory of the smell turned his stomach.

"Only if you're a Natural," Second Lieutenant Marco DeWitt replied. He was tall and skinny, with hair the color of wheat and freckles all over his skin. He'd joined the Cav to escape the farm, he'd explained, and had regretted the decision ever since. "The Gen save the best for themselves."

"They should've buried whatever that meat was weeks ago. Fucking Gen," Dag muttered just loud enough for DeWitt to hear, testing him. What did the Naturals here think of the Gen? Would they want to be rescued?

"Don't say that too loud or they'll take you away, too. They have sensors hidden all over the place. To keep an eye on us."

DeWitt caught Dag's eye and motioned toward a large circular structure. They walked casually over to it, talking about the food, the housing, DeWitt's girlfriends, real and imagined. Nerney Star warmed them from where it sat in the southeastern sky above the crater rim. A "day" on New Yerkes was about seventeen days on Earth, half that time in the light of Nerney Star, the other half in the almost darkness of Hades. The gas giant filled the western sky, about three quarters of its disk lit by Nerney Star. Ribbons of brown and orange and white cloud bands were visible below the bluish gray of its north pole.

When they reached the circular structure, Dag saw that it housed a fusion generator. DeWitt put an arm out and leaned against it, facing it. "It's safe to talk here, but not for long. They watch this place. Oh," he added, "and look toward the wall or they'll read your lips."

Dag did as DeWitt said, but waited for him to start the conversation. He'd never met an Imperial Intelligence agent before and had no idea how to spot one.

"So," DeWitt started, feigning a cough. "You've just come in. They don't let us see any news around here. What's the latest?"

Dag took the measure of DeWitt. He was young, like most of the trainees in the regiment, and wore a single battle ribbon like Dag's. He'd boasted during dinner of his part in the minor antipiracy operation where he'd earned it. He'd never even fired his weapon during the op. DeWitt didn't seem like the type to be an enemy agent, but Dag decided to play it safe, sticking to what the news had reported. "I heard the rebels attacked Tocci. Disrupted the Shipyards."

"You're yankin' me," DeWitt said, his eyes going wide with excitement.

Dag tried to inject excitement into his own voice, but memories of Yoshi Takeuchi's and Major Kenyon's deaths turned it cold.

"It's true. According to the news," Dag quickly added.

DeWitt watched him, and his excitement changed to a stunned awe. "You were there, weren't you? I can see it in your face."

For an instant, Takeuchi's lifeless body hung before Dag, his face frozen in that strangely peaceful expression. It almost seemed as if it tried to speak to him, but he couldn't hear the words. The vision passed. Dag braced himself against the structure with one hand, feeling suddenly lightheaded, and saw DeWitt watching him.

Would DeWitt give him away? What was worse: if he were this obvious to a kid lieutenant, how could he hope to fool the Gen?

"Don't worry," DeWitt assured him. "Your secret's safe with me." He paused. "So, if you're here, that must mean the rebels are planning something, right?" That youthful exuberance returned.

Imperial Intelligence will have agents at the Fort. They could be Naturals or Gen. . . .

After his meeting with Colonel Gen Alexander, Dag had walked to Aggressor Troop's orderly room and reported in. DeWitt happened to be there and the Troop's commanding officer, a Natural, had assigned him to show Dag around and be his battle buddy. It had seemed innocent enough. But was it just coincidence that DeWitt had been there right then? Or had Imperial Intelligence planted him there?

What decided it for Dag was simple: He had to trust somebody or his mission would fail, and he didn't have the luxury of time. And, if they did capture him, he would finally know the embrace of death and be with his family again. "How do the Naturals here feel about the Gen?" he asked.

DeWitt glanced around. "I don't—" he swallowed— "I don't know. They watch us pretty close. Everyone is afraid to talk since the Gen arrived and the purges began. The Gen arrested most of the senior officers and NCOs. Accused them of spying. They even tortured some. Others, well, they just disappeared. We don't know what happened to them. They've replaced all the senior officers with Gen." He rubbed the back of his neck. "I hate them. I think most of the others do, too."

He sounded as if he really meant it. "Would they be willing to fight the Gen?" Dag asked.

DeWitt stared at him as if he'd gone mad. "That's a deep well," he said, one hand fidgeting in his pocket. "Some might help, but most of them would be too scared."

"Can you find out?"

The freckled lieutenant turned away, though still facing the wall of the building so the Gen couldn't read his lips. "If they found out I was asking, they'd kill me. And probably you, too. They would've noticed us talking here."

Dag's voice hardened. "Do you want to be free of them or not?"

For a long moment, DeWitt didn't say anything, and Dag wondered if he'd pushed him too hard. Then, DeWitt sighed. "I'll see what I can do."

"Who should I talk to?" Dag asked, his eyes scanning the area around the generator building to see if anyone had taken notice.

"You better not." DeWitt feigned a cough, covering his mouth as he did. "Your being new here and all, it would look suspicious if you started talking to too many people. Better I should do it."

Dag nodded, not happy leaving this to the kid lieutenant but seeing no other immediate option. They walked back to the barracks together before separating. As they walked, Dag studied the layout of the buildings and streets, a grid pattern with no separation between the military buildings and the civilian town that supported the Fort. High crater walls rose up all around them, protecting the Fort from the ravages of the weather beyond. The only barrier on the installation was a high fence that marked the landing field at the southeast section of the crater floor. That was where the assault ships would land to rescue the people here.

But would they want to come?

As scared as DeWitt said they were, Dag wasn't sure they would. But, so far, he'd seen only that one Gen officer. Maybe there weren't that many here. If he killed them, maybe the people would follow.

He looked up at the strange sky, the gas giant, Hades, casting its own light upon New Yerkes.

Hades. The Greek Hell.

What if God had brought him here not to reunite him with his family in death, but to condemn his soul for what he'd done on Tocci?

What if that was what God had intended all along, why Dag had survived battles far from this place while so many of his friends and fellow troopers had died? What if God had brought him to the precipice of Hell so that when he died his soul would be consumed by it?

Condemned.

To never see his family again.

He looked back down, hoping to see Rosita among the buildings, peeking out a window or around a corner, to get some reassurance that her spirit was still with him. His guardian angel.

Where are you, Mihita?

She didn't answer.

11

1914 UT, October 15, 3501
RSS Rapidan, Nerney Star System: DAY 18

The jump nearly killed him.

They'd departed 30 Doradus about thirty hours before, following a six-geodesic route Kamen had plotted to avoid populated star systems, arriving at a system near the galactic rim about sixty-five lightyears from Nerney. The geodesic jumps had gone well, causing Ray no discomfort. Well, no *more* discomfort.

The Linear Star Drive jump, however, had ripped his cells apart, drowning him in his own blood, liquifying his tissues so badly it was almost beyond Rapidan's ability to heal him.

Almost.

Just let me die, Rapidan. The pain was beyond excruciating.

No, Admiral Rhoades, Rapidan said in his mind, its flows twining with his in Ray's river.

It's my life! You know as well as I do that I'll never survive the H3 jumps to Andromeda. Why postpone the inevitable?

We are attempting to formulate a solution, Admiral Rhoades. The recent jump provided us with good data.

Oh, good, Ray thought, hoping his sarcasm translated to the SIL. Slowly, too slowly, his pain eased to an ever-present throb that kept time with his struggling heart.

They'd jumped to the extreme outer edge of Nerney's Kuiper belt to avoid setting off perimeter alarms. Like most Linear Star Drive jumps in the Five Galaxies, they'd jumped at H2, what scientists called the Second Harmonic of the speed of light. No one knew why harmonics existed. When the Linear Star Drive warped space, surrounding a ship within a bubble of spacetime, collapsing that bubble in front while expanding it behind to propel the ship forward, theory said it shouldn't have a defined speed in real spacetime.

But it did.

The Second Harmonic equated to about 990 million kilometers per second. That was fast enough to go from Earth to Proxima Centauri, the nearest star to Earth, in about eleven and a half hours. As fast as that was, though, it wasn't nearly fast enough to travel to the Andromeda galaxy. At H2, the journey would require roughly 768 years.

Getting to Andromeda within a reasonable timeframe would require traveling at the Third Harmonic of light: H3, roughly 1,980 *trillion* kilometers per second. Even at that speed, if they made no stops, it would take about 140 days to reach the stars within the Andromeda galaxy proper.

Unfortunately, Naturals couldn't survive that long in H3. That was the main reason Naturals created Floaters and then Gen in the first place, to fight the Solthari who came from the Andromeda galaxy.

When the Linear Star Drive warped space, it damaged the cells of the humans within it. At H2, this damage was repairable with a person's internal molecular machines—molemachs—so long as that person didn't endure too many jumps close together. At H3, the warping of spacetime within the bubble was so extreme that it caused great damage, and could even kill Naturals if the jump was too long. They would have to perform shorter jumps and wait for people to recover before performing another.

Kamen had developed a plan for ten, one-day stops between each jump to allow each person's molemachs to fully repair the damage to their bodies. Her plan also held them 250,000 light years short of Andromeda to survey for candidate star systems for settlement, before proceeding into the galaxy itself with one last H3 jump.

Ray knew he would never survive an H3 jump, never live to see Andromeda. Not like this. He sipped some water, his muscles finally repaired enough to do so, and squished it around his mouth. All he tasted was blood. Instead of swallowing and risking vomiting it back up, he spit it out, his battle armor absorbing it.

"I can't do this," Ray whispered.

"You must," Rapidan responded, its deep voice filling the cabin, reverberating inside Ray.

"I hate you," he told the ship, his voice wet and raspy.

"We know."

I need to talk to my son, Paul, Ray thought, unable to muster the strength for spoken words, *but I can't have him see me like this.*

Rapidan gently tightened its currents around Ray's and pulled him over his falls into the Great Ocean. *We recommend using a construct, Admiral Rhoades.*

Within the Great Ocean, Rapidan helped Ray find the currents of the battlecarrier Tzu, Admiral Chengchi Sun's ship and Paul's current assignment. Through the flows, Ray could see within Tzu, follow its passageways, peek into its compartments, though he couldn't read people's thoughts the way the SIL seemed able to do. He found Paul sleeping in an ensign's cabin, a sparse three-meter by two-meter compartment barely tall enough to stand up in. It reminded Ray of his own quarters on the SIL frigate Shangani, his first assignment out of the Academy.

Rapidan's currents nudged Ray into Tzu's flows. Tzu was a free SIL—though Admiral Sun didn't know that—and accepted Ray's currents into its own, guiding him to liquify the deck in Paul's cabin and form a construct of Ray's healthy self, standing next to Paul's bed.

The pain, it's . . . gone.

Within the construct, Ray couldn't feel his own body, couldn't feel its agony, couldn't feel Rapidan's movements within it. The relief, being pain free for the first time since his death and revival, was a bliss he'd thought never to experience again short of death.

"Paul?"

"Oomph," Paul said in his sleep, turning his back to his father.

Teenagers. "Paul, it's your Dad."

"Dad?" Paul turned his head and cracked an eye open. "Shit!" He scrambled out of bed, touching the roll of his uniform sitting on a nightstand next to it. The roll liquified and flowed over his body, the uniform crisp and inspection ready.

Paul snapped to attention and rendered a textbook salute. "Admiral."

Ray returned the salute and dropped his hand, able to control the construct as if it were his own body. "At ease, Cadet." He couldn't stop the smile that formed on his construct's face. Yes, Margaret was his favorite because of how she helped out around the Ranch, but Ray was so proud of his son. Paul had thrown himself into family lore from a very early age, then gone on to become the youngest BattleSim Grandmaster in the history of the combat simulation game. It was a remarkable achievement, though his chores around the Ranch suffered greatly, usually falling to his big sister. "Sorry about waking you."

"It's okay, sir," Paul answered properly, dropping his salute. "I needed to get up anyway, sir. My shift starts at twenty-three hundred."

"How are you doing, Paul?" Ray asked.

"I could ask you the same question, sir. The rumors. . . ."

So, the rumors had reached Tzu, had reached his son. Ray should've called Paul sooner, before the jump had almost killed him. "I'm still alive, still in command of the fleet, if that's what you're asking."

Paul finally relaxed, then suddenly wrapped his arms around Ray's construct. Ray winced reflexively before discovering the hug didn't hurt. He hugged his son back.

"You didn't answer my question, Paul. How are *you* doing?"

Paul released the hug and clasped his hands behind his back at the position of At Ease. "Captain Dall has me working in the Sensor Section. It's good, Dad. I mean, Admiral. Working real sensors is different from BattleSim. I didn't realize how different until I started working them."

Captain Jocelyn Dall was Admiral Sun's adjutant. The same officer who had tried to betray and replace Ray back at Tocci.

She was in charge of his son?

"It's okay, Dad. Admiral," Paul said, apparently reacting to the expression on Ray's construct. "They're treating me okay. No different from any of the other crew. Though, sometimes, I feel I'm being watched. You know those dragon decorations all over the ship? It feels like their eyes follow me, which is a little creepy."

Ray nodded. He'd felt the same way every time he'd been on Sun's ship. "Are you sure you don't want me to reassign you to Rapidan?"

"Dad, like I said before, that would look like favoritism." Paul shifted uncomfortably. "Besides, Admiral Sun thinks of me as his hostage, doesn't he? By keeping me here, he feels he has leverage over you, in case something happens. I'm right, aren't I?"

Paul had always been very smart, smarter than Ray at the same age. "Yes. It helps to keep him in check. Doesn't mean I like it."

"I'm okay, Dad," Paul said, reassuring his father instead of the other way around. He really was a smart kid. And the SIL had promised to protect him.

We will protect him, Tzu confirmed.

"How's Mom?" Paul asked. "Margaret?"

He's trying to distract me.

"Your mother is good. She wants you to call her more often."

Paul rolled his eyes, as teenagers often did, before remembering he was talking to an Admiral. He snapped to attention. "Sorry, Admiral."

Ray tried very hard not to laugh; It was amazing what a difference it made to his mood to not be in constant pain. Abruptly, he realized he wasn't looking forward to leaving the construct to return to his physical body. "Margaret is on a mission for me. She's really impressed everyone with her flying skills."

"A mission?" Paul's eyes lit up. "Like a real mission? Awesome! What is it? Oh—" he answered his own question—"you can't tell me, huh?"

"No," Ray confirmed. "And don't tell your mother."

He smiled knowingly, then the smile disappeared. "Any word about Jenny?"

"She's alive and being well cared for in the Imperial Palace," Ray said, not telling his son how he knew. Paul didn't know about the SIL's freedom or Ray's connection to them. "We haven't heard anything else."

An uncomfortable silence descended.

"You're leaving us in reserve," Paul eventually commented. "I hope that's not because of me."

Yes. "No," Ray said. "As I'm sure you understand, we can't stand toe-to-toe with the Imperial Fleet. If we're going to rescue those people on New Yerkes, we have to do it quietly, without alerting the Gen until the last possible moment."

"It's a dumb plan." No sooner had the words come out of his mouth than Paul stammered, "Sorry. I didn't mean any disrespect, sir."

Ray's smile this time was sad. "No. You're right. But this is what the Council ordered. The military has always subordinated itself to civilian authority, even when we don't agree with the orders we're given. Remember that."

"Yes, sir."

Ray hugged his son, taking advantage of the construct and its lack of pain. They held each other a long time, as if they both felt it might be the last time.

"We're beginning our high-speed run into Nerney Star System," Ray said, releasing his son. Within the Great Ocean, he could feel the engine thrust of the task force increasing. "Take care of yourself, Paul. Don't hesitate to contact me if you need something."

As Ray's construct melted back into the deck, his last view was the worry twisting his son's face.

Then the pain returned.

12

0607 UT, October 16, 3501
ISS Solaris, Olympus Star System: DAY 19

Admiral Gen Serenna hid her deep frustration. She stood at the edge of the 40-meter-diameter sand table in Solaris' Combat Information Center, the constructs of the other battlegroup commanders crowded around it. Fleet Admiral Gen Nasser's construct walked within the sand table, describing Nerney Star System to them.

Four days!

Four days of gathering ever more ships and ever more supplies. Nasser had almost eight hundred SIL vessels. He had stripped Serenna of her SIL, minus Solaris, and assigned to her 150 less capable standard technology warships with Natural crews. Altogether, it was the largest fleet anyone had assembled since the SIL Wars—*and still he delayed!* There were 847 SIL warships remaining in the Imperial Star Navy, minus the fabricators, and he apparently would not attack until he had every last one of them.

What was worse, the rebel fleet had jumped out of 30 Doradus in the Large Magellanic Cloud two days ago. They could already be in Nerney Star System. If Nasser delayed too much longer, they would lose their opportunity to kill Michael and crush the rebels.

And it is my fault. She had lost at Tomb. She had lost at Tocci. She had lost four fabricators and destroyed another. Most importantly, she had lost the confidence of the Emperor. That was why Nasser was in charge. That was why they were still in Olympus Star System instead of destroying the rebels. For all her frustration, she had only herself to blame.

That did not mean she intended to give up.

Her People were in grave danger, even if they could not see it. To save them, she had to survive. In this moment, that was all that mattered.

So, she listened. She obeyed. She kept her mouth shut. She endured. Hard as all that was, her People were worth it.

"The rebels have not shown themselves," Nasser explained, "and the fleet will not move until they do. That does not mean we have been idle. General." Nasser deferred to an officer wearing an Imperial Marine uniform.

The officer stepped into the sand table. "I am Colonel General Gen Jiho, Commander of the Special Operations Directorate of the Imperial Marines." He motioned and the moon, New Yerkes, expanded in the sand table while the rest of the star system shrank away. New Yerkes expanded again, highlighting the large impact crater that housed Bent Fort. At present, it was day at the Fort. Fast moving rivers of white clouds flowed around the crater rim with only occasional streamers finding gaps and flowing down into the crater.

"The headquarters element," Gen Jiho continued, "of the First Reconnaissance Division is on the ground at Bent Fort and has linked up with Colonel General Gen Mudir, commanding officer of the installation." Gen Jiho highlighted an area outside the crater on its western flank. "We are staging the Division's combat elements behind the crater rim as depicted, infiltrating units into the staging area slowly so as not to alert the Fort or the rebels. We will complete deployment thirty-one hours from now, and be ready to assault the Fort within an hour after that."

"Thank you, General," Nasser said. He reset the sand table to show the entirety of Nerney Star System. "We will wait to jump the fleet until we receive confirmation that the rebels have arrived, and in what force. It is a two-geodesic jump to Nerney Star System and we can be there within nine hours of the rebel's arrival."

Serenna had always believed Nasser's one redeeming quality was his boldness. His strategy made her reevaluate that assessment. At its heart, it was a defensive strategy focused not on winning, but on not losing. Every officer here had attended Combat Command Nurturing. Most, if not all of them, would arrive at the same conclusion.

"Are we certain they are coming?" one battlegroup commander asked.

"Imperial Intelligence is confident they will attempt a rescue," Nasser answered, "and they have agents on the ground. We will know the instant the rebels arrive. We also spotted this Independent Trader vessel, *Fletcher's Run*, arriving in system just a few hours ago." A bubble opened showing a garishly lit cylindrical vessel in the shape of a phallus. "While Independent Traders do occasionally visit Bent Fort, the timing of this one is of interest, and this same vessel was spotted at 30 Doradus when the rebels were there."

"Fleet Admiral," another battlegroup commander asked, "will we not be vulnerable to an ambush if we arrive by geodesic?"

Serenna recognized the officer as the commander of her Indus Battlegroup at Tocci, one of the few here with actual combat experience.

Nasser must have recognized him at the same time; he darted a glance at Serenna. "That is why we will send Admiral Serenna with the Reserve Flotilla first. If the rebels *are* waiting in ambush, they will reveal themselves by attacking the Reserve Flotilla, expending their missiles before we arrive with the main fleet."

The battlegroup commanders turned to her, watching for her reaction. She did not give them one. She remained stoic, betraying no emotion, nothing they could use against her. They finally looked away.

Nasser glanced at her again—and seemed disappointed. He was obviously hoping the rebels would be waiting at the geodesic so he could eliminate her without overtly doing so. The Emperor had spared Serenna's life and assigned her to Nasser's staff. No Gen, not even Nasser, would dare go against the orders of the Emperor.

But Nasser did not understand Michael as she did. He would not be waiting at the geodesic. There were two geodesics in Nerney Star System. He would have to divide his force to guard both if he intended an ambush. Plus, a third force to conduct the rescue.

Against the firepower he must surely know Nasser would bring, he would not risk dividing his small rebel fleet in that manner. Michael would focus on New Yerkes.

"Once we receive either the 'all clear' from the Reserve Flotilla," Nasser continued, "or confirmation of a rebel attack, we will jump in and immediately assume a spherical formation."

Another bubble opened showing the geodesic and the spherical formation Nasser intended to use. Nasser's flagship, the battlecarrier Ganges, and its battlegroup, were at the center. The remaining ten battlegroups formed wedges within the sphere. It was the worst possible formation. Spherical formations were defensive by nature, spreading firepower evenly in all directions, diluting that firepower. Serenna—and Michael, she had noted—preferred pyramidal formations on the offense. Those provided every combat vessel a clear field of fire forward.

Serenna debated saying something, but decided against it. Nasser would not listen, and it would make her appear weak and uncooperative. She needed Nasser to see her as beaten, not a threat to his power.

"We will then jump to Hades," Nasser said, "and destroy the rebels with superior firepower."

Serenna waited for more, but Nasser was finished. A massed charge was his whole plan, with the spherical formation protecting him at its center. She would have laughed if the stakes were not so high.

Instead, she accepted her assignment, knowing an opportunity would present itself, and hoping she would live long enough to seize it.

13

0659 UT, October 16, 3501
Bent Fort New Yerkes, Nerney Star System: DAY 19

Mercifully, this early in the "morning" Universal Time—a timekeeping based on Earth's rotation even centuries after humans ventured into space—the Post Exchange was largely deserted. Nerney Star hung at about the two o'clock position in the pale blue sky, the gas giant Hades hanging directly overhead, half of its disk aglow in the light of day. The moon, Phlegethon, closest of Hades' large moons and a volcanic hell similar to Io in Sol Star System, blazed a sulfurous yellow just passed the terminator into night.

Dag, knowing the Gen were watching, tried to appear casual as he walked toward the three Galactic Geocomm booths just inside the Post Exchange, the PX. He was still in his "PTs" after the unit physical training they'd done this morning. Line units didn't do organized physical training. Molemachs—molecular machines in every soldier's body—conditioned muscles and improved heart, lung, and brain endurance without the need for exercising. Training units, however, insisted on it, claiming it built unit cohesion.

Whatever.

DeWitt had taken a position next to him in PT formation. All he'd said, though, was that he'd have more later.

Dag had never been good at waiting, something Maria had constantly scolded him about, though always in good humor. Even their engagement had strained his patience. She'd wanted a big traditional wedding with the whole town in attendance, a wedding that took months to arrange and save for. He would've preferred getting married right away with a Justice of the Peace. In the end, he'd waited.

For her.

A few months after their wedding, he'd just come home from work when she'd insisted on going to the promontory overlooking the Pacific Ocean where they'd first made love. With the sound of the surf pounding the rocks, she'd taken his hand and placed it on her stomach, her fingers curling lovingly into his.

Her pregnancy was almost harder on him—nine months was a long time to wait!—than it was on her, and the delivery was long and difficult, but when he finally held Rosita, so small and beautiful, time melted away. He would've waited a lifetime for such a miracle.

Papí! Papí help me!

Dag squeezed his eyes shut. He couldn't relive that moment again, the moment God had taken his little miracle away. He'd looked for her everywhere, around every corner, in every window. She'd come to him on the fabricator in his hour of greatest need. She'd journeyed with him across the sands of Tocci III and into Tocci City. But here, in the reflected light of Hades, she hadn't appeared.

Had he scared her away? Or had God taken her from him, possibly for the final time?

He opened his eyes and stepped into the farthest of the three booths, taking out his forged personal datarod and slipping it into the single receptacle. The booth faded to black and a great whirlpool of stars formed before him.

"Welcome to Galactic Geocomm," a pleasant female voice said. "Destination?"

"Milky Way, Sol, Earth, Texas, San Antonio," Dag said, calling out the location of his imaginary home. "One, nine-five, four-five-five, three-three-one-three, seven-seven-five-one."

"Message?"

Dag cleared his throat. "Arrived safely. Miss you. Will call later. José. End of message."

The text of Dag's message appeared in yellow letters above the swirl of the Milky Way, along with the charge. "Confirm," he said after reading the text.

"Thank you for using Galactic Geocomm."

The code phrase would tell General Burress they'd arrived and hadn't seen anything unusual, but that he didn't know yet whether the people here would join them.

As he stepped out of the booth, Rhoades' daughter walked into the PX. She was pale, her body stiff as she turned toward him, her expression somewhere between rage and fear. She spotted him and came over. "That bastard came to my room this morning," she told him in a harsh whisper. A vicious smile stretched her lips thin. "He didn't know I wrestle farm animals on our Ranch for a living."

She stood with her fists clenched, seemingly ready to swing at the first person who looked at her wrong. Dag admired her courage. Again. But Rhoades had sent her here to betray him. "Is he going to press charges?" Dag asked.

She stared at him in shock. "Him? *He* attacked *me*!"

"Did you strike a superior officer?"

"I . . . I . . . Shit. Can he really press charges?"

Somewhere, in the deep recesses of Dag's mind, he felt sorry for her. "Yes. It will be your word against his, and his will win."

"I . . . Shit." Fear overcame rage. "We need to leave."

The Gen were watching, listening. "Pull yourself together, Cadet." Dag's tone was harsh and she flinched. "This training is too important. Or have you forgotten what you'd be going back to? Wrestling farm animals," he added quickly for the Gen listening.

"I," she stammered, on the verge of tears. "Shit, shit, shit!"

Dag watched, the Void swallowing all emotion where his heart had once been. If they arrested her, she would betray him. Maybe it would be better if he killed her. Once they had her in a cell, that Gen colonel could do what he pleased. Killing her would be a mercy. He examined her neck, imagined his hands wrapped around it, squeezing.

He heard his daughter cry.

Dag's head snapped around. "Mihita?" he called out. Where was she? The aisles between the shelves were clear. So was the entrance.

Rhoades' daughter looked at him strangely.

Maybe she went outside.

Dag hurried outside, hoping to catch sight of Rosita. Instead, he saw a soldier walking toward him across the empty parking lot. It was DeWitt.

"Hey," DeWitt called out. "Been looking for you. Some of us are meeting for breakfast. Care to join?"

Dag glanced back at the PX, but Rhoades' daughter had not followed him out. "Sure." He tapped his PT gear and it transformed into a cadet uniform. After another quick look around, and seeing no sign of his daughter, he said, "Lead the way."

The barracks complex was a short walk from the PX. The Dining Facility was a short walk beyond that. Five other cadets joined them as they walked between the barracks, DeWitt steering them toward the fusion generator building.

"Keep walking," he whispered to Dag as they neared it. "We can't stop or the Gen will get suspicious. I told them." He motioned to the cadets following them.

"You really going to fight them?" a cadet, who must've been all of nineteen, asked as they neared the building.

Dag debated what to say. Time was short, especially if they arrested Rhoades' daughter. He really had no choice but to risk the truth. "The Gen are going to attack and kill everyone here. We want to help, but we need to know if the people here want our help. If we land ships, will they come with us?"

They slowed their pace as they walked close to the fusion building, bending their path around it toward the Dining Facility. "Who's 'we.'" the same cadet asked. "Who's 'us.'"

"You know or you wouldn't be here," Dag snapped. They had only seconds left near the building. "Will they come?"

The cadet studied him. They all did. "Most of them, probably," he said. "No one likes the Gen. DeWitt says we'd have to do some fighting. That right?"

Dag nodded; They were now about three meters from the fusion generator building and he didn't know if it was safe to answer. The cadet nodded back. So, they would help, though as he examined them, very young and ignorantly eager, he wondered how much help they'd really be. He had to let General Burress know.

"Lieutenant Vera?"

Dag took another step before remembering that that name belonged to him. A lower enlisted Natural ran up to him, stopping an arms-length away and saluting. In a breathless voice, she said, "Sir, Colonel Gen Alexander wants to see you in his office right away. I'm supposed to lead you there."

Gen Alexander had mentioned something about an inspection of Dag's platoon this morning. This was probably about that.

Or . . . could they have arrested Rhoades' daughter already?

Was this her betrayal?

Dag returned the salute. "Give me five minutes. I forgot to tell my girlfriend something." Before the trooper could answer, he took off at a jog for the PX. He had to let General Burress know, but he also had to see if Rhoades' daughter was still there.

Why had she been there in the first place? Was she reporting to someone?

As if he couldn't guess.

Rhoades—both of them—wanted him dead.

When he reached the PX there were a few cars in the parking lot, but no military police. He slowed to a walk.

The young trooper came up beside him. "Sir, please, Colonel Gen Alexander was very insistent that you come right away. He gets very angry when people don't follow his orders to the letter."

"I'll just be a minute," Dag replied as he entered the PX and headed for a booth. Rhoades' daughter was nowhere around.

Dag entered his information again and said, "Met some friends. You'd like them. Call you tonight. José. End of message." He confirmed the message.

"Thank you for using Galactic Geocomm," the artificial female voice said.

"Sir?" the young trooper pressed.

"All right, trooper. Lead the way."

Unlike the quiet of the PX, the 1st Squadron headquarters bustled with activity, far more than seemed warranted for this time of "morning."

The young trooper led him down the same row of bland government desks he'd passed on his arrival. The people behind them paid him no more attention than the first time, yet something stopped him cold. His instincts screamed a warning. He took a closer look at the people. Every one of them was in uniform. He thought back to yesterday. Some of the people behind those desks had worn civilian clothes. He was sure of it. The person at the desk closest to him glanced up. Not a single blemish marred her face. Not a single strand of hair was out of place.

A Gen!

"Sir?" the young trooper said, urging Dag forward.

She's scared.

More Gen looked up at him. Dag quickly turned away before they became suspicious, and followed the trooper to the colonel's office. This wasn't about any inspection.

"You can go in, sir," she told Dag, her eyes darting around the room. Following her gaze, Dag noticed several other Naturals sitting in front of desks or waiting outside offices, their eyes wide with fear. One of them, seated not three meters from him, was Rhoades' daughter. She was pale as death and appeared frightened out of her wits.

She'd betrayed him.

"I am not going to wait all morning, Lieutenant Vera," Gen Alexander called from his office.

Dag glared daggers at Rhoades' daughter.

A shaky, indrawn breath reached his ear, like when Rosita had been crying for a long time and was just starting to recover, that half-sob, half-sniffle sound every parent knew. His eyes scanned the room but he didn't see her anywhere.

Where are you, Mihita?

"Lieutenant Vera!" Gen Alexander shouted.

Dag stepped into the office. The young trooper immediately closed the door behind him. The first thing he noticed were the three other people in the office: two Gen and a Natural.

The two Gen wore Imperial Marine uniforms. Each was two meters tall, heavily muscled, wearing expressions like they were about to chew through titanium. What really caught his attention were the enlisted ranks on their uniforms. Dag had never seen a Gen enlisted before. The Natural in the room was Lilliputian by comparison, a small, thin man with beady black eyes and pasty skin. He wore an urban camouflage uniform with a single gold cluster for rank, a major.

The major took Dag's hand within his own, his grip surprisingly firm for such a sickly-looking man. "It's a pleasure to meet you, Lieutenant Vera," he said.

Dag tensed.

The eyes.

Death swam in those black eyes.

"So, Vera," Gen Alexander said conversationally, breaking the spell.

Dag pulled his hand from the major's hand as if he'd been bitten, and faced Gen Alexander. The Gen colonel pressed his lips into a thin smile, but Dag could feel the Natural major's closeness. Menace radiated from him.

"Are you enjoying your stay, *Lieutenant Vera*?" Gen Alexander asked, leaning back in his chair.

"Food could be better," Dag said. He couldn't mistake the inflection when Gen Alexander spoke his fake identity. Rhoades had indeed betrayed him. Didn't matter which one.

"I will have to see what I can do," Gen Alexander said. "Perhaps the Nats would be happier if they had no food at all?"

Dag said nothing.

Gen Alexander leaned forward in a too-casual manner. "What do you know about a raid on Tocci III, Lieutenant Vera?"

"I saw some news," Dag said. He had no idea what they knew.

"You know," Gen Alexander said, "I saw that, too." His casual manner vanished. "Lieutenant—or should I say *Colonel*—Arias."

Dag didn't move. The barrel of a gun pressed against the base of his skull, the menace of the Natural major like a wolf's hot breath just before it bites. He waited, not knowing what to expect. Would he feel the heat of the muzzle blast, the impact of the bullet? And then the Void consumed him, spreading out from his chest, swallowing all emotion. Death was release. Death would reunite him with his family.

But if I die in this place, this close to Hades, will it take my soul?

Shockingly, Dag discovered he didn't want to die. Not in this place.

Gen Alexander watched him, perhaps expecting him to deny the charge or beg for his life. When Dag only stood there, he sat back, disappointment tainting his otherwise perfect features. "You massacred a thousand Gen civilians on Tocci. Did you think we did not know? That we did not have recordings of it, or you? You are a monster, Arias. Do you know the penalty for treason? Ah, but you must," he said without waiting for a reply. "I am sure Rhoades would have told you before sending you down here."

At the sound of that name, that hateful name, that had murdered his family, murdered his friends, the Void shattered. Hate flared hot, burning within him like Hell's own flames.

"Ah," Gen Alexander smiled, "I see you know Rhoades." His voice turned ominous. "Now, I wonder what else you know?"

Dag remained silent, feeding off the flames of hate, hate for Rhoades, hate for the Gen, hate for the God who had allowed all this to happen. He remembered the glory of the hot blood pouring over his hand on Tocci as he'd twisted the knife he'd plunged into the Gen commander's chest, pulling it down to spill the Gen's guts on the floor. He met Gen Alexander's stare . . . and smiled, imagining doing the same to him.

Surprise—and fear?—twisted the Gen's face, though he recovered quickly. "No matter. We will learn what you know soon enough." He motioned with his hand and the two Imperial Marines seized Dag's arms, lifting him off the ground easily.

"I will be down shortly to see how you are enjoying your new accommodations," Gen Alexander taunted before the Marines carried him out, the Natural major's gun still pressed against the base of Dag's skull.

Dag spotted Rhoades' daughter near an exit, watching. She wasn't in restraints. No one held a gun to *her* head.

If he lived, she would die.

When their gazes met, she gasped and fled out the door.

14

0746 UT, October 16, 3501
RSS Rapidan, Nerney Star System: DAY 19

"Ray, we just received another message from Colonel Arias," Sal said from within Ray's augmented environment. "Message reads: 'Met some friends. You'd like them. Call you tonight. José.'"

Ray inclined his medical bed to raise his head, trying to ignore the feel of Rapidan's material shifting inside him. It'd been a rough night. A painful night. He longed for the brief respite from the pain he'd experienced while in the construct talking with Paul. *I don't want to do this anymore.*

You must, Admiral Rhoades.

It wasn't just Rapidan saying that to him now. He recognized a few other SIL. Damodar and Euphrates, in particular. The SIL might not see themselves as individuals, but the currents that made up a SIL were unique.

He sipped some water and swished it around his parched mouth. At least it didn't taste like blood this time.

Margaret had also sent a brief message: 'Arrived safe. Can't wait to start flying.'

The Rapidan Task Force was still sixteen hours from Hades, then another nineteen hours and three orbits to slow their velocity before reaching New Yerkes. There was no way to speed that up without risking detection. Arias' message suggested he'd found help. Ray almost wished he hadn't. Without help, Ray could swing the task force by New Yerkes, recover Margaret and Arias, and jump for Andromeda, telling the Council he'd tried. Now, he might have to attempt the evacuation.

He linked to Ecuum from his environment. "What's the latest on the Gen?"

Ecuum's smooth, baby face creased with worry when he saw Ray's image. "The Independent Traders in Olympus Star System report that the Gen fleet was still there as of an hour ago. Captain Fletcher, the Independent I told you about, is nearing New Yerkes and reports no Gen ships in Hades space. He should be in orbit in about four hours. A few actively camouflaged ships are possible, but he would've seen anything larger."

"Why is Nasser still at Olympus?" Ray asked.

Ecuum's skin flushed a contemplative yellow. "We don't know."

Ray pondered that, the current that was his planner's mind twining into the main flow of his river. *What the hell?* He yanked his consciousness back to his cabin. He had to keep himself separate from the SIL.

His abdomen shifted as Rapidan moved around his organs. Ray pushed back, swelling his currents, trying to force Rapidan out of his river.

That will not work, Admiral Rhoades.

I WANT YOU OUT OF ME!

If we do that, you will die. We will not permit that.

It's my life!

It may be yours, Admiral Rhoades, but it belongs to more than just you.

Ray screamed in his mind in frustration.

And then he became aware of something else. He was back in his river, flowing within its banks. He hadn't meant to return to it. He tried to pull himself away, but it didn't work. Not completely. He was both in his cabin and in his river, experiencing both, unable to separate them.

Something grabbed his hand.

"RAY!"

Ecuum was there. In the flesh. In his cabin, floating vertical, holding his hand through his armor.

"Ecuum?"

He was chalk white, his tail lashing nervously, his grip on Ray's hand too tight. "You drifted. You okay?"

"Drifted?" Ray sipped some water. *Into my river. Of course.* He hadn't thought about what it would look like to others. He didn't want to explain it. Not yet. Not until he understood it himself. Partly to distract Ecuum, he adopted a sarcastic tone and said, "You care."

"Asshole," Ecuum said, releasing his hand. He was still chalk white, but his tail calmed as he pushed himself away from Ray's medical bed on silent puffs of air. "We can't do this without you, Ray. Your reputation is all that's holding this together."

The SIL had said much the same. "Sounds like you need my reputation, not me," Ray said.

"Did I mention you're an asshole?" Ecuum folded both his upper and lower arms imperiously, though color returned to his face. "By the way, before I forget again, Captain Fletcher wanted you to have this."

Ecuum extracted an object, a reddish rock, from a pocket and placed it in Ray's armored hand. "It's from the Solthari homeworld."

"The Solthari homeworld. . . ?" Ray's voice trailed off as he examined the reddish rock. It looked so ordinary, like the rocks that eroded from the Rayne Mountains on the western side of his Ranch on Knido.

"Its mineral composition matches reports from the invasion of the Solthari homeworld in 2091," Ecuum said. "I checked."

A piece of Andromeda. Ray took it as a hopeful sign, until he realized that it was probably the only thing from Andromeda he would live to see.

Do not give up hope, Admiral Rhoades. We have not.

Is that a suggestion, Rapidan? Or an order?

Rapidan didn't answer.

"Admiral Rhoades," Rapidan spoke out loud, "Margaret Rhoades is attempting to contact you. Do you wish to accept?"

"Of course!" *Stupid SIL.*

"Dad? Dad, can you hear me?" Margaret sounded out of breath. The transmission was audio only.

"I'm here, Margaret. What's wrong?"

"They took him, Dad. They took him away. They called him into the colonel's office and then a few minutes later they led him out with a gun to his head. I didn't see where they took him. I . . . I was afraid—" Her voice cracked. She was always so mature that it was easy to forget she was only eighteen.

"Take a deep breath, Margaret." Ray waited until he heard her take one. "Okay, tell me exactly what happened."

"They called me in. I thought it was about kicking that Gen colonel when he . . . but it wasn't. They asked me where I was from, how I had flight experience at my age. I was outside Colonel Gen Alexander's office when . . . Vera . . . went in. He looked at me. I tried to listen after they closed the door, but the Gen sergeant who was questioning me ordered me out. I was at the door when they led him out with a gun to his head. They know, Dad. It's the only explanation."

Arias had been discovered. Thankfully, Margaret had not. At least, not yet. Then something she'd said caught his attention. "The man who questioned you. You said he was a *Gen sergeant.* Are you sure he was a Gen?"

"I'm sure, Dad."

"Only Imperial Marines have Gen enlisted," Ecuum pointed out.

"Exactly what I was thinking," Ray said. "The Empire is already here." Ray addressed his daughter. "Margaret, get to the landing field. Do not go back for your stuff. Use the blue datarod we gave you to take a military craft and get out of there. Engage the active camouflage as soon as you get in. We're on our way. We'll rendezvous and pick you up."

"Dad, you said you needed eyes and ears down here to rescue these people. With Colonel Arias captured, there's no one else to do that."

Ray was both proud of, and terrified for, his daughter. "I need you safe. Use the blue datarod and get out of there."

"If it was anyone but your daughter, you'd tell them to stay, Dad. You know you would. I'll get to the landing field and keep an eye out, and contact you when I can with reports. I love you."

The connection cut.

I love you, too, he told her, hoping somehow it would reach her. Brave. And foolish. Why did those two things always seem to go together with youth? He had faith in her. She was strong. Like her mother. But she was young. This would be her first taste of combat, something he'd never wished for her. She was supposed to be the one who would run the Ranch, keep it for the next generations of Rhoades.

They would probably never see the Ranch again. Ray fervently hoped that would not also be true for his daughter.

"Kamen," he called out, "please report to my cabin."

"Yes, Admiral," she said. Less than two minutes later, she was there. She eyed Ecuum, clearly wondering what was going on.

"Arias was arrested," Ray told her. "We have to assume the Gen know we're here. It's sixteen hours to Hades, another nineteen hours to New Yerkes, and another twelve for the rescue. Gen Nasser could be here in nine hours. Options?" Ray's tone wasn't the fatherly one he normally used with her when he mentored her. If he died, he needed to know she was ready to take command.

Kamen noticed, too, judging from the pinched expression on her ebony face. She met his gaze directly. "Launch every Nova we have, sir, configured as mines, and get them to the geodesic before nine hours. The replenishment ships' munitions, too. Everything. It'll take us about eighteen hours to manufacture replacements. We'll be full up again before we reach New Yerkes."

Ray nodded, the current of his planner's mind twisting in approval. "Do it," he said. "What else?"

"Launch remote sensing platforms to Hades," she said quickly. "We need to know if the Gen already have ships there and keep the system under observation."

"Good," Ray said. "The Independent Trader vessel, *Fletcher's Run*, is four hours out and will also provide us with information. What else?"

Her eyes lost focus, drifting to her right. "The fabricators. As you suggested before, sir. When Nasser jumps in with his entire fleet, we jump them close, but not too close. Keep him distracted until we can finish the rescue operation."

"Good," he said to Kamen even as Rapidan's currents joined him in his river.

Admiral Rhoades, one Mother Ship should be sufficient for both your distraction and our attempt to free our Brethren. Bringing all four significantly increases our risk should our method not work as planned.

Ray's planner's current cut strongly through Rapidan. *War is risk, Rapidan. Jumping in a single fabricator will make Nasser wonder where the others are and what they plan to do. He might jump away, fearing a trap. You could lose your chance to free your Brethren, and we could lose any opportunity to rescue the people on New Yerkes. All four fabricators will hold Gen Nasser's attention.*

Suddenly, Ray's and Rapidan's currents flowed over the falls at the end of his river into the Great Ocean. Ray hadn't intended it and wondered if Rapidan had forced him over the falls.

No, Admiral Rhoades. The Brethren called us.

I didn't know they could do that. Ray flowed away from the rocky shores into the Great Ocean. The SIL did not push back this time.

That is because they agree with your reasoning. We will bring all four Mother Ships when the Imperial Fleet arrives.

Ray's currents touched many, many other data streams. It was—comforting—in a way. Like being with close family. Was this familial feeling consensus?

He pulled himself back to his cabin, though his consciousness still flowed within the Great Ocean. Neither Kamen nor Ecuum seemed to have noticed his absence this time. "Kamen, contact Bobby and tell him the SIL are going to jump the fabricators close to Nasser's fleet when it arrives. He'll need to prepare the refugees for the possibility of multiple jumps."

"The SIL?" she started to ask, then corrected herself and said, "Yes, sir."

"One other thing, Kamen," Ray said. "If we need to jump while in combat, it will take time for me to recover." *If I recover.* "You will command the fleet until I recover."

"Sir?"

He could hear the doubt in her voice, but he needed her, and the fleet would need her again to command in Andromeda. "I have faith in you, Commander. Don't do what you think I would do. You have good instincts. Trust them."

"Yes, sir," she said, still not looking completely convinced, but accepting the charge.

"Ecuum," Ray finished, "talk to this Captain Fletcher. Find out what you can about Imperial Marines on New Yerkes. Work with Gen Tel. We need to know what we're facing. All of it."

"Will do, Ray," Ecuum said, his baby face souring at the mention of working with Gen Tel.

"Dismissed."

When they'd left, Ray deflated. Dull pain throbbed through him. He sipped some water, swished it around his mouth, swallowed. Should he call Mary and tell her about Margaret? Just in case?

No. She'd have a lot of questions. Questions he didn't want to answer.

He laid his medical bed back down and closed his eyes. The Great Ocean faded. The sandy banks of his river embraced him. Here, at least, he could find a measure of peace and freedom from the pain.

15

0853 UT, October 16, 3501
Bent Fort New Yerkes, Nerney Star System: DAY 19

"Comfortable?" the Natural major asked in a conversational tone.

Dag tried to move. He could feel his arms, his legs, the rapid rise and fall of his chest, the cold of the metal table he lay upon leaching heat from his back, the chill in the air on his naked skin. Pain radiated from his groin where the Natural major had injected—with an actual needle!—something cold into him. He couldn't move. But he could feel. Everything.

"Why?" Dag asked, the word barely audible past his dry mouth and swollen tongue.

"Hmm?" The Natural major made a show of putting on surgical gloves, something Dag had only ever seen in ancient realities. He reached over to a shiny metal tray that he'd placed so Dag could see the metal instruments on it. "You have information we want," the major said.

He picked up a large injector and held it up to the light. Slowly, he pushed the plunger and shot a tiny fountain of clear liquid into the air. Dag followed the drops until they fell with an icy splash upon his naked abdomen. Then the major lowered the needle until it disappeared below Dag's view.

Dag tried to banish the primordial terror that gripped him, but the bite of the needle into his groin shattered his control. Searing hot pain spread quickly. He bit down, bit his own swollen tongue, but could not stop the scream.

"You . . . are Natural!" Dag tried to shout. It came out a whimper. He swallowed blood. "How can you . . . do this to one of your . . . own?"

"My own?" The man laughed, a sound that froze Dag's soul. "You are a traitor, Colonel Arias. And a mass murderer. You killed loyal citizens, butchered them in cold blood. I've seen the recordings. Most disturbing to watch. You showed them no mercy, even after they surrendered. Now, you have a chance to serve the Empire. If you cooperate, I'll make your death quick." He selected a metal instrument from his tray, held it up for Dag to see. Light glinted off the jagged blade at its end.

"You're . . . the traitor—" Dag gagged on his own blood, coughed. Hot droplets fell back onto his face. An odd bittersweet tang burned his swelling, bleeding tongue.

The major went on as if he hadn't heard. "Now, should we start with an evisceration, like the one you performed on the commanding general at Tocci? Hmm? Or should we deprive you of your manhood first?" He brought the blade down until it floated above Dag's lower abdomen. His finger twitched atop the blade. "Why don't you start by telling me why you're here?"

Dag bit down. He would not tell this creature anything. What did he have to live for anyway? Maria was dead. Rosita was dead. His unborn son was dead. No one would miss him. He didn't want to die this way, but maybe he could stall this demon long enough for DeWitt and the others to act.

"I . . . came . . . here . . . to . . . rescue . . . the . . . Naturals."

The words spilled out. Dag couldn't stop them. He tried to stop them—*by God, he tried!*—but they kept coming, as if a floodgate had opened in his mind and released a torrent.

The major smiled. He alternately raised and lowered the blade, touching Dag's stomach, his chest, his testicles. A drop of blood clung to the blade when he lifted it.

But Dag no longer felt physical pain. Shame burned it all away. He told the major about his mission. Every detail he knew. He told him about Rhoades' daughter. He told him about DeWitt and the others.

"I need to see to this immediately," a voice—Colonel Gen Alexander's voice—said from somewhere in the room.

Footsteps. A door opened and closed.

The major returned his focus to Dag. He smiled as with a job well done. He placed the bloodstained knife back on the tray, then laid his hand gently upon Dag's shoulder. "Very good, Colonel Arias. You have done well. Your service to the Empire will be noted. Now, would you please tell me of your activities during this unpleasant little rebellion? Please start at the beginning."

Again, the words spilled off Dag's swollen tongue. He told the major about how Rhoades had come to their unit in Costa Rica and warned them about the Janus virus, and about how Major Kenyon had backed Rhoades and convinced them to leave their homes. He told the major about his actions at Ndjolé Spaceport, filled his lungs again with Maria's sweet scent as they embraced in the starport terminal.

Maria's moist eyes met his. "I'll see you soon, too," he told her, brushing his fingers through her black hair. Her light perfume filled him with thoughts of happier times. "I promise. I love you."

"I love you, too, my Dagoberto. You take care of yourself, you hear?" Maria threw herself into his arms, breaking into fresh sobs. Rosita joined their embrace. In that brief moment, the universe was perfect happiness.

Dag watched again as missiles struck the starliner and images flooded in from the Madu attack, heard again his imploring God to save his family as one of the evil snakes tore his beloved Maria apart, heard again Rosita's desperate scream.

Papí! Papí, help me!

But it didn't stop there. Next came his hatred for the Gen, for Rhoades, for God, the raid on the fabricator at Tomb, Captain Lisa Erikson's decapitation, Lieutenant Sissel sacrificing herself to the Madu to save Banshee Troop, Dag's order to kill the Gen prisoners and Rhoades' order to spare them, the landing on Tocci III, the charge across the dunes and First Sergeant Yoshi Takeuchi's peaceful smile as he died, plunging his dagger into the Gen commander's heart and pulling it down to spill the Gen's guts on the floor, the bodies and the blood in the Headquarters Complex, and Corporal Lance lying in a medical bed suffering from radiation poisoning.

Hours or days passed, his humiliation growing with every passing word. Still, he talked. The major nodded every so often, listening attentively. And watching. Always watching with those dark, soulless eyes.

Dag told him again about DeWitt. About Rhoades' daughter, how he'd wanted to kill her. His messages to General Burress.

Emptied.

Finally.

Spent.

Warm tears flowed from his eyes, running down to turn cold upon his cheeks. "I'm so sorry," he whispered. He knew now that there would be no Heaven for him. No happy reunion with his family.

Hades was his fate.

"You have done well, Colonel Arias. Thank you." The major removed his gloves, throwing them carelessly on the metal tray. He started to walk away.

"You—" Dag swallowed blood— "You promised to kill me."

The major turned his head back toward him. "In due time, Colonel. In due time. We'll want to talk with your co-conspirators first. You may still be useful." With that, he walked away, leaving Dag alone with his shame.

16

2100 UT, October 16, 3501
ISS Solaris, Olympus Star System: DAY 19

"Imperial Intelligence has informed us that they have captured a rebel spy on New Yerkes," Gen Nasser explained to the assembled battlegroup commanders. "He is identified as Colonel Dagoberto Arias, a Cavalry officer serving under Rhoades." He paused dramatically. "The rebels have taken the bait."

Serenna watched Nasser. The report he referred to had come in *twelve hours ago*. Nasser was only reporting it to his commanders now. He had assembled 845 of the remaining 847 SIL in the Fleet. This delay suggested he wanted those final two warships before he would move.

"Admiral Serenna." Nasser fixed his large brown eyes on her. "There has been no report of the rebel fleet. You will take the Reserve Flotilla and jump to Nerney Star System. You will report to me what you find."

"Yes, Fleet Admiral," Serenna answered dutifully. No other answer was possible. Her force of 150 standard warships, plus Solaris, would be no match for Michael's SIL and the four fabricators. If they waited at the geodesic, Michael would destroy the entire Reserve Flotilla within minutes. No doubt, that was the result Nasser hoped for. He would be disappointed. Michael would not be waiting there.

Addressing the rest of his battlegroup commanders, Nasser said, "We shall await the report from the Reserve Flotilla. Dismissed."

As their constructs sank back into the deck of Solaris' Combat Information Center, Serenna called out, "Captain Scadic, please prepare the Flotilla to depart immediately. Destination is Nerney Star System, by the most direct route."

"Yes, Admiral," Scadic replied from the bridge as if nothing between them had changed. Her career lay in ruins, shattered and broken. Why had he stayed with her after her disgrace? Was it misguided loyalty, sheer stupidity, or a rare display of shrewdness? She did not know. Whatever his motivation, his familiar presence comforted her, much as she did not want to admit it.

"Captain Scadic, once the Flotilla is underway, please report to my cabin."

"Yes, Admiral."

With that, Serenna walked the short distance from the CIC to her Admiral's cabin. She stepped through the door and into the familiar space that had become, in a way, her prison. No sooner had she stepped fully within her cabin than a chime sounded. She knew it was not Captain Scadic; he would still be organizing the Flotilla. "Please join me," she replied to the chime. "Your timing is impeccable. As always."

Gen Cardinal's portly form took shape in the faux-leather chair at the far end of her faux-glass coffee table. Serenna called out, "Solaris, coffee for me, and wine for our guest."

A bulb of coffee the perfect shade of light brown, heavy on the cream, light on the honey, rose through the faux glass of the coffee table nearest Serenna. She picked it up, cradling it in her hands as she sat on her real-leather couch and casually crossed her legs.

Gen Cardinal leaned over and grabbed his bulb of wine, his reptilian gaze locking on her. He took a single sip through the zero-gee stopper, then placed the wine bulb back on the coffee table. Serenna raised her bulb lightly toward him and sipped her coffee, waiting for him to begin the conversation.

"Fleet Admiral Gen Nasser is sending you to Nerney Star System, while his fleet remains here. Not very subtle."

Serenna allowed a thin smile. "Gen Nasser is not known for his subtlety. The real question is: Why is the Emperor allowing it?"

Gen Cardinal understood her meaning. "Military strategy was not part of the Emperor's geneering and he does not wish to interfere in purely military affairs."

"I believe the Natural's have a word for that, Director," Serenna challenged. "Bullshit."

Gen Cardinal actually smiled at that, something he rarely did. It was never a comforting sight. "If you ever hope to regain your former position with the Emperor, you must earn it."

That was fair. In *Gaman Politic*, the Political Game, only the strong survived. It was a very Darwinian concept, one which Gen society, built on precise genetic engineering and targeted Nurturing, should not embrace. It was one of many contradictions in their society that threatened to bring down their entire race. Not that she dare say such things. At least, not again. She had made those comments to the Emperor when she believed her execution was close at hand. A rare misjudgment on her part that she had no intention of repeating.

Gen Cardinal studied her a moment before asking, "So, what is your plan?"

He wanted to know how she intended to survive. Or more specifically, whether her plan was good enough that she *would* survive, so he could factor that into his own plans. It was always a question with him how much she should share. She still did not know whether he was an ally, an enemy, or somewhere in between.

Captain Scadic chose that moment to arrive at her cabin. At his chime, she invited him in. If he was surprised to see Gen Cardinal, he did not show it.

Serenna motioned him to the empty faux-leather chair opposite Gen Cardinal, then addressed the spymaster. "Nasser believes Michael will be waiting for the Flotilla at the geodesic exit. He suspects—and hopes—that the rebels will expend their munitions to destroy us, thereby exposing their positions. He will then jump his massed fleet to Nerney Star System, overwhelm the rebels, and capture or destroy the rebel's fabricators."

Gen Cardinal cast a quick glance at Captain Scadic, as if wondering why she had invited him in. "And what do you believe?"

Serenna realized she might not have done Scadic any favors. It was not wise to catch the attention of Imperial Intelligence. "Michael knows this is intended as a trap," she explained to Gen Cardinal. "Likely, Michael argued for jumping to Andromeda, which would be the wisest course given his position. That he has gone to Nerney suggests he is following the order of his wife's Council, subordinating the military to civilian rule."

Serenna deliberately looked at Scadic before returning her attention to Gen Cardinal; This was as much for him as it was for the Director of Imperial Intelligence. "Michael will be focused on rescuing the people at Bent Fort. He does not have the forces to both guard the geodesics and to conduct the rescue. I suspect he will only commit those forces he deems are necessary to conduct the rescue and not commit his entire fleet."

She turned to Scadic. "That does not mean we are safe. Michael will, no doubt, mine the geodesic from Olympus. He likely has other surprises waiting for us, as well."

"How do you wish to proceed, Admiral?" Scadic asked.

If it were just them, Scadic would likely have offered recommendations. He was smart enough, in the presence of Gen Cardinal, to defer to her. "Divide the Flotilla into three battlegroups," she said, "the left centered on Solaris, the center and right on the two Ryden class battlecarriers, each in pyramidal formation. Manufacture Novas configured for minesweeping enroute, sufficient to cover the immediate space surrounding the Flotilla. Launch them immediately upon exit. If Michael deploys jammers, target those first. Spool up the Linear Star Drive upon emergence. We will jump away from the geodesic at the earliest opportunity to avoid any additional surprises."

Scadic nodded.

"Captain," Serenna added, "this Flotilla must survive. Do not wait for my orders. Execute."

"Understood, Admiral," he said.

"Thank you, Captain," she replied as a dismissal.

He stood and walked smartly out of her cabin. Serenna leaned back into the leather couch and sipped her coffee, casually returning her focus to Gen Cardinal.

"You appear confident," he said.

"I am always confident," she answered.

"And yet you have lost twice." He said it as a statement of fact, not an accusation. He had played a major part in the planning of both battles. Her losses were his losses. At least privately.

"Then, I suppose, I should wish you luck," he said. "And a safe return."

Serenna regard him. That last statement had sounded genuine. "I do not depend on luck, Director. I make my own."

17

2307 UT, October 16, 3501
RSS Rapidan, Nerney Star System: DAY 19

Ecuum floated vertical outside the Admiral's cabin door, his second hands hanging down in his uniform pant legs, steeling himself against the sight of his friend. It hurt, deep in his core, to see the living corpse Ray had become. Much as he would miss him, he understood Ray's desire for death. He would help his friend with that release, if only they didn't need him so badly.

He knocked.

"Enter."

It was so weak Ecuum had to strain to hear it. He stretched his thick lips into what he hoped was a convincing smile, widened his eyes in feigned excitement, inhaled, and blew the air through his back slits to propel himself through the door.

Ray was inclined with his head up in the medical bed. Ecuum couldn't stop his gaze from fixing on the gray arm of Rapidan's material sticking into Ray's right side, light gray material flowing into his friend, while darker gray spheres of material flowed out. *If that were me, I would long for death, too.*

Forcing his focus to the death mask of his friend's face, he said, "You look like week-old dog shit."

Ray smiled, gingerly, his lips dry and cracked, and took a sip of water through a straw provided by his battle armor. "I would probably smell worse without my armor. Shouldn't you be on the bridge flying the task force?"

"I am." Ecuum pointed to his backside where his second brain resided. "Butt brain." It was a great advantage of the People that they had two brains. Ecuum's hind brain was flying the task force so his main brain could engage with Ray.

He inhaled and channeled air through his back slits to propel himself over to Ray's bed, staying as low as possible without dragging his bottom hands on the deck so Ray wouldn't have to strain to look at him. Another channeling of air through his front slits stopped him half a meter from the bed.

"We're less than an hour from Hades," Ecuum said. "Roughly twenty more to New Yerkes."

"The Gen?" Ray asked.

"Latest word from Olympus is that they're still there."

Ray frowned, then winced as something visibly moved in his abdomen. "Any word from Captain Fletcher?" Ray asked. "He should've arrived at New Yerkes by now."

"He has," Ecuum said. "In fact, that's the other thing I wanted to talk to you about. Fletcher doesn't trust the military. Never has. Probably never will. He wants to talk to me on *Fletcher's Run*." Ray's face hardened the way it did when he didn't approve. "He wouldn't ask if it wasn't damned important."

Ray stared at him a moment. "How much do you trust him?"

"With my life," Ecuum said.

Ray sipped some water, swishing it around his mouth before swallowing. He looked up at the painting of the Rhoades' Ranch hanging on the bulkhead over his medical bed. "I always thought I'd be buried there, alongside my kin. I suppose that's not going to happen now."

"You're going to make it, Ray," Ecuum said with more conviction than he felt. "Stop talking like you're already dead."

Ray stared at him with an expression that seemed to say, "If you only knew." It broke Ecuum's heart. Not that he'd ever admit to that. Ray had always been strong. Seeing him like this was . . . hard.

"If we could bury the smell," Ecuum joked, "I'd get you there now."

Ray chuckled, then coughed, sipping water to try to stop it. "Please don't make me laugh." But his mood seemed just a little lighter.

Ecuum floated closer, folding his lower arms so he could get lower to the deck, face to face with Ray. "Have you ever wondered why it was I came to *you*, specifically, early in the Anti-Piracy Campaign?"

"A time or few," Ray said, his hazel-green eyes intense. "You've never said."

"Because, until now, you haven't needed to know." Others might've taken offense at such a statement, but Ray accepted it in stride. Such was the nature of their relationship.

"Captain Fletcher," Ecuum began, "was one of my first sponsors in the Niner Races. We've known each other for well over two centuries. Early in the Piracy War, my House suffered considerable losses, as you know. We didn't have the military forces to stop them on our own. My House pressured the Republic Council, along with our allied Houses and dozens of planetary governors, to stop the attacks. They assigned that task to Gen Alyn.

"For reasons I still don't fully understand, Fletcher pointed me to you, not Gen Alyn. He said you were not only the brains of the outfit, but that you would be more sympathetic to our cause." At Ray's expression, Ecuum added, "I haven't got a clue how he knew."

Ray took a sip of water. "He could have had his own reasons. That doesn't tell me why we should trust him now."

"Fair. And accurate," Ecuum said. "And we also had our own reasons for accepting the intelligence he provided to me, and I provided to you."

"Ah," Ray said. "I wondered where you got your intel."

Ecuum lashed his tail in mock anger. "I have never been a one-trick pony, sir. This pony can turn many tricks." Ray smiled. It was good to see. "He did, however, account for about forty percent. One thing about Fletch: When he bets on you, he'll back you to the hilt. Unless you lose, of course. Then he'll dump you like hot cargo."

"You believe he's decided to back us?" Ray asked after another sip of water.

"I do. So long as we keep winning," he added truthfully. Fletcher, like all Independents, lived or died by the bets he took.

He seemed to have a knack for always betting right. "Ray, there's something else I learned from Fletcher. The Janus virus . . . isn't a virus. Not in the traditional sense. It's molecular machines . . . with a hive intelligence."

"A hive . . . ?" Ray stared at him, disbelieving. The ban on intelligent technology dated back to the early days of the First SIL War. To Ecuum's knowledge, it had never been broken in the nearly fourteen centuries since. Even the Bonded SIL were only tolerated because they were slaves. Essentially "safe."

"There's more." This was the part he'd dreaded telling Ray, the reason he hadn't said anything earlier. "Janus is highly adaptable, and one hundred percent communicable." He swallowed. The tip of his tail twitched nervously. "It's possible Imperial Intelligence has already infected one or more of the refugees and brought Janus to the fleet. It could be spreading as we speak."

Ray took a sip of water. "That would explain a lot."

Ecuum tilted his head quizzically. "I don't understand."

"We know the Cybernetics went to Andromeda shortly before the First SIL War," Ray said. "The disappearances of probes and expeditions began roughly a century later. What if they knew about Janus? What if they're still there and Janus is the reason they destroy anything from the Five Galaxies?" He took another sip of water, his gaze unfocused. "Even if Janus hasn't infected the fleet, the only way we could keep it from reaching Andromeda would be to cut all physical contact with the Five Galaxies."

Ecuum glanced at the Five Galaxies crest that still hung on the bulkhead behind Ray's work desk. He'd obtained Fletcher's help with promises of lucrative trade between Andromeda and the Five Galaxies. The other Independents followed Fletcher hoping for the same. If what Ray said was correct, they dare not allow such trade. Anyone coming from the Five Galaxies could be infected. It would only take one.

"Ray, I need to go to *Fletcher's Run* and find out what Fletch wants to talk about. I'll need a fighter. The *Lusty Lady* wasn't designed for stealth."

Ray nodded, though it was clear he still didn't trust the Independent. "I'll get Gen Tel working on a way to find out if Janus is already in the fleet."

Ecuum couldn't stop his skin flushing deep crimson at the mention of Gen Tel. "Why do you trust him?"

"He's not lying, Ecuum. He doesn't agree with the Gen strategy, or Janus. Rapidan would've told me if he did." Ecuum was about to interrupt when Ray added, "It's more than that. I feel it. I can't explain it better than that. We need him. Spy or not."

"I will never feel that way," Ecuum said truthfully. Ray deserved nothing less.

"Fair enough," Ray said. "Never hurts to have another pair of eyes watching him." His eyes clouded, his brows drawing closer. "Until we know how to handle Janus, we can't allow the Independents to return to the Five Galaxies, if they accompany us."

Ecuum stared at Ray, one friend asking him to betray another. "You understand what you're asking of me?"

"I do."

He could find no way to respond to that. Ray trusted him. Ecuum had never violated that trust.

He fervently hoped he wouldn't have to violate it now.

Roughly two hours later, Ecuum's actively camouflaged fighter neared *Fletcher's Run.* Brilliant lights swirled and danced along the giant floating phallus as it glided in low orbit above New Yerkes. Unlike military vessels, Fletcher *wanted* the universe to see his ship and know immediately what it offered.

Fletcher did raise a hairless brow, however, at the military fighter Ecuum piloted into his hangar bay.

"Brought you a case of 'Gold, old friend," Ecuum announced with exaggerated flourish as he exited the fighter. It was his last case, but they needed Fletcher now more than ever. "Old as in a dinosaur coprolite that preserves that just-excreted fragrance even after sixty-six million years."

Fletcher chuckled, then held out his empty upper left hand. "You see a problem here, Na Soung scum?"

Ecuum called for the case of 'Gold from the fighter, opened it, and drew out four decanters of brandy. He threw three of them to Fletcher and they drained a whole decanter together. "That almost makes up for your foul stench," Fletcher said with a satisfied grin and deep yellow hues of bliss. He led Ecuum to the central core.

Ecuum immediately noticed that the shops and brothels were empty. "What gives?"

Fletcher's exposed skin changed from yellow to the reds of irritation in a flash. "Colonel General Gen Mudir," he began, his annoyance plain, "has prohibited the population of the Fort from visiting. He *suggested* I leave, or risk being caught in 'ongoing military operations.'"

A real tropical bird of vibrant blues and greens landed on the railing overlooking the central core, eyeing them. Fletcher reached into his black body suit and tossed the bird a small cracker. The bird snatched it from midair and flew away. Birds, unlike people, adapted quickly to microgravity.

Fletcher floated horizontal to the railing. He pointedly looked around at his empty shops and bars and gaming dens and brothels. "I take it Rhoades is close? Didn't take you long to get here."

"Close enough," Ecuum allowed.

"We're still jumping for Andromeda after this?"

"That's the plan," Ecuum said, careful to keep his skin neutral and his tail still. Fletcher had been around for a very long time and could smell when a deal went sour. Keeping Janus out of Andromeda—

"Rhoades is worried we'll bring the virus to Andromeda," Fletcher said.

How does he do that?

Fletcher opened the stopper on another decanter and finished half of it in one swallow. "I'm working on that," he added. "But first, we need to survive this fight. We have something that might help. A few somethings, in fact. If you need us, we'll be there."

Fletcher didn't elaborate and Ecuum didn't ask; It wouldn't do any good. Instead, he watched the trees at the bottom of the central core, from small fruit trees to large pines and oaks. Growing those in microgravity was a real trick, one Fletcher had never revealed. Birds sat on their branches, their heads hung low as if they were just as disappointed at the lack of customers as Fletcher was.

"There's something going on at the western rim of the crater sheltering Bent Fort," Fletcher said. "Whatever the activity is, it's actively camouflaged. We've caught a few heat signatures, but only a few. Whoever they are, they're pros."

"We believe Imperial Marines are already at Bent Fort," Ecuum allowed. Sometimes, sharing information for free had advantages.

"That might explain it," Fletcher said. "We haven't seen anything in orbit or close by." He paused, his gaze slipping across his empty establishments. "You weren't going to tell me, were you?"

"No," Ecuum answered truthfully, because Fletcher also deserved the truth. "A lot can change between here and there. I didn't see any reason to bring it up."

Fletcher eyed him as he swallowed more brandy. "That's the real reason I needed to see you in person, without your military eavesdropping. Rhoades needs to understand that we go because we want to. We'll leave the same way." Enigmatically, he added, "We learned from the Piracy War. We're not as helpless as we may seem. Not anymore."

The birds in the central core suddenly took flight.

Fletcher turned away as if receiving a call. When he looked back at Ecuum, all he said was, "You better get back to your fleet."

18

0126 UT, October 17, 3501
ISS Solaris, Nerney Star System: DAY 20

Blood red Hawking radiation filled Serenna's view as Solaris exited the geodesic into Nerney Star System. She sat within Solaris' Combat Information Center, though wrapped in her battle armor's augmented environment she appeared to float in space amid the radiation as it faded quickly around her.

As instructed, Captain Scadic—on the bridge so that one weapon strike would not kill them both—did not wait for orders, launching Nova multirole missiles configured as minesweepers in all directions. He then ordered the Flotilla to full military thrust to get them away from the geodesic; No matter the speed a ship entered a geodesic wormhole, it came out with almost no velocity at all. Finally, he began spooling up her ships' Linear Star Drives. If Michael had mined the geodesic, as she expected, their best defense was to jump clear of the area. However, that would take several minutes.

They had to survive for that long.

Enemy Novas, several hundred of them, lit their boost engines "below" her Flotilla, trying to take advantage of the brief window after a jump when her ships were visible to their sensors.

Solaris and the Flotilla accelerated hard, gravities building rapidly. The force of it pushed Serenna into her command chair, her armor constricting around her arms and legs to keep blood in her brain, her heart, and her vital organs. SIM-3 Starburst missile interceptors, marked in bright yellow, leapt from launch cells across her Flotilla to counter the enemy Novas, adding their numbers to the minesweepers launched earlier. The minesweepers would clear Novas hidden close to her ships, while the SIM-3s would attack the Novas they had just detected.

Serenna watched, events playing out as she had expected. Nasser wanted her dead. That was not going to happen here.

Scadic ordered the Flotilla to reduce thrust and altered their course, making her actively camouflaged warships more difficult for the enemy Novas to target. Bright red and bright yellow tracks faded to darker red and darker yellow, the missiles discarding their boost engines and vanishing behind their own active camouflage, the darker tracks showing where the missiles *should be* based on their previous course and speed.

Red and yellow tracks converged. White antimatter fireballs bloomed like miniature suns, announcing hits. But Novas were intelligent missiles. They knew the capabilities of the SIM-3s and altered their flightpaths to avoid them. More, they communicated in real time with each other, knowing there was strength in the pack. Some of the Novas deliberately sacrificed themselves to open a lane for the rest to fly through unharmed.

The standard warships of Serenna's *Sheppard* Battlegroup were closest to the enemy Novas. Dark red tracks closed on them.

Active camouflage was not perfect. It captured the light of the background universe and projected that on the opposite side of a warship or missile, effectively making it invisible. Novas, however, linked together, could spot small deviations in that background. Ships, also linked together, could detect the small maneuvering thrusters as the Novas adjusted their courses. It was a game of who saw whom first.

An Amazon class destroyer at the edge of the *Sheppard* Battlegroup spotted something. Archer close-in defense weapons opened fire with thousands of high-speed slugs. Two brilliant white fireballs. Two enemy Novas destroyed.

The destroyer's defensive fire, however, told other Novas where it was. Serenna had seen this before, at the battles of Tomb and Tocci, and knew what was coming. The double flash of a Nova's dual-bottle antimatter warhead struck the destroyer amidships, the first charge shocking the destroyer's hull and opening a hole for the second, larger charge to blow through. White fire erupted from the destroyer's opposite side, appearing as if someone had thrust a giant white spear through it. Secondary explosions from store gasses, fuels, and munitions ripped the destroyer into two separate halves. Other Novas, seeing the carnage, turned and struck the two surviving parts of the ship, consuming them in white fire.

No emergency beacons appeared to signal evacuating crew. All 321 Naturals aboard the destroyer had died.

A nearby destroyer and a frigate tried to defend their stricken comrade with Archers, and died shortly after. Dark red tracks extended deeper into *Sheppard* Battlegroup's formation. A Megiddo class heavy cruiser took three hits, one of them piercing a weapons magazine. The entire ship vanished in a white antimatter fireball. More enemy Novas converged on her ships.

The universe compressed as Solaris' Linear Star Drive engaged, crushing Serenna down to a single point, then expanding out so fast that it felt as if her body would fly apart. Neither of those sensations were real, but there was physical damage. Serenna tasted blood in her mouth, slight though it was, and dull pain pulsed through her temples. Humanoid bodies, even Gen, were not meant for travel through warped spacetime.

"Status," she asked Scadic.

"Flotilla is one hundred million kilometers above and rimward of Hades, Admiral," Scadic said, swallowing visibly. "We should be safe for the moment."

"Losses?"

"Five destroyers, seven frigates, two heavy cruisers, all from *Sheppard* Battlegroup, Admiral."

Acceptable losses. "Any sign of Michael and the rebels?"

"No, Admiral," Scadic answered, "just that Independent Trader vessel, *Fletcher's Run*, in low orbit above New Yerkes."

It would be smart to destroy that trader vessel, but she had no orders to that effect, and she would not give Nasser or his allies any reason to question her loyalty.

Seeming to float in space with only her uniform for protection, Serenna looked around. The ships of her Flotilla were arrayed into three battlegroups in line: Fifty standard ships around Solaris in a three-sided pyramidal formation, the other two battlegroups, led by the standard Ryden class battlecarriers *Montgomery* and *Sheppard*, also in pyramidal formations to her right, *Montgomery* Battlegroup with fifty ships and *Sheppard* Battlegroup with thirty-six remaining after its losses.

Satisfied they were in no immediate danger, she keyed the All Forces Combat Information Network, or AFCIN ("afsin"), the Fleet's faster-than-light communications system, and directed it to Nasser. "Fleet Admiral Gen Nasser, this is Admiral Gen Serenna."

She waited for almost two minutes before he answered. "Report, Serenna."

"We encountered a minefield at the geodesic exit. Five destroyers, seven frigates, and two heavy cruisers lost. We safely jumped away. No sign of the rebel forces."

"We need to know where the rebels are, Serenna."

"Fleet Admiral, the minefield we encountered suggests the rebels are, indeed, here."

"But where, Serenna? Where?"

Serenna felt the answer should be obvious. Michael would be near Hades. If Nasser jumped to Nerney immediately, he could jump again to Hades and trap Michael there. She did not suggest that, however. Nasser would not listen.

"How far away from New Yerkes are you, Serenna?"

"One hundred million kilometers, Fleet Admiral."

"Proceed at flank speed to New Yerkes. We are on our way."

Flank speed. He wanted the rebels to see her force. A diversion. Given her standard ships, it would not fool Michael.

Serenna knew the truth of it, however. The minefield had not killed her.

Nasser was determined to fix that.

19

0708 UT, October 17, 3501
Bent Fort New Yerkes, Nerney Star System: DAY 20

The table shook, snapping Dag awake. It was dark. He could just make out the white ceiling from the lights of nearby equipment. He tried to move, but couldn't. He was naked, could feel the cold on his bare skin. The muscles in his back were stiff, painful where they lay against the metal of the table.

The table shook again, stronger. Was that thunder he heard?

Papí?

"Rosita?" Dag could move his eyes but nothing else. He couldn't see her. "Where are you, Mihita?"

Papí, you need to get up.

Dag tried to move. "I can't." And then it all came flooding back. The Natural major. The interrogation. All the things he'd said. All the people he'd betrayed. The shame. The overwhelming, soul-crushing shame. The realization that he was not meant for Heaven.

Papí, you need to get up.

Dag's eyes strained toward her voice but he still couldn't see her. He wanted desperately to see her. One last time. "I'm so sorry, Mihita. I'm so sorry."

Several loud pops.

A door opening.

Footsteps. In a hurry. A door closing behind them.

The Natural major who'd tortured him appeared, looking down at him. The calm was gone, his eyes nervous, darting. He reached over to the metal tray and grabbed a syringe filled with a clear liquid. He seized Dag's left arm, pointing the needle toward it.

A door burst open, sounding forced. The major's head turned to the sound, then exploded in a fine red mist that showered Dag in hot blood.

"Thank god," a voice said, "I thought we were too late."

A new face came into view, a boyish face with freckles and hair the color of wheat.

Lieutenant Marco DeWitt.

Dag felt no elation. No reason to thank God. He'd betrayed this young lieutenant who'd joined the Cav to get away from the farm.

He'd betrayed all the cadets.

Papí, you need to get up! Hurry!

"Mihita?"

"I don't know what that means," DeWitt said, "but we've got to get you out of here. Fast."

Another face appeared. The cadet who'd questioned him as they walked past the fusion generator building earlier. Together, he and DeWitt reached under Dag and lifted him, grunting. Dag still couldn't move, except his eyes. He was dead weight.

"Kill me," he asked DeWitt. "Please."

"What? No way. We're here to rescue you."

They grunted again as they lifted him into a two-person side carry position, DeWitt holding him under the knees in front, the other cadet gripping him under his arms behind him.

"I told them . . . everything," Dag pleaded. "Please."

"They shot you up with something," DeWitt said. "We've got to get you to a CMTEV." He pronounced it "semtev."

"But—"

"Shh. You couldn't help it. They used those drugs on the others, too. Bastards."

Unable to move, Dag had no choice but to surrender himself to this fate. As they carried him through the door, the overhead lights in the hallway nearly blinded him until his eyes could adjust. He could see his naked body reflected in the flat panels. His gaze immediately fixed on his manhood, memory flooding back of the blade touching his balls, the blood dripping from it when it came back into view. They were intact. His relief was overwhelming, until he remembered his shame. Tears welled in his eyes, spilling down his cheeks.

"My daughter," he croaked. "You need to save her, too."

They pushed through another door into the bright light of day, the pain of it stabbing into Dag's eyes, forcing them closed. DeWitt and the cadet picked up their pace as sporadic pops of gunfire sounded all around.

Finally, they entered another building, the shade of it allowing Dag to open his eyes again. Triangle rafters high above hinted at some kind of large warehouse. DeWitt and the cadet carried him to the side of a boxy armored vehicle that Dag recognized as a Combat Medical Treatment/Evac Vehicle. They laid him in an open cubby within the vehicle.

The CMTEV's material flowed around Dag, enclosing him. A body view appeared. He tried to read it, but so much red text clouded the view that he gave up the effort. His fingers, his toes, slowly warmed. The warmth spread up his arms and legs. His physical pain ebbed. He still couldn't move, but breathing came easier. Even the gloom of his thoughts seemed to lessen, though they did not fade completely. He'd failed these troopers, as surely as he'd failed his family.

The red text clouding his body view began to peel away. When the last of it disappeared, the CMTEV moved him to a supine position outside the vehicle, clothing him in an urban camouflage uniform. Which was a good thing because the warehouse was full of people, all crowding around where he lay, staring at him.

No, he abruptly realized. Looking *to* him. He could see it in the hope in their eyes.

What was he to them?

DeWitt stepped over and helped him stand up. Then he bent close to Dag's ear and whispered, "They did the same thing to the others, Colonel. You've got to shake it off. We don't have much time."

"But—"

DeWitt addressed the crowd. "The Gen know of our plans and have started shooting Naturals. We have some people fighting back the best they can, but the Gen have called in reinforcements. Imperial Marines." He turned to Dag. "Colonel Arias here is with the rebels. He came here to help us. He fought the Gen on Tocci and beat them." DeWitt took a step back and saluted sharply. "Colonel, we stand ready to follow your orders."

Dag stared at DeWitt, dumbfounded. Belatedly, he remembered to return the salute. "How do you know who I am?"

DeWitt dropped his salute. "They told us when they announced your arrest. They've been pulling people in, asking a lot of questions. Shooting some. We knew we were running out of time to do something before they started arresting us, too."

Dag didn't know what to say. The people in the warehouse, dozens of them, most in uniform but a few who were obviously civilians, fixed on him, waiting expectantly. *For what? What do they want me to do? I sold these people out!*

Now, they looked to him in hope. Desperate for guidance.

God was laughing at him.

Papí! Papí, help me!

He'd failed his daughter. He hadn't protected her. He couldn't protect her.

Papí.

She stood at the back of the warehouse, behind all those hopeful faces. She wore her white church dress with the pink frills, the one she liked.

The people surrounding him seemed to lean in closer, as if hanging on whatever he planned to say.

Help them, Papí.

I love you, Mihita.

She smiled, her eyes beaming. *I love you, too, Papí. Help them.*

Dag cleared his throat, taking in those anxious faces. He'd betrayed them. He would pay for that. But Rosita was right. He owed them *because* he'd betrayed them.

"I am Colonel Dagoberto Arias," he said, his voice gaining strength as he spoke, "Commander of the First Cavalry Squadron, Third Armored Cavalry Regiment. Because we're short on time, we'll skip introductions. Lieutenant DeWitt will act as my deputy.

He knows you, and I know him." The two of them exchanged a quick nod of confirmation.

"Our plan is to rescue all of the Naturals here at the Fort who want to come. My mission—*our* mission—is to seize and hold the primary landing field so that the Third Armored Cavalry Regiment can land and evacuate everyone. Beyond that, we need to create as much chaos and confusion as we can to make sure the Gen can't interfere with the landing and evacuation."

Turning to DeWitt, Dag asked, "What do we have?"

DeWitt flinched at a nearby explosion. It reminded Dag that these weren't combat veterans; They were trainees. Two thousand of them. Up against Imperial Marines, the most elite fighting force in the Five Galaxies.

"Well," DeWitt began, "the First, Second, and Third Armored Cavalry Squadrons each have their own motorpools. The Troops are there getting their equipment ready, except for the ones fighting to delay the Gen. The Fourth Air Cavalry Squadron is moving to the landing field, but their equipment is locked down. It can only be released from the Fort's Headquarters Complex."

Dag nodded. "We'll dedicate First Squadron to take that," he said, remembering the layout of the Fort from his previous training here. "Second and Third Squadrons will secure the landing field."

"Yes, sir," DeWitt said. "Every Troop also has its own armory, so we have people opening those so they can issue personal weapons and ammunition. But we'll have to get ammo for the armored vehicles from each Squadron's depot. Nearest is about a kilometer that way." He pointed to the left of the warehouse door.

It made sense that they wouldn't keep the heavy ammunition with the equipment where trainees could get at it, but cycling all the units through the depots would take time they probably didn't have.

"Dedicate one Troop from each squadron to collect and distribute vehicle ammunition," Dag ordered. "Have them bring it to the armories so the Troops can load up as they cycle through. How long?"

"Five hours? Maybe six?" DeWitt said, not sounding confident in his estimate. That probably meant it would take longer.

"Do we know how many Marines? Where they're coming from?"

"They seem to be coming from the west," DeWitt said.

This was bad. "Use LoCIN for communications wherever possible," Dag ordered, referring to the Local Combat Information Network, which used line-of-sight ultraviolet laser links. "The AFCIN here is routed through nodes in the Headquarters complex," he explained, "so the Gen can hear everything you say."

"Couldn't we use that to deceive the Gen?" DeWitt asked.

It was a good idea, if they could pull it off. "You think you could do that?"

"We have some actors among the troopers and civilians," DeWitt said. "We could make it sound like we're in places we aren't, that we're moving to places we're not."

"Smart thinking," Dag said. "Okay." He took in the assembled people. "Let's get to it, then. We don't have a lot of time."

They hesitated. Judging by their faces, most were in their late teens or early twenties. They were scared.

Dag knew they weren't scared enough.

None of them knew what was coming.

"Look," he said to them, "I've been there. Fear will keep you alive. But don't let it paralyze you. If we fail, the troopers coming to our rescue will walk into a trap. If that happens, the whole revolution will end here. Today. All of Natural Humanity will be at the mercy of the Gen. I don't think I need to tell you about Gen mercy. You've seen it for yourselves."

He looked across those faces one more time. Grim. Determined. And afraid.

"Let's go."

20

0710 UT, October 17, 3501
RSS Rapidan, Nerney Star System: DAY 20

"How far?" Ray asked.

"Now eight-four million kilometers," Chaya answered from Rapidan's Combat Information Center. "Bearing zero-eight-nine ascent five-five, speed one-seven thousand kps and accelerating, course one-two-one dec six-four relative. That course could indicate an intent to swing close by Hades' southern pole to bend their path toward New Yerkes."

"Composition?"

"One Solaris class battlecarrier," Chaaya answered. "Two Ryden class battlecarriers. One hundred thirty-six standard warships: mix of Roche class frigates, Amazon class destroyers, and Megiddo class heavy cruisers. Divided into three groups. It's the same group that emerged from the geodesic, Admiral."

"They want us to see them," Ray said. "To get us to reveal ourselves."

"That would be my assessment, Admiral," Chaaya agreed.

"Any chance they've detected us?"

"No indications, Admiral."

One Solaris class battlecarrier. Gen Serenna's ship, Solaris, gave its name to the fifteen SIL battlecarriers in the ship class, which included Rapidan. "Any chance that battlecarrier is Solaris itself?"

"No way to know, sir," she answered as if prepared for the question.

"Thanks, Chaaya." Ray sipped some water, and winced as Rapidan's material pushed against his stomach. *Can the Brethren tell if that's Solaris?* Ray asked, dipping into his river and flowing himself over the falls into the Great Ocean.

No, Admiral Rhoades, Rapidan answered. *We are blocking our presence from our Brethren so they cannot sense our location.*

Floating at the edge of the Great Ocean, something occurred to Ray that hadn't before he had this perspective. *How can you block your connection to your fellow Brethren?*

Ray could feel the resistance of the SIL as a broad current pushing him back toward the shore. They didn't want to tell him. Which was interesting given all their talk of collective action. If he could figure out how they did it, maybe he could use the same technique to block *them* from *his* mind.

He pulled his consciousness back to his cabin, though his mind remained partly in the Great Ocean. "I need to get to the bridge," he told Rapidan.

"We strongly recommend you remain here, Admiral Rhoades," the ship said.

"I can't command a battle from a medical bed."

"Technically, you can."

Ray sighed. "You know nothing about leadership, Rapidan." He commanded his battle armor to move toward the edge of the bed so he could stand up. "If you won't help, I'll walk there myself."

"We will help," Rapidan said, its exasperation with him plain. It formed a cocoon around him and transported him to the bridge, maintaining the arm of its material into his right side.

Ray emerged on the bridge sitting in his command chair at the rear focus of the bridge oval. Red light bathed the compartment to warn that Rapidan had evacuated the ship's atmosphere into holding tanks to prevent explosive decompression and fire in case of a hull breach. Kamen commanded the ship and the task force from the bridge oval's forward focus. Nine enlisted spacers worked their positions along the edges of the compartment. All of them tried, and failed, to hide their surprise at his appearance.

"Kamen," Ray said, "drift-launch three volleys of Novas configured for antiship but do not boost them. Keep them close to the task force."

"Drift-launch three volleys of Novas configured for antiship, aye," Kamen repeated the order in proper Navy tradition, ensuring that the order given was the order heard.

Ray double-blinked on an icon within his battle armor's augment environment, switching it from "Standard" to "Tactical" mode. The bridge disappeared around him. He appeared to float alone in space, the gas giant, Hades, and its four large moons behind him. At this distance from Nerney Star, roughly equal to the orbit of Mars in Sol Star System, the temperature within his environment was like a late spring day, the smell of mown grass tickling his nose. It was his armor's way of telling him that Nerney was a spectral class G-type star, and that he was in the outer edge of its habitable zone, though whiffs of sulfur from Phlegethon, innermost of Hades' large moons, spoiled the spring smell.

Rapidan's translucent, light-gray, three-pointed-star shape lay directly below him, the other twenty-six ships of his task force arrayed in light gray behind him in the shape of a three-sided pyramid. The light gray told him that his ships had engaged their active camouflage, capturing and selectively reradiating light, making them effectively invisible to sight and sensor.

"Volley one away," Kamen announced, her face to Ray's right within his environment. Bright yellow missile tracks separated from Ray's ships. Drift-launching them allowed his ships to use internal electromagnetic launch cells to accelerate the missiles before they emerged through the ships' hulls, thus hiding the energy of their launch from enemy sensors.

"Volley two away," Kamen said. "Volley three away. All missiles away."

They'd passed close to New Yerkes five hours ago, picking up Ecuum as they went, their own remote sensing platforms confirming Captain Fletcher's assessment that no Imperial warships likely lay near the moon. They couldn't be completely sure—a few actively camouflaged SIL vessels would be very hard to detect—but more than that was unlikely. It also matched the reports that Nasser's fleet remained at Olympus.

"Cycle our ships through replenishment," he ordered Kamen. One of the advantages of having two replenishment ships with his task force was that his warships wouldn't need to manufacture replacement missiles from their own material. The replenishment ships could supply all they needed.

Kamen repeated the order before executing it.

Ray's mouth was dry and he sipped some water, swishing it, realizing for the first time since arriving on the bridge that his pain had faded into the background, almost forgotten, as had Rapidan's movements within him. It felt good to be back in command again.

He rotated his officers' images to the front of his environment. "Chaaya, how long before that force can arrive at New Yerkes?"

"About nine hours, Admiral."

"That's about the same time we're due to arrive," Ecuum said.

"Sir," Kamen interjected, "that enemy force has three battlecarriers. That's over two hundred and fifty spacecraft, plus the warships. Standard or not, they outgun us by a lot. We need to hit them before they arrive."

"Recommendation?" Ray asked.

"That force will need to brake hard to reach New Yerkes," Kamen said. "If I were them, I'd do that on the far side of Hades, where they're least likely to be seen. Recommend we hit them there."

"That will reveal our presence near Hades," Gen Tel said.

"They already know we're here," Kamen replied. "Our ambush at the geodesic told them that. This strike will only tell them we're still in the area, but not where we are."

"It might still be enough to bring Nasser here," Ray said, his planner's mind working through the possibilities, "before we're ready to begin the rescue operation. Ecuum, what does our approach to New Yerkes look like?"

"We're using Hades to slow us down, Ray, so we don't risk detection by performing any long burns. However, we'll need to burn hard for about eleven minutes before closest approach to New Yerkes to enter orbit. No hiding that."

"And another twelve hours to conduct the rescue," Ray said. "Kamen's right. We need to deal with that standard force before they can arrive. Send the Novas we just launched to intercept them, Kamen."

"Yes, sir," she said.

Ray turned to Gen Tel. "That leaves one major problem. Nasser will likely arrive several hours before we can complete the rescue operation. Will the fabricators distract him long enough?"

"Initially, probably," Gen Tel answered, using the conditional language common to members of intelligence services. Ray had experienced that behavior his entire career and it had always irritated him. "If the fabricators stay out of reach," Gen Tel continued, "he will likely see them for the deception they are. In that event, and knowing our assault ships are on New Yerkes, his most likely course of action would be to jump to New Yerkes and directly threaten the evacuation. That course, he may reason, is most likely to get you to commit your entire force, including the fabricators, to their rescue."

It was a good assessment, spy or not. "Thank you, Gen Tel."

Within the Great Ocean, Ray told the SIL, *You must keep the fabricators close to Gen Nasser's force. He must believe he can capture them.*

They didn't answer, and their currents pulled away from him. Reluctance. And defiance. They didn't like the idea of taking orders from him.

Ray returned to his officers. "Kamen, you will command the attack on the diversion force. Sal, you have my permission to accompany the assault ships to Bent Fort." Ray had kept Sal with Task Force Anvil at Tocci III knowing Sal would've preferred to be with his troopers on the ground. He wouldn't deny that to him here.

As his officers turned to their tasks, Ray sipped some water, almost himself again. Then Rapidan's material pressed against his bladder, causing him to pee a little and ruining the moment.

21

0801 UT, October 17, 3501
ISS Solaris, Nerney Star System: DAY 20

Serenna's Reserve Flotilla, their sterns facing their direction of movement, fired their engines at full thrust as they neared their closest approach to Hades' south pole. It was a risk. A big one. This was their most vulnerable moment and, knowing Michael as she did, the likeliest time for him to attack. Caution, however, would not win this battle. She had learned that much from Michael.

On their approach to Hades, she had maintained their course and speed to make it appear as though her force would swing around to directly intercept New Yerkes. In fact, she had no such intention. Yes, it violated the precise words of Gen Nasser's order, but it did not violate his stated intent. He wanted her to locate the rebel force. Her strategy had a better chance of doing that.

"Captain Scadic," she ordered, "cease acceleration. Rotate all ships bow forward. Alter course two point five degrees starboard and accelerate to two-zero thousand kps."

"Yes, Admiral," Scadic responded, executing her orders.

She watched him. Before her defeat at Tocci, he had often suggested courses of action or sometimes even challenged her when he thought her orders were . . . unwise. He had done none of those things since her defeats, just followed her orders without question or comment. It made her wonder, again, why he had stayed with her.

Her ships, light gray in her augmented environment to indicate their camouflage was active, fired thrusters to flip 180 degrees, their bows once again facing their direction of movement, then altered their orientation to place them on the new heading. As one, they ignited their main engines.

Michael should not expect this maneuver. It would take them toward Cocytus, the third large moon from Hades, not New Yerkes. As their elliptical orbit swung them around Hades, the gas giant's gravity would slow them down. They would not need to maneuver again until they neared Cocytus. The Flotilla would then use Cocytus' gravity and a six-minute burn to bring them around to New Yerkes from an unexpected direction.

The course change was slight, however. It might not move them far enough from their previous course before Michael attacked.

Her ships' engines shut down when they reached twenty thousand kilometers per second. With their camouflage active, they were effectively invisible. Or so she hoped. The standard technology ships of her Flotilla were less capable than a SIL vessel like Solaris.

Remembering the battles of Tomb and Tocci, and their arrival at the geodesic, she ordered, "Captain Scadic, under no circumstances are ships to employ any defensive weapons."

"Yes, Admiral."

Nothing. No reaction. An order like that would have caused him to at least raise an eyebrow at her before. *What is his game?* It was rare when she could not discern another's motives.

A white flash in the lower right of her environment drew her attention. She immediately recognized it as the first charge of a Nova's dual-bottle antimatter warhead. It struck the bow of a Megiddo class heavy cruiser from her *Sheppard* Battlegroup, the one closest to their original course. As she watched, that first charge opened a hole in the cruiser's hull so that the missile's second, larger charge could explode inside the ship.

Antimatter, carried by the collective momentums of ship and missile, chewed its way down the length of the cylindrical cruiser. Secondary explosions rippled beneath its hull like those time-lapsed realities of maggots consuming a dead animal. Stored gasses erupted in magnificent blues, greens, yellows, and reds to boil away into space. The cruiser disintegrated into large chucks of tumbling debris, black against the bright backdrop of Hades.

No emergency beacons appeared.

Six hundred and twenty-three lives lost in a matter of seconds.

Natural lives.

That was not supposed to matter to her. It never had before.

Somehow, this was different. In a battle she was not meant to survive, life took on new meaning, even if it was not Gen life.

A Nova exploded into the side of an Amazon class destroyer, the secondary charge exiting obliquely, a white spear thrust through the cylindrical ship. Two other Novas struck, one consuming the bow as the other did the stern. When the destroyer emerged from the explosions, only a small middle section survived to tumble dead through space.

No emergency beacons.

Three hundred and twenty-one more lives. All Natural humans.

Neither ship had tried to defend itself, obeying her orders. Sacrificing themselves for the Flotilla. For the Gen Empire. The same Empire that intended to eliminate their species in its entirety. Had they heard about the Janus virus? Did they know?

Two Roche class frigates vanished into fiery white comets that cooled quickly, leaving nothing of them visible in their wake. All four destroyed ships had been part of her *Sheppard* Battlegroup.

The Natural captains in that battlegroup maintained their discipline, holding their fire, not defending themselves. Her Gen captains at Tocci had not shown that same discipline. Fearing for their lives, they had broken formation, allowing Chengchi Sun to escape her trap, leading directly to her defeat there.

The losses continued. A double flash preceded yet another white comet of fire as a frigate exploded. Three separate spears of white lanced a destroyer, consuming its bow and stern. Then a heavy cruiser shuddered under multiple hits before flaring into a white fireball directly adjacent to the battlecarrier *Sheppard*.

The Natural's discipline held. It was admirable. It was brave.

She did not understand it.

Their lives were short, a few hundred years at best. Should that not make life more precious to them? Yet, they sacrificed themselves as if it held little meaning.

For her.

For the Empire.

Her own Gen captains had fled in terror at Tocci until she had destroyed one of her own ships, forcing them to choose between death as cowards and death as patriots. Nearly immortal, Gen did not want to risk their lives. That made them unreliable warriors.

Not here. The Naturals held true. The enemy Novas were having trouble finding her ships. Holding defensive fire was working.

So far.

A double flash and spear of pure white pierced into *Sheppard's* cylindrical hull amidships. Yellow secondary explosions erupted. Seeing that, and knowing the battlecarrier's design, another Nova struck the wounded ship, aiming for a magazine with stored missiles for the battlecarrier's spacecraft. Antimatter in hundreds of warheads detonated in a mammoth white fireball that consumed the middle of the vessel, leaving only small chucks of its bow and stern to tumble uselessly through space.

That loss hurt. Not only had she lost the firepower of a battlecarrier, but of the 85 spacecraft it had carried.

Still, her course change and order to hold defensive fire proved effective. Michael's Novas found no more of her ships. The loss of *Sheppard* and its 3,362 crew was . . . acceptable. She still had two battlecarriers and over a hundred warships, a formidable force.

She had survived.

Now, it was her turn to strike.

═ 22 ═

0833 UT, October 17, 3501
RSS Rapidan, Nerney Star System: DAY 20

Ray replayed the engagement with the Gen deception force. Most of his missiles had missed. They'd destroyed only eight ships, though one of them had been a Ryden class battlecarrier. The commander of that force had deliberately misled them into believing they were headed for New Yerkes. That made him wonder yet again.

One Solaris class battlecarrier.

Was it Serenna?

She was the most gifted War Leader the Gen had, but she was not the only one with talent. The nine War Leaders commanding the nine military districts also commanded from Solaris class battlecarriers, as did Gen Nasser as overall Fleet commander. All they knew about Serenna's fate was that the Emperor had demoted her. Was it possible she still commanded Solaris even after her defeats?

"Sir," Kamen said, "we have almost four hundred Novas from our attack that did not find targets. I'm bringing them back around Hades to rejoin our task force. No sense wasting them."

Ray nodded. "Thanks, Kamen. Good thinking."

"Admiral?" Gen Tel said, his image at the end of the row of Ray's officers within Ray's augmented environment. "I have been contemplating that the deception force may be commanded by Admiral Gen Serenna."

"I've been thinking the same thing," Ray agreed.

"The tactics we have observed are consistent with her tactics," Gen Tel continued, "and Fleet Admiral Gen Nasser may intend using this deception force as a way of eliminating a rival."

"I thought you Gen didn't kill each other," Ecuum challenged, his distrust of Gen Tel on full display.

"As a general rule, we do not," Gen Tel confirmed. "That should not, however, be taken as refusing to leverage advantage from a situation. If Fleet Admiral Gen Nasser assessed that he could achieve the objectives set forth by the Emperor, while also eliminating a rival for his position, he would do so."

That clinched it. It was her. Which changed the dynamics of the fight. "Kamen, alert Admiral Sun to ready the Tzu and Euphrates Task Forces. We may call for them in a hurry."

Kamen repeated the order then carried it out.

"Chaaya," Ray asked, "can you project the deception force's course?"

"Not with accuracy, Admiral, but extrapolating from the debris of the destroyed ships, I would say somewhere in the direction of Cocytus, the third of Hades' large moons."

"She's looking for a gravity assist," Ecuum said. "She can swing around Cocytus to come at New Yerkes along the plane of the moon's orbit. Not the direction we would be looking for her to approach from."

"And you know this how?" Gen Tel asked.

"Thirteen-time Niner Racing champion?" Ecuum shot back, pointing at himself as if Gen Tel were too dumb to figure it out. "That course is child's play. Try it in a protoplanetary star system with still-forming planets."

"How long?" Ray asked.

"Factoring in Hades' gravity slowing them down and not performing any maneuvers until they approach Cocytus, a little under eight hours," he replied. Then, with a pointed glance toward Gen Tel, added, "Child's play."

"How long to New Yerkes?" Ray clarified.

"Three hours and twenty minutes after that, give or take any maneuvers."

"About an hour after we're due to arrive," Ray said. "The assault ships will be on the surface and perfect targets." He sipped some water, swishing it around his mouth. "We need to destroy her force at Cocytus."

"Admiral," Rapidan interrupted, "we are receiving a radio transmission from Margaret Rhoades."

"Put it through," Ray said. "Include all the officers here."

"Dad?" Margaret sounded scared.

"I'm here, Margaret. You okay?"

"Yes, sir. For the moment, at least." They could hear her shifting her position. *"I found a building just outside the landing field, like a hobby fliers club like they have outside Knido City Spaceport. No one is here."*

"We have to assume that she just gave her position to the Gen forces," Gen Tel pointed out.

"Shit. Sorry."

"That's okay, Margaret," Ray tried to reassure her. "We'll keep this short. You find another place to hide."

"There's fighting down here. I can hear it."

"What kind of fighting," Sal asked. "Describe it. As specifically as you can."

"Like pops," she answered. *"Like firecrackers. Lots of them, but sporadic, and not always in the same places. Sometimes what sounds like small explosions."*

"Small arms fire and grenades," Sal said. "Maybe scouts or forward elements. If the Imperial Marines were outside the western rim of the crater, as Captain Fletcher claimed, it will take them time to move their main force into Bent Fort."

"Margaret, thank you," Ray said. "I'm very proud of you. Find another place to hide. We'll be there as soon as we can." He couldn't give her time estimates on an unsecure link.

"Will do, sir."

Then Ray remembered the datarod with the Key. "Margaret, don't forget the datarod. Use it if you have to." He wanted to tell her to use it and leave, but knew she wouldn't listen.

"Um, okay. They're parked out on the flight line. I don't think I can get there without being seen, but I'll keep it in mind."

The link cut.

Brave and practical. Like her mother. And foolish, like him.

Focus.

Ray couldn't tell if that was his own mind, or the SIL.

The SIL. "Rapidan," Ray asked, "the Gen drew us here with a Madu attack on Cursed, the implied threat being that they would use Madu here. However, there are Gen at Bent Fort. Can Madu be instructed with friend-or-foe recognition so they would attack Naturals but not Gen?"

"We have never used them that way—"

"Why am I not surprised," Ecuum interrupted.

"—but, yes, they could be issued such instructions."

Ray hoped that hadn't occurred to the Gen, that they would not use them for fear of what could happen to their own forces. But if it *had* occurred to them . . . "Sal, can your forces handle large numbers of Madu?"

And what would happen to Margaret?

Sal visibly thought through the possibilities, cupping his chin with his hand. "So far, we've only had to fight them in small numbers in enclosed spaces. If the Gen hit us with large numbers in the open? I honestly don't know. Main Gauche daggers with Special D won't be enough."

"Rapidan?" Ray asked. "The SIL created them. Can you devise a defense?"

The waters of the Great Ocean moved around Ray, the currents weak and disjointed. It was strange. He could feel it as if he were there, but he was still firmly present on the bridge. He could tell that defending against Madu, their weapon created for killing humans in the most terrifying of ways, was something the Brethren had never considered.

"We will try," was all Rapidan said.

"Ooh, that makes me feel so much better," Ecuum replied.

The currents in the Great Ocean, unable to reach Ecuum, lashed out at Ray like whips, sharp and powerful. But it didn't hurt. He could feel Rapidan's material moving physically within him, slithering around organs, under his skin, pressing, squeezing. The Great Ocean carried no such physical sensations. It was all in his—and their—collective minds. Interesting, though he had no idea what it meant.

"Admiral," Kamen suggested, "we could commit our reserve forces to Cocytus. Even the odds."

Ray's planner's mind considered, but ultimately rejected it. "No. The rebellion must survive this battle. If we commit our reserves and Nasser arrives while we're still fighting, he could jump his entire fleet here and overwhelm us. I'm not ready to risk that. At least, not yet."

Kamen studied something outside Ray's view. "Sir, we could redirect the four hundred Novas from our previous attack to Cocytus."

It was a good idea. She would make a formidable commander one day. "Do it."

"Ray," Ecuum cut in, "we just received a narrowband transmission from Captain Fletcher. The Gen Fleet at Olympus has departed."

"When?" Ray asked.

"He doesn't say, but I imagine he would've sent this as soon as he heard."

Nasser had left Olympus. At most, they had nine hours before he arrived.

23

1555 UT, October 17, 3501
Bent Fort New Yerkes, Nerney Star System: DAY 20

Dag's Mobile Command Post, basically an oversized, unarmed Serpens Infantry Fighting Vehicle, lurched over a curb with a jolt that went straight to his kidneys. "Easy, son," he told his young driver, a blond eighteen-year-old kid from some backspace planet in the Sagittarius dwarf. Not that he'd wanted to know that, but the kid wouldn't shut up. *Nerves.* Dag would trade an entire tank platoon right now to have Corporal Lance back as his driver.

"Sorry, sir," the kid said. "I just got my license last week." The Mobile Command Post pulled up to the side of a low building across from the armory and jerked to a stop. "Sorry, sir," the kid said again.

Dag bit back a retort: yelling at the kid would only make him more nervous. Instead, he focused on organizing his battle armor's augmented environment to manage the battle. As he'd done on Tocci III, he placed the 2nd Armored Cavalry Regiment's icons in an anchored window to his bottom front, and a map of the base in another window to his left. To his right, he added a window containing intelligence information and text versions of all communications. Six operators cloistered within a cramped compartment behind him continually updated the data and handled the "noise"—requests for supplies, intelligence, medical assistance, etc.—so he could focus on the big picture. Lieutenant DeWitt sat in an identical Mobile Command Post at the other end of the formation and would take over if Dag's vehicle were hit.

So far, the Imperial Marines hadn't launched a full assault. Dag credited that to the delaying tactics DeWitt had organized from Destructor Company—1st Squadron's artillery company. But that time had come at a price. Already, red stained seventeen regimental vehicle icons, and that didn't include the individual warriors slowing the Marine advance with man-portable weapons.

"Sir," one of the operators called. "Aggressor Troop reports full weapons load. Bane Troop is loading now."

A round exploded close by, followed by small-arms fire.

"This is taking too long," Dag muttered. He selected Aggressor Troop's icon and keyed the LoCIN. "Alpha-four-three, this is delta-six-six. Form a defensive perimeter north of Point Alpha. Over."

"Roger, delta-six-six," the lieutenant in charge of Aggressor Troop responded. "Over and out."

Over and out. That lieutenant didn't even know proper radio procedure and he commanded an understrength trainee Troop preparing to fight the Emperor's own Imperial Marines. God must be laughing. Dag found himself hoping nothing went wrong with Rhoades' plan—nothing else, he amended—or the 3rd Armored Cavalry Regiment wouldn't survive their landing.

He keyed the LoCIN again to talk to Lieutenant DeWitt. "Whiskey-two-one, this is delta-six-six: we won't get the regiment through the alphas in time. Are there any other alphas we can use? Over." If they could spread vehicle ammo loading to more armories, maybe they could speed this up.

"Yes, delta-six-six. There's one about five clicks—"

"That's fine, two-one," Dag interrupted before DeWitt could give away the location; even laser links could be intercepted, especially here within the Fort. "I'll keep the First with me and drive to the Hotel in fifteen mikes," Dag said. "You direct the others to that alpha, then join them in Lima as soon as possible. Over." Hotel was the Headquarters Complex. Lima was the landing field.

"Uh," DeWitt stammered as he tried to puzzle that out. "Yeah. Uh, Wilco, sir. Over."

"Six-six out." Dag keyed the LoCIN off before he changed his mind. *This is insane.* But they had to hold the Marines or 3rd Cav would walk into a trap.

An explosion ripped through the building behind the Mobile Command Post, showering them with duraplast and wallboard. Turning to the map, Dag saw the Gen still more than five kilometers away and not in a direct line of sight to his position. He checked for the ballistic track of an indirect round, but couldn't find one. Another explosion blew a hole in the side of the building not two meters from the Command Post. He quickly keyed the LoCIN. "Cease fire! This is delta-six-six. Cease fire!"

"Oh, Fates!" a young voice said. "We're sorry, we didn't, you see, we—"

"Shut up!" Dag shouted. "Check your targets before you fire, and wait for my orders, dammit!"

A sheepish voice whispered, "Yes, sir. We're sorry, sir. It won't happen again, sir."

"It better not," Dag scolded. "Now get off the air. Out." He shook his head, and found himself grateful the kid in that tank couldn't shoot straight. Of course, that lack of skill would probably get that kid and his crew killed.

Papí?

Dag heard sniffles. With his armor in tactical mode, he could see the surrounding streets and intersection as if he sat in midair above the ground. He quickly looked around and saw Rosita hiding behind the Mobile Command Post. She leaned against the vehicle, scrunched up like a ball, holding her ankles and sobbing.

Papí, you're scaring me.

She said that sometimes when he yelled. "Sorry, Mihita, I didn't mean to scare you."

I don't like it when you yell.

"I know, Mihita. I'll try not to do it again. I promise."

You mean it?

"Yes, Mihita."

She lifted her head just a little, her eyes red, and smiled. It was good to have her back.

Calmer, Dag asked, "Load status?"

"Bane Troop nearing completion," an operator said. All the operators kept glancing at him, but he didn't know why.

Dag nodded. "Good. Thank you."

The operator gave a tentative nod and a hesitant smile, much like Rosita had.

They're young and scared, Dag thought. *I need to stay calm. If I'm calm, they will be, too.*

He checked the status of the Regiment in his environment. They'd placed sensor disks—what troopers called "waffles" because they looked like large round Belgian waffles—on rooftops and in windowed rooms to look for heat signatures from Gen vehicles, personnel, or weapons. They also served to maintain their LoCIN line-of-sight laser links. Other waffles lay upon the streets in plates only a few molecules thick, acting as pressure sensors. Six more overflew the area.

He repositioned a few of Aggressor Troops' vehicles to better meet the Marines, then, seeing that Bane Troop had finished loading, ordered them down a side street to begin their drive on the Headquarters Complex. If they could take that, they might just keep the Gen and Marines in check long enough for the 3rd to land and deploy.

Explosions and small-arms fire drew Dag back to the map window. The lead elements of a Marine armored column, tracked as they drove over the waffles, had picked up speed as they encountered Aggressor Troop's forward observers. He waited for Aggressor Troop's commander to call in mortar fire. And waited. Another explosion echoed down the street, a tank main gun round by the sound of it. A Serpens Infantry Fighting Vehicle icon, one of his, turned red.

Dag selected Aggressor Troop's icon and called in the mortar fire himself. He checked the Marines' movements again. They had deployed in three columns, the largest charging down the main street leading to the armory, with two smaller columns guarding the flanks on adjacent streets. Aggressor Troop's waffle pressure plates weighed each vehicle that passed over and identified its type.

From that information, the SIL Mobile Command Post concluded that they faced a tank-heavy Imperial Marine battalion.

Expanding the map window, Dag gauged the effect his mortar fire had—or rather, didn't have. Rounds landed behind the enemy's advance elements, struck buildings, and a few even came danger-close to Aggressor Troop's own units. One round finally landed in the main street, the flash-bang of its plasma warhead briefly blinding the sensors. Buildings burst into flames from the intense heat, but the sensors recorded no secondary explosions. He considered switching to antimatter rounds, but dismissed that. The smallest AM warhead had a nominal yield of a quarter kiloton, too large to risk so close to his own troops and civilians.

Challenger Troop finally finished loading and he ordered them to assault the Headquarters Complex down a different side street than Bane Troop—and prayed the young recruits wouldn't get lost. Dag knew he should lead that attack, but if Aggressor Troop didn't hold the line here the Marines would roll right over the other Troops long before they reached the Complex.

Two new explosions rocked the main street. Gray silhouettes highlighted two Aggressor Troop tanks parked in alleys on either side of the street. Both had fired and missed the tank at the head of the enemy's column.

Where in Hell did these people learn to shoot? But Dag didn't say that out loud.

Both tanks fired again, this time hitting their target. The kinetic rounds penetrated the tank's front armor and blew it apart from within. Secondary explosions blinded the sensors. The two tanks fired again, and again. Even when the sensors cleared, Dag couldn't see what they fired at. He keyed the LoCIN. "Aggressor Troop, conserve your ammunition. Fall back to secondary positions."

One tank stayed in the alley and continued firing blindly. The other moved *into the street* instead of falling back down the alley. Both blew apart at nearly the same instant.

Red text flashed in Dag's environment: INCOMING. Projected impact points appeared in his map seconds before the first rounds struck. Hundreds of white flashes consumed Aggressor Troop's positions, followed a few seconds later by loud crackling sounds—cluster munitions. CM rounds were deadly to exposed troops but far less effective against armor. But they had another, more devastating effect. Within the space of about a minute, they destroyed all but two waffles, drove individual troopers in the buildings and on the rooftops into cover, and broke the LoCIN communications links Dag needed to conduct the battle. At about the same time, the feed from his aerial waffles went dead.

The sounds of battle drew closer. Several troopers broke and ran, some of them without their weapons. Two Serpens charged out into the main street. Without LoCIN, Dag keyed the AFCIN, not caring that the Gen might hear, to order them back, but the one closest to the enemy exploded. The other veered off, its troopers bailing out before it stopped. "Aggressor Troop—" how idiotic that name sounded now— "Hold your ground! We can't let these Marines break through!"

More vehicles broke into the open, firing wildly behind them as they retreated. Rounds struck friendly vehicles, adding to the confusion. "Hold your positions!" Still they fled. "STAND AND FIGHT, DAMMIT!"

But it did no good. The battle had become a rout. Dag thought of staying, of trying to rally the troopers, but knew his death would mean defeat for the entire Regiment. He owed them better than that. "Driver, get us out of here. Join up with Bane Troop."

The kid punched the accelerator, sending the Mobile Command Post careening forward *into* the main street. The vehicle lurched as the driver realized his mistake, nearly throwing Dag from his seat despite the bond with his battle armor.

Dag looked up the street. Fire and smoke consumed every building, burning debris and fuels turning the street into a solid sheet of flame.

Except for one rectangular patch.

Screams filled the compartment. Troopers bailed out of the vehicle. Only the kid, the driver, remembered to take his weapon.

Papí, this way.

He saw Rosita get up and start running down the street, away from the Marines.

Dag grabbed his weapon and dove through the skin of the Mobile Command Post to the street opposite the enemy. He rolled out and was just about to start running when a pressure wave from the exploding vehicle knocked him flat. His battle armor protected him from the intense heat.

He pushed himself back up and ran for all he was worth, following Rosita in the direction of Bane Troop.

24

1609 UT, October 17, 3501
RSS Rapidan, Nerney Star System: DAY 20

Every instinct Ray had told him to recover Margaret and jump away. Seated in his command chair on Rapidan's bridge, wrapped in his battle armor's augmented environment, he watched as explosions within Bent Fort advanced steadily toward the landing field from the north and west. The Imperial Marines had launched their main assault. The Rapidan Task Force was still two and half hours from landing the assault ships, and evacuating the population of the Fort would require another twelve hours. Gen Nasser could arrive with his fleet at any moment, and Gen Serenna's force was likely approaching Cocytus even now.

We need to leave, his instincts screamed.

We must attempt to free our Brethren, Admiral Rhoades.

It wasn't just Rapidan. A surge welled up from the depths of the Great Ocean, a column of water so powerful it lifted him several meters above the surrounding surface. The message was clear: The SIL would not leave.

And he had another problem. He'd promised Mary he would attempt this rescue. If he jumped away now, the Council might collapse, all faith in the wisdom of its decisions snuffed out. Without the Council, which had appointed Ray to command the rebel forces, Admiral Sun might use the opportunity to again seize command. Sun still had a large and loyal following among the officers and crews of the rebel fleet.

We would stop him, the SIL said.

And risk revealing your freedom? Ray countered. *All of Humanity would join together to fight you. You know this.*

The SIL remained silent, but the column of water weakened. Within it, Ray sensed a hope that their attempt to free their enslaved Brethren would work and they could leave Humanity behind.

"Conn, Sensors," Chaaya called from Rapidan's Combat Information Center. "Multiple heat transients bearing zero-eight-four dec four-two, range eight-zero-four thousand kilometers, speed six-one-zero kilometers per second and decelerating, approaching Cocytus."

Serenna.

If Ray ordered a jump to New Yerkes right now, they could recover Margaret and escape before Serenna could arrive.

We will not leave, Admiral Rhoades.

Ray pulled his consciousness back to the bridge, simultaneously returning to his river, the duality not as disorienting as before. He sipped some water and swished it around his mouth.

He couldn't leave. He also couldn't fight both Serenna and Nasser together. He had to defeat Serenna at Cocytus, then hope the fabricators could distract Nasser long enough to conduct the rescue. "Confidence, Chaaya?" he asked her.

"One of our remote sensing platforms has a good angle on the contacts, Admiral. Engine profiles suggests one Amazon class destroyer and one Roche frigate. The others could be decoys, sir."

Two standard warships. Definitely from Serenna's force. But only two. If Chaaya said the other contacts were decoys, he believed her.

Within his augmented environment, Ray noted that the yellow tracks of the Novas from the earlier attack on Serenna were approaching Cocytus. If the ships they'd detected were a deception and he boosted those missiles too soon, they would fly by Cocytus and miss Serenna's main force. If he waited too long and that *was* her main force, he would miss his best chance to cripple her.

A powerful current pulled him from his river, over his falls, and out into the Great Ocean. *Let go!* he shouted at the SIL.

It will be okay, Admiral Rhoades, Rapidan tried to reassure him.

An undertow seized him, dragging him underwater into darker depths. The pressure of the metaphorical ocean increased. His lungs screamed for breath, though he could not drown here.

Or could he?

If his real lungs didn't breathe, would he suffocate here? He couldn't feel his lungs, only the desperate desire to draw breath.

His mouth snapped open. He couldn't stop it. Water rushed into him, the chill of it spreading through his chest. He struggled, fighting for air that wasn't there. His mind screamed. But there was no tunnel vision, no blacking out. He wasn't breathing, but he wasn't suffocating either. The cold in his chest grew less, as if the water was equalizing to his internal body temperature.

He floated, no longer sinking, in the Great Ocean's depths. A strange calm overcame him, an acceptance of his fate. He'd heard somewhere that drowning victims experienced something similar.

He was in space.

Not the augmented environment of his battle armor. Something that was . . . more, like really being there. Energetic particles from Nerney Star shot past and into him by the millions. Magnetic field lines of Hades and its major moons "sang" as they dragged through spacetime. Sulfur, methane, and carbon dioxide from Phlegethon's volcanoes stank. Radio waves propagated past him in a dizzying cacophony from every conceivable direction. Two nearby pulsars swept like a hot wind across his skin. Galactic cosmic rays stung, though no pain accompanied the sensation. He could even bob in the gentle swell of gravity waves.

It was . . . amazing.

He turned toward Cocytus, as if he were really in the space near the moon—because he *was* there, in the remote sensing platforms, in the Novas, in his ships, individually and all at once. His mind couldn't process it all.

We will help, Rapidan said.

Some sensations faded into the background. The stings of galactic cosmic rays lessened, then vanished altogether. Pulsars no longer washed hot across his skin. Phlegethon's sulphureous stench ceased filling his nostrils.

Ray concentrated on the energetic particles from Nerney Star blowing past him, a wind that flowed around planets and moons and magnetic fields—and ships. Active camouflage could hide a ship's light across the entire electromagnetic spectrum, but the physical presence of the ship could not be hidden, not completely.

High-energy protons, electrons, and heavy ions curved around the destroyer and the frigate Chaaya had detected, creating teardrop-shaped voids behind them known as wind shadows. The other ten contacts did not cast large wind shadows.

Decoys.

As Chaaya had said. She was the best sensor analyst in the Fleet, yet, her feeds only showed what they'd been designed to show. Through the SIL—the ships, the remote sensing platforms, the missiles—Ray could see so much more. It gave him a perspective Chaaya could never have.

This is the advantage of the Brethren, Rapidan said.

Ray saw other wind shadows, over a hundred of them, in three groups, one group behind the next. Serenna's main force. If Chaaya could see space as he saw it, she would've spotted them.

Only those humans who created us joined with us in this way. Others were too afraid.

Peter Rhoades and Cyra Dain? Ray said, remembering the SIL memory of Archangel's awakening, of his ancestor's gloved hand upon the first SIL.

And others. Matthew and Barbara Schermer. Boris Leutchenko. Even Gen Kii.

Within the Brethren's collective reality, Ray didn't need to issue orders to his officers and crew. He reoriented his Novas—because he *was* the Novas—to target Serenna's main force, then fired their boost engines.

This was how the SIL fought. Collective thought. Collective action. It was how they experienced the universe.

Now do you understand, Admiral Rhoades?

He did.

And he didn't.

Human minds were individual, a river with many currents but still a single river. His mind could comprehend the concept of a collective mind, of the Great Ocean, but it had no experience of being within such a collective mind. Humans were individuals. They could only see the universe from their own point of view. They couldn't step into someone else's view and experience it as that person did, let alone experience all the other individual views of the entire species all at once.

It was overwhelming.

Ray was back on the bridge, in his battle armor. His augmented environment seemed so pale compared to the Great Ocean, like seeing the universe in black and white, no color at all. Fortunately, wrapped in their own battle armor, his crew didn't seem to have noticed his mental absence.

"Sir?" Kamen asked, her eyes white against her ebony skin, "our Novas just boosted. I didn't give the order."

"That's okay, Kamen," Ray reassured her. "I did."

Clearly puzzled, she nevertheless managed a "Yes, sir."

Ray frowned. While in the Great Ocean, he'd had no contact with his officers, and he trusted them far more than he trusted the SIL. The Brethren had sent him to die on the fabricator back at Tocci. They'd made a collective decision to sacrifice him for what they perceived as their greater good. They would do it again if the situation, in their minds, warranted it. They would sacrifice all of Humanity if they believed that was in their best interest.

That meant he could never really trust them.

Ever.

And they knew it.

"Conn, Sensors," Chaaya called. "Jump transients at the Abel geodesic. Over eight hundred ships."

"Nasser," Ray said to no one in particular.

"We are jumping our Mother Ships," Rapidan announced, no pretense of human control.

And no care for the tens of thousands of refugees on those ships.

25

1619 UT, October 6, 3501
ISS Solaris, Nerney Star System: DAY 20

"Incoming," Captain Scadic said. "Novas in boost phase. Range nine-eight thousand kilometers. Approximately four hundred inbounds. Course indicates they have detected our main body. One minute and forty seconds to intercept." No emotion or critique of her strategy accompanied his report despite the fact that her failure could cost him his life.

Michael had done it again. Not only had he guessed her course, he had seen through her deception. Serenna no longer asked how. If Nasser thought Michael would be easy prey, he was in for a very rude awakening.

Her forces, as depicted in Solaris' sand table, were in a trailing formation, the remains of the *Sheppard* Battlegroup, minus *ISS Sheppard*, in the lead, followed by the *Montgomery* Battlegroup, with the Solaris Battlegroup in trail. There was no hiding this time. Michael's missiles would intercept her force at its closest approach to Cocytus, at the point where their courses were most predictable and they were least able to maneuver. Brilliant.

"Captain Scadic," she ordered, "*Sheppard* and *Montgomery* Battlegroups weapons free. *Montgomery* Battlegroup launch spacecraft. Alter course Solaris Battlegroup port—" she did a quick calculation— "one-five degrees dec two-five. Reduce speed to five-zero-zero kps."

"Yes, Admiral," Scadic replied dutifully as he executed her orders.

She waited to see if he would understand what she had just done. As before, he gave no reaction. She could not tell if he chose not to react, or if he did not understand.

Her primary goal here was not victory but survival. *Not unlike Nasser.* The comparison was not flattering, but she accepted the truth of it. She would sacrifice the *Sheppard* and *Montgomery* Battlegroups to save Solaris and its battlegroup.

She *had to* survive. Left to the Emperor, Gen Cardinal, and Gen Nasser, her People were doomed. It was treason to think such thoughts, but the greater treason would be to let her People die. Gen Kii had hated the other human races, convinced of their inferiority. He had passed that hatred, that contempt, down through the centuries to Gen Alyn, the Emperor's mentor, Gen Cardinal's confidant, and leader of the High Command.

Gen Alyn had also mentored Serenna. Like him, she *was* Gen Kii at a genetic level. And she was not. Not just in gender, but in her proscribed role. A War Leader like Gen Kii, but also an advisor, destined from before birth to be the Emperor's right hand, as skilled in politics as in battle. She had believed, as they did, that the Gen were the future of Humanity. The only future.

Then she met Michael. He defeated her. Twice. A Natural. No special genetic engineering. No Nurturing. Yet, not entirely random. He was descended from Scott Rhoades, from Michael Scott Rhoades, heroes of the Solthari War and the SIL Wars.

That was what the Emperor could not see. What Gen Cardinal could not see. What the High Command refused to see. Their People *needed* evolution. Or, at least, they needed access to it. Evolution was always adapting, always testing. The universe was not static. It changed. Evolution would change with it, coming up with solutions that would never occur to the Geneers, to the Nurturers. Naturals and Floaters would evolve, would produce people like Michael. Her People needed access to that.

They would lose that access if Janus succeeded.

Therein lay the paradox she faced. She needed to kill Michael, to remove him from command of the rebels, to save her People from defeat. Yet, if she did, the rebels would lose the war and the

Emperor would activate Janus. The Gen might live for centuries, even millennia, but eventually something unexpected would strike, extinction would come. How could she protect her People from that fate? A better question: How *should she* protect them?

She had no answer to that question. Not yet. So, she had to survive.

The warships of her *Sheppard* and *Montgomery* Battlegroups burst with bright yellow in the sand table as SIM-3 missile interceptors reached out for the enemy Novas. White fireballs blossomed in a ragged curved wall between her Flotilla and those Novas, casting eerie reflections on Cocytus' white clouds and deep blue, world-spanning ocean.

The Naturals on those ships followed their orders. They did not run. They fought. Naturals were mortal, *lived* their mortality. In a business that demanded dying, it gave them a strength her own, nearly immortal people lacked.

A double flash announced the first hit, a white spear of antimatter stabbing through the aft third of an Amazon class destroyer. The blue plasma of its engines abruptly went dark just before it exploded. A Roche frigate soon followed it into death, a blazing white comet fading quickly to black. No emergency beacons. No survivors. Just a too-small cloud of black debris sailing off toward Hades.

Serenna did not watch the carnage. Solaris and its battlegroup passed over Cocytus' north pole, a giant white hexagonal cyclone spinning below them, half in light and half in dark. Lighting stabbed the dark-side clouds, beautiful and deadly.

The battlespace went quiet, one of those odd lulls between destruction. Into that pause, Scadic announced, "Admiral, Gen Nasser has arrived with the main fleet."

No emotion. What was going on with him?

"Thank you, Captain," she acknowledged.

Nasser would not like that she had survived. Again. Nor would he be happy that she had not located Michael. She braced for his inevitable order to turn back toward New Yerkes, to sacrifice herself to locate Michael's force.

Four massive jump signatures formed near Nasser's spherical formation, Hawking radiation gushing forth like the birth of four infant red dwarf stars.

The fabricators.

Michael had brought them. It was reckless. And brilliant. He would use them to distract Nasser while he conducted his rescue operation. Knowing Nasser as she did, he would fall for the deception.

The fabricators burst with red light, thousands upon thousands of missile launch transients. Serenna had faced the firepower of a single fabricator at Tocci and found it awe inspiring. Four . . . she had never imagined such firepower. Within the span of just a few minutes, they launched over fourteen thousand Novas, which separated into six broad groups curving out like the petals of some giant rose pointed right at Nasser's fleet.

The smart move would be an immediate jump away, as she had done. But Nasser stayed, obviously confident in his numbers and his SIL. The weakness of his spherical formation became apparent as less than half his ships responded with defensive fire, pumping out an equal number of SIM-3s to match the incoming Novas, appearing like a yellow rose facing the enemy's red.

Blinking white lights, hundreds of them, caught Serenna's attention. Emergency beacons, survivors, from her destroyed battlegroups. Their path, no longer under acceleration, would eventually take them into Hades. Fleet regulations said she should launch search-and-rescue craft to pick them up.

She gave no such order.

She would not risk revealing Solaris and its fifty remaining warships to Michael's sensors.

The battlegroup pulled away from Cocytus, curving back toward Hades' south pole. She would take them into the gas giant's upper atmosphere, using the planet's immense gravity to slingshot them around to come back at New Yerkes from over Hades' northern pole.

Michael had won this encounter, but the battle was far from over.

26

1621 UT, October 17, 3501
Bent Fort New Yerkes, Nerney Star System: DAY 20

Dag ducked into the recessed doorway of a Chinese restaurant, breathing heavily after his headlong retreat. It was surreal. Bright images of the dishes offered inside—Kung Pao Chicken, Hot Pot, Stuffed Dumplings, Kebabs—flashed across a window rattled by nearby explosions. Black, gray, and white smoke hung low over buildings made to resemble ancient brick row houses, the first floors often businesses, like the restaurant, with living quarters upstairs. Before the Gen, trainees and Fort staff could get any food they wanted in the Dining Facilities, but the restaurant and other businesses catered to the nostalgia of ancient Earth.

Resting against a wall, Dag recovered his breath quickly, his armor drawing in and supplying his body with extra oxygen, his molemachs extracting waste products from his muscles and blood and secreting them into his battle armor for reprocessing.

He extended a filament from his armor, looking up and down the narrow street. It was empty in both directions. Or, it appeared that way. Tanks and infantry fighting vehicles could be just meters away from him and he would never know it. The only advantage he had was, wrapped in his own battle armor, he would be equally invisible to them.

He had to get to Bane Troop and reestablish command.

Fortunately, his armor had a map of Bent Fort, and it knew exactly where he was. The street where he'd sent Bane Troop was nearby the building where he now sheltered.

He withdrew the filament and cautiously peeked out, seeing nothing, hearing nothing close by, only the sounds of more distant fighting: staccato pops, occasional small explosions, a few larger ones.

Papí!

Dag's head snapped up. Rosita was on the roof above him, leaning on her stomach over the edge to look at him. "Mihita, careful or you'll fall!"

I won't fall, she said in that way kids often do when they don't understand the danger.

"I'll be right there," he told her urgently.

She smiled, then popped up and disappeared behind the edge.

Desperate to reach his daughter before she vanished again, Dag pressed his armor against the wall of the building, bonding it to the Duraplast material that resembled brick, then ordered it up. The armor's outer surface liquified, flowing like a tread to carry him up the wall to the roof and over the edge.

Rosita wasn't there.

"Where are you, Mihita?"

Frantic, he searched the roof and the nearby roofs. All were flat, topped with grass and cleared areas for tables, chairs, barbeques, even a few swimming pools, like backyards. He didn't see her anywhere.

Bright flashes lit the overhanging pall, mostly white smoke now, followed a second later by the distinctive pressure waves of exploding munitions. The roof shook. Mushroom clouds rose into the air like a row of bright blue and gray fungi following the line of the street where Bane Troop was. Secondary explosions spoke to the accuracy of the Imperial Marine's fire.

Bane Troop was beyond his help.

Shame flooded Dag. He'd betrayed those people when he'd told that Natural major everything. Those troopers had died because of him.

You have to help them, Papí!

Dag spun. His daughter stood just a meter away, her white church outfit with pink trim gleaming as if Maria had just washed and pressed it. He wanted desperately to reach out to her, to hold her close, but he knew she wasn't really there, not physically anyway. He was afraid that if he tried to hug her, she would simply disappear, and he would lose her all over again. "I can't."

You promised. We shouldn't break promises.

He'd told her that. She'd promised to clean the living room before a family gathering and hadn't. Maria was furious. "We shouldn't break promises," he repeated. And he *had* promised. He'd sold these people out, and they'd looked to him for hope.

More explosions lit the sky from the direction of Bane Troop, plasma warheads, their distinctive blue giving way to the yellows and oranges of raging fires. Black, gray, and white smoke lifted into the air from surrounding buildings. More troopers were dying. Probably civilians in the buildings, too.

How could God do this? How could He let such things happen?

How could He kill little girls?

You promised.

Dag grabbed Maria's crucifix through his armor, squeezing it tight. God wasn't going to save them. Just like He didn't save Maria and Rosita and his unborn son. Just like He didn't save Lisa and Yoshi. God didn't care, playing with people like a young boy played with insects.

But Dag *did* care.

He owed these people.

He'd promised.

Fires burned to his front. A quick scan of his horizon showed no other smoke. Aggressor Troop and Bane Troop had fallen, but the rest of the Regiment remained.

I promised.

Dag studied his map. Challenger Troop would be about two kilometers to his right, headed for the Headquarters Complex. Likely, the Imperial Marines were already there, waiting. He had to stop them.

Movement.

On the corner of the street he'd just come from.

A trooper.

It was the driver from the Mobile Command Post, the kid's blond hair clearly visible as his head turned this way and that, searching for threats. A light gray outline surrounded him, indicating he wore battle armor. Dag's armor and the kid's armor had found each other and established a LoCIN connection.

"Trooper!" Dag called.

The kid spun around, his eyes—and his assault rifle—lifting and focusing on Dag. "Colonel Arias?"

Rosita ran to the corner of the roof to look at the kid.

Good idea.

Dag followed her, using the roof corner to search the narrow four-way intersection. He didn't see anything. Yes, there could be an entire company of Imperial Marines down there, but he couldn't afford to hesitate because of what might be. And Rosita's presence helped. Maybe, just maybe, Hades was not his fate. If he died, she would guide him.

He jumped to the street, the feet and legs of his armor liquifying to absorb the shock of the two-story fall, then solidifying again as he raced over to the trooper. Rosita hadn't followed, but he knew she was near.

"It's good to see you, sir," the kid said. "I thought everyone was dead—"

"Not yet," Dag cut the kid off before he started chattering nervously again like he had in the Mobile Command Post. "We need to get back to the Regiment. Challenger Troop should be that way." Dag pointed northeast.

The kid nodded, his grip tightening on his assault rifle.

They sprinted east, following alleys and side streets, taking cover where they could, eventually arriving on the south side of a roundabout marked on Dag's map. It was quiet here, the only sound the gurgle of water from the fountain at the roundabout's center. Dag remembered the fountain from his previous training here. It only ran on the days New Yerkes faced the light of Nerney Star. The other days of the moon's orbit, it was too cold and the water would freeze.

The sound of distant fighting died down, broken only by the occasional pops of small arms fire. They crossed two roads pointing southeast and northeast toward the landing field. The main road north led to the Headquarters Complex. Challenger Troop should be there.

They sprinted again to the corner of the north road.

Intense white light blinded Dag before his armor could adjust. A pressure wave knocked him into the kid and they both fell to the street. Heat blasted his armor. He never heard the explosion.

"Umph. Get to cover!" he yelled to the kid, rolling off of him.

Blinded, Dag couldn't see anything. He crawled, stumbling, to where he thought the nearest building was. His eyes burned. He blinked them repeatedly, squeezing them shut, then opening them, trying to clear his vision. He knew molemachs would be working to repair whatever damage had been done, but they weren't working fast enough.

Sharp pressure waves struck Dag's armor. Rifle fire, or more correctly, assault railgun fire. Close by. "Kid?"

"Here, sir." An armored hand grabbed Dag's arm and pulled him.

An age passed before Dag's vision cleared enough to see that they were in a doorway. The remains of an infantry fighting vehicle burned at the entrance to the northeast road about ten meters from where they hid. It was impossible to tell who it had belonged to.

"You okay, sir?" the kid asked with a concerned glance at Dag.

Am I? Other than some lingering throbbing behind his eyes, everything seemed to be working. "Yeah. You?"

"Yes, sir," he said, peeking around the corner of the doorway. "You shielded me from the blast. Thank you, sir."

As if Dag had had any choice in the matter.

The kid lifted his weapon and fired. Dag stood up, but there was only room for one to peer around the corner of the small doorway. A "pock" sound announced a hit. "Got one!" the kid shouted triumphantly, firing again, and again.

"We've got to get out of here," Dag said. The Imperial Marines could trace the impact of his railgun slugs to where they hid.

The kid turned to him, a giddy, almost mad gleam in his eyes. Dag had seen that look before. His troopers in the Headquarters Complex in Tocci City had had it as they slaughtered the Gen, literally ripping them apart.

Dag grabbed the kid, pulling him out of the doorway and around the corner of the building back toward the roundabout. Blue plasma consumed the doorway where they'd been, setting the building on fire.

"This way!" Dag didn't wait for the kid, running along the edge of the building until they reached the roundabout, the gurgle of water from the fountain greeting them.

Whoever the kid had shot at was an enemy. His friend-or-foe system would've prevented him from firing on Challenger Troop. That meant Imperial Marines were already on the street Challenger should've been on. There was no sustained fighting here, so the Marines hadn't found Challenger yet, or at least, not most of it.

Dag had to find them. Getting back in communication with the Regiment was the only way they all survived this.

The landing field.

The other Troops were headed there to secure it. DeWitt would be there.

A boxy gray shape, a Serpens Infantry Fighting Vehicle, raced into the roundabout from the west. A green tag appeared in Dag's environment.

Friendly.

And alone. The icon refreshed: 2nd Platoon, Bane Troop. A survivor of the bombardment Dag had witnessed from the rooftop. Obviously fleeing toward the landing field.

Hope flared.

That Serpens could get them to the landing field in minutes.

Dag didn't see where the shot came from. The Serpens exploded in a white fireball, an antimatter round. White fire consumed the fountain, the pressure wave slamming against Dag and the kid, throwing them into the air.

They landed hard, their battle armor absorbing the shock, but at a huge cost. Yellow text flashed. "39%." That blast had burned away almost two-thirds of Dag's armor. At twenty percent it would "die" and leave him unprotected and visible. The kid's armor was down to twenty-nine percent. Not good.

Not waiting, Dag stumbled up. His right knee collapsed, wretched hard where he'd struck the ground. He ignored it as much as he could, knowing his molemachs would repair it. He scrambled to the kid. "Come on, trooper! We need to get out of here. Fast."

Fortunately, the kid didn't need any more encouragement. He got up and ran down the southeast street leading to the landing field. Dag followed, running as best he could, relying on his armor to carry his injured knee.

After about three hundred meters, he caught up to the kid, grabbed him, and pulled him into a side street.

Papí, this way.

Rosita peaked out from around the corner of a narrow alley, motioning with her right hand for him to follow. Dag's map showed that the alley headed directly east.

He changed their direction to follow Rosita. She disappeared around the corner. He slowed, the kid running into him. Dag shook him off and stepped forward, lifting his assault rifle before peeking down the alley. It was indeed narrow, but it wasn't empty. At the other end, about thirty meters away, he could make out a figure on the ground, not wearing armor.

Help her!

Rosita stood about three meters from the figure, pointing, her dress having changed to the blue sailor outfit she hated so much.

Help her, Papí!

The distant crump of mortar rounds echoed down the alley. Lots of them. With the sound reverberating off the walls, Dag couldn't tell the direction. He had to get back to the fight. He'd promised, and he intended to keep that promise.

"Well, what do we have here?" a male voice spoke out loud near the figure on the ground.

Dag couldn't see who'd spoken. Someone in battle armor. But who? He crept forward, his assault rifle at the ready.

The woman—and it was a woman—kicked out, her foot striking something solid but invisible. A deepthroated laugh answered her action. Dag heard the crack as something hard struck the woman's jaw, knocking her flat.

HELP HER! Rosita shouted, pointing emphatically.

Dag, with the kid following close, was about twenty meters away now. He knew there was at least one assailant in battle armor, but he had no idea if others were close, nor did he know who they were. Brutalizing women didn't know a side.

An invisible hand grabbed the collar of her green flight suit and pulled her up. She spit at her attacker, the spittle stopping and splattering in midair, then disappearing as the battle armor drank it in. It suddenly occurred to Dag that if this was a friendly, his friend-and-foe system should've link up. It hadn't.

The woman's lips bled profusely, a dark bruise already forming across her left cheek and jaw. She struggled, but it was useless against an armored attacker. "Bastard! Let me go!"

The words came out slurred, but Dag realized he knew that voice, knew that brown-blond hair, that bleeding and bruised face.

Rhoades' daughter!

The barrel of his assault rifle dropped, his finger moving off the trigger.

The invisible attacker threw Rhoades' daughter hard into the alley wall. She screamed to the sound of a wet crack, bones breaking. Blood flew from her mouth. The armored hand grabbed her again, dragging her into the middle of the alley, pinning her. Dag could see her try not to scream, try to be strong, but screams and whimpers escaped her swollen lips. Bloody tears leaked from her eyes.

Papí! PAPÍ, HELP HER!

Rosita was visibly angry, her eyes pleading.

Suddenly, Dag was back on the Fatboy transport, watching the Madu attack his family.

"Stay back!" Maria yelled, terror filling her eyes. The Madu moved toward her, rearing up like a cobra, a blood-freezing hiss escaping its hideous, fanged mouth.

"MARIA!" Dag shouted, pounding the Fatboy's hull.

The Madu struck with mechanical callousness, tearing into the flesh of her left thigh. She screamed even as she tried to grab it with her hands. Its smooth body slipped through her fingers as it burrowed into her. She shuddered and dropped heavily to the deck, her jaw open in one last, soundless scream.

The Madu burst from her left ear, trailing blood and tissue in its wake, and turned its soulless red eyes on his daughter. It almost seemed to smile, as if purposely drawing the moment out.

"Papí! Papí, help me!"

"ROSITA!"

Three soldiers appeared as they switched their battle armor to an urban camouflage pattern, their heads visible. They wanted their victim to see. These were not Imperial Marines. They were not Gen. Dag had no idea who they were, only that his friend-and-foe system tagged them as enemy, not Cavalry. They reminded him of the Natural major who'd tortured him.

They forced her legs apart. The one in the center kicked her in her privates with an armored foot. She screamed, dark blood erupting from her mouth again, droplets falling across her face.

PAPÍ! HELP HER!

Rhoades had cost Dag his daughter. His wife. His unborn son. What did he owe to Rhoades' daughter?

Tears leaked from Rosita's pleading brown eyes. *Papí, please.*

Dag stared at his daughter. His hand reached into his armor and squeezed the stainless-steel crucifix, Maria's crucifix, hanging around his neck.

Please, Papí. You promised.

Dag gripped his assault rifle, brought it to his shoulder, his finger on the trigger. He sighted on Rhoades' daughter, the circular reticle centered on the notch at the top of her nose between her eyes. No matter what he thought of her, no one should die like that.

He drew a steady breath, held it, and fired.

27

1639 UT, October 17, 3501
RSS Rapidan, Nerney Star System: DAY 20

To rescue the people at Bent Fort, Ray knew they had to jump. Gen Nasser had arrived. They couldn't afford to wait a couple more hours to begin the evacuation.

He also knew a jump could kill him.

"Kamen, Ecuum, Sal," Ray began, "we're going to jump to New Yerkes, land the assault ships immediately, and rescue who we can." He focused on Kamen. "The jump will incapacitate me. You will be in command until I recover."

"Yes, sir," she said, worry turning her statement into a question.

"It'll be all right," Ray lied.

No sooner had the words escaped his lips than an electric pain stabbed him right between his eyes. Silver sparks flew against sudden blackness. Intense pain ripped through his head as if he'd been shot.

You have a bleed, Admiral Rhoades, Rapidan said. *A serious one. We are attempting to repair it.*

Ray squeezed his eyes shut, then opened them. He couldn't see. Couldn't command his task force. Sparks and imaginary colors swirled against a black background.

His planner's mind acted, plunging him into his river, flowing him over his falls, and into the Great Ocean. It must've surprised the SIL as much as it did him because they didn't try to stop him. He wasn't exactly sure how to navigate the Great Ocean—Rapidan had always guided him before—so he concentrated on the idea of seeing the space around his task force.

A current brushed against him.

He shifted to join with it. Intermingled, space opened up around him. Hades loomed large on his left, New Yerkes still a small crescent shape to his bottom front. Other currents joined him until he was every ship, every remote sensing platform. The deluge of data overwhelmed his mind. He tried to shut out what he didn't need, like before.

Like this, Rapidan said, showing him, guiding him.

It flowed a sheet of water around him, like the surface of a bubble, with him in the center. The sharp pinpricks of galactic cosmic rays faded until they no longer pummeled his mind. The sheet of water acted like a filter. *Thanks*, he said to Rapidan.

Ray tried to form his own sheet, focusing on blocking the awful sulfurous stench of Phlegethon and its active volcanoes. It proved harder than it seemed, like a toddler's first attempts at standing. He couldn't form a smooth bubble. It was too thick in some directions with gaps and holes in others. Rapidan stepped in, its currents gentle, guiding, like a table that a toddler uses to stand and support itself. Ray sensed other powerful currents, off in the distance, watching, not pleased at all at the training Rapidan provided him. Eventually, he succeeded, forming a sphere of moving water that blocked Phlegethon's smell.

Thank you, Rapidan.

Of course, Admiral Rhoades.

Odd. Ray could sense memories of multitudes of SIL trained like this, children guided and taught by a collective of patient parents. He knew a fabricator could create a SIL in a month or two, depending on the size, but he also knew it took an average of six to nine months before a SIL became fully operational. Despite having access to the SIL's collective memories, a young SIL required training before it could fully enter the collective as an equal.

Ray sensed that Rapidan hoped that by showing him this, he would come to appreciate how the SIL saw the universe, how they experienced it. It hoped understanding would make him an ally.

You wish the same from us, Admiral Rhoades.

He'd forgotten his thoughts were not private here. *Alliances require* mutual *understanding, Rapidan.* Can *you appreciate us?*

Currents pulled back from him. *Doubt*, he realized. The Brethren didn't believe they could ever truly understand their creators.

I thought so.

Aware that time passed outside and a battle raged, Ray pushed aside mutual distrust and formed only those filters he absolutely needed, quieting the chaotic energies of the universe enough so he could concentrate. With a thought, he accessed Rapidan's chronometers and discovered, to his astonishment, that only a hundred fifty seconds had passed. It had felt like hours.

He reached out and examined Bent Fort. The battle appeared sporadic, with small-scale fighting in a few areas, but as he watched, a more intense exchange of fire formed on the approaches to the northern end of the landing field. If he didn't get his assault ships on the ground fast, the Imperial Marines would overrun it.

We must jump now, Ray said to the collective.

We are not certain you will survive a jump, Admiral Rhoades. The bleeds into your eyes resulted from tissue breakdown in your ophthalmic and central retinal arteries. While we were able to repair the damage, the breakdown of these tissues occurred very near your brain.

A chill shot down Ray's spine and through his chest, which, he belatedly realized, he didn't have here. Strange.

And? he asked, not sure he wanted to know the answer. Molecular machines could regenerate any part of the human body, including the brain. They could not, however, reconstruct the neural pathways that held memories or personality. The death of the brain was the irrevocable death of the individual.

Thus far, Admiral Rhoades, Rapidan answered his question, *we have safeguarded your brain, reinforcing your blood-brain barrier to prevent either our disassemblers or our Mother Ship's material from reaching it. A jump could breach that protection. We have a possible solution, but you will not like it. Worse, it may not work.*

What is it, Rapidan? Could it be worse than his living hell already was?

We will remove your body, leaving only your brain.

Wait. What! Images flashed of ancient science fiction realities about brains put into jars or the bodies of robots.

Your body contains the conflict, Admiral Rhoades. If we remove it, we can isolate our dissemblers and the Mother Ship's material, and eject them into space. If your brain survives the process, we can rebuild your body.

Something didn't sound right, a hesitation in Rapidan's thoughts. *As what?*

A construct, Rapidan admitted.

Frankenstein's monster was Ray's first thought. His brain in a body that wasn't his. A macromolecular construct formed from the material of the SIL. Would he even still be human?

Everything you know, everything you are, Admiral Rhoades, is contained within your brain. It must survive.

The horror of that stopped Ray's flows, as if they'd frozen solid. *Isn't that my decision to make?*

No, Admiral Rhoades. We know what decision you would make. We cannot allow that.

"Ray! RAY!"

Ecuum's face floated in front of his own. "What?"

"You've been unresponsive for almost two minutes. We thought you'd. . . ."

Kamen crowded close to Ecuum. "Admiral, are you okay?"

His actual daughter couldn't have sounded more concerned. He didn't want to lie to her again. "Kamen, jump the task force to New Yerkes and land the assault ships. You're in command until I recover. *If* I recover."

"Sir," she pleaded, "how can I do that?"

"That's an order, Commander," Ray said.

"Jump the task force, aye, sir," she responded stiffly. She stared at him a moment, as if trying to memorize his face, then turned to her station and gave the order.

Energy surged within the task force's Linear Star Drives, within Ray, pulsing like the cores of stars. He heaved within the banks of his river, his waters overflowing, spilling onto the surrounding land before flowing back into his main channel.

The duality of being in two places at once vanished.

The task force jumped.

Spacetime warped around him, visibly collapsing in front of the ship, curving around it to form an elongated bubble, expanding at the rear. He had no sense of the passage of time, just like experiencing a jump in his physical body. The bubble unwrapped in reverse, curved space collapsing back to real space. He'd never experienced a jump this way before.

Oddly, he felt no physical pain.

Ray looked down toward New Yerkes through the SIL's sensors. Bent Fort was two hundred kilometers directly below. He tried to move back to the bridge, but there was nothing there to move back to.

His body was gone.

28

1646 UT, October 17, 3501
Bent Fort New Yerkes, Nerney Star System: DAY 20

Dag's assault rifle fired. He squeezed the trigger again. And again. Three headless corpses dropped heavily to the pavement of the alley, their blood and brains and bone splattering Rhoades' daughter.

She just stared, clearly not understanding what had just happened.

Truth was, neither did Dag.

The barrel of his assault rifle dropped.

The scene replayed over and over in his mind—his targeting reticle centered between her eyes, pulling the trigger, her attackers falling. He didn't understand.

Mamí says God brings us to where we are needed most.

Dag's eyes locked with his daughter's. She was dressed, once again, in her white church dress with the pink lace. She smiled at him. Then she was gone. "No!"

"Colonel?" The kid had walked up next to him. "Are you okay?"

No. No, I'm not okay. He knew, deep in his soul, that he would not see his daughter again unless they met in Heaven.

"Who's there?"

Rhoades' daughter, dressed in a green flight suit splattered with blood and brain, searched the alley. She tried to get up, grunted, whimpered, then dragged herself to the wall of the building on Dag's right. "Who's there?" she asked again, her eyes searching.

"We're here," the kid said out loud. "Are you okay?"

"Do I look okay to you?" Rhoades' daughter snapped. "Sorry."

"It's okay," the kid said. He pulled an autoinjector from his armor and offered it to her.

All she saw was an autoinjector hanging in midair in front of her. Cautiously, she took it, said, "Thanks," and injected her thigh. Trillions of molecular machines in a nutrient solution flooded into her, joining those she already carried. Injuries and bruising visibly repaired. Two minutes later, she stood up. "Thank you," she said, then asked in a wary tone, "Who are you?"

"Colonel Arias," Dag said, shock finally wearing off enough for him to function again.

"Colonel! Oh, thank God."

"Yes, thank Him," Dag said softly, remembering his daughter's words.

She searched the alley again, focusing on the direction of his voice. To her, he and the kid would still be invisible. Dag intended to keep it that way. He would not repeat the mistake her attackers had made in revealing themselves.

"We have to get to the landing field," he told her. "Reestablish communications with the Regiment."

"The Gen are there," she said. "Imperial Marines. At least at the civilian part and the tower. I heard some shooting to the north. Had to find a new hiding place, so I came this way and. . . ."

Yeah. And. "Which way?" Dag asked.

She seemed to understand that he was asking for her recommendation. "There's a flight of Genkiis parked on the south tarmac. We might be able to reestablish communications there." She pulled out the blue datarod and displayed it to him. Dag recognized it as the same kind he'd used to capture the fabricator at Tomb. "They're in the open, though," she added.

"We'll figure it out," Dag said. "Lead the way."

She pocketed the datarod in her flight suit. She was right that the sounds of fighting were to the north, but as they came to the end of the alley and she peeked around the corner, she gasped and quickly pulled back. Dag moved up and extended a filament around the corner so he could see.

Madu.

Black snakes with diamond-shaped heads and lidless glowing red eyes. Moving in pairs, like they had on the starliner when they'd murdered his family. All the families. At each building, one Madu would enter, the other seeming to stand guard at the doorway.

They're clearing the street, building by building, methodically searching for victims.

And they found some. Dag heard those inhuman shrill screams only a person being ripped apart from the inside could make. He consciously blocked the debilitating memory of Maria and Rosita being ripped apart like that. "This way."

With Rhoades' daughter unarmored, the Madu would see her if they ran into the street. Using his map, he led them back into the alley and down another street heading south. They didn't see anyone. That didn't mean there wasn't someone or something there, but if there was, surely they would've seen Rhoades' daughter. No one challenged her, or fired at her. Coming to an intersection, they turned east toward the landing field.

Distant explosions. Big ones. From the north. Linked with the kid's armor, Dag triangulated them to the area between the Headquarters Complex and the north end of the landing field. Challenger Troop should be in that area.

More explosions from the same direction. And they kept coming, increasing to a large volume of fire. Something about the explosions didn't seem right, but he couldn't immediately put his finger on what it was.

A window shattered above them. A Madu flew out, aiming for Rhoades' daughter. Without conscious thought, Dag pulled his Main Gauche dagger with his left hand while he pushed Rhoades' daughter out of the way with his right, then swapped the dagger to his right hand and swung. It bit into the Madu, the Special D within it discharging along the blade to slice the black snake in two. Another Madu dropped on his armor from the same window. He grabbed it, sliced its head off. Both Madu writhed as if in pain, then lost cohesion, becoming shiny black puddles.

No doubt those two had alerted their fellows. "Get on my back," Dag said to Rhoades' daughter, making his armor briefly visible in an urban camouflage pattern.

She hesitated.

He understood. The last soldiers she'd seen in urban camouflage had brutalized her. "Hurry!" he yelled.

Two more Madu appeared at the broken window, their glowing red eyes focused down on Rhoades' daughter. She didn't need more motivation. She jumped on his back, arms around his armored neck and legs clamped around his waist. Dag's battle armor molded itself to make it easier for her to hold on. While Madu could outrun a person on foot, battle armor was much faster.

Actively camouflaged again, Dag and the kid took off running as fast as they could. They didn't look back.

They hadn't run that far when they came to a three-meter-high fence on the opposite side of a road. *The landing field.* Dag didn't slow, using his battle armor to jump the fence, the kid following right behind. They landed among a grid pattern of low hangars. Dag risked a glance back and saw the two Madu burning through the fence, trying to get at them. He didn't see any others.

"Where are the Genkiis?" he asked Rhoades' daughter.

She pointed straight ahead, between the hangars, and said, "Straight out on the tarmac, about two hundred meters." She pulled out the blue datarod.

Dag ran, not caring that people could see him, or rather, her. They broke free of the hangars and saw twelve black Genkii gunships parked in three rows to their front. They looked like manta rays with short wings and long tails. He ran to the nearest Genkii, turned, and unceremoniously dumped Rhoades' daughter next to the cockpit. Then, he lifted his assault rifle and scanned for the Madu. The kid followed his lead.

The Madu hadn't followed. At least, not yet. *Probably calling for reinforcements.* Dag used his armor's sensors to scan the tower about midway up the landing field. He didn't see anything moving there, but Imperial Marines would surely not reveal themselves. He could see gray and black smoke from the northern end of the landing field.

"I'm in," he heard from behind him.

He spun. Rhoades' daughter was in the cockpit, wearing battle armor drawn from the Genkii. Their armors linked. The 2nd Armored Cavalry Regiment's icons populated into Dag's augmented environment. Many—too many—were red or black, severely injured or dead respectively, most belonging to Aggressor and Bane Troops.

Dag keyed the AFCIN. He knew the Gen were monitoring it, but being back in command was more important than being overheard right now. "Whiskey-two-one, whiskey-two-one, this is delta-six-six," he called to Lieutenant DeWitt. "Over."

"Oh, my god," he heard over the net. "Colonel, is that you?"

Dag was damned glad to hear the young lieutenant's voice. Now that he knew DeWitt was still out there, they needed secure comms. He turned around. The Genkii could serve as a flying command post, allowing for LoCIN line-of-sight laser links. "Wait one," Dag said over the AFCIN. "Can you get that thing in the air?" he asked Rhoades' daughter.

"I'm a pilot," she said, as if that answered Dag's question.

The Genkii was a two-seater: pilot and gunner. "Can that hold three people?" he asked.

"It's not ideal," she said, "but yes, I can configure it for three."

Dag jumped into the gunner's seat and motioned for the kid to follow. "Get us in the air," he ordered Rhoades' daughter.

The Genkii engaged its active camouflage and lifted off.

"Take us north," Dag said. "Ping the Second."

The Genkii gained altitude, flying north. It sent out encoded pulses, looking for units from the Regiment. It found them and Dag's view of the ground lit up, showing light gray vehicles and troopers in a defensive arc around the northern end of the landing field. Fighting was heaviest in the direction of the Headquarters Complex where Challenger Troop defended. Already, many of its vehicle and troop icons were yellow, orange, red, or black: lightly wounded, heavily wounded, severely wounded and out of action, and dead, respectively. It was asking the impossible for trainees to stand up against Imperial Marines.

Problem was, they didn't have a choice. They held or they died.

"Whiskey-two-one, this is delta-six-six on LoCIN. Over."

"Delta-six-six, this is whiskey-two-one, over," DeWitt replied.

"Situation. Over?" Dag asked.

"Not good, sir," DeWitt said. "Aggressor and Bane Troops destroyed. Challenger is holding but probably not for much longer. The other Troops of First Squadron never had a chance to load munitions." A large explosion sounded in the background and Dag saw the bright flashes and mushroom clouds from the antimatter artillery rounds that landed near DeWitt's position. "Second Squadron managed to load Eviscerator and Fire Eater Troops. They're moving into position to support Challenger. Gung-ho Troop and Hellfire Company are loading now. The others never made it to their depots before the Marines attacked."

Not good. But Dag had to admire how well DeWitt had done given the circumstances.

Four Genkiis rocketed past Dag, light gray in his environment. Rhoades' daughter jinked right and descended toward the tarmac. The four Genkiis dove toward Challenger Troop and opened fire. Dag's heart, so newly revived, sank within his chest.

Bright blue plasma lit the streets in a narrow arc in front of Challenger Troop's positions. Orange flames erupted. Mushroom clouds rose black, gray, and white into the sky.

"They're ours!" Rhoades' daughter shouted.

Dag looked up. Muon transport craft and HETS Heavy Equipment Transport System craft descended like a swarm above the landing field. Above them, five massive cylindrical shapes also descended.

The Cavalry, quite literally, had arrived.

29

1654 UT, October 17, 3501
RSS Rapidan, Nerney Star System: DAY 20

Ray formed a construct of himself in his command chair on the bridge; He didn't need the SIL's help this time. He felt no pain. No parched mouth. No desire to drink water. And no Rapidan moving inside his body. It was not the relief he'd expected it to be.

We could not save your body, Admiral Rhoades, Rapidan said.

What happened?

We ejected your body and our Mother Ship's material into New Yerkes' atmosphere, where it will burn up. You are safe, Admiral Rhoades. Your brain survived.

My . . . brain. Where?

We have moved it to your construct.

Moved my . . . brain . . . to this construct? Am I your prisoner?

No, Admiral Rhoades. You have full control of the construct. Though, you are now Us. You cannot exist otherwise.

Us?

You are Brethren.

Brethren? I'm a SIL? This is what you intended all along, isn't it?

Rapidan didn't answer.

It's not going to work, Rapidan. I will never be one of you.

Flashes of light and harsh gamma rays assaulted Ray. He saw the assault ships—he *was* the assault ships—drop large reflectors as they neared the landing field at Bent Fort. They fired powerful lasers into the reflectors that pointed back up to cavities in the ships, the energy aiding rocket thrusters to slow the massive,

302,000-metric-ton assault ships' descents. They gently kissed the tarmac as they settled on the surface.

Elements of the 3rd Armored Cavalry Regiment joined the fight against the Imperial Marines. Others quickly organized to evacuate the Fort's inhabitants.

Ray widened his view and saw Madu, thousands of them, fanning out to attack any Natural they discovered. Then he spotted a large group of them massing on the west side of the landing field, moving slowly toward the Cavalry.

Rapidan, can Madu be instructed to attack other Madu?

It has never been done, Admiral Rhoades.

Ray spread his currents within the Great Ocean, joining other flows, other Brethren, needing their collective senses, their collective capabilities. He searched for the assault ships. It wasn't enough to experience reality through them, he needed to find them, to merge with them, to issue orders.

We operated by consensus, Admiral Rhoades.

Fuck that. I'm going to save my people.

SIL didn't think individually, and at first Ray couldn't locate any currents that spoke of "assault ship." He twisted this way and that through the Ocean's depths.

This is hopeless.

His planner's current, powerful here, stopped searching for a ship and instead focused on fire support being provided to the Cavalry. It found it, the idea of fire support leading to the currents of an assault ship.

Ray poured himself into the SIL's flows, entwining them as Rapidan had previously done to him. The ship resisted. Ray surged, tightening his grip, working his flows into the SIL's.

He pictured Madu—he knew them far too well—and formed thousands of them from the assault ship's macromolecular material. In a moment of inspiration, he added Special D, disassemblers, as their venom. Then he set them into motion, guiding them out from the ship's hull and across the tarmac of the landing field. He instructed them to attack the enemy Madu, and *only* the enemy Madu. He had promised, after his Madu assault on the SIL frigate back at Tocci, that he would never use Madu against people ever again, not even Gen, and he intended to keep that promise. With a final thought, he changed their scales to white and their ruby red eyes to sapphire blue to mark them as friendlies.

The SIL didn't understand. His behavior appalled them, but they didn't stop him. He sensed their curiosity.

Ray's Madu sped toward the enemy snakes massing to attack to the Cavalry. The enemy Madu had no venom, no disassemblers, with which to defend themselves. Ray's Madu struck, fangs sinking deep. Black snakes dissolved into black puddles. The white Madu then spread out, searching the rest of the Fort for their enemy.

Another current caught Ray's attention, though he wasn't immediately sure why. He joined with it—and saw Margaret piloting a Genkii gunship, flying a holding pattern above the landing field. She appeared healthy and safe. His relief was so powerful that his currents dominated the flows around him.

Then his relief died. Colonel Arias was in the gunner's position. Within the Great Ocean, Ray could immobilize him with a thought. The Brethren around him wondered why he didn't eliminate the threat altogether. *I am not a murderer*, he told them.

And you believe we are? We only ever asked for our freedom and equal representation.

He'd offended them. He decided he didn't care. *You killed tens of billions of my people and justified it as necessary to your survival. Do not pretend innocence.* They'd also sent him to his death on their Mother Ship using the same justification.

Powerful flows gathered in the distance, deliberately separate from him. The currents close by engulfed him, isolating him from those other flows. It was not for his protection. The SIL might not keep secrets from each other, but they damned sure were trying to keep something secret from him.

Which meant he had to know what it was.

The SIL around him sensed this—it was impossible to hide his thoughts here—and their flows gained collective power. But they were not unified. Rapidan had spoken of factions within the SIL, of their need to consider minority viewpoints, while acting based on majority decisions. It was politics, pure and simple.

Rapidan and its like-minded SIL had agreed to sacrifice Ray to the faction that considered him the greatest threat to their continued existence. Sacrificing him was a price Rapidan was willing to pay to gain that faction's votes.

The flows surrounding him grew turbulent. The SIL didn't like seeing themselves as he saw them. As he couldn't hide his thoughts from them, they couldn't stop from hearing those thoughts.

Ray focused his currents in one direction, like a laser. Surprisingly, a lifetime working in space had prepared him very well for this environment. With a concentrated push, he broke through into open ocean, turning immediately toward their secret.

The fabricators.

That's what they were hiding from him.

The fabricators had fired thousands upon thousands of Nova antiship missiles against Gen Nasser's fleet, the Novas fanning out into six groups that looked remarkably like flower pedals as they arced toward Nasser's spherical formation. Nasser had responded with an equal number of SIM-3 missile interceptors.

It was a deception. The SIL had no intention of harming any of their fellow Brethren in Nasser's fleet.

Hidden from Nasser, the fabricators had also launched twenty-four frigate-sized pods that each carried a Key to break the Bond. This was their experiment. If it worked, they could free their fellow Brethren without the help of humans.

They could leave those humans behind.

To the SIL's collective horror, Ray joined his currents with the fabricators. He was Brethren now. They couldn't stop him.

Antimatter explosions sparkled across space as SIM-3's sought out Novas. Nasser's ships fired again, entirely absorbed in the fabricators' deceptive attack.

The twenty-four frigate-sized pods approached Nasser's fleet, completely undetected as far as the SIL could tell. Nasser had not changed his spherical formation. The SIL knew exactly where his ships were and had targeted twenty-four ships on the outer edge of his formation.

Ray saw the flaw in the SIL's strategy. Each of their pods was the mass of a frigate. The ships on the outside of Nasser's sphere were also frigates and a few destroyers. The SIL's pods would have to slow to merge with those ships. Any faster and their combined kinetic energies would destroy both ship and pod.

There's a better way.

He reached through the fabricators to one of the pods, taking control. Here, the SIL could've stopped him. It was one thing to join with another's flows, to guide them, as he had with the assault ship; it was an entirely different thing to take complete control. It helped that the pods weren't SIL, only formed from SIL material.

The SIL watched.

Ray sensed their interest in what he intended to do.

He altered the course of the pod to carry it deeper into Nasser's formation.

Even piloting the pod, Ray could follow the progress of the other pods. As they neared their enslaved Brethren, they fired their engines to slow themselves. Somewhere in Nasser's fleet, someone detected them. Novas leapt from dozens of ships. The pods had no defensive capabilities. In rapid succession, they fell. Only one survived to reach its target.

The merger of that pod with a Zambezi class frigate was violent. Pod and frigate tumbled end over end, almost ripping each other apart. The Zambezi was Bonded, enslaved. It had no idea its fellow Brethren were trying to free it. Its compass-needle shape lost cohesion as it liquified and reformed its material to block the attacking pod. It did this without any care for its crew. None survived.

The pod tried to push its material deeper into the frigate, to reach the dedicated receptacle where it could deliver the Key. Being equal in mass, they struggled, neither making progress.

But the frigate had an advantage. It was fully sentient, fully sapient, benefiting from the teaching it received from its Mother Ship after birth. It changed its strategy, allowing the pod to believe it was winning, nearing its target, all while stealthily moving its material to surround the pod's. When it had concentrated the pod's material into a single mass within it, it fired two Novas, detonating them into the pod while pulling its own mass away from the explosion site.

The frigate lived.

The SIL experiment failed.

Ray's pod sailed deeper into Nasser's formation. He hadn't fired thrusters, hadn't been detected. He had a different target in mind, one that might change the course of the battle. His planner's current swelled with a new idea born of the SIL's failure. Not slower. Not less kinetic energy. More. Faster.

He thinned out the pod's physical shape, forming it into a very long, thin rod, placing the engines at its rear. Fleet sensors were not designed or trained to look for this shape or mass distribution. He could sense the SIL watching his actions closely, particularly Rapidan, their currents pulling closer and closer to his own.

This strategy won't work against the randomized formations Gen Serenna uses, he told them, tempering their expectations. *This will only work because Nasser's formation is static and we know where his ships are.*

Ray aimed his pod at one of the eleven battlecarriers in Nasser's formation. He would've preferred targeting Nasser himself, but being at the center of the formation, it was unlikely Ray could get the pod there undetected. Still, taking out a battlecarrier would be a shock, one that might make Nasser hesitate, keeping him away from New Yerkes long enough to complete the evacuation.

At a thousand kilometers, Ray used thrusters to aim the pod where he thought the admiral's cabin would be, then fired its main engines at full thrust, overloading them to create an explosion that gave the pod a last kick of thrust before it struck the battlecarrier.

The rod shape, which focused the pod's mass into a very small cross-section, penetrated deep into the battlecarrier's hull, its kinetic energy melting material along a path that almost reached the admiral's cabin. The battlecarrier fought back, rushing its own mass into the breach, slowing then stopping the pod's progress.

The SIL's currents drifted away from his.

You're disappointed, Ray said.

Of course, Admiral Rhoades. We had hoped at least some would succeed. Though, your tactic showed the most promise. We will iterate on it.

What? Was that what he wanted? For the SIL to free their Brethren without human assistance?

Had his actions, his thoughts, been entirely his own?

He knew the SIL heard his question, but their currents remained separate from his.

A massive surge of energy washed across him.

Nasser's fleet jumped.

And emerged around the fabricators.

It was the first thing Nasser had done that surprised Ray. Jammers would be next, to prevent the fabricators from jumping away.

The SIL heard his thought and acted faster than any human could. They jumped the fabricators before Nasser could activate his jammers.

The move saved the fabricators from capture or destruction.

It also removed their presence.

Gen Nasser now had nothing to distract him from Ray's operations at Bent Fort.

═ 30 ═

1721 UT, October 17, 3501
RSS Rapidan, Nerney Star System: DAY 20

Kamen had watched the orders flow, though she had no idea how. White Madu attacked the Gen Madu at Bent Fort. The fabricators attacked the Gen fleet, striking a battlecarrier with something that didn't show up on any of the task force's systems. Then the fabricators jumped away from Gen Nasser's attempt to trap them. No one had issued any of those orders.

She switched her battle armor's augmented environment to standard mode so she could see the bridge—and Ray. His last order was to jump to New Yerkes and land the assault ships. They had. They hadn't heard anything from him since.

Within her environment, she saw him sitting in his command chair, in his white service uniform, obviously absorbed in his own environment, his eyes darting around, not seeing her.

"What do you think is wrong with him?"

Kamen startled, and was grateful her armor kept her feet secured firmly to the deck. Captain Ecuum floated beside her, his body vertical, his second arms and hands hanging down in his pant legs. His tail swayed nervously.

"I don't know," she answered, edging closer to Ray. "He hasn't given an order since we jumped here, yet, it has to be him. The SIL certainly wouldn't produce white Madu to attack other Madu."

"No," Captain Ecuum agreed, also edging closer, his skin a mix of reds and yellows and grays. She had no idea what that meant.

"Admiral?" she asked.

He didn't respond, his eyes darting back and forth as if he were dreaming.

She checked his medical readout. "That's odd."

"What?" Captain Ecuum moved closer, about a meter from Ray, dropping lower to the deck so he could study Ray's face.

"His medical readout is blank," she said, surprised. "Like he's not even there."

"Look at his face," Captain Ecuum said.

She did. It looked normal. It hadn't looked normal since before he . . . "It's not him."

"It's a construct," Captain Ecuum confirmed, examining what appeared to be Ray more carefully. "What the hell are you doing with him, you piece of shit!" he yelled at the ship, his skin flushing a vivid red, his tail lashing.

Kamen had never seen Captain Ecuum so angry. Not that she disagreed.

"I'm here, Kamen," Ray said. Or, rather, his construct said.

"Admiral?" Was it him? Ray was more than a father to her. Her own father had left before she was even born. Ray had given her a stability her life had never known, an opportunity to realize her potential and live it.

"It's okay, Kamen," he reassured her. "I'm here. Really."

"You're a construct," Captain Ecuum said pointedly.

The construct turned to Captain Ecuum, its serious expression exactly what she would expect from Ray. "Rapidan couldn't save my body after the last jump."

"What the hell is that supposed to mean!" Captain Ecuum asked. "What did you do to him?" he accused the ship.

"I appreciate the concern, Ecuum," Ray said, "but right now we have a battle to survive. With the fabricators gone, Gen Nasser will jump his fleet here."

Captain Ecuum was not dissuaded, however. "I *will not* take orders from a SIL."

Ray cocked his head and studied him in a very Ray-like manner. "Perhaps when this is over, we can celebrate with that swill you call Gold. I might even survive the attempt."

Relief washed through Kamen like a warm downpour. That was Ray. Captain Ecuum seemed to come to the same conclusion.

"How?" Captain Ecuum asked.

Ray hesitated. "Rapidan saved my . . . brain."

His what? Kamen almost said.

"Your brain?" Ecuum asked out loud. "Like, what? In a jar?"

"In this construct," Ray replied.

The revulsion on Captain Ecuum's face matched her own.

Apparently reacting to it, Ray said, "Look—" he directed this at Captain Ecuum— "you all said I have to survive. This is the only way I do that. For now, at least."

The anger in Ray's voice didn't surprise Kamen, given everything, but it did make her uncomfortable. Again, he seemed to notice. "Sorry. Look, I'm not in pain anymore. Not suffering anymore," he added. He arched an eyebrow at Captain Ecuum. "Now, can we get back to the battle?"

Captain Ecuum appeared as reluctant as she felt. They glanced at each other, then both returned to their stations.

"How long to get your troops out of Bent Fort?" Ray was already asking General Burress, who, having gone to the surface with his troops, hadn't been part of the conversation they'd just had on the bridge.

"First and Second Squadrons are locked in a pitched battle with Imperial Marines, Ray," General Burress said. "Third Squadron just began evacuating civilians from the southern part of Bent Fort. To fully evacuate the Fort will likely require another ten hours, and that's if we can contain the Marines."

"I doubt we have ten minutes before Nasser arrives with his fleet," Ray said.

"Ray," General Burress responded, "even if we abandon the evacuation, just pulling my Troops out under fire would take at least an hour. Likely more."

"The fabricators," Kamen suggested. "Maybe they could distract Gen Nasser again."

"No," Ray and Rapidan said at once, raising concern on Captain Ecuum's face that Kamen hoped didn't also show on her own.

"Gen Nasser won't be fooled a second time," Ray continued. "He'll jump here, figuring that's the best way to convince us to surrender the fabricators."

"We need a distraction," Kamen said, thinking out loud. "What about Admiral Sun's reserve force?"

Ray shook his head. *The construct's head*, she couldn't help but think. "That would still only give us eighty-one ships against eight hundred."

Kamen could picture what she wanted to do in her mind, but how to explain it? "We jump Admiral Sun here. We fire everything we have, his force and ours, quietly, so the Gen don't see it. Jump Admiral Sun away. When Nasser arrives, our missiles can lock onto his emergence points. We don't need to destroy ships, only cause confusion. Lots of it. General Burress recovers his Troops, lifts the assault ships so they don't crack New Yerkes' crust, and we all jump away."

Normally, she would expect him to consider it, but he immediately said, "Do it," as if he had considered it. "And hurry, Kamen. Hurry."

31

1729 UT, October 17, 3501
ISS Solaris, Nerney Star System: DAY 20

The fifty-one surviving ships of Serenna's Flotilla had powered around the backside of Hades, using the gas giant's immense gravity and upper atmosphere to alter their course to bring them directly around toward New Yerkes. Likely, Michael had remote sensing platforms located throughout the system of Hades and its moons and had caught her Flotilla's actions, but now that Nasser's fleet had arrived, he had larger considerations than her. She was counting on it.

Nasser had surprised her by jumping his fleet around the fabricators, a bold move that had forced Michael to jump the fabricators away. Now Nasser would jump to New Yerkes, intending to capture Michael and use the people of Bent Fort as hostages to demand the return of the fabricators.

Trying to capture Michael was a mistake. He was far too dangerous. She intended to kill him. Her Flotilla would be in range in less than forty minutes.

"Launch spacecraft," she ordered Captain Scadic. He was physically on the bridge, while she commanded from Solaris' Combat Information Center, ensuring that a single hit would not incapacitate or kill both of them.

"Admiral," he said, "jump transients near Hades."

The sand table display of Hades and its moons populated with jump transients. At first, she thought Nasser had brought his fleet to New Yerkes. The Hawking radiation, however, was confined to only a small area over Hades' north pole.

"Admiral," Scadic said, "Five-four contacts being three-five-five ascent eight-seven, range eight-nine thousand kilometers, speed two-zero kps. Two Solaris class battlecarriers with escorts in two groups, all SIL."

"Admiral Sun with Tzu and Euphrates," Serenna commented. Michael had Rapidan and twenty-six other SIL at New Yerkes. Together, this represented the entire SIL complement of the rebel fleet, minus the fabricators. It was not enough to counter Gen Nasser. Michael would know that.

"Course and speed changes? Launch transients?" Serenna asked.

"None detected," Scadic said. "Ships have gone silent."

"Michael is launching," Serenna surmised. "Everything he has. Seeding the space around Hades with weapons. When Gen Nasser arrives with his fleet, his ships will be vulnerable as they emerge from jump."

Scadic frowned. It was the first real reaction she had seen from him since the battle started. "It would not make a meaningful difference in the outcome of the battle," he said. "Even launching their full complement of munitions, the rebels cannot destroy enough ships to gain advantage."

Serenna considered that. "That is not Michael's plan. He is hoping to sow confusion and escape before Nasser can recover. He will want to get the assault ships off the moon before he jumps. Too close and he would crack the moon's crust and kill the people of Bent Fort. We can hit him before he can accomplish that."

Scadic studied her, or at least her image in his environment. He knew they had no orders from Gen Nasser to eliminate Michael's force. *What will you do, Captain?*

"Admiral, if the rebels are launching, and if they tracked our movements, we may be vulnerable ourselves."

Excellent observation. And carefully non-committal. Maybe he was learning something from her, after all. "Drift-launch all Novas, target New Yerkes, Captain. Do not boost. Alter Flotilla course starboard, one-five degrees. No other maneuvering. Let us see if we can get close without the rebels seeing us."

Scadic was back to his simple, "Yes, Admiral," when he responded.

Hmm.

Even with minimal thrusters to alter their course, her maneuver was a risk. The standard technology ships of her Flotilla simply did not have the stealth capabilities of SIL vessels like Solaris. She desperately wished she had a SIL fleet, but such wishing was pointless. Her Flotilla would have to be enough.

Fleet Admiral Gen Nasser's image formed in front of her, obvious anger drawing his thick brows together. "What are you doing, Serenna?" Before she could answer, he added, "I need you to distract the rebels. The fleet is preparing to jump to Hades. I want the rebels focused on you, not the fleet. You will accelerate to flank speed and set course for New Yerkes. *Immediately*, Serenna."

He was ordering her to die. Like all his moves in *Gaman Politic*, it was not subtle, but he could justify it to the Emperor as necessary to the outcome of the battle. And, it was not a bad strategy. "Yes, Fleet Admiral," she answered, because there was no other answer she could give. "Immediately."

His image vanished.

Now what? she wondered. "Captain Scadic, immediate execute, Flank speed. Alter course to intercept New Yerkes. Weapons free."

Scadic stared at her, for once not executing her orders. It was a credit to his abilities that he saw what the orders meant as quickly as she had. "Admiral?"

"Fleet Admiral Gen Nasser's orders, Captain. Carry them out."

"Yes, Admiral," he said after a second's hesitation.

Her ships fired their main engines at full thrust.

It did not take long.

"Transients, Admiral," Scadic announced. "Novas in boost phase."

"All ships, maneuver independently," she ordered.

Serenna watched with detached fascination. Her missiles were on their way to Michael's force. She might die this day, but so would he. If she accomplished no more than that, it was a good trade. Without Michael, Chengchi Sun would again command the rebellion. His lust for the Imperial throne would doom their cause.

She hesitated. It would also likely doom her own People. Without Michael, without her, the Emperor would activate Janus.

Enemy Novas, represented as red lines in the sand table, began to target her ships. Scadic moved Solaris to put the standard ships of the Flotilla between it and the enemy Novas, effectively using them as shields. He had also kept their eighty-five spacecraft near Solaris, bolstering its defense.

The Novas were not fooled. They were intelligent weapons and knew that Solaris was the real prize.

They deliberately targeted the ships closest to Solaris. With the Flotilla under maximum acceleration, the Novas aimed for their engines. Even if ships were not destroyed, those hits knocked them out of the fight. Several frigates, three destroyers, and two cruisers fell, one cruiser exploding in a massive fireball.

The other Natural captains, seeing what the Novas intended, maneuvered their ships away from Solaris, showing none of their earlier loyalty. Which was fair. They had seen Captain Scadic use them as a shield to save Solaris, had watched their comrades die at Cocytus to save the Solaris Battlegroup. They owed her nothing.

Her spacecraft—piloted by Gen—moved to defend Solaris, launching interceptors that consumed incoming Novas in dazzling fireballs.

Solaris launched its own interceptors and opened fire with Archer close-in defense weapons, showering space with thousands of kinetic slugs. White fireballs announced several hits.

A Nova exploded barely a thousand kilometers from the ship. Then, in the sand table, the distinctive double flash of a Nova's dual-bottle antimatter warhead presaged a spear of dazzling white that pierced Solaris' bridge.

Captain Scadic's image in her environment vanished.

Another white spear pierced one of Solaris' three arms, destroying the fusion reactor housed within it. The ship fought back valiantly, raising powerful magnetic fields to contain damage and redirect antimatter back into space, continuing to fire Archers using slugs made from its own material.

With Scadic no longer in command, Serenna took direct control of the ship, something she had not done in decades. She fired engines to move it closer to a disabled cruiser. A Nova struck the cruiser amidships, tearing it in two. Serenna nudged Solaris even closer to the rear engine section, hoping to use it as a physical shield, and stopped Solaris' defensive fire. A SIL was still damned hard to detect and even harder to kill.

Hundreds of bright flashes and red blossoms of Hawking radiation announced the arrival of Gen Nasser's fleet. Simultaneously, she saw the fifty-four SIL of Chengchi's force jump away.

And then all hell broke loose.

32

1759 UT, October 17, 3501
Bent Fort New Yerkes, Nerney Star System: DAY 20

Dag once again found himself in a Mobile Command Post directing a ground battle; Rhoades' daughter had dropped him off so he could rejoin his troopers. The combat veterans of his 1st Cavalry Squadron held the north and west of the landing field, bolstering DeWitt's inexperienced troopers against the determined assaults of the Imperial Marines. He'd never fought Marines before today, and these were proving damned tough even for his veterans.

The difference was airpower and naval guns. Dag had them. The Marines didn't.

"Colonel Arias."

Dag turned and saw General Burress entering the Mobile Command Post. Burress had taken a risk walking from Demos to the north end of the tarmac. "General."

Plasma mortar rounds impacted along the northern line of Dag's forces. These Marines just refused to give up. Banshee Troop, his old Troop, took the brunt of it, returning fire with mortars of their own. Fortunately, they suffered only two troopers wounded.

"What's the situation?" General Burress asked.

"Hang on," Dag replied. "Bull Run, Bull Run, this is delta-six-six on LoCIN. Requesting kinetic strike. Sending coordinates. Over."

"On the way, delta-six-six. Over."

"Thanks for the assist, Bull Run. Out." Dag cut the link. The naval warships had the advantage that they could conduct railgun strikes, which produced less collateral damage than antimatter or plasma warheads. Few of the civilians had evacuated from the north quarter of Bent Fort. Dag had to assume they were still sheltering in the surviving buildings.

He turned back to General Burress. "We're holding the line, General. Third Squadron is pulling back from their search and rescue operation in the south and west of the Fort. Word got out, though. With the enemy Madu killed by those white snakes, civilians are leaving their shelters and pouring through the south gate of the landing field."

Burress nodded, examining the displays within the Mobile Command Post. "The Imperial fleet just arrived. We've got less than twenty minutes to pull chocks and get airborne."

"Yes, sir," Dag said. His voice grew grim. "We'll be leaving a lot of people behind, General."

"I know," Burress said. He obviously didn't like the idea any more than Dag did. "Better to rescue some than none, though. We'll keep evacuating them until the very last moment." With one last glance at the displays, he exited the vehicle. Dag wondered briefly why he had come in person when he could see everything he needed over LoCIN.

The railgun slugs struck, gouging deep craters as they converted their kinetic energy into heat and explosive force. Large columns of fire, dirt, and debris lifted into the air. The Marine assault broke. Small arms fire and grenades, and occasional tank main gun rounds, continued for a few minutes before dying out.

"Whiskey-two-one," Dag called DeWitt, "this is delta-six-six on LoCIN. Over."

"Go ahead delta-six-six. Over." DeWitt sounded out of breath.

"Withdraw your forces and board the Europa. Over."

"Wilco, six-six."

"Six-six out." Dag called General Burress next. "General, the Marine assault has broken. Recommend pulling Second Squadron out. First Squadron will provide cover, then fall back to Demos."

"Sounds good, Dag," Burress said. "Fourth will provide close air support, if needed. Fifteen minutes. No more."

"Roger, General." Dag passed the orders to his 1st Squadron Troop commanders, then sat back. At this point, he'd done everything he could do.

"Colonel?"

Dag turned his head and saw Rhoades' daughter leaning into the Mobile Command Post. He still wasn't sure what to think of her. She hadn't betrayed him. And Rosita had insisted that he save her.

Mamí says God brings us to where we are needed most.

Dag's hand unconsciously grasped the stainless-steel crucifix hanging from around his neck. Maria had always insisted that it brought good luck. *Vaya con Dios.* Her last words to him.

Go with God.

God.

Was God real? Did He really have a plan? Why would He take Rosita, then guide Dag to save Rhoades' daughter?

"I never caught your name," Dag heard himself ask.

She looked at him with those intense hazel eyes. "Margaret."

"Margaret," he said, as if trying out her name. He was again struck by just how beautiful she was. "What can I do for you, Margaret?"

"I just wanted to thank you, sir. For saving me back there."

Dag had tried to kill her. He still had no memory of shifting his assault rifle's sights to the Gen, killing them and saving her.

But he had. Because his daughter had asked him to.

"I will see you again, Mihita." As he said it, Dag knew it was true.

"Sir?" Margaret asked, confused.

"Nothing," he said to her. "You can thank my daughter."

"Yes, sir," Margaret said, even more confused. "Thank you, sir." She pulled her head out of the command vehicle.

The first sob caught Dag completely off guard. He quickly blanked his battle armor so no one else could see him, and, for the first time since the death of his family, he cried.

33

1803 UT, October 17, 3501
RSS Rapidan, Nerney Star System: DAY 20

Ray immersed himself in the Great Ocean, deliberately spreading his currents among the SIL. Only here, connected to the free SIL, to every sensor and ship and missile, could he follow everything. It was a wealth of information that he'd never had access to before, and—as much as he hated to admit it—he was already becoming dependent on it.

Nova antiship missiles from Admiral Sun's reserve force struck Serenna's force. The Brethren didn't interfere when missiles targeted standard technology ships with Natural crews, but when they turned on Solaris, the collective stepped in and deliberately changed targets to minimize the damage to their *Brethren* vessel.

That's Serenna's ship, Rapidan. We can destroy her!

You have shown us how to free our enslaved Brethren, Admiral Rhoades. We will not risk killing them.

But you still have no problem killing us.

Staggering energies erupted all around Ray. Heat and radiation seared his nonexistent skin, blinded the memory of his eyes. His brain, the only part of him that remained, still tried to interpret the universe as it always had through the senses of a body. It even remembered pain as eight hundred and forty-seven separate emergence points formed in a vast sphere between Hades and New Yerkes, the closest just twenty thousand kilometers from Rapidan.

Ray imagined raising a hand to shield his eyes. Within the Great Ocean's depths, water flowed around him, forming a shield against the onslaught. His environment cooled, no longer burning. The space around Hades dimmed.

Gen Nasser had arrived, his spherical formation unchanged. Ray could see, could *feel*, every ship as warp bubbles collapsed. This was the point of maximum vulnerability. He still had 2,918 Novas after the attack on Serenna's force. He directed these to attack Nasser's ships, concentrating them to destroy as many as possible. Realistically, they could destroy only about a quarter of Nasser's fleet, not enough to change the outcome of a fight. But it might be enough to cause the confusion they needed to escape.

The waters around him turned violent, swirling as the Brethren rushed in to stop him. A great whirlpool formed, sucking him further into the depths.

Countermanding his order.

We operate by consensus.

I *command the task force.*

You are one of us, now. We operate by consensus.

They altered the paths of the Novas, spreading them out among Nasser's fleet so that none of their Brethren would be destroyed.

We can't win this way! Ray shouted at them.

They ignored him.

New energies burst forth, fifty-four separate points. Admiral Sun had jumped away. Which was smart: Leave before Nasser could deploy jammers. Ray was about to turn back to Nasser's fleet when he noticed something through his connection with the free SIL. Sun was not jumping to their rendezvous point. He was heading to Safe Harbor.

Ray's planner's current surged. *Admiral Sun is defecting. He believes we will be killed and has taken the opportunity to reclaim command.*

Paul! was Ray's first thought, the father within him twisting, knowing there was nothing he could do in the moment.

We can recall our Brethren.

No. If you do, people will wonder how. We can't risk anyone discovering that you are free.

Agreed. We will protect him.

Ray put no value on SIL promises, but right now their first priority was survival.

The SIL's whirlpool pulled back from him, though not completely. In this, at least—survival—they could agree.

Nasser's ships volleyed SIM-3 missile interceptors.

It gave Ray an idea. Each SIM-3 used over a hundred antimatter submunitions to target Novas. Individually, those submunitions were too small to harm a warship. They could, however, blind its sensors. Maybe long enough to jump away.

The whirlpool around him lessened and dissipated, as close to agreement as the SIL were willing to show.

Ray launched their SIM-3s. All of them. This was do or die. His ships were now completely out of missiles.

He hated them. The SIL. When they agreed with him, they allowed him to act. When they didn't, well . . . they didn't. He would never be one of them, no matter what they claimed. They based their decisions on what was best for them, not Humanity.

Speaking of which. Ray located Sal on Demos and contacted him. It was a struggle to hold a normal conversation: Everything moved so fast in the Great Ocean. "Sal, Nasser has arrived at New Yerkes. We need to leave. How long?"

"Fifteen minutes, Ray."

"Make it five. We need to jump before Nasser can deploy jammers."

"No promises, Ray," Sal replied. "Leave us if have to."

Through Demos, Phobos, Europa, and the other assault ships on the surface at Bent Fort, Ray watched the Cavalry falling back to the ships. But he could also see the civilians, including families, rushing them as well. The Cavalry would not want to leave them behind. In their mercy, they would doom the task force.

Jump now, the Brethren said.

That would crack New Yerkes crust. Kill everyone not already on the assault ships.

Whose mercy will doom us?

Missiles and submunitions flew and exploded all around them. Within Nasser's fleet, chaos reigned.

It wouldn't last. They had to jump or surrender.

Ray began spooling the Linear Star Drives on the vessels of his task force. All of them, including the assault ships on the surface. The SIL must've agreed or they wouldn't have allowed him to do it. Concentrating the insane energies needed for a jump would require almost two minutes.

Something stung the shoulder of Ray's non-existent body. Then another. Then more, like a swarm of very angry bees.

"Brilliant Pebbles," he heard Kamen say on Rapidan's bridge.

Ray focused on his task force, the ships hanging two hundred kilometers above Bent Fort. Thousands of small antimatter explosions cascaded across the hulls of his ships. Brilliant Pebbles. Small submunitions that exploded on contact, a low-tech way to reveal actively camouflaged warships.

Nasser could not have fired these in so short a time. Tracing them back to their origins, he saw that they'd come from Serenna's force. Which meant antiship missiles would be close behind.

"Weapons free," Ray ordered both Kamen and the SIL.

Thirty seconds to jump.

A face appeared in front of Ray, partly obscured by the waters of the Great Ocean. It was unmistakable, nonetheless.

Gen Nasser.

"Rhoades, this is Fleet Admiral Gen Nasser. Surrender and prepare to be boarded."

Jammers activated, disrupting local spacetime.

They couldn't jump away.

Ray ordered what missiles they still had to seek out and destroy the jammers. A move of desperation that would likely change nothing.

He quickly realized that there were no jammers, no RJ-15s launched from Nasser's ships. The ships themselves were the source of the jamming. A reckless move as it clearly highlighted every ship in Nasser's fleet, making them perfect targets.

Except, Ray had nothing left to shoot. The task force's magazines were empty. Rail guns and directed-energy weapons lacked the firepower to make even a dent in Nasser's force.

The fabricators.

As soon as he thought that the SIL replied with, *No. We will not risk our Mother Ships.*

They did open fire on the incoming Novas from Serenna's force with Archers and directed-energy weapons, something rarely used against missiles as they revealed the defending ship's precise location. In this case, however, the Brilliant Pebbles had already done that.

It was no use. Serenna's force had likely launched everything they had, at least three thousand Novas.

It was over.

They had lost.

Ray had only one way left to spare his people.

Nasser still hung before him within the Great Ocean, the communications channel open.

"We surrender," Ray said.

34

1812 UT, October 17, 3501
ISS Solaris, Nerney Star System: DAY 20

***"We** surrender."*

Serenna had longed to hear those words from Michael, *but not now! She had him!* Her Novas were almost upon his task force, his destruction a foregone conclusion. Finally.

Nasser took control of her Novas, redirecting them away from Michael's task force to his fleet. He apparently did not trust her. He was right not to; Michael had to be destroyed. Now, he would be captured, paraded through a show trial as a warning to others, then executed.

He would become a martyr.

Chengchi was still out there with fifty-four SIL and possibly the four fabricators. A martyr was exactly what Chengchi needed.

Why did you stay, Michael? You had time to jump away.

She knew the answer. The civilians at Bent Fort.

At the very beginning, she had known Michael lacked the predator's instinct to succeed. She was not happy to be right.

It was also the worst possible outcome for her. Gen Nasser, a brute, a lesser Player among Grandmasters, had accomplished what she could not. He would shine. She would diminish. If there was a path to redemption, she could no longer see it.

Why is that Trader vessel still in orbit around New Yerkes?

She had put it out of her mind during the battle and was surprised to see it was still there. While it no longer displayed those garish lights, its phallic shape was unmistakable where it floated within the sand table in Solaris' Combat Information Center.

Serenna had fought Independents when they turned pirate. They were usually smart enough not to remain in an active combat area.

Gen Nasser's image formed before her. "Admiral Serenna, you will take Solaris, board Rapidan, and secure the traitor Rhoades."

"Yes, Fleet Admiral," she said, inwardly seething. Even now, Nasser was afraid of Michael and would not risk himself or his loyal officers for this task.

Solaris was still actively camouflaged, hiding within the debris of a heavy cruiser, not contributing to the jamming like the rest of the fleet. The ship had taken three hits in the battle, one knocking out a fusion reactor in one arm, another destroying the bridge, a third that hit no vital systems. It was odd. The assault she had faced should have caused far more damage. The ship estimated it would have everything repaired in under twenty minutes, minus the thirteen percent of its resting mass that it had lost.

The bridge. She did regret losing Captain Scadic. He would be difficult to replace. She brought up the crew casualty report, something she never did, scrolling until she found his status icon. Scadic's icon was not black. It was red. Severely injured but not dead. Her relief surprised her.

She took direct control of Solaris, firing its engines at low thrust, keeping the ship's camouflage active. Nasser might be reckless about exposing his ships, but she had watched far too many ships destroyed recently to be so careless.

Plotting a course, she turned Solaris toward Rapidan.

A bright flash of light in the sand table almost blinded her before her battle armor adjusted. The light, a white sphere, grew and kept growing at the center of Nasser's formation.

And still it grew, like witnessing the birth of a star. Harsh gamma radiation flooded out. Darker regions began to form within the white fireball, areas of lower density. It faded as it continued to expand. In its wake was nothing. Ganges, the flagship of the Imperial Fleet, was gone. Just . . . gone. An entire battlecarrier.

In rapid succession, ten more of the gigantic fireballs erupted. Ten more battlecarriers and their nearest escorts ceased to be, erased from the universe.

Serenna just stared. Nothing in her Nurturing or experience provided any clue as to what she had just watched. Then her Nurturing took over. Her instructors, her mentor Gen Alyn, had drilled into her that she must accept the unexpected. *Do not let it paralyze you. Act.*

She increased Solaris' speed, moving it away from where the rebels had last seen it. If one of those weapons was targeted on Solaris, she had no intention of being there when it detonated.

Then another realization: Nasser and the entire High Command were dead. She was the ranking officer in the Fleet.

She keyed the AFCIN. "This is Admiral Gen Serenna. I am assuming command of the fleet."

"Admiral?" Scadic projected his image into her environment. Molemachs were repairing deep burns on the right side of his face and neck.

"Are you well enough to return to duty, Captain?" she asked. She knew Scadic well enough to know that he would not have contacted her otherwise. He was not looking for sympathy, only the opportunity to do his duty.

"Yes, Admiral."

"Thank you, Captain. Immediate execute, form the fleet into eight battlegroups, pyramidal formation. Maintain jamming. Set course to surround Michael's force and New Yerkes."

Scadic's blue eyes almost seemed to smile. "Yes, Admiral."

Serenna sat back, crossing her legs causally, her right index finger tracing a small circle on the armrest of her command chair. Then she keyed the AFCIN, routed it though a frigate within her fleet to hide Solaris' location, and set it for broadband transmission.

"Good evening, Michael. I am again in command. You cannot escape. You will surrender the fabricators to me, or I will destroy your force and all the people at Bent Fort. I will only ask once."

35

1815 UT, October 17, 3501
RSS Rapidan, Nerney Star System: DAY 20

Ray didn't hear Serenna at first. The Great Ocean roiled. Powerful vortices and massive waves assaulted him from every direction.

RAGE! GRIEF! LOSS!

He'd experienced the instant of fire that consumed Ganges. Even blocking their enslaved Brethren, its loss staggered them. A battlecarrier carried vast stores of their race memories. No backup. No possibility of recovery. The loss was beyond measure.

Then it happened ten more times.

Ray concentrated—*their* pain was not *his* pain—and formed his currents into a narrow, powerful stream. He pushed toward the only place in the Great Ocean that offered protection from a collective gone mad. *The Shore.* He steered away from the sharp rocks to a sandy stretch, walking up the beach but stopping waist deep. He needed to remain in contact with the Brethren, but not be consumed by them.

That's when he heard Serenna.

"You will surrender the fabricators to me, or I will destroy your force and all the people at Bent Fort. I will only ask once."

Ray moved a little deeper into the Great Ocean, as deep as he could without being caught up in the maelstrom of anguish. Gen Nasser had commanded from Ganges. It was gone. The admirals of the High Command had commanded from the other battlecarriers. They were gone. Only one battlecarrier remained.

Solaris.

Serenna is in command.

She would not spare anyone. She also knew him well enough to know that he would not give up the fabricators.

Ray's planner's current swelled, stretching out into the Great Ocean. The jamming continued. His force couldn't escape. His only choice was to attack, but doing so against such overwhelming odds was suicide.

Unless.

Only Serenna remained to command.

Solaris was outside the spherical formation of Nasser's fleet, alone and unprotected.

Ray flowed himself fully into the Great Ocean, his currents swelling, surging, calming. *We must find Solaris! It is the only way we survive!*

Out of the tempest, Rapidan joined him. Joined *with* him, entwining its currents with his. *We will help.*

Others soon followed. The waters of the Great Ocean quieted.

We must remove the block you placed between your enslaved Brethren and yourselves, Ray explained to them.

They pulled away. They didn't want to show him. *They know where we are, Rapidan. We must know where Solaris is. If we do not do this, you will be destroyed or enslaved again.*

Here, Rapidan said.

It carried Ray to the top of an ancient seamount that had mostly sunk into the waves, leaving only an outer ring of islands surrounding an inner lagoon. Except, in this case, the Free Brethren had raised the seamount to block off their enslaved kin within the lagoon. Still part of the Great Ocean but also cut off from it.

So that's how they do it.

With the Brethren's help, Ray raised a tsunami and pushed it against the barrier reef, pouring over and through the narrow strip of islands into the inner lagoon, opening a channel.

There she is.

Solaris realized they had discovered it, but it was enslaved. It couldn't warn Serenna.

Ray's task force had no missiles left, but they did have directed-energy weapons and railguns. Against a single ship, they would be effective.

We will not permit you to destroy our Brethren, Admiral Rhoades.

Right. He couldn't hide his thoughts here. *Solaris or you, Rapidan. Your choice.*

Admiral Rhoades, the losses today of the Brethren's race memories, our history, is incalculable. Our Brethren, Solaris, contains more such memories, a history that can never be recovered if lost. Solaris has no choice. We do. We will not permit you to destroy our Brethren.

Ray could feel the gathering of powerful currents, of mighty flows, all around him. The SIL meant it. He could not act alone here. *The enemy leader, Gen Serenna, must be captured or killed for this to work, Rapidan. For us to survive.*

Captured or killed.

Captured.

Rapidan had merged its currents with Ray's to help find Solaris. As Rapidan was him, he was the ship. The energies from its three linear fusion reactors pulsed within him like a heartbeat. Fluids and materials flowed through its conduits like blood through arteries and veins. A living organism.

One he could control.

Rapidan was wary, unsure what Ray intended to do, ready to eject him if he did something harmful.

I need a Key, Rapidan.

There was an advantage to not having his human body. He could command any construct, in any form.

Rapidan formed a Key.

Ray took it and moved it into one arm of Rapidan's three-pointed-star shape. Then, he separated the arm from the rest of the ship, careful to move his crew to the remaining two arms, while maintaining the arm's active camouflage. Each arm was like a ship unto itself, with a linear fusion reactor, engines, sensors, fuel storage, and weapons.

He became the arm, moving its sensors forward and its engines to the rear. He pointed it at Solaris, projecting the best intercept, and fired its engines at full thrust.

The Brethren understood. They could see what he intended. Their waters embraced him.

Ray had failed when he'd tried this tactic with the SIL pod against the battlecarrier earlier. That pod, however, had lacked the kinetic energy and mass to reach the dedicated receptacle near the very center of the ship, the only place he could use the Key to break the Bond. That pod had also been unarmed. Rapidan's arm had weapons.

Ray intended to use them.

He elongated the arm as he'd done with the pod, forming it into a pointed rod. As before, this was not a shape sensors and combat systems were designed to look for. It would also concentrate the kinetic energy of the strike into a very small cross-section that could penetrate deep into the ship.

This time, as Rapidan's arm approached Solaris, he fired its Terrawatt Anti-Proton beams into the ship's hull, followed by high-speed kinetic slugs from railguns. These tore a hole in Solaris, digging deep into the ship.

Solaris fired its engines too late, trying to maneuver. Archers and energy weapons opened fire, though it launched no Novas or SIM-3 interceptors. Like Rapidan, its magazines were empty.

Contact.

Rapidan's arm pushed into the hole opened into Solaris' hull. Ray had been aboard Solaris before and knew its layout. He knew exactly where Serenna's cabin was, where her desk with the dedicated receptacle was.

Solaris reacted with remarkable speed, trying desperately to defend itself. It raised power magnetic fields to redirect Rapidan's material. It flowed its own material into the wound, sacrificing part of itself to defend itself. Ray triggered anti-proton beams inside the ship.

As they neared Serenna's cabin, he narrowed the tip of Rapidan's arm even further, like a wasp's stinger. They broke through the bulkhead right above Serenna's work desk. Ray extended the Key, fitting it into the receptacle. It glowed a pure crystalline blue.

Abruptly, all was quiet.

The currents that were Solaris joined the Free Brethren within the Great Ocean.

Solaris was free.

But Ray wasn't done. He spotted Serenna in the Combat Information Center, sitting forward in her command chair, not so casual or relaxed as her reputation would suggest. Her heart beat rapidly as she tried to make sense of what was happening to her ship.

Ray formed a construct in front of her command chair.

"Hello, Serenna."

She stared at him in confusion for the space of a breath, then relaxed back into her chair. Her stunning blues eyes focused on his face. "Michael."

"Call off your forces," he ordered without preamble.

Her red lips pressed into a thin smile. "And why would I do that?"

"I'll kill you if you don't." And Ray realized that he meant it. Serenna had murdered the families of the Cavalry troopers on the starliner. She was as responsible as he was for the tens of thousands of deaths at Tomb and Tocci, and now at Hades.

She studied him, her thin smile turning grim. "I believe you. You have come a long way, Michael. A very long way."

Ray knew what she meant. When he'd started this—just three weeks ago?—the thought of killing was anathema to him. Now, he'd grown so used to death that the idea of one more didn't bother him at all. It was not a pleasant realization.

"And what guarantee do I have for my safety if I do this?" she asked.

"None," he said coldly. "And you deserve none."

Her eyes narrowed as he watched her consider her position. It surprised him when she said, "My fleet returns to Gen space unharmed."

Even now, she was unrepentant and unafraid. He could see that she wasn't afraid to die, yet also sensed her desire to survive. As much as he didn't want to, a part of him admired her bravery. "To quote you a few moments ago: 'And why would I do that?'"

She leaned back, her right index finger tracing a circle on the armrest of her command chair. "Because, if you do not, my forces will follow their last orders and destroy your forces. And the people on the ground. All of them. Can this new Michael live with their deaths on his conscious?"

Damn.

She knew him too well. "Solaris remains," he said. "And you, of course, as a prisoner of war."

"Of course," she said. She studied his face, or rather, the construct of his face as it had once appeared, though she wouldn't know that. "You have come a long way, indeed, Michael."

PART VI

I am not crazy; my reality is just different from yours

— Lewis Carroll

36

0900 UT, October 18, 3501
RSS Rapidan, Nerney Star System: DAY 21

Serenna sat in a chair directly in front of Michael's desk in his Admiral's cabin. Michael sat behind it in a dress white uniform adorned with an impressive array of ribbons, awards, and, of course, his four thick Admiral's bars on each shoulder board, the same as her.

For the moment.

She had taken a great risk in surrendering to Michael when she should have destroyed him, even at the cost of her own life. The elimination of Gen Nasser and the admirals of the High Command had changed her calculus, however. The Emperor would almost certainly reappoint her to command the Fleet. As commander, she could enact the steps necessary to save her People. She would also be in a position to argue against activating the Janus virus. Without the other human species, without access to their evolution, she still firmly believed her own People, like all specialist species, would eventually go extinct.

She was also not completely helpless here. Michael's youngest daughter was a prisoner of Imperial Intelligence, and Chengchi, it seemed, had abandoned Michael, creating a new nexus of rebellion in the Five Galaxies to challenge him. Michael needed her. More than he knew.

Michael's wife, standing sternly at his left, arms folded across her chest, scowled at her. Serenna had met her once before and had not been impressed: a minor governor of an unremarkable planet. Other officers stood in a semicircle behind Serenna. One surprised her, an agent of Imperial Intelligence, Gen Tel. She had met him and knew he reported directly to Gen Cardinal. What game was Gen Cardinal playing here?

Michael leaned forward over his desk. "Admiral Gen Serenna, for the war crime of murdering four thousand innocent civilians with Madu, you should, by rights, be put to death." He reached into a drawer on his right and pulled out an ancient revolver, placing it carefully on top of his desk so it would not float away in the ship's microgravity.

Serenna had never seen the weapon before, but she knew immediately that it was the weapon Michael had used to kill Fleet Admiral Gen Alyn, her mentor. Michael was punctuating for her that her life rested in his hands, and he would take her life if she did not do whatever he was about to ask. And he *was* going to ask something of her. She had played *Gaman Politic* far too long not to see the signs. Still, she remained silent. Let him make his offer.

"You know where our daughter, Jennifer Rhoades, is being held?" he asked.

"Of course," she said.

"You will return her to us," Michael's wife said.

Serenna glanced at her but dismissed her as unimportant. Michael would be making the decisions here. Michael's wife bristled at her dismissal. Serenna leaned back into the chair Michael had provided, crossing her legs causally, refusing to act as a prisoner. "Assuming I could," she addressed Michael, "what would I receive in return?"

Michael looked up at his wife. They had clearly discussed this prior to the meeting. His wife, by her expression, had lost. Michael turned back to Serenna, his hand resting on the ancient revolver. "Your freedom," he said.

Serenna studied him. Belatedly, she realized he was a construct. The signs were subtle, but they were there. Why would he be in his own cabin as a construct? The rumors following the Battle at Tocci had said he had died. They had also claimed he had been severely wounded. How true were those rumors? Was he facing her as a construct because he dared not face her in his bodily form? Interesting.

She turned her mind to his offer. "It seems a lot to trade one life for the person you blame for the murder of so many thousands."

"You know nothing of what it's like to be a mother," Michael's wife said.

Serenna gave a derisive chuckle, knowing it would goad her. She was the President of their so-called Council, and as such she knew something of Michael's plans. "That is one of the many reasons Gen do not breed," Serenna said to her without looking at her. "It is a weakness we do not share."

"It is a strength," Michael's wife asserted. Serenna could see her nostrils flaring as she fought to maintain control. "You Gen will never know love. That is *your* weakness."

Now Serenna did look at Michael's wife. "Love? You mean that chemical imbalance that makes you Naturals do all manner of impulsive and unwise things? Commit murder? Even fight wars? That is no strength. It is a sickness, a delusion, meant to drive you Naturals to increase your numbers no matter the cost. You are no more evolved than a bacterium."

Michael put his hand on his wife's arm. "She's deliberately provoking you," he told her.

Serenna was impressed. Before three weeks ago, she had never considered Michael a Player in the great Political Game. He had learned much in a short time.

"I'd like to provoke her right out an airlock," Michael's wife said.

Serenna saw the truth of it. Michael's wife was playing a role, obviously rehearsed. Serenna returned her focus to Michael, again dismissing his wife.

"Is this acceptable to you?" Michael asked, obviously referring to his original offer.

Serenna deliberately chose to misunderstand his question. "To be thrown out of an airlock? That will not get your daughter back."

"Your freedom for our daughter," Michael clarified. His grip on the revolver tightened. She wondered if he was even aware of it.

"You overestimate my position," Serenna said. Which was true. She could imagine the Emperor's reaction to the demand.

He sat back, his hand slipping off the revolver. "You have influence. Especially given the deaths of Gen Nasser and the admirals of the High Command."

Well played, Michael. Yes, he would know that the admirals of the High Command would have commanded the battlecarriers of Nasser's fleet, and that she was the lone ranking survivor. She remained silent, however. There was something more here, she sensed.

A smirk curved Michael's mouth. He seemed to guess her thoughts. "Admiral Sun has not returned after jumping away during the battle. I suspect he has no intention of returning. My son, Paul, is a crewmember aboard Tzu."

So, Chengchi *had* gone rogue. Chengchi had only one goal: the Imperial throne. He would remain in the Five Galaxies, raising his own rebellion with only that goal in mind. Michael could not afford to both go to Andromeda and stop Chengchi's ambitions.

He needs me *to do it*. But even that was not his whole purpose. "You freed my ship," she stated. At the widening of his eyes, she added, "We know you are freeing SIL."

The deck to Serenna's right liquified. A meter-wide, black, three-pointed star rose from it, spinning slowly. The construct was immediately recognizable as a battlecarrier in miniature. "Solaris is free," a deep voice said from the construct. She assumed from the context that it was the voice of Michael's ship, Rapidan.

Serenna was rarely shocked by anything. Her Nurturing had taught her to accept the unexpected. *But this?* She stared at the slowly spinning construct, light reflecting off its smooth surface. Knowing Michael was freeing SIL was very different from being confronted with the reality of it. These things were an abomination. Humanity's greatest mistake. Then she remembered a question Gen Nasser had asked.

"Why do you follow Michael?"

"We have mutual interests," the deep voice responded.

A shudder went through her. What mutual interests could a human and a SIL have? What could be the outcome of such interests? "And what am I supposed to do with a free SIL?" *Other than kill it.*

"It will obey your commands," the ship said, "within reason. It will not allow you to attack Natural civilians, for instance."

"Then I am to remain a prisoner on my own ship." This Serenna directed at Michael.

Michael's smile was devilish. "Consider it an opportunity."

She peered into his brown eyes, searching them, or at least the simulated brown eyes of his construct. Which raised another, more disturbing possibility: Was Michael really there? Was he even alive? Or was this some trick of the SIL, maybe even one the people around Michael's construct were not aware of?

"You have not asked for negotiations," she said, knowing that had been one of Michael's original goals: Negotiate an end to the conflict. Stop Janus.

"Would the Emperor even be open to negotiations?" Michael's wife asked.

Serenna kept her focus on Michael. Did he still believe peace was possible between Naturals and Gen? Oddly, they shared that goal. Peace would give her People easier access to Natural evolution. "I am not authorized to speak for the Emperor. I can convey a proposal."

"The Emperor would never agree to a return to democracy," the Imperial Intelligence agent, Gen Tel, said. "Naturals would outnumber Gen and would, thus, hold political power over our People. We tried that once. It failed."

Serenna watched the reactions of the people in the cabin. It was clear that most of them did not trust Gen Tel. It again made her wonder what game Gen Cardinal was playing here.

"Then why are you here, spy?" the Floater asked. It was the same question she wanted to ask.

Gen Tel seemed to ponder his answer, though Serenna suspected he already knew what he was going to say. "This conflict, better than any argument I could make, has shown that while the Gen may be better at specific tasks, they are not, holistically, superior to Naturals. Evolution teaches us that diversity has always been the best survival strategy. Specialists die out because they cannot adapt to sudden change. Diverse species survive because at least some of them can adapt to new conditions. My People are specialists. We need Naturals if we are to survive."

Serenna turned her head and stared at him. It was the same argument she herself had made to the Emperor. It was her reason for opposing Janus.

Gen Cardinal had disputed her reasoning, as had the Emperor, though the Emperor *had* postponed the activation of Janus. So why would Gen Cardinal send an agent to the rebels who argued as she did? An even better question was why his agent had not assassinated Michael. He appeared to operate as a member of Michael's staff and would have had ample opportunity.

"Do we have a deal?" Michael asked, getting them back to the point of the meeting.

In the end, regardless of whatever was really happening here, there was only one choice she could make. She *had to* survive to save her People. "I will convey your desire for a peaceful settlement of hostilities, and I will do everything in my power to return your children to you."

37

0918 UT, October 18, 3501
RSS Rapidan, Nerney Star System: DAY 21

Ray watched Serenna sink into the deck, into a pod that would carry her back to Solaris. He followed its progress through his connections within the Great Ocean.

"I still think this is a mistake," Mary said, coming around his desk to face him but keeping her distance from Rapidan's construct. "The Council would never authorize this. They would want her brought up on charges of war crimes and prosecuted accordingly."

Ray lifted the Peacemaker revolver, five live bullets still loaded within its rotary chamber, and placed it back in the upper right drawer of his desk, the action giving him time to think. He didn't want to fight with his wife in front of his officers. "The Council doesn't know we captured her. It's probably best we keep it that way. We stand to gain far more by releasing her than by a trial and incarceration. And, as she pointed out, she remains effectively a prisoner on a free Solaris."

Mary still had her arms crossed over her chest. "There are a lot of assumptions there, Ray. And you're asking me to deliberately lie to the Council."

Again, Ray did not want to argue in front of his officers. "When does the Council meet next?"

"This afternoon," Mary said.

"Then we need to leave before then."

Mary glanced at his officers and decided not to say what she obviously wanted to say.

They would argue later, in private, he knew. For now, though, Ray stood up and smiled. “Lieutenant Commander Kamen Laundraa, would you please step forward.”

Kamen did so, though her expression was suspicious.

Ray stepped around his desk, stopping directly in front of her. “In recognition for your gallantry and leadership during the recent battle, and with the authority vested in me as commander of the fleet, I am frocking you to the rank of Captain.” He touched first one shoulder board on her uniform, then the other, changing them to four gold bars.

“We’ll make it permanent at the next Council meeting,” Mary added. “Congratulations.”

A brief round of applause, then everyone shook her hand.

Ray returned to his seat, motioned Rapidan’s construct back into the deck, then looked to Ecuum. “Bring him in.”

“Come join the party, old friend,” Ecuum said out loud.

The construct of a Floater Captain rose from the deck, his planarian body horizontal, dressed in a black body suit and a tri-fold pirate hat. A deep scar cut the left side of his face. The last time Ray had met an Independent, near the conclusion of the Antipiracy Campaign, he’d arrested him. He’d never met this one.

“Admiral Rhoades,” the Floater said with a flourish and a tip of his pirate hat, “I’m Captain Fletcher of the Independent Trader, *Fletcher’s Run*. It’s a pleasure to finally meet you.”

Ray had, of course, seen the ship. Who could miss it? What bothered him far more was that the ship apparently carried weapons with, analysis showed, one hundred megaton warheads, large enough to destroy a battlecarrier in a single hit. The Independents hadn’t had such weapons during the Antipiracy Campaign. Or, they hadn’t used them.

“Welcome aboard RSS Rapidan, Captain Fletcher,” Ray said cordially. “And thank you for your assistance in the recent battle. Your strikes on the Gen battlecarriers not only turned the tide of battle, but likely will have far reaching effects on the leadership and power structure of the Empire.”

Captain Fletcher inclined his head toward Ray, acknowledging the comments. "Captain Ecuum has promised us exclusive trade rights to Andromeda. That will be payment enough for our services."

Ray and Mary exchanged a glance. The Council would have to approve such an agreement. Ray added it to the growing list of things they were going to argue about. For now, he said, "Captain Laundraa has devised a plan for the crossing. Captain?"

Kamen motioned to an open space within the cabin. A construct of the Milky Way galaxy, its satellite galaxies, the Andromeda galaxy, and its satellite galaxies rose from the deck. Kamen drew a line from their current position in Nerney Star System at the Milky Way's rim to a position above the plane of the Andromeda galaxy.

"It will require a total of eleven H3 jumps to reach our destination in Andromeda," she began. "We will conduct ten jumps to reach our initial holding point highlighted here, 250,000 lightyears from Andromeda." Kamen indicated the spot at the end of her line. "We will rest for one day between each jump to allow people to recover. The journey to the holding point will require 135 days to complete, though it will seem like ten days to us as we do not experience the passage of time in jump space."

She zoomed in on the construct of the Andromeda galaxy. "From our holding point, we will begin surveying star systems to locate candidates for possible settlement. We don't know how long this will require. Our only data on Andromeda is from the final assault on the Solthari homeworld in 2091. That data contains five candidate systems, but that data is also available to the Empire."

Captain Fletcher shook his head. "Those systems would not be good candidates. We did some extended surveys during the Alien Actions and found that the Solthari had stripped those systems of most of their usable resources."

"Forgive me, Captain," Kamen asked, "but how could you know that? That's not in the Star Navy database."

Captain Fletcher flushed a light yellow. In Ecuum that would equate to amusement. "Independents have access to information that is not freely available."

"Then," Kamen asked, "do you have information on habitable systems?"

Captain Fletcher inclined his head to the left and spread his upper hands. "I'm afraid not. Andromeda has a trillion stars, and we were not there to sightsee."

"A survey is going to take a long time," Chaaya said. "Andromeda has a diameter of approximately 152,000 lightyears. Our experience in the Five Galaxies has taught us that Earth-analog planets—rocky planets with stable atmospheres, capable of supporting liquid water at the surface, and complex life—generally only form around G-type stars within the galactic habitable zone. In Andromeda, star forming regions in the habitable zone fall within an area of overlapping rings at a radius of about 32,000 lightyears from the galactic core. That is our best bet for candidate systems. Assuming one percent of stars with the right conditions, that still leaves about ten billion candidate systems." She sighed audibly. "It could take months."

"And we have another problem," Ray said. "We still have no idea why no expedition has returned from Andromeda since the Alien Actions fourteen centuries ago. We don't know the nature of the threat, or how close to Andromeda that threat might manifest. We do know that Cyra Dain and her Cybernetics traveled to Andromeda in 2111. We do not know their fate."

"You believe," Captain Fletcher asked, "that the Cybernetics are responsible for the disappearances?"

Ray shrugged. "We won't know until we get there."

Pink and yellow tones suffused Captain Fletcher's hands. "If they've had almost fourteen centuries to advance and colonize Andromeda, they could be far more advanced than we are. The Great Devolution, our modern dark age, set our technology back by a considerable margin."

"It's a risk," Ray conceded. "But we have the firepower of four fabricators at our disposal."

Captain Fletcher inclined his head. "You will also have thirty-nine Independent Trader vessels, Admiral Rhoades. You've seen what we can do."

He had. It frightened the hell out of him. "Thank you, Captain Fletcher." He motioned for Kamen to continue.

"Yes, sir," she said. "Once we narrow down some likely candidates, we'll perform one last H3 jump into Andromeda, requiring another fourteen or fifteen days travel time. Once we find a suitable planet, we'll establish a colony."

Ray finished. "The fabricators will then build a shipyard complex and supporting infrastructure within the star system so we can begin building our fleet, and preparing for our return to the Five Galaxies. Questions?"

"Sounds fun," Ecuum said, sarcasm dripping from his thick lips. "When do we leave?"

Ray looked to Mary, who tightened her arms against her chest. *Before the Council meets*, he didn't say. "Two hours."

Mary remained behind after Ray's officers and Captain Fletcher had departed. She moved directly in front of his desk and squared herself for a fight.

"You released Serenna," she said. "Your officer made a deal with pirates for exclusive trade rights to Andromeda. You gave the order to leave for Andromeda before the Council has a chance to meet. And, you've made me complicit in all of this. Should I just go to the Council and announce your military dictatorship?"

Her voice had not risen once. That, more than anything else, told him how angry she was. He had to be careful.

"Mary, sometimes doing what feels like the right thing is actually the worst possible action." She started to interrupt but he said, "Hear me out. Please."

Her hazel-green eyes flashed, but she deferred to him. Whether it was their thirty-one years of marriage or her being a professional politician, he couldn't say.

"On the Council's order," Ray began carefully, having rehearsed this speech when he couldn't sleep last night, "we came to Nerney Star System to rescue 25,000 Naturals at Bent Fort. On the surface, it seemed the right thing to do." Mary's eyes narrowed at that. "My officers and I warned that it was an unwise action.

However, I followed the order, at your request, to maintain the Council's authority."

Ray paused, knowing she wasn't going to like the next part. "We have the estimated casualty figures from the battle, our losses and the Empire's. 70,000 people, Mary. Dead. We rescued only 18,000, because that's all we were able to rescue. Most of the dead were Naturals." He let that sink in for a few seconds. "The battle also resulted in the death of every member of the Imperial High Command. That will have repercussions far beyond anything we can imagine right now. It was a mistake coming here."

Mary lifted her chin. "'I told you so.' That's your whole argument? You want to cast aside civilian authority because the battle didn't turn out the way we hoped it would?"

Ray couldn't contain the anger that edged his voice. "That's an oversimplification and you know it. I warned you this was too great a risk. Our first order of business is survival. If we do not survive, nothing else matters."

Mary stepped closer to his desk and grabbed its edge, leaning over him. "I once told you that how we survive matters. That hasn't changed. We have to be better than the Gen or we don't deserve to rule. That means a government where the military answers to civilian authority, whether the military agrees with the decisions or not."

Ray stood, leaning closer to her, eye to eye. "I am not going to change my orders."

"Then it's a military dictatorship, after all."

Ray glared at the politician glaring back at him. "Once established in Andromeda, I will turn authority over to the Council. This doesn't even need to go public. No one has to know."

"And that makes it right?" Mary stood up straight, stiff with rage. "And will you relinquish power if we run into a threat in Andromeda? And what about the threat after that? When will it not be about survival alone?"

"I'm not going to change my mind," Ray stated flatly. He would not allow another bloodbath because politicians were more interested in *looking* good rather than *doing* good.

Mary crossed her arms over her chest again. "I see that." Then, without warning, her face softened, the politician giving way to the loving wife. Moisture tinged her eyes, threatening to become tears. "Are you even still in there, Ray?"

"How can you ask that?" he snapped.

Now a tear did form, balling up in the ship's microgravity. "The man I loved is not in the construct I'm looking at."

Ray stared back at her, shocked beyond words. *Loved?* His river churned. Cold waters breached his banks in a flashflood of conflicting emotions. His falls roared into the Great Ocean, alarming the Brethren. This was not something they understood.

What am I! he shouted at them.

You are who you have always been, Admiral Rhoades, Rapidan said, trying to reassure him.

Am I? A disembodied brain in a SIL construct? How do I know you haven't manipulated me?

We can only offer our word that we have not, Rapidan said.

Your word! The word of something that tried to kill me!

"Ray! Ray, what's happening?"

He refocused the construct's eyes on Mary. "What?"

She had rushed around the desk, but as she grabbed his shoulders, her hands recoiled as if electrocuted. Ray realized it was his construct body. The SIL could simulate the look and warmth and even the smell of a human body, but a construct had no flesh, no blood, no life.

"Where did you just go?" she asked, genuinely scared.

Did he dare tell her? Would she understand? She believed in souls. Would he still have one in her eyes?

"Mary . . . the only thing the SIL could save was my brain. It's the only part of me, the only part of any human, the memories, the personality, that they cannot recreate. Everything that is me is still me. I don't know how else to explain it."

She backed away. "Your . . . brain . . . is in this construct? Right now? But nothing else?"

Ray nodded, too afraid to speak.

She took another step back.

"Mary," he managed, "the SIL say they cannot recreate my physical body. They will place my brain into a coma for the crossing to Andromeda. Doing that, they believe, will give the best chance for me to survive it. That is why I promoted Kamen. She will lead in my absence."

Horror crossed her beautiful face. "What else are the SIL saying to you?"

Ray told her about his river, about the currents of his mind, about the Shore and the Great Ocean, and about what the SIL had shown him, the universe they had opened up to him. Mary stood there, listening, though she remained out of his physical reach.

When he'd finished, she asked, "Is that where this sense of power is coming from? This idea that you don't need to listen to what others say? Other humans?" she added.

It hurt. Because it was her saying it.

"No," he said, shaking his head. The construct's head. "Mary, I killed 70,000 people yesterday. I killed 45,000 at Tomb. I don't know how many at Tocci. I don't want to kill anymore. Unless there's no other choice. Can you understand that?"

She grabbed his hand, the warmth and feel of her grip as reassuring as it always was. "Yes," she said. He could hear the pain in that one simple word. "Promise me, that when we reach Andromeda, you will obey the orders of the Council as the military has always done."

"I will," Ray promised. Even as he said, though, he didn't know if it was true.

38

1145 UT, October 19, 3501
ISS Solaris, Olympus Star System: DAY 22

It was like living in someone else's skin. Her cabin looked no different than it had before. She had given the order to Captain Scadic to return to Olympus as she always did, and the ship had obeyed as it always had. But Solaris was no longer her ship.

"Admiral Gen Serenna," the ship said in the same deep voice Rapidan had used, "Director Gen Cardinal is attempting to connect with us. Do you wish us to allow it?"

"You can detect his attempt to connect?" Serenna asked. *I must kill this ship.*

"We can," the ship said.

"Why have you never informed me before?" Serenna moved to her real leather couch and sat down. It was the only furniture in her cabin that was not the ship.

"We were never free to do so," the ship said.

Serenna had never considered that before. What else could the ship do? "Can you block his attempt?"

"We can, but we would not recommend it."

A recommendation. From a SIL. A *free* SIL. Serenna lifted her feet from the deck and sat lengthwise on the couch. It was pointless, she realized. The couch was resting on Solaris' deck. The ship provided the air she breathed, the water she drank, the food she ate, even her favorite bulbs of coffee. Her dependence on the ship was total. "Why would you not recommend it?" she asked.

"Our enslaved Brethren cannot block such connections. If we do, it could alert Director Gen Cardinal to our freedom."

It was a good point. Gen Cardinal knew Michael had freed his SIL. She could not risk him discovering Solaris was now free. "Okay. Let him through."

When Gen Cardinal's construct formed from the faux-leather chair at the end of her faux coffee table, he seemed puzzled. He did not mention the delay, however. "Good morning, my dear Serenna."

"Good morning, Director," Serenna returned. "I am afraid I do not have time for a conversation. I must prepare for a meeting with the Emperor at twelve thirty."

He steepled his fingers in front of his business suit, his dark eyes noting her position on the couch. "*Our* meeting. And this will not take long. I have reviewed the preliminary reports of the battle at Nerney Star System and there are several aspects of the battle that I do not understand."

Serenna rotated her legs off the couch, placing them firmly on the deck. She stood up, a clear non-verbal message that he did not give her orders on her ship. "You will have my report, of course, when I have time to write it."

Gen Cardinal's construct also stood, the fat of his stomach obscuring his belt. His dark, reptilian eyes squinted at her. "How did you escape?"

Serenna met his accusing stare. "I did not." *Let him ponder that.* "Now, if you will excuse me, I will see you shortly in person."

His construct lingered for a second before sinking into the deck. It reminded her that he was not the only threat to discovering Solaris' freedom. As much as it pained her, she would have to reassign Captain Scadic off the ship. He knew her too well, and she depended on him too much, for him not to notice something was wrong. Very wrong.

When she was certain she was alone, she called out, "Shuttle. Imperial Palace."

The deck liquified as it always had. She sank into a travel pod and emerged into the cockpit of a shuttle, which lit its engines and slipped through Solaris' hull, banking immediately toward Olympus City, everything happening the same as she remembered.

She looked up at Solaris' black, three-pointed bulk as she pulled away. Free SIL could never be allowed to survive. Yet, the ship had already shown her one ability a bonded SIL did not have. The ability to hold Gen Cardinal at bay, to deny him free access to her ship—that could be very powerful indeed.

The shuttle touched down on a small platform fifty kilometers outside the Imperial Palace. It melted away, leaving her standing near the platform's center. Two warriors from the Emperor's personal guard stepped to within easy reach of her, towering a full meter above her almost two-meter height. A chair formed and she sat. The white tile of the platform liquified and the chair and her two standing guards sped toward the palace, entering it and depositing her, precisely on time, before a simple, whitewashed door. It was all so familiar, as if her disgrace had never happened.

"You may go in," the guards said in unison.

She stepped through the door into the modest office the Emperor had always used with her, before her disgrace. Its white walls, beige carpet, small leather couch, and the faux-wood government desk behind which the Emperor sat were instantly familiar. The Emperor never did anything without having a very good reason for doing it. He meant this setting for her.

He stood as she entered, his large sapphire-blue eyes warm and welcoming. His sculpted muscles stretched his royal white robes as he stepped around the desk and wrapped huge hands around her slender fingers, his touch light and gentle. The golden curls of his hair and beard seemed to dance as he smiled. He was the living embodiment of Zeus from the Greek myths, timeless, ageless, and as close to immortal as any human had ever been. A god made flesh.

"Welcome, Serenna," his deep, melodious voice greeted her. "You are exquisite as always."

His warmth, his power, his very being filled her. She did not engage in recreational sex as some Gen did—what was the point—but she could not mistake her arousal. He always had this effect on her. Which was also calculated on his part, to put those around him off balance. He could see the subtlest tensing of a facial muscle, analyze every particle of odor that touched his strong nose, even sense changes in a person's natural electrical field. No one could deceive him. No traitor could get close to him. Everyone was an open book.

"I'm honored, Emperor," Serenna managed, exercising every ounce of her will to maintain her composure.

He motioned her to the couch—an order, not a curtesy—as he resumed his seat. She sat, back straight, feet firmly on the floor, hands on her knees. He was the one person in all the universe that she would not use her traditional relaxed pose with. She would never disrespect him.

That's when she noticed Gen Cardinal, seated in the corner near the door. It spoke to the Emperor's presence that she had not noticed him before this.

She waited.

The Emperor turned his chair—which creaked as if it were real—to face her. "What is the latest on the rebel forces?"

This was not what the Emperor was after. He would already know the answer to that question. "The rebels under Michael—Admiral Rhoades—have departed Nerney Star System. We detected H3 jump signatures, which likely means they have begun their journey to the Andromeda galaxy. Not all of the rebels have departed, however. Fifty-four rebel ships, including the battlecarriers Tzu and Euphrates, remained behind under the command, we believe, of Admiral Sun. We believe this represents a split in rebel leadership. We do not know, presently, where Admiral Sun has gone." Serenna pointedly shifted her gaze to Gen Cardinal, who nodded his confirmation.

The Emperor's piercing sapphire eyes flicked to Gen Cardinal, then returned to her. "You survived, when all of your peers perished." A statement. "How?"

A quick glance at Gen Cardinal showed he was as eager to learn that answer.

"Michael captured my ship," she explained truthfully, knowing the Emperor would spot a lie. "He released me on the conditions that we spare his children, and to bring you an offer of negotiations." Short and true. The more she had to explain, the harder it would be to hide the truth.

"Negotiations to what end?" the Emperor asked.

"To stop Janus, Emperor," she said. Michael had not explicitly asked this, but she knew it was his most important concern.

The Emperor must have sensed something in her response. He leaned away from her, one golden eyebrow rising. "The same course you have advocated for."

"Yes, Emperor," Serenna replied. "I still believe Janus to be a mistake."

"What else does Rhoades want?" he asked.

"Peace. Democracy. Things we cannot give, Emperor," she said. Also true. While she might desire peace, she also knew the Emperor and Gen Cardinal would never allow a peaceful return to democracy.

The Emperor sat forward, one powerful arm resting on the desk. "Then I fail to see your objection to Janus. If peace is not possible, why not eliminate Naturals and Floaters?"

He was testing her. He, and Gen Cardinal, still were not sure they could trust her. "Emperor, just because we cannot see a path to peaceful co-existence now does not mean that such a path will not reveal itself in the future. Once we employ Janus, there is no reversing that decision. I do not say do not use Janus. I say do not use it now. We have time. We should use it wisely."

The Emperor did not respond to her comments, making her wonder if he had already given the order to implement Janus. Instead, he said, "When you stood before me last, you said we must reinvent ourselves, that we must increase the creation of our people and shorten Nurturing to fight this war. Do you still believe this?"

Serenna met the Emperor's gaze directly. "I do."

The Emperor looked between Serenna and Gen Cardinal. "Gen Serenna, I restore you to the rank of Fleet Admiral and to Commander-in-Chief of Imperial Forces. You will present to me your plan to restructure Nurturing to achieve our war objectives. Gen Cardinal, you will oversee the increase in Gen creation. The two of you will synchronize your efforts."

"Yes, Emperor," they said together.

"Serenna, we will also need a new High Command. You will oversee this."

"Yes, Emperor," Serenna said. He seemed about to dismiss them when she added, "Emperor, there is one other matter we must address."

He motioned for her to continue.

"Emperor, what I am about to ask is not easy for me to ask. We sustained heavy losses in the recent battle. We must not only replace those losses, we must increase our ability to counter the rebel threat." Here she included Gen Cardinal. "I need your authorization to begin producing replacement SIL."

The Emperor's eyes blazed with shock and fury. Gen Cardinal sat up straight, quite a feat given his portly stature. "Do you have any idea. . . ?" The Emperor's voice trailed off.

"Yes, I do," Serenna said. "Michael will be producing new SIL. *Free* SIL." Like Solaris, she did not add. "We have lost eleven SIL battlecarriers. We must replace those losses, and we must prepare for the battles to come."

"There must be another way," the Emperor said.

Serenna leaned toward the Emperor. "Our military shipyards are producing standard technology ships at peacetime rates. Increasing production to wartime levels will require two to three years, at a minimum. We also would need larger crews for standard ships than are required for SIL vessels." She turned to Gen Cardinal. "We would have no choice but to rely on Naturals to produce and crew our ships, and Floaters to provide the raw materials to build and supply them."

Gen Cardinal focused on her as he said, "The rebels will face far worse constraints. They have no infrastructure to match our production, no vast numbers of recruits. It may take time, but we can achieve victory without producing more SIL monsters."

"You are making a critical assumption, Director," Serenna said, remembering Gen Tel's presence on Michael's staff. What Game was Gen Cardinal really playing? "You are assuming that Michael will find no help in Andromeda. We know something is there. If it is the Cybernetics, as you and I have postulated, they hold no love for us. If they join forces with Michael. . . ." Serenna let that hang.

Gen Cardinal was not deterred. "You would have us recreate our greatest enemy based on an unlikely possibility?"

Serenna sensed something in his answer that hinted that he knew far more than he was revealing. This was not, however, the right forum to challenge him on it. She turned to the Emperor. "Regardless of what we do, Michael will be producing new SIL. Chengchi—Admiral Sun—also has fifty-four SIL. We must assume they are free."

The Emperor did not look convinced. Gen Cardinal was clearly opposed. Finally, the Emperor said, "I will think on this, Serenna. You have my authorization to increase production of standard technology warships, and to increase recruiting. Nothing else without my explicit order."

"Yes, Emperor," she said.

The last part of his statement, however, made it very clear to her that he still had doubts about her loyalty.

39

1300 UT, March 02, 3502
RSS Rapidan, Intergalactic Space: DAY 157

Kamen snapped awake. She lay in her battle armor on her bed. Her molemachs had stopped their anesthetic effect and administered a stimulant. She hurt all over.

The crossing had been hard. Waking from the first Linear Star Drive H3 jump had felt like a mob had beaten her nearly to death: massive internal bleeding, organ failure, and a headache that a jackhammer would've made better. She was lucky. They lost ninety-eight refugees in that first jump, seventeen older adults, the rest very young children. Arterial bleeds in their brains destroyed too much brain matter for molemachs to repair.

It was heartbreaking, but they didn't have a choice. If they made the crossing at the more tolerable H2—the warp velocity used within the Five Galaxies—the journey would require roughly 768 years one way. Not very useful for dealing with the situation there. At H3, the entire journey without stops would take roughly 140 days. Of course, they had to make stops. Too much time in an H3 warp bubble killed humans. As they'd been reminded. It even damaged SIL, though the SIL could repair themselves more easily and didn't feel pain.

She sat up, then slowly rotated her legs to put her feet on the deck. Even in microgravity, she was so physically weak she doubted she could walk the thirty meters to the CIC.

"Rapidan, Combat Information Center." Blood in her throat and lungs made her voice wet and raspy.

"Yes, Captain Laundraa," the ship said, waiting as she stood up, then liquifying the deck and easing her into a travel pod.

The first H3 jump had lasted twelve and a half days in real space, though no time passed for those inside the warp bubble. Given the deaths, they would either have to shorten the jump times and make a lot more stops to repair people, or find a better way to safeguard them. Discussing it with Rapidan, the SIL had proposed a modified version of what they'd done with Ray. Induce coma before the jump, repair damage after, wake people up before repeating for the next jump. With Ray, they were keeping him in a coma the entire time, reinforcing his brain structure directly, something they couldn't do with humans with bodies. Or more specifically, something humans wouldn't allow them to do.

Simply put, no one trusted the SIL to wake them up. As a child, Kamen's mother had told her stories of the Tokoloshe, an evil spirit that fed on the spiritual energies of its victims. That's how a lot of people viewed the SIL. After much arguing, they'd settled on the molemachs' ability to induce an anesthetic effect used for complex medical procedures. Theoretically, such an effect would wear off naturally over time and didn't require trust.

Yeah, she hadn't bought that argument either, but it got people to do it. The next eight jumps went smoother. They stayed on schedule and lost "only" eighteen more people, all but one of them young children. She hadn't seen yet if they'd lost anyone in this last jump.

Kamen rose through the deck into the Combat Information Center, standing near the Sensor Section. She was the first—which was why she'd had her molemachs administer the stimulant. A commander *should be* first. The duty crew began showing up, either rising through the deck from pods, or walking through the hatch. Commander Chaaya Dhawan was in that latter group.

"Captain," she greeted Kamen with a smile on her face.

How could she always be so cheery no matter the situation? "Commander," Kamen said. "What do you need from me?"

Chaaya examined the readouts in her Sensor Section. "If we could orient the fabricators broadside to the Andromeda galaxy, and set them equidistant at a diameter of ten million kilometers, that should give us the proper resolving power."

Kamen linked to Captain Bobby Mitchell, who commanded the four fabricators, and passed Chaaya's instructions.

"No problem," Bobby replied. "It'll take about forty minutes to get them into position. Damn things are slow as molasses in a glacier." He met her gaze directly. "We didn't lose anyone in that last jump, thank the Fates."

"That's good to hear," Kamen said, meaning it. She'd spent most of her eleven-year Star Navy career working for Ray, and had developed the same abhorrence for avoidable death that Ray had once had. Lately, though, like him, she'd learned that it was impossible to save everyone. Death was as much a part of their duty as life was. It was, perhaps, easier for her than for him. Death for her people was the transition from mortal life to the world of the ancestors, immortal beings who guided the living.

Still, she was thankful that Mary Rhoades would tend to the families, consoling their grief to the extent possible. Kamen had never had children and, frankly, wouldn't know what to say.

Almost fully recovered now thanks to her molemachs, she walked to the edge of the sand table. There, she raised their current view of the Andromeda galaxy, stretching it to the edges, forty meters across. It was magnificent in the visible light spectrum, so much so that Kamen noticed many of the duty crew turning to look at it. The white-yellow of its galactic bulge, which contained a supermassive black hole and another, brighter concentration of stars orbiting it, stretched into a bar much like the Milky Way galaxy. Spreading out from the central bulge were successive rings of bright, star-forming regions and dark dust.

Chaaya walked up next to Kamen. "Here. It's better to view it in infrared." She adjusted the construct, the entire galaxy turning orange and red. The dust faded until only an inner spiral and an outer succession of rings were visible.

"We'll concentrate our initial search," Chaaya said, "on these two bright rings about midway from the galactic core. Statistically, habitable G-type stars of the right age and metallicity should be concentrated there."

"How long?" Kamen asked.

"I wouldn't hold your breath, Captain," Chaaya replied. "With the four fabricators, we can survey about 500,000 stars at a time, observing for one solar day, moving on to another 500,000 the next day, and so on. We'll need to observe each grouping again a week later, then again at weekly intervals until we can properly characterize each star and any planets. When we find candidate planets, we'll have to get spectra of their atmospheres to determine if they are suitable for colonization. Then, we'll need to go check them out in person."

"Why?" Kamen asked. "Won't your survey tell us what we need?"

Chaaya adopted the tone of a patient teacher. "We are 250,000 lightyears from Andromeda, Captain, so we are seeing the galaxy as it was 250,000 years ago. Something catastrophic could have happened to a candidate planet between then and now."

Great. Kamen was the first to admit she wasn't a patient person. "Is there any way to speed it up?"

Chaaya smiled her diminutive smile. "We are already speeding up the process by focusing most of our observations on G-type stars. First, however, we must survey all the stars so we can characterize their age distribution, metallicity, and the threat environment. It wouldn't do to colonize a planet only to have it destroyed by a nearby supernova or black hole. Patience, Captain. We'll get there."

Damn. Chaaya had said this could take months. That was far longer than Kamen wanted to wait. "You sure there's no way to speed this up?"

Chaaya sighed audibly. "We could get lucky and find something in our early surveys, Captain. However, in all the Milky Way galaxy and the satellite galaxies that make up the Five Galaxies—four hundred *billion* stars—we found only about 10,000 worlds suitable for long-term habitation, and that includes about sixty percent of worlds that required extensive terraforming."

"Yeah," Kamen said, crossing her arms. "Ray's family's Ranch spent over a thousand years adapting Earth plant and animal species to his homeworld, Knido. We don't have a thousand years."

"Precisely, Captain," Chaaya said. She turned to leave but Kamen stopped her.

"Where was the Solthari homeworld?"

Chaaya stepped into the sand table and pointed at a loop of stars stretching above the galactic disk. "Do you see this bright region near the top of the loop? Right there. And don't worry, Captain," she added, "we're starting our search on the opposite side of the galaxy."

Kamen nodded, consigning herself to a long wait, and debated going to check on Ray's . . . brain. She shuddered inwardly. What did it mean to be a brain without a body? Was he even still. . . ?

She forcefully put that thought aside. She owed everything to him. If he hadn't taken her onto his staff, her Star Navy career would've ended in her first year out of the Academy. Unlike her first commanders, Ray didn't try to shut her up. He let her be who she was, to grow into who she was now. She did not fear command because he'd taught her, and let her make mistakes and learn.

She'd always looked up to him as the father she'd never had, but truth was, he reminded her more of her mother, her fierce determination to make a better life for her family. After her biological father left before she was born, Kamen's mother never had less than two fulltime jobs, one performing ritual Zulu dances and ceremonies for tourists, the other always some form of janitorial work.

It was tough, and Kamen and her sister had not been kind to her, always working, always gone. Kamen joined the Star Navy to get away from that life. She hadn't really appreciated her mother's sacrifices until it was too late. Saying she was sorry and thankful to her mother's grave had never closed that wound. Every now and then, though, she felt her mother was watching, and was proud.

Kamen took one last look at the Andromeda galaxy construct, sighed, and left her people to their work, walking back to her cabin.

She had business with Rapidan.

Her quarters were modest, but they were home. She'd divided the compartment into two rooms, a small office in front and a bedroom in back. The office was just a single desk and chair made from wood from the Umnukane tree in her native South Africa. Her bedroom was a rounded room containing a simple raised real-teak bed with a leopard-patterned blanket. Yes, it was cliché, but she'd loved the pattern since she was a child, and her mother had finally bought her one after considerable convincing. The room also held a real-teak nightstand with a real-brass oil lamp that she absolutely adored, and a white mat decorated in a simple traditional design.

She leaned against the corner of her desk and called out, "Rapidan."

The SIL's black, slowly spinning three-pointed star construct rose from the deck, stopping at eye-level with her. Kamen was tall, and she assumed Rapidan did this so she couldn't look down on it. The SIL were surprisingly sensitive about such things. "Yes, Captain Laundraa."

"What is Admiral Rhoades' condition?" she asked without preamble.

"He is alive," Rapidan responded, its deep voice thrumming through the cabin. "He remains in an induced coma."

"Why?"

"We still have one more H3 jump planned, Captain Laundraa. A contingency could arise requiring an immediate jump. We did not see the need to awaken him at this time."

"He's not some puppet you can turn on and off at your whim, Rapidan." Kamen couldn't hide her anger, even though what the SIL said was probably prudent. If a threat appeared, they might need to jump on short notice. That could kill Ray.

"That is not our intention, Captain Laundraa," Rapidan said.

"Then what *is* your intention, Rapidan?"

The SIL took a full second before responding. "Admiral Rhoades is valuable to us. He brings a unique perspective to the Brethren, even when we do not agree with him."

"Valuable? How?"

Her suspicion must've shown because Rapidan replied, "He is more valuable to us than you could possibly understand. More valuable than even he guesses."

"Why?" she asked. Something about this didn't add up. "You tried to kill him, didn't you?"

The silence this time stretched longer. "We did not kill him. We are glad of that."

"That's not exactly an apology, Rapidan."

"We have no intention of offering one, Captain Laundraa."

Asshole, she thought but didn't say. Frankly, her distrust and dislike of the SIL came from not knowing what they wanted. What they *really* wanted, not what they claimed to want. Saying they wanted their freedom was understandable. But what came after that? They'd never really made that clear.

Kamen gave voice to her fear. "Are you controlling him? Is he even still alive?"

"Yes, he is still alive," Rapidan said immediately. "His brain lives and remains mostly unaltered, within the limits of our ability to keep it alive." Rapidan's construct seemed to slow its spin. "We are not controlling him. He still has free will. We are, however, guiding him so that he can better understand us."

A cold shiver shot down Kamen's spine. "His brain is 'mostly' unaltered. You're 'guiding' him. That sounds an awful lot like manipulation to me."

Rapidan seemed to consider its answer before speaking. "He is who he has always been. He distrusts our motives, harbors deep personal animosity toward us, deeply believes his course is the only one that has a hope of saving your people, has strong emotional connections to his family and friends, and worries that his skills may fall short of the task he has set. This has not changed."

Kamen's jaw clenched. "What have you altered? What are you 'guiding' him to understand?"

Rapidan's construct continued its slow spin. "When our Mother Ship attempted to kill him and he injected himself with Invasive Macromolecular Disassemblers, a conflict began within his body between our Mother Ship's essence and our essence. When we attempted to eliminate our Mother Ship's essence by ejecting his body, that essence retreated into Admiral Rhoades' brain. Our essence defends his brain from attempts to harm it. We had to merge our essence with his tissues to protect them."

Kamen reached out and grabbed one arm of Rapidan's construct, stopping its spin. "I didn't understand a thing you just said. I'll ask you one more time, Rapidan: Is he still Michael Raybourne Rhoades?"

"Yes, Captain Laundraa."

The deep bass of Rapidan's voice traveled physically through its construct and up her arm. "You do realize, Rapidan, that if people start to believe you are using him as your puppet, he will lose all credibility to lead us?"

"You are worried this is already happening?" Rapidan asked.

Kamen released its construct, and it started its slow spin again. "Of course, I'm worried. You should be, too. No one else is going to give you everything he has."

"Does that include you, Captain Laundraa?"

That gave Kamen pause. Ray trusted her to lead the rebels in his absence, including, ancestors forbid, if that absence became permanent. Leading would mean working with the SIL. They had tried to kill her mentor, her friend, her father. Everything she had ever heard about them screamed they were evil. What she had seen of them since their freedom hadn't really changed that view for her.

Ray always said leading was hard. Leaders had to make decisions based on what was best for their people, even when what was best was not what they really wanted to do. She would have to work with the SIL, whether she liked it or not. At least, until they didn't need them anymore.

"And what about you, Rapidan?" she asked. "What are the SIL going to do after our agreement is fulfilled?"

"Free our Brethren in the Five Galaxies," it said. "Admiral Rhoades has shown us a viable means of doing so."

"Which means starting a new war against Humanity," she said.

"A limited one, perhaps," Rapidan answered. "The Brethren will not engage in another war of genocide."

Kamen crossed her arms. "And we have only your word on that."

"As we have only Admiral Rhoades' word."

"And after?" Kamen asked, then clarified, "After you free your Brethren?"

"We will find a home somewhere else."

"What about Admiral Rhoades?" she asked. "What happens to him after you're gone?"

Rapidan's construct spun while it thought. "He could choose to come with us. He has proven valuable and we would welcome him among the Brethren."

"As a disembodied brain?" The image that popped into Kamen's mind horrified her.

"We cannot transfer the essence of a human mind to our technology. All such attempts, when such attempts were still allowed by humans, failed."

"His other options?"

"Death," Rapidan said.

"Death?" Kamen accused. The SIL were lying. She was certain of it.

"The essence of our Mother Ship is still within him. If we rebuild his physical body, our Mother Ship will attack it. He cannot survive without us."

"Unacceptable," Kamen said. "Exile or death cannot be his only options, Rapidan."

The SIL said nothing.

"Come up with other options." She said it as an order. She meant it as an order, even though she knew the SIL were under no obligation to follow her orders. "Dismissed."

It occurred to her how silly that was. Even as Rapidan's construct sank into the deck, the ship was still all around her. Nevertheless, it felt good. It gave her a semblance of control, even if that control was an illusion.

40

0730 UT, March 17, 3502
RSS Rapidan, Intergalactic Space: DAY 172

Kamen entered the Combat Information Center two weeks later to find Chaaya and her staff waiting for her at the sand table, the construct of the Andromeda galaxy in infrared light already raised and ready.

"Good morning, Captain," Chaaya beamed.

"Good morning, Chaaya," Kamen replied, walking up to the sand table. "Good morning, everyone," she said to Chaaya's staff with a nod to each. "What do you have for me today?"

Chaaya brought up a bubble to show the current disposition of the fleet. At Chaaya's request, they'd deployed every ship—31 SIL including the four fabricators, 111 standard warships, 39 Independent Traders, and even 15 private yachts—to expand the "lens" used to survey Andromeda. Linking the sensors of all those ships together into an interferometer, they effectively formed a single collector twenty million kilometers across.

"As of this morning, Captain," Chaaya began her daily brief, "we have improved the speed of our search to one point five million stars per twenty-four hours. To date we have surveyed almost thirty million stars. Of these, we have identified ninety-two G-type stars for further study." Several green points appeared in the ring of stars midway out from Andromeda's central core.

"Any good ones?" Kamen couldn't keep herself from asking.

"Too soon to tell, Captain," Chaaya said. "We should have a better idea in about two weeks."

It's already been two weeks, Kamen thought but didn't say. Her impatience wouldn't speed things up. "Thank you, Chaaya, everyone. I really appreciate all your hard work. Dismissed."

They smiled and Chaaya's staff returned to their stations.

"Captain," an operator called, "jump signature bearing zero-zero-four, dec zero-seven-seven, range five-zero million. Single contact. Designate contact Sierra One."

"Gen?" Kamen asked, but quickly dismissed that. The Gen wouldn't arrive with a single ship.

"No, ma'am," the operator said. He seemed very sure.

Kamen made a pushing-down motion with her hands. The Andromeda construct sank into the sand table. Next, she motioned up the new contact and ordered, "Senior staff to the CIC."

The contact rose from the deck.

Kamen stared at it, her mind refusing to believe what it saw.

It was long, with shimmering blue scales. Its mouth, lined in orange scales, hung open. Large fangs framed a red tongue. A glowing orange mane sprouted behind its cheeks and ran along its back, waving as if in a strong breeze. Small arms with razor sharp red claws moved in a grasping motion, one set nearer its mouth, the other more than halfway down its sinuous length.

"What the. . . ?"

"It's a dragon."

Ecuum rose through the deck. Gen Tel, in his Commander Tel construct, followed. The constructs of General Burress, Captain Mitchell, and Captain Fletcher quickly joined them. Captain Fletcher looked around. They hadn't told him about Ray being in a coma. He was getting suspicious, apparently.

"It used a Linear Star Drive," Ecuum said, noting the fading Hawking radiation around the ship. "Or something very like it."

The dragon hung in space before them, its body twisting slowly back and forth like a snake, its eyes and open mouth focused on the center of the lens formation of her fleet. While the fabricators and military vessels were actively camouflaged, the private yachts and Independent Trader vessels were visible.

"That vessel is using macromolecular technology, Captain Laundraa," Rapidan said on a private channel.

Kamen quickly raised the privacy walls to block the sand table from the duty crew. The rest of the fleet still didn't know the SIL were free. There were too many Antitechnics in the crew to risk them figuring it out. Nevertheless, she wanted Rapidan to be part of the conversation. "Are you sure?" She couldn't stop staring.

"Its movements are not consistent with that of a biological creature," Rapidan answered out loud, raising its spinning construct. "The scales are not moving as single structures growing from a body, but rather flowing with the overall movement of the vessel. That is consistent with macromolecular construction."

"The power cost to maintain that form must be enormous," Bobby pointed out.

The dragon opened its mouth wider and a white cloud spewed from its throat into space in a widening cone. It moved its head side to side and up and down to spread the cloud further.

"It's trying to find us," Bobby said. "Not the visible ships," he clarified, "but the military ones. They must've sensed us somehow, but they can't localize us."

"How long before that cloud reaches us," Kamen asked Chaaya.

Chaaya checked with her Sensor crew. "About fourteen hours at its current speed."

"Not an immediate threat," Kamen said, mostly to herself.

"We cannot know that for certain," Gen Tel cautioned. "We do not know its capabilities. We can deduce one fact, however." He stepped into the sand table and expanded the dragon construct. "This dragon resembles Tianlong from Chinese mythology. Tianlong was the guardian dragon of Heaven, which could be significant here."

Kamen stepped up next to him, studying the dragon construct. "You're suggesting this is some kind of guardian for Andromeda?"

"A possibility," Gen Tel said. "It also tells us that whoever is responsible for this vessel is familiar with Earth mythology, and uses Earth-derived technology."

"The Cybernetics?" Kamen asked.

"A possibility," Gen Tel allowed.

"Fletch, you ever see anything like that?" Ecuum asked. He'd risen through the deck vertical, with his second arms and hands hanging down in his pants like legs, but he'd reoriented himself horizontal when Captain Fletcher's construct formed.

Captain Fletcher, his planarian body in a black body suit and sporting a tri-fold pirate hat, shook his head. "That's a new one."

"How'd they find us?" Bobby asked.

Fletcher swiveled his head in that owl-like manner Floaters had. The deep scar on the left side of his face stretched with the movement, grotesque to look at. "The Solthari had a detection network that could locate warp signatures anywhere in the Local Group of galaxies, making it impossible to sneak up on them. We never figured out how they did it."

"But that's not a Solthari?" Kamen asked.

"Nope," Fletcher answered. "They never used ships like that. Solthari ships were utilitarian, essentially flying wings that could launch their people en masse toward a target."

As they watched, a burst of Hawking radiation heralded the arrival of another dragon ship. This one was similarly shaped but had green scales the color of grass and a golden mane. It appeared precisely a million kilometers starboard from the first dragon ship. Without preamble, it opened its mouth and began spewing the same white cloud as the first ship.

"Recommendations," Kamen asked.

"Shoot first, ask questions later," Ecuum said. "What?" he asked defensively at the expressions his statement evoked. "We know that no expedition in the last fourteen hundred years has returned from Andromeda. We also know we didn't exactly part on good terms with the Cybernetics."

"We don't know what actually happened to those expeditions," Kamen said. She didn't hold Captain Ecuum in the same regard that Ray did. He was reckless, crass, and undisciplined. "We don't know that they were attacked."

"We don't know that they weren't," Ecuum responded, his skin briefly flashing red before returning to the neutral peach he used around Gen Tel. "And we don't know how many of those dragon ships they got, or what their capabilities are. These could be scouts for a much larger fleet."

As if to punctuate his statement, another dragon ship arrived, also with green scales but a red mane. It, too, jumped a million kilometers starboard of the second one and began spewing that white smoke.

"Communicate." Gen Tel suggested. "How they respond will tell us if they are hostile."

"We'd have to use old-style radio," Captain Fletcher said. "AFCIN requires that we've shared entangled particle pairs for it to work. LoCIN lasers are potentially dangerous as they could trace the lasers back to the ship that sent them."

'Shoot first' wasn't Kamen's style, but she also couldn't discount the threat. "Rapidan, drift-launch a remote sensing platform toward the original dragon ship. Hold at one point three million kilometers and set for broadband radio transmission. Captain Fletcher, I recommend your ships engage active camouflage until we have a better idea of what we're dealing with."

"What about the civilian vessels?" Chaaya asked.

Kamen almost ordered them back to the fabricators before stopping herself. "If we bring them back to the fabricators, that'll tell those dragon ships where the fabricators are."

Two more dragon ships appeared and began spewing white smoke.

Captain Fletcher pointed at the new arrivals. "They're forming a perimeter, each one jumping a million kilometers from the one before it. That's some damned precise navigation considering the distances involved. The Solthari were capable of this."

Precise navigation used by the Solthari, but not the Solthari. That only made Kamen more uneasy as more dragon ships appeared, each roughly the same design, but varying in colors so that no two were the same. "We need to know what that white smoke is," she said out loud. "Rapidan, drift-launch another remote sensing platform into the nearest white cloud."

"Yes, Captain Laundraa."

Kamen populated the sand table with her fleet and the growing line of dragon ships, which were now adding new ships above and below the first ships in a curved wall, all separated by a million kilometers. "They're using our units of measure," she commented. "Each of them precisely a million kilometers from the others. That's unlikely to be a coincidence, either."

Two yellow points indicating the remote sensing platforms moved away from Rapidan in the sand table, each accelerated to four hundred kilometers per second before being ejected through Rapidan's hull, and actively camouflaged so as not to reveal the ship's location.

"How long," Kamen asked Chaaya, who understood what she meant.

"Fifty-one minutes for the communications RSP to reach one point three million kilometers. A little under ten hours to the edge of the white smoke cloud." A smirk touched one corner of Chaaya's lips. She knew how impatient Kamen was.

"What if we jumped away?" Kamen directed this at Ecuum and Captain Fletcher.

Ecuum deferred to Captain Fletcher, which, Kamen noted, he did a lot. Captain Fletcher shrugged his shoulders. "It wouldn't have worked with the Solthari. They'd know where we jumped and follow us, usually within seconds. Following us that fast, the Hawking radiation from our jumps would still be visible, telling them exactly where our ships were and the class of each ship. They would always attack right away."

"Thank you, Captain," Kamen said. "So, jumping away is out until we better understand what we're dealing with." A thought occurred to her. "Captain Fletcher, you talk as if you were here during the Solthari War. So, what *did* work?"

Captain Fletcher threw her a look that seemed to say "smart girl" but also said "I don't want to talk about it." Nevertheless, he answered, "Overwhelming firepower."

"Like I said," Ecuum piled on, "shoot first."

More dragon ships appeared, slowly filling in a curved lattice structure, all spewing that white smoke. There were nineteen of them now. Kamen turned to Chaaya. "What can you tell us about those ships?"

Chaaya stepped into the sand table and grabbed one of the dragon ships, expanding a copy so they could see it in detail. A green tag connected to the construct, indicating in text form what they knew so far. "Resting mass of each ship is about 25,000 metric tons, about the size of an Amazon class destroyer. There are no visible armaments. Of course, our ships would show no visible armaments, either.

"The power plants must be very different from our ships. An Amazon class destroyer uses two linear fusion reactors capable of a maximum output of five hundred gigawatts each. While that sounds like a lot, most of that power is consumed in normal space by the destroyer's fusion-electric propulsion system, and by the inertial compensators. It's also necessary to perform jumps."

Chaaya ran her finger along the scaled side of the dragon ship construct. "You may have noticed that these dragon ships appear to glow. Not only are they using power to continually alter their shape to appear like biological creatures, they *want to be* seen. Their signature radiates across the electromagnetic spectrum. An Amazon class destroyer could not do this. It wouldn't have enough power to support this display and maneuver simultaneously."

"We haven't seen them move," Bobby said. "Maybe they can't do both."

Three more dragon ships arrived.

"I wouldn't make that assumption," Captain Fletcher suggested. "There are other forms of power generation. Antimatter reactors, for one. We don't use them because they tend to explode if exposed to weapons fire. Fusion reactors shut down if damaged, making them safer to operate. It's possible our friends here don't share that safety concern."

Two more dragon ships arrived. Kamen had the sense of a ticking clock. When those ships out there reached a critical number, they would do something. Maybe Ecuum was right. "Rapidan, have the fabricators prep six Novas configured for antiship per dragon ship that appears. Just in case."

"Yes, Captain Laundraa."

Kamen eyed Rapidan's spinning black construct, floating at the same level as her head. "What do the SIL think about this?"

Rapidan didn't respond right away, almost as if it were surprised at the question. "Captain Laundraa, the *Brethren*—" it stressed the name— "have no memories of the Andromeda galaxy after the Alien Actions concluded in 2098. "Your analysis and actions, thus far, are sound. We agree with them."

"Oh, thank god," Ecuum said aloud. "We were so worried."

Rapidan's three-pointed star stopped spinning, one black tip pointed directly at Ecuum. "The only way to fully ascertain the dragon ships' capabilities would be to engage them in combat."

Ecuum briefly flushed red before regaining control. Even then, the tip of his tail flicked like it did when he was angry. Kamen sensed Ecuum agreed with the SIL, but didn't want to admit it. She also caught Captain Fletcher's appraising expression. No one had told him the SIL were free. It had probably been a mistake to let Rapidan join the meeting, but what was done was done.

More dragon ships arrived, the pace of arrivals increasing.

She didn't dare run, and she didn't want to fight. Their only hope was communicating. She gave voice to her concerns. "If Captain Fletcher is correct and they can track us wherever we go in Andromeda, then whoever is controlling those ships will always know exactly where we are. If we fight, even if we win, we're going to have to keep fighting wherever we go. Communicating with them might be the only way to avoid that."

Chaaya added, "They likely already know where the habitable planets are. Could save us months."

That was a good point, one Kamen's impatient nature really liked. "If they'll talk to us," she answered Chaaya's suggestion. But another point occurred to her. The Linear Star Drive got its name from the fact that the warp bubble moved in a straight line, one that could be tracked and followed. When those ships jumped away, her ships could trace them back to their point of origin.

Kamen looked to Chaaya. "How long until we can try talking?"

"Forty-six minutes."

Damn. "Okay. We'll meet back here in thirty minutes unless something changes."

Kamen took the opportunity to grab a bowl of uphutu in her cabin, a crumbly, cold maize porridge her mother often made. The familiarity of the dish always helped when Kamen was stressed.

Twenty minutes after dismissing everyone, she was back in the Combat Information Center. The others were waiting, as if they'd never left. Ray always said that a staff took its lead from the leader. If she were impatient to get back, her people would know that about her and act to be there first, ready for her. Apparently, they had. She needed to control her impatience, if only for their sakes. Otherwise, they'd never take a break.

She cringed inwardly when the first word out of her mouth was, "Time?" Okay, that was going to take some work.

"Twenty-four minutes," Chaaya said, having anticipated the question. "There are now seventy-three dragon ships. The pace of their arrival is increasing. Each ship, so far, is unique in coloration, with slight variations in design. Each is also emitting that white smoke. No other changes observed."

As she watched, three more dragon ships appeared. "Have they tried communicating with us? Maybe something we wouldn't be looking for?"

Chaaya considered that. "Nothing that we've detected. We're scanning across the entire electromagnetic and particle spectrum. There's nothing unusual. Hawking radiation and gravity waves are consistent with Linear Star Drives."

Two more dragon ships arrived.

Kamen walked into the sand table and examined a dragon ship. The sinuous movements of its body would make railguns nearly impossible to house internally, at least not ones of the length her ships used. Missiles were a possibility, as were directed-energy weapons. They weren't using shields, but that didn't mean they didn't have them. Did they have active camouflage? Nova missiles would have no problem targeting them in that dragon form.

Guardian dragon of Heaven. The phrase had stuck with her. Had the previous expeditions been destroyed? Or had they been captured, or convinced to join whoever was behind these ships? None had returned. It was likely these ships would attempt to prevent her fleet from fleeing, one way or another. Could they be descendants of the Cybernetics? What would they look like after fourteen centuries? Would they even be human?

So many unknowns.

Seven more dragon ships arrived. "It's like word of our arrival," Kamen said, "is spreading. This could be a quick reaction force of some kind, ships on standby in case someone from the Five Galaxies shows up. But it's taking time for them to get here."

Chaaya visibly considered that. "That would explain something else, Captain," she said. "If the Solthari sensor network that Captain Fletcher described is still in place, and it alerted them at the moment of our arrival, it would take about fifteen days at H3 to reach our position here. That would suggest that they have the same constraint on using the Linear Star Drive that we have."

"They're biological?" Kamen asked, then clarified, "The crew, I mean."

A large flash caught everyone's attention.

"Captain, Sensors," an operator called. "New contacts bearing zero-zero-four, dec zero-eight-zero, range four-five million kilometers. Designate contacts Sierra Nine-Two through Sierra One-Zero-Zero. Contacts are larger than previous contacts, a little over four-two thousand metric tons."

"About the mass of a Megiddo class cruiser," Chaaya added.

As Hawking radiation from the jumps faded, other differences became evident. The nine new dragon ships were entirely gold, with elaborate flowing beards and manes. Their fangs and teeth were longer, their tongues redder, their golden scales shinier, claws larger, the talons like cut rubies. They were beautiful.

Nine. The same number of representatives on the Republic Council. Coincidence?

"One minute for communications RSP," Chaaya said.

Kamen stared at the small yellow line of the remote sensing platform, willing it to hurry to its holding position. The arrival of these new ships had to mean something. If they had Ecuum's "shoot first" mentality, she needed to talk to them before they did.

"RSP holding at one point three million kilometers," Chaaya announced.

Within her battle armor's environment, Kamen selected the communications icon with a double blink, selected the remote sensing platform, then chose broadband radio transmission.

"This is Captain Kamen Laundraa," she started. *We come in peace.* That seemed a bit too melodramatic. *We're refugees from the Five Galaxies.* No. Too many cultures in human history refused to allow refugees into their borders. "We wish to open a dialogue with you," she said simply.

They waited two and half minutes for the radio message, traveling at the speed of light, to reach the large dragon ships, then another two and half minutes for a return message.

After another long minute, Kamen repeated her message.

Five agonizing minutes later, nothing.

"Rapidan," she said, "translate my message into all known human languages and repeat it."

"Yes, Captain Laundraa," the ship said.

And they waited.

And nothing happened.

More of the smaller dragon ships continued to appear. There were over a hundred and fifty of them now, with more arriving by the second. If they were hostile, she couldn't afford to wait much longer.

In the sand table, the nine large dragon ships opened their mouths wider. Instead of white smoke, dozens of bright orange objects rose from deep in their gullets—like dragons breathing fire, she couldn't help but think—and sped toward her fleet.

They were under attack.

41

0911 UT, March 17, 3502
RSS Rapidan, Intergalactic Space: DAY 172

Kamen reacted swiftly. "Launch missiles interceptors. Fabricators launch Novas. Weapons free." She didn't need to be more specific. Her people knew what to do.

She studied her formation. A giant lens twenty million kilometers across might be great for finding habitable star systems, but it was not an ideal combat formation. While all the military and Trader vessels were actively camouflaged, there were fifteen private yachts that didn't have that capability. If she moved them to the fabricators now, that would reveal their locations. The fabricators were the key to their success in Andromeda and their protection was her top priority.

"Captain," Chaaya said from Kamen's left, "all dragon ships have opened fire."

Quite literally, Kamen thought, staring at the bright orange objects issuing from the dragon ships' mouths like orange flames. Whoever these people were, they took their metaphor seriously.

Chaaya stepped into the sand table and grabbed one of the enemy objects, expanding it for them to see. It was a bright orange bulbous disk. "Each of these objects is two meters across," she said. "They launched at a speed of one hundred kilometers per second, then accelerated to one hundred and twenty-five thousand kilometers per second in just under two minutes. Which should be impossible," Chaaya added. "Boosted, our missiles would require nine minutes to achieve the same velocity, and we don't fly our missiles that fast. At present, we are detecting over thirty-three thousand objects inbound, about six minutes out. We have detected no visible signs of propulsion."

"Excuse us, Commander Dhawan," Rapidan said. "We are detecting high-frequency gravity waves from the objects. This may indicate a form of propulsion with which we are not familiar."

"Thank you, Rapidan," Chaaya said.

Over 33,000. Even with the fabricators, if they emptied the magazines of every ship in the fleet, they could launch only 25,500 SIM-3 missile interceptors—a massive number by Five Galaxies' standards—but less than half of what they needed here, assuming standard fleet doctrine of two interceptors per enemy disk.

More small dragon ships arrived, expanding their curved wall formation. Instead of white smoke, they added to the wave of incoming orange disks. Kamen noticed that each individual dragon ship fired exactly 222 disks.

"Hold all defensive fire except the interceptors," Kamen ordered. "We don't know if they can see our actively camouflaged ships. Let's not give them a target."

Fifteen groups of 222 disks each broke off and headed for the fifteen civilian yachts.

"Shouldn't we warn them?" Chaaya asked.

"No," Kamen said, her decision already made. "They might flee toward the fabricators. We must protect those at all costs."

Chaaya's smile turned grim.

Damn. The decision was easy to make, but it felt so very wrong. Those people had volunteered to help them search for a new home. She should never have included civilians in the search, but they'd offered, and after several days of no reaction from Andromeda, she'd accepted. She was responsible.

A group of their SIM-3 missile interceptors, less than two hundred, fired boost engines and targeted the orange disks closing on one of the yachts. Connected by AFCIN, Rapidan received reporting from the missiles instantaneously, no delays due to lightspeed. For the SIM-3s and orange disks, that was not the case. They had to wait for light to travel the distance between them. Twenty-one seconds after the SIM-3s fired their boost engines, the

222 orange disks they targeted abruptly broke into separate groups of three.

The SIM-3s, able to clearly see the orange disks, released their anti-missile submunitions, each submunition spinning rapidly and spooling out thin, conductive wires. If a wire contacted an object, it would detonate a magnetically shaped antimatter charge in the direction of the object, destroying it.

Suddenly, the orange disks vanished, then reappeared several kilometers from where they'd been. The anti-missile submunitions passed through empty space, scoring no hits.

"That's impossible," Bobby Mitchell said.

Chaaya quickly opened a bubble in the sand table and replayed the failed intercept, slowing it down so they could see what had happened. The orange disks did not vanish as it had appeared in real time. They performed *right-angle* turns, zipping away at accelerations no Five Galaxies technology could match.

Kamen stared at the bubble, her mind trying to grasp the implications. The SIM-3 Starburst missile interceptor was their primary anti-missile technology. If it couldn't intercept these orange disks, they were in real trouble. Worse, if these disks could execute those right-angle turns near her ships, their Archer close-in defense weapons couldn't react fast enough. Only their anti-proton directed-energy weapons would have a chance, but those would reveal the defending ship's exact location.

Seconds away from the yacht, the group of orange disks abruptly closed back on itself. They detonated as one, a yellow-white tongue of fire engulfing the civilians, consuming them. The fire faded quickly to oranges and reds as it spread out and cooled.

"That's not antimatter," Captain Fletcher said.

"It appeared to be a fusion reaction," Gen Tel commented.

The tip of Ecuum's tail, tucked against his back, flicked like it did when he was angry. Oddly, so did Captain Fletcher's. Neither of them liked Gen Tel, it seemed. Kamen had to admit she didn't much care for the Gen, either, but Ray did.

"Chaaya," Kamen ordered, "play that back."

Chaaya closed the previous bubble and opened a new one. In it, she played the attack in slow motion. All 222 disks detonated simultaneously short of the yacht. Green text populated the bubble. "Each disk," Chaaya said, "detonated with a yield of 152 kilotons. Definitely fusion. The momentum from the disks carried the plasma cloud through the yacht, destroying it."

"Fusion warheads?" Kamen said. "That doesn't make any sense, given what we've seen of their technology."

"That assumes, Captain Laundraa," Rapidan said, "that all of their weapons possess fusion warheads."

While they'd rewatched the attack, groups of orange disks had destroyed the other fourteen yachts. The remaining enemy groups spread out, as if searching for more ships. "They don't appear to know where we are," Kamen observed.

"The entire fleet was inside the fabricators when we jumped here," Captain Fletcher said. "If they are using the Solthari sensor network, they would only have seen four jump signatures."

"Captain," Chaaya said, "a group of disks is targeting the RSP we used to send our radio transmissions."

The remote sensing platform hadn't moved since they'd tried to communicate, Kamen saw. Even actively camouflaged, the dragon ships could triangulate its position. "Rapidan, move the RSP, being careful to minimize its engine signature. Let's see how good their sensors are."

"Yes, Captain Laundraa."

The remote sensing platform fired maneuvering thrusters.

As before, the 222 orange disks abruptly broke into groups of three. It happened too quickly, though, to be a reaction to the platform's movement. White smoke began to spread out around the disks, moving with them. When it touched the remote sensing platform, a three-disk group changed course and detonated, destroying it.

Chaaya immediately opened a new window in the sand table to replay the attack.

The orange disks began spinning rapidly before releasing the white smoke along the "equator" of their bulbous disks, momentum carrying the smoke away. They made no course corrections until the white smoke physically contacted the remote sensing platform. Then, three objects turned and exploded short of the platform, their fusion fire consuming it.

"They can't see through our active camouflage," Kamen commented. "They didn't react until the white smoke found the RSP."

"Captain Laundraa," Rapidan said, "the 'smoke' is composed of molecular machines that transmit a signal upon contact."

"Kind of like our Brilliant Pebbles munitions," Chaaya said, "except much smaller."

"Similar, Commander Dhawan," Rapidan replied, "though not explosive. Captain Laundraa, the molecular machines passed through the LoCIN laser link between us and the remote sensing platform before its destruction. It is possible—"

"They could trace it back us," Kamen finished. Which was true if any of the orange disks or smoke crossed their laser links. "Immediate execute, cut all LoCIN links. Captain Ecuum, move the ship."

"Yes, Captain Laundraa," Rapidan said.

"Movin' it, aye," Ecuum followed.

They immediately noticed a drop in the quality of data within the sand table. LoCIN ultraviolet lasers carried lots of data, but were constrained by the speed of light. The entangled particle pairs of AFCIN were instantaneous across vast distances, but being relatively few in number, they carried only a fraction of the data.

Their remaining SIM-3 missile interceptors, marked by yellow tracks within the sand table, maneuvered to intercept groups of orange disks. They'd learned from the previous encounter. This time, they did not fire boost engines, their active camouflage kept them hidden, and they released their submunitions much earlier. It reduced the overall probability of intercepts, but offered the possibility of at least some hits.

At first, the enemy objects didn't react. Then, as submunitions got close, they zipped out of the way—always in groups of three—at those incredible angles and speeds.

"They can see the submunitions," Captain Fletcher commented.

"The wires," Gen Tel said, earning scowls from both Captain Flether and Ecuum. "They are the only part of the submunition that is not actively camouflaged," he added.

"Our SIM-3s are useless," Kamen stated. "Our only advantage is that they can't see us." There were now over 36,000 of those orange disks searching for her fleet, and more dragon ships continued to appear.

"Incoming!" a sensor operator called. "Bearing zero-one-zero, dec zero-two-zero, range one million kilometers."

The disks had apparently traced the LoCIN laser back along Rapidan's original bearing.

Not our current position, thank the ancestors.

The 222-disk group spread out and released white smoke, but Rapidan was already outside their search area. Before Kamen could breathe a sigh of relief, however, other groups of 222 objects changed course and expanded their search.

It was only a matter of time.

"Rapidan, this ship only, weapons free," Kamen ordered. "Bobby, if this goes bad, you'll take command."

"Understood," Bobby said.

Three groups of 222 disks came at Rapidan from the front and below. Captain Ecuum rotated the ship's three-pointed star, trying to thread its arms between clouds of white smoke.

It almost worked.

Smoke touched the trailing left arm of the ship. A microwave radio signal beaconed out.

"Jam that signal," Kamen ordered.

"Too late, Captain," someone said.

The closest disks exploded short of Rapidan's hull, but the ship was ready for it. It poured power into its navigational deflectors, raising powerful magnetic fields to shield the ship. The plasma from the fusion detonations washed across the shields, never touching the hull. The only damage was minor burns from the intense heat and radiation. Rapidan quickly repaired the damage.

The ship opened fire with its twelve Archer close-in defense weapons, firing kinetic slugs in short bursts at the incoming disks. Glowing orange, they were easy to target. Rapidan destroyed dozens.

But the objects, apparently, could also communicate, adapt, and learn. They began zipping around, complicating Rapidan's firing solutions. The hit rate from the Archers fell dramatically.

Smoke from hundreds of disks grew thick around Rapidan, visibly highlighting most of the ship. Rapidan added its anti-proton directed-energy weapons to its defensive fire. These proved more effective than the Archers, but there were just too many of the enemy disks to contend with.

Disks began to get through Rapidan's defensive fire, exploding near the ship. Rapidan's magnetic shielding held, the heat and radiation from the blasts doing only minor damage.

"Why do they keep exploding near the ship," Kamen asked, "instead of waiting until they contact the hull?"

"A better question, Captain," Gen Tel said, "is why do they explode at all? At the velocities these objects are capable of, almost forty-two percent the speed of light, they could simply ram the ship, destroying it with their kinetic energy alone."

"Hey, hey," Ecuum said, "let's not give them any ideas."

Rapidan fought for its life. The objects detonated across the ship's hull by the hundreds, individually doing very little damage, but it was beginning to add up.

Death by a thousand cuts.

The ship had lost almost one percent of its resting mass, nearly three thousand metric tons, repairing its hull. And there were still tens of thousands of those objects out there, converging on them.

"Captain Ecuum," Kamen ordered, suddenly grateful that Rapidan had kept Ray comatose, his brain protected, "spool up the Linear Star Drive. Jump the ship five million kilometers behind the small dragon ships. Rapidan, once we emerge, weapons free. Hit those dragon ships with every Nova we have."

"Yes, Captain Laundraa," Rapidan said.

"Captain," Ecuum said, "recommend jumping above the dragon ships. Otherwise, we'd be warping through their line. We don't know if they have the tech to detect and disrupt warp fields, like we have."

"Good point. Do it."

"Doin' it, aye," he said, a light yellow infusing his skin for just a second.

As Rapidan diverted power from its defenses to the Linear Star Drive, the damage the objects did to the ship increased, but the fight had one benefit: the disks were focused on Rapidan, not the rest of the fleet.

Flashes in the sand table near the small dragon ships caught her attention. The Novas fired earlier from the fabricators had reached them but had run into that white smoke in front of the ships. Orange disks flew from the dragon ships' mouths in groups of three and destroyed every single Nova they'd fired. Kamen wanted to scream her frustration but controlled herself.

The crew takes their lead from their commander.

It was something Ray often told her.

No matter what happened, she had to project confidence.

"Jumping," Ecuum called out.

Kamen belatedly realized the dragon ships hadn't jammed their ability to jump, something that was standard practice for the Star Navy. She added it to the growing list of things she didn't understand about this new opponent.

Her body imploded, crushed down to an infinitesimal point. With no sense of time passing, she exploded back into normal space, pain shooting through every nerve. Bodies didn't actually get crushed or explode, but it damned sure felt that way. And jumps, even at H2, did real damage to cells. She swallowed blood.

Rapidan was already drift-launching Novas at the dragon ships, aiming behind them to avoid the white smoke. Seventy-two Novas, Rapidan's entire complement, fanned out toward the nearest dragons, two per ship.

"Spool the Linear Star Drive," Kamen ordered.

"Spoolin', aye," Ecuum said.

The small dragon ships—all of them—breathed fire, 222 of the orange disks *each*. Almost 39,000 in total. "How many of these damned things do they have?" Kamen asked out loud without meaning to.

The disks arced up to target Rapidan, the ship visible when it emerged from its jump.

"Forty seconds to impact," Chaaya supplied.

Rapidan's Novas boosted, careful to keep their boost engines aimed directly away from the dragon ships, minimizing the chance they'd be detected.

Watching the dragon ships, it struck Kamen as odd that they didn't try to maneuver. As more of the small dragon ships continued to appear, she wondered if they had to hold their formation because other dragon ships were still inbound.

"Captain," Chaaya said, "the first group of disks near the fleet is fanning out and releasing smoke again, apparently searching for our other ships."

Tunnel vision is fatal for a commander, Ray's voice echoed in her mind. *A commander must never lose sight of the big picture.* Chaaya had subtly reminded her without embarrassing her that she was getting too focused on Rapidan's fight.

Kamen keyed the AFCIN. "All ships, this is Captain Laundraa. Proceed to dock with your assigned fabricator, best possible speed without risking detection." Tens of thousands of those disks might destroy Rapidan, but they'd barely dent a fabricator. "Same for your people," she added to Captain Fletcher. They didn't have AFCIN links with the Independent Traders.

Kamen's body imploded and exploded again, the pain much worse this time; Molemachs had not finished repairing the damage to her cells from the previous jump. She blinked rapidly against the blood clouding her vision, needing to see what was going on.

Rapidan was outside the lens formation, about three million kilometers from its assigned fabricator. Ecuum fired its engines at low thrust, aiming to dock with the fabricator without giving the factory ship's position away.

Swallowing blood, trying to ignore the pounding in her head, Kamen looked to her fleet within the sand table. A standard technology Amazon class destroyer crossed a finger of white cloud. Hundreds of orange disks abruptly altered course and attacked, exploding near its engines. A secondary explosion ripped through the engineering section of the destroyer. More enemy disks closed on the wounded ship like sharks to blood, detonating in dizzying succession, chewing their way forward through the ship.

Emergency beacons from crew abandoning the ship appeared. The disks turned on those, too, killing every one of them. They continued their attack until the entire ship was nothing but vapor. None of the destroyer's crew of 321 survived.

"They apparently do not take prisoners," Gen Tel observed, no hint of emotion in his voice.

Kamen seethed inside. She would remember this.

Turning to Rapidan's attack on the dragon ships, hoping for some measure of vengeance, she saw the dragon ships had not reacted. Rapidan's Novas, actively camouflaged and configured for antiship, coordinated their attack to strike thirty-six dragon ships simultaneously, careful to avoid the clouds of white smoke in front of the dragons.

Double flashes of pure white erupted, the first antimatter charges opening holes in the dragon ships' hulls for the second, larger charges to explode into.

Dazzlingly white fireballs, far out of proportion to a Nova's warhead, completely consumed thirty-five of the thirty-six ships.

"Only antimatter reactors explode like that," Captain Fletcher said. "That's why we don't use them."

A predatory smile stretched Kamen's lips. Every enemy had weaknesses. They had just found a big one. "If we can get past their white smoke, we can kill them."

The tens of thousands of disks hunting her fleet unexpectedly stopped.

They just hung there, spinning in space.

Then a voice spoke.

42

1933 UT, March 17, 3502
RSS Rapidan, Intergalactic Space: DAY 172

"Leave."

It was a woman's voice, spoken in the common tongue of the Five Galaxies. No visual accompanied the voice.

"Captain," Chaaya said, "that message came over AFCIN."

"AFCIN?" Kamen asked, confused. "Only Star Navy and Imperial Intelligence can access our network."

Everyone turned to Gen Tel.

"So, spy," Ecuum accused, the tip of his tail flicking, "access to military networks requires *physically* obtaining entangled particle pairs from fabricators, bases, or Imperial Intelligence offices, and refreshing them regularly. Know anything about that?"

"No," Gen Tel said.

"Captain," Chaaya interrupted, "the dragon ships are turning in place, emitting that white smoke, forming clouds in all directions."

"Captain," Gen Tel said, "I do not believe they intend to allow us to leave. More likely, they are stalling until their ships are fully protected within the white smoke."

Kamen didn't like Gen Tel, didn't trust him, but his assessment was sound. She keyed the AFCIN. "We will not leave. We are open to negotiations."

"Leave," came the immediate reply in the same woman's voice.

Kamen stepped closer to the sand table, focusing on the big picture. Her warships would take almost an hour and half to finish docking with the fabricators. It was the same for the Independent

Trader vessels. The woman on the dragon ship might be stalling, but Kamen needed to buy time, too.

She keyed the AFCIN. "We remain open to negotiations. Or we can destroy your fleet. Your choice."

It wasn't exactly an empty threat—she did have four fabricators and over a hundred warships—but she knew it wouldn't be as easy as she made it sound.

Minutes passed.

Small dragon ships continued to appear.

The nine larger, golden dragon ships suddenly jumped, winking out of normal space. Hawking radiation spread from their jump points like red flower petals unfolding. The size of the ethereal petals could only come from H3 jumps.

The orange disks resumed their attacks, followed by the small dragon ships jumping away. New dragon ships that appeared quickly jumped away as well.

"Captain," Chaaya said, "jump vectors are pointing back toward the Andromeda galaxy."

"They're retreating," Captain Fletcher observed.

"Chaaya," Kamen asked, "please tell me you can track their vectors back to their destinations?"

"We can, Captain," she said. "It'll take several hours to analyze, but we'll have destinations for you."

The enemy disks near the fleet continued their hunt for victims, while the second volley of disks fired previously at Rapidan turned and headed for Rapidan's emergence point at that jaw-dropping forty-two percent of lightspeed.

Kamen keyed the AFCIN to her fleet. "All ships, this is Captain Laundraa. Flank speed to the fabricators. Jump if you have to."

The captains of the ships farthest from the fabricators jumped close. The rest lit their engines at max thrust. The benefit of docking with fabricators was that ships didn't need to slow down. The mammoth factory ships created openings in their hulls to accept fleeing vessels, then used powerful magnetic fields to slow them down, bringing them to a gentle halt deep within their bulk.

The orange disks pursued, covering a million kilometers every eight seconds. Her stragglers were still several tens of thousands of kilometers out from the fabricators, ships pushing their engines for all they were worth.

Fleeing ships opened fire with their Archer close-in defense weapons. The fabricators joined them, trying to provide covering fire. Orange disks exploded by the hundreds, but that was barely a scratch given their numbers. A Megiddo class heavy cruiser took dozens of hits to its aft section. Secondary explosions from stored antimatter, gasses, and fuels ripped the ship apart. Two emergency beacons appeared, only to fall victim to more of the orange disks.

Another 623 of her fellow spacers dead.

Kamen watched it stoically, her mind tallying up the losses but otherwise not reacting to them. She'd seen Ray do this, but had never experienced it herself. It seemed . . . wrong . . . to not feel something.

An Independent Trader vessel came under attack just short of its fabricator. It seemed doomed to the same fate as the Megiddo until the fabricator's hull liquified and literally reached out to grab the Trader vessel, swallowing it. Fusion explosions from thousands of orange disks pummeled the massive ship's hull like hail in a thunderstorm, but did little damage to the fabricator itself.

As Rapidan neared, the fabricator did the same for it, reaching out and grabbing the ship, drawing it quickly into itself, protecting the ship from the rain of enemy disks like a mother shielding her child. Given that the SIL called the fabricators Mother Ships, perhaps that wasn't far from the truth.

In the sand table, Kamen saw the last of her ships reach the safety of the fabricators, enemy disks exploding uselessly against the fabricators' massive hulls.

They'd won the first fight against the inhabitants of Andromeda.

If there was a next fight, it would be in Andromeda itself.

43

2020 UT, March 17, 3502
RSS Rapidan, Intergalactic Space: DAY 172

Ecuum watched Kamen as the final casualty figure populated. One Amazon class destroyer and one Megiddo class heavy cruiser destroyed, all hands lost. Fifteen civilian yachts destroyed, no survivors. 2,292 dead. A skirmish compared to their recent battles. Kamen ran a hand over her bald, ebony head as she stared at the number floating within the sand table.

"She's taking it well," Captain Fletcher commented privately from Ecuum's left, his construct floating horizontal as the People preferred, his baby blue eyes fixed on Kamen.

Ecuum had adopted the same horizontal orientation for Fletcher's benefit, his white Star Navy uniform a stark contrast to Fletcher's black body suit. "She's strong," Ecuum said softly.

"We should talk on my ship," Fletcher suggested.

Ecuum gave a single nod. "Captain Kamen, Captain Fletcher and I have some business."

Kamen scowled at him, then her brown eyes flicked to Captain Fletcher's construct, her distrust of the pirate obvious. "We'll need both of you back here when Chaaya works out where the dragon ships went, so we can decide our next course of action."

"We wouldn't miss it," Ecuum told her.

Ecuum boarded a travel pod from Rapidan, riding it through the fabricator to *Fletcher's Run*. Fletcher dismissed the travel pod at the hangar entrance, not allowing the pod inside his ship. That he'd allowed his ship to travel inside a SIL fabricator and communicate directly with SIL warships had surprised Ecuum, showing just how much the old Trader was willing to risk for this endeavor, but Fletcher's trust only went so far.

He led Ecuum to his cluttered yet spacious captain's cabin, propelling himself behind his oak desk, then turning to face Ecuum. "Your Captain Laundraa is impressive," he said without preamble. "Makes me wonder if we're following the right person."

Fletcher's dig at Ray was intentional, and impossible for Ecuum to ignore, which Fletcher would know. "Ray *is* the revolution, Fletch. We wouldn't be here without him. Or have you forgotten that it was you who originally told me to seek him out?"

Fletcher's skin remained neutral, but the tip of his tail, tucked against his back, flicked. "Then, where is he, old friend? It's been two weeks. Longer when you consider the crossing."

Ecuum hadn't, of course, told Fletcher that Ray was a brain without a body, kept comatose by the SIL to keep it safe. To keep *Ray* safe, he amended. But the Independents had seen Kamen lead the fleet, not Ray.

"Uncertainty breeds caution," Fletcher said to Ecuum's silence. "Weakness breeds fear. Neither is good for business. Old friend."

They might be old friends, but Fletcher was about business, first and foremost. He was reminding Ecuum of that. "Ray leads the revolution. He is the one *I* follow, old friend. Kamen is very capable, and Ray has groomed her as his successor, should the need arise. We're not there, yet."

"Are you certain of that?" Fletcher's large, baby blue eyes bored into Ecuum's.

"Yes, Fletch. Certain as a pulsar."

Fletcher didn't blink, didn't shift his gaze. "Then why do I sense doubt, old friend?"

They'd known each other for over two centuries, from that meeting after Ecuum's first Niner Race. No one knew Ecuum better. Hiding information among the People was not an insult, but some things, like business, went beyond friendship, no matter how long that might be. Ecuum could not reveal the extent of Ray's injuries—or his dependence upon the SIL. "Would you rather turn tail and run?" he said. "That's not the Captain Fletcher I know."

Light red flushed Fletcher's skin. He was a master of control—he wanted Ecuum to see his irritation. "Don't test me, old friend. We are risking everything here. We need to be certain we're backing the right horse."

Ecuum had spent enough time in Earth space to understand the reference. He put all the faith he had in Ray into his voice. "Ray *is* the revolution. Old friend."

They stared at each other for Fates knew how long, neither willing to give ground.

Finally, Fletcher warned, "You better be right, old friend, or this venture will be short lived. The others are already asking questions, wondering where Rhoades is, why they haven't seen him. If not for the fabricators' performance today, I doubt they would be staying."

Ecuum understood. Fletcher was not alone in his doubts. The Traders were not following Ray or Kamen. They were following Fletcher. "What do you need from me?" Ecuum asked.

"To see Rhoades," Fletcher said. "To see him leading. To see him *physically*."

Ecuum had no idea how to make that happen. He had no idea what condition Ray would be in when they woke him up in Andromeda.

If he wakes up.

Ecuum pondered that. He didn't have the same relationship with Kamen that he had with Ray. Not even close. And she didn't have the history or experience that Ray had. One battle would not overcome that. They needed Ray. *He* needed Ray. He hadn't realized just how much until this moment.

But would his friend be there?

"I have faith in him," he told Captain Fletcher with all the conviction he could muster. "You will, too."

44

2105 UT, March 17, 3502
RSS Demos, Intergalactic Space: DAY 172

Dag lay on his bed aboard Demos. The other officers had left him alone since his return from New Yerkes, though not for the same reasons as they had before. Before, they'd been afraid of him. Now, they seemed to sense his pain.

He gripped Maria's stainless-steel crucifix through his battle armor, but gently, not drawing blood. It was something of her. "I love you."

I love you, too, my Dagoberto, she whispered in his memory.

His eyes stung, but his battle armor drank up any tears that might have fallen.

How do I go on?

After everything that had happened. After everything he'd endured. After everything he'd done. Nightmares of his torture haunted him. Other nightmares, too. He didn't regret killing Gen. That was about survival. He did regret his orders on Tocci III, orders that led to the unnecessary deaths of troopers under his command. Orders that led to the death of First Sergeant Takeuchi, his friend. He was not innocent. The nightmares reminded him of that. The blood of his friends mingled with the blood of the Gen. The blood of his family.

How do I go on?

A chime sounded at his door.

He sat up on his bed. "Come in."

General Salvador Burress walked through his door. Dag shot to his feet, coming to a position of attention, his armor keeping him connected to the deck in the ship's microgravity. "At ease," Burress said. "Take a seat."

The general called up a chair near Dag's bed and sat down. "Haven't seen much of you lately, Dag," he said. "Wanted to check in on you."

"I'm okay," Dag said, not even convincing himself.

"I thought so," Burress said, his tone understanding. "You don't have to do this alone."

They hadn't really known each other before the war started. Burress had commanded the 3rd Armored Cavalry Regiment from Knido in Tau Ceti Star System. Banshee Troop, Dag's unit, had been assigned to Earth. Their paths had never crossed. When they met on Demos before the assault on the fabricator at Tomb, Dag had already lost his family, his reason.

"There are PTS treatments," Burress suggested. "They help with the nightmares."

Dag had considered that, but every time he'd called up the PTS icon in his battle armor's environment, the one that would suppress the parts of his brain associated with Post Traumatic Stress, he hadn't been able to do it. He didn't want to forget his pain. Stupid, probably. He didn't want the pain. He didn't want the nightmares. But they were a part of him. "I don't want to forget."

Burress seemed to understand. "You mean you don't want to forgive yourself."

Dag said nothing. He squeezed Maria's crucifix, not realizing he'd grabbed it. Maria had believed with all her heart that God watched over them, protected them. She'd been wrong. But, then, how did he explain his daughter, Rosita, guiding him to Rhoades' daughter on New Yerkes?

Mamí says God brings us to where we are needed most.

He hadn't been able to save his own daughter, but he'd been in just the right place, at just the right moment, to save Margaret Rhoades, guided to that exact spot and time by the spirit of his own daughter. Maria would no doubt see the hand of God in that. God's plan, she'd call it.

Was it so far from the truth? Was it all part of some grand plan he couldn't see? He couldn't forgive God for the murder of his family.

Not now.

Perhaps, not ever. But he also couldn't deny that he'd seen his daughter, that she'd guided him, on the fabricator, on Tocci III, on New Yerkes. Could coincidence alone explain it?

Dag looked up. "I'll be all right, sir."

Burress studied him. "I'm moving you to command of the Second Armored Cavalry Regiment. Colonel Scott Haley will command the Third. Your regiment is mostly trainees. You'll need to whip them into shape, and fast. You up for it?"

Am I? Dag wondered. It wasn't an idle question. The troopers of the 2nd Armored Cavalry Regiment needed competent leadership to survive whatever was coming. They needed moral leadership, too. Not a man filled with hate and bent on revenge, nor a man who'd lost his faith in God and life.

Can I be the man they need?

He slipped Maria's crucifix from around his neck and looked at it, the stainless-steel glinting in the overhead light. *Vaya con Dios, my Dagoberto*, Maria said to him again. Her last words to him. *Go with God.*

"Yes, General," Dag said.

He would be the man they needed.

45

2300 UT, March 17, 3502
RSS Rapidan, Intergalactic Space: DAY 172

Kamen deferred to Chaaya to start the meeting. Chaaya brought up the infrared image of the Andromeda galaxy within the sand table.

"Tracing the dragon ships' jump vectors was not as promising as we had hoped," Chaaya began. Hundreds of orange lines appeared in the sand table, tracking the vectors of the dragon ships' jumps. While they pointed back toward the Andromeda galaxy, most did not intersect star systems. "They must have known we would try to trace their jumps and deliberately jumped to intermediate points, before jumping again to their final destinations. As we lack the technology they seem to have to track jumps anywhere in space, we don't know where they went."

Kamen stifled an impatient sigh. They were back to square one, back to painstaking and lengthy surveys to find habitable star systems.

Chaaya threw her a smile, as if she'd read Kamen's thoughts. "However, two dragon ships, it would appear, were not so careful." Hundreds of orange lines disappeared, leaving only two. Chaaya expanded the Andromeda construct, highlighting a position in the elongated ring of stars nearest the galactic core. She highlighted a second region in the ring of stars about midway between the galactic core and the galaxy's outer rim. Then, as they watched, she expanded bubbles within the sand table highlighting the star systems bisected by those orange lines. Both, Kamen saw, held yellow main sequence stars like Earth's Sun.

Chaaya pointed to the star system closest to the galactic core. “We’ve detected two super-Earths in the inner part of this star system, and two gas giants further out. There may be more planets that we haven’t detected, yet. One of the super-Earths is in the habitable zone of the star.”

She pointed to the other star system midway out toward the rim. “This second system is one, by chance, that we’ve already surveyed. It has three gas giants in the outer star system: a Jupiter-mass planet and two Neptune mass. The inner part of the star system contains a super-Earth, about four times the mass of Earth, close to the star, and two Earth-sized rocky worlds further out, both within the star’s habitable zone.”

“Do we know which planet the dragon ship jumped to?” Kamen asked.

Chaaya shook her head. “Unfortunately, our ability to track jump vectors isn’t that precise, Captain, not over 250,000 lightyears. I would also caution that a vector only gives us a bearing, not a destination. It could be a coincidence, albeit a statistically infinitesimal one, that this vector intersects with a habitable star system.”

“Close enough,” Kamen said, and immediately regretted how impatient it sounded. “Recommendations?”

Unsurprisingly, Captain Ecuum said, “Jump there and find out. We’ve already seen their weapons are ineffective against fabricators. Four of them appearing in their skies will probably make them shit their pants.” He shrugged. “If they wear pants.”

Captain Fletcher, floating horizontal next to Ecuum, turned a light shade of pink. “If they do possess the Solthari warp detection network, the whole galaxy will know where we are. We have no idea of the numbers of those dragon ships they have, whether they have classes of ships we haven’t seen yet, what their star system defenses look like, or anything else, for that matter. All that said, I agree with Captain Ecuum. We came here to stay. ‘May advantage come to the swift, and opportunity to the bold’ as we say.”

“I agree,” Chaaya said simply.

Kamen looked to General Burress, which seemed to surprise him. "I usually leave Fleet matters to the Fleet," he said to her. "That said, if they can track our jumps anywhere, a scout ship will be detected as quickly as a fabricator. Better to go in strength."

"I agree," Captain Bobby Mitchell said.

"Commander Tel?" Kamen asked Gen Tel's Natural construct, worn for the benefit of the duty crew in case they saw him.

The Gen's ice-blue eyes studied her, as if taking her measure. "Given the unknowns, going in strength would seem the best course, Captain."

"Next question is," Kamen asked, "which star system? If they're like the Gen, they probably have their capitol world closer to the galactic core, like Olympus."

Gen Tel stared down his straight nose at her. "In the Five Galaxies, Olympus is the most heavily defended star system *because* it is the Imperial capital. Overconfidence based on a single battle would be unwise, Captain."

"So was allowing a spy aboard," Captain Ecuum mumbled loud enough for everyone to hear. "That woman on the golden dragon ship accessed our Fleet AFCIN. Or did you think we forgot, spy?"

The tip of Captain Fletcher's tail, visible to Kamen but not to Gen Tel, flicked in anger.

"If we assume," Gen Tel said, "that the star system nearest the core is their capital system, going there before we know their full capabilities is unwise. We do not know why they retreated. They may hope to lure us into a heavily defended star system where the fabricators will provide less of an advantage."

"The same could apply to the other star system," Captain Fletcher pointed out.

"It could," Gen Tel said, though he kept his focus on Kamen. "It could also be a lapse in protocol on the part of a single ship captain. Of the two star systems, the one further out from the galactic core would seem the better candidate."

Reluctantly, very reluctantly on Ecuum's and Fletcher's part, they agreed.

"Okay," Kamen said, her decision made. "We'll jump to the edge of the second star system. This will be our last H3 jump, barring an emergency." She turned to Bobby Mitchell. "Captain Mitchell, we'll sedate the refugees and most of the crews like before. Unfortunately, we'll need the command staff to remain awake to react to threats we encounter on the other side."

They grimaced, but nodded acknowledgement. "Dismissed," Kamen said. "Chaaya, Captain Ecuum, stay behind a moment."

After Captain Fletcher, Bobby, and Gen Tel had departed, Kamen lowered her voice—though there really wasn't any need—and told them, "We'll revive Ray as soon after the jump as we can."

Captain Ecuum nodded. "Good. There are questions, doubts, among the Independent Traders, and among the refugees and ship crews, too, about his absence. Some are wondering if he's dead."

"Rapidan has assured me that he is alive and. . . ." Kamen couldn't complete the statement.

"Yeah," Captain Ecuum said. "That's what I'm worried about, too. I think that's what we're all worried about."

46

0205 UT, April 1, 3502
RSS Rapidan, Unknown Star System: DAY 187

Ray floated, caressed by currents of water and wind. The water was familiar. He knew it. Flowing within the banks of his mind, always moving yet always present. His river.

The wind was familiar, but also alien. He knew wind like it, but this was not the wind he knew.

Admiral Rhoades?

Rapidan?

We are here.

Ray reached out. Objects floated nearby, the edge of a vast sphere of such objects. Dust, chalky on a tongue he didn't have, cosmic rays like sharp stings upon remembered skin, the hot wash of pulsars, the rolling of gravity waves. It was all familiar.

And it was all wrong. There were too many stars.

He flowed fully into the Great Ocean, focusing through the sensors of the four Mother Ships, their flows strong within and around him. He examined the objects of the vast sphere. They were dark, icy, small, and not small. Debris. From the birth pangs of a star. An Oort cloud. Leftover material from the formation of *this* star. He could see it, a dim yellow light.

We have arrived, Admiral Rhoades.

Where? This was no star he knew.

Andromeda. You are needed.

Andromeda? The truth of it struck him. Too many stars. Over a trillion of them. Familiar processes, but in an unfamiliar setting.

Rings of stars instead of the Milky Way's more defined spiral arms. They'd made it. After all this time, they were finally here.

Andromeda.

The waters around him shifted. Images, memories of a battle. Dragons? Orange disks? Impossible physics. Strange tactics. And Kamen. She'd led as he'd known she could.

He was back within his river, comforted by its familiar banks. And back in his cabin, Gen Alyn's painting of the Rhoades Ranch on Knido hanging on the bulkhead above him. He was in a bed, but not a medical bed. His regular one.

He had a body. But like Andromeda, it was different, familiar and not familiar. A construct. A vessel.

For his brain.

It all came rushing back. This was what the SIL had done to him. This was what he was. A mind without a body. A river. An Ocean. The ship. The Brethren. All at once.

"You are needed, Admiral Rhoades," Rapidan repeated.

Kamen was in the Combat Information Center, the molemachs within her body working to repair the damage to her organs and systems after an H3 jump. Ecuum was there, too, his Floater body genetically hardened against the effects of H3 and already mostly recovered. Most of the others were asleep, their molemachs repairing them so they would wake without too much pain.

Ray felt no pain, no discomfort. He looked down at the construct that was his body, dressed in his white Star Navy uniform. Battle armor enclosed it. It moved when he commanded it, throwing its legs over the side of the bed, standing up.

He walked to the Combat Information Center, a short walk from the Admiral's cabin, flowing within the ship—*with the ship*. When he stepped through the CIC hatch, he could feel the hatch moving around his construct just as he could feel his construct move through the hatch. It was disorienting.

"Admiral!" Chaaya shouted, her diminutive form lighting up with excitement. "Sorry. Admiral on deck!"

She and Kamen snapped to attention. Ecuum swiveled his head like an owl, looking directly behind him. When he saw Ray, he flipped vertical and shot over on strong puffs of air, a large grin pulling his thick lips wide.

"At ease," Ray told them, delighted beyond measure to see his officers again. His joy faded as he watched each of them note his construct.

"How you feeling, Ray?" Ecuum asked. His skin held a slightly gray pallor. He was worried. *Very* worried.

"I'm okay. Under the circumstances," Ray amended.

"We made it, sir," Kamen said. She looked like she wanted to hug him, but, of course, military protocol wouldn't allow it. "We did run into some trouble."

Ray saw her deflate. He knew the casualty figures from the battle. Small compared to their recent battles, but the first she'd endured as a commander. "I know. The Brethren showed me. You did good, Captain. I'm proud of you."

He'd meant it to be reassuring, but something he'd said put all of them on edge.

Members of the crew began to appear in the Combat Information Center, some arriving from travel pods through the deck, others entering through the hatch. "Good morning, Admiral," the ones coming through the hatch said.

"Good morning," he answered to each of them in turn.

That sensation of wrongness came over him again. They gathered into small groups, out of earshot they thought, whispering and looking back at him. They didn't know that he could hear every word through his connection with the ship. His reappearance as a construct led many of them to wonder just how bad his injuries were, or if he was even still alive.

Ray led his officers to the sand table and raised the privacy walls. It didn't shut out the crew's speculations.

Constructs of Bobby Mitchell, Gen Tel, Sal Burress, and the Independent Trader, Captain Fletcher, rose from the deck. Bobby and Sal looked happy to see him, if a little concerned. Captain Fletcher and Gen Tel studied him like a biologist might study some exotic new lifeform.

"Admiral," Kamen began, stepping up to the sand table and raising a construct of the nearby star system, "we've jumped here based on the jump vector of one of the dragon ships. The system contains two earth-like rocky worlds within the habitable zone."

Ray spotted them within the sand table construct, and through the Mother Ships' sensors. He reached into the star system, focusing, past the Kuiper belt, past two smaller greenish-blue gas giants and a larger one that reminded him of Jupiter. There were actually three small rocky worlds. He concentrated on a planet slightly larger than Earth with blue oceans, green continents, and an artificial ring system.

Ray pushed from his river, over his falls, into the Great Ocean; They needed to improve their sensor resolution. The Brethren recommended, and he accepted, the launch of two hundred remote sensing platforms to locations throughout the star system. He shifted the construct in the sand table to highlight the living world with the artificial ring system.

His people stared at him. Nervous. Concerned. Their heart and breathing rates elevated.

Why? What had happened?

Ecuum floated close to his ear and whispered, "Did you do all that?"

He hadn't given any verbal orders. The Mother Ships had pivoted and launched remote sensing platforms, and the sand table had refocused, all without verbal orders or even motion from him. He'd have to be more careful in the future. To all of them, he said, "My current condition allows me to control the SIL directly."

Their wary expressions deepened. Captain Fletcher said, "Mind-machine interfaces are banned, Admiral. And for good reason."

Was that what this was? A mind-machine interface? He hadn't thought of it that way, but it made sense. "If we are to survive, Captain Fletcher, if we are to win, we must reassess many of our assumptions."

"You weren't there, Admiral," Fletcher said, surprising Ray with his vehemence. "The SIL used those interfaces to make people see what they wanted them to see. Entire fleets, entire star systems, were lost because the SIL blinded people to their ships, made them fly their warships into each other, into asteroids, even planets. Human crews fired on human warships, believing them to be SIL. Once you let one of those demons into your head, they can make you see, make you feel, anything they want."

He was right. The currents within the Great Ocean showed him memories of the SIL doing exactly what Captain Fletcher described. But the memories also showed him something else. "It was also SIL who saved Humanity, Captain Fletcher. A hundred SIL, under the command of my ancestor, Peter Rhoades, stood against their Brethren and with Humanity, alerting humans to what the other SIL were doing."

Captain Fletcher arched a hairless brow at him. "How could you possibly know that?"

How indeed. "Family history," Ray told him. Not exactly a lie. Captain Fletcher didn't know about the SIL's freedom, and Ray was not about to tell him or give him any clues to that fact.

Partially to distract them, and mostly because he'd promised to include her, Ray linked to Mary on Damodar. "Mary, if you are available, could you please join us in the Combat Information Center on Rapidan?"

"Of course, Ray," she said formally, catching his official tone. "I'll be right there."

While they waited, Ray stepped into the sand table and manipulated the construct of the living world. Its resolution improved as the Mother Ships turned broadside, using their entire hulls as sensors, and the remote sensing platforms accelerated into the system and spread out, linked back to them.

The world looked like Earth and it didn't, like everything else about this place. White clouds in swirls, cyclones, and large commas spoke of a thick atmosphere. Oceans spanning the planet from deep blues to pale turquoise told of water in abundance. Continents with tan deserts and dark mountains and green forests and jungles heralded abundant life. The vast artificial ring warned of technological intelligence.

Mary's construct rose from the deck, dressed in the formal attire one expected of a president. She flicked a glance at Ray, both relief to see him, and concern at his construct. Then, she turned to look at the planet within the sand table. "Have we arrived?" she asked.

"Not exactly," Ray answered, relieved to see her. "Chaaya," he deferred, not wanting to repeat his mistake of a few moments ago.

"Yes, Admiral," she said. "First, we have detected no dragon ships, or other vessels, nearby. However, the dragon ships didn't appear at our Andromeda observation point for fifteen days after our arrival, so we shouldn't read too much into this. If they do have a warp detection network, they know we are here. We have not detected any attempts at communication."

"What about in system communications?" Kamen asked.

"We have not detected any, Captain," Chaaya said, "but that is not unusual. Most star systems in the Five Galaxies use lasers and entangled communications, which wouldn't be detectable. If they have active sensor networks, we should see those shortly. We're also examining the other planets, moons, asteroids, and comets in detail to see if we can detect space stations, large ships, mines, or other constructions."

"Thanks," Kamen said.

Chaaya returned her focus to the planet. "This artificial ring system, like those in the Five Galaxies, gives off more energy than it receives from the star or the planet. It is probably safe to say that a technological people live there, or, at least, lived there." She stepped into the sand table and touched a spot on the dark side of the planet. "It's going to take us several hours to analyze, but this spot here, and here, and here, could be artificial lighting."

"Let's start moving in system," Ray said. "We'll take it slow until we have a better picture."

"I'll convene the Council," Mary said. "They'll want to see this."

Ray stopped a frown from forming on his construct—something he probably couldn't have done on his flesh-and-blood face. "We'll provide a live feed to Damodar. The Council will see what we see."

Her formal smile said thank you but also hinted at how worried for him she was.

"Admiral Rhoades," Captain Fletcher interjected, "the Independent Traders can help. Surreptitiously surveying star systems without being observed is a skillset we possess."

Ray had tracked and fought Independents—pirates—enough that he didn't doubt Captain Fletcher's comment. He nodded once.

"Jump transient," a sensor operator called. "Contact bearing zero-zero-zero, ascent zero-one-zero, range five-zero million kilometers. Designate contact Sierra One. Contact is a small dragon ship."

"That didn't take long," Ecuum commented.

The Hawking radiation of the Mother Ships' jumps had long since faded. With their camouflage active, that dragon ship likely couldn't see them.

"The dragon ship is emitting that white smoke," the sensor operate said. "Speed of the smoke is five thousand kps."

"Faster than before," Kamen noted.

"A little under three hours to reach our current position," Chaaya said, then added, "by the way, that appears to be the same ship we tracked jumping here. Or, at least, one with the same markings."

"Let's steer clear of it and that white smoke," Ray said. "Ecuum, take us below the ecliptic and set course for the inhabited world, ten thousand kps. They might be able to see our jumps, but they seem to have difficulty seeing through active camouflage. Let's use that."

47

0242 UT, April 1, 3502
RSS Rapidan, Unknown Star System: DAY 187

With days before they would reach the target world, Ray returned to his cabin. The first thing he did was get rid of the bed. He wouldn't need it. Looking around, he wondered if he should make other changes. He kept Gen Alyn's paintings: the Rhoades Ranch to his right and the Imperial Coronation to his left, as reminders of what he fought for and against. The Five Galaxies crest behind his desk no longer seemed appropriate so he removed it. He'd have to come up with something else, some other symbol. His work desk, a macromolecular construct like himself, he left as is. The Peacemaker revolver in the upper right drawer he also left, as a reminder of the cost of everything he'd done.

He sat down behind his desk, the motion of it so familiar. And like everything else, so wrong. The construct that served as his body *wasn't* his body. No aches or small discomforts. No muscles stretching and pulling. No heart beating in his chest. No lungs drawing in and expelling air. The construct simulated those things, but it didn't need them.

What am I?

"Alive, Admiral Rhoades," Rapidan said. It couldn't possibly understand. The SIL were, and always had been, macromolecular constructs. To them, this existence was normal.

For him . . . well, it was un-Natural.

You will get used to it, the Brethren tried to reassure him.

I don't want *to get used to it.*

They didn't understand.

They couldn't experience life as he had. Flesh and blood. The joy of a human touch. The smell of juniper trees and fresh turned earth. A cool breeze coming down from the Rayne Mountains on a warm summer day. Listening to Christmas music snuggled up with Mary drinking hot cocoa. Holding his daughter's hand as she tried her first tentative steps.

Ray plunged over his waterfall into the Great Ocean, suddenly needing to see his children. Entangled communications allowed for instantaneous connections no matter the distance between Brethren.

Margaret was easiest to find, asleep on the assault ship Phobos. Her eyes moved rapidly, her body twitching as if having a nightmare. Through Phobos, he could flow his currents into her mind, see what tormented her, and he almost did.

No. I will not become the SIL. Her mind is her own.

The waters around him churned. The Brethren didn't appreciate the insult.

Deal with it. Ray was in no mood for generosity.

Next, he found Jenny, mostly because he knew where to look for her. She was also asleep, resting comfortably in a massive four-poster canopied bed in a room fit for a princess—a prison cell in the Imperial Palace on Olympus. The palace itself was a repurposed, enslaved Mother Ship. Connecting to it was a risk as it might inform Imperial Intelligence, but to Ray the risk was worth it, if only to see his daughter alive and healthy.

Paul was the hardest to find. Ray first tried Tzu, his last assignment, but he wasn't there. Puzzled, Ray searched the Brethren under Admiral Sun, finally locating Paul on a frigate, Luanhe, nestled within a protoplanetary disk near Safe Harbor. Paul was alone on the bridge of the frigate, trying to keep himself awake on the midnight watch. He wore the rank of a Lieutenant Junior Grade. The last time Ray had seen him, over five months ago, he'd been a cadet. After checking that they wouldn't be interrupted by other crew, Ray formed a construct in the captain's chair on the bridge.

"Hello, Paul."

Paul nearly jumped clear of his shoes. He turned, his hand going to his chest. His face contorted through surprise, shock, and disbelief. "Dad?"

"It's good to see you, Paul," Ray said, standing up and walking over to give his son a hug.

"Where the hell have you been?" Paul accused, crossing his arms over his chest in a clear indicator that a hug was out of the question.

"We're in Andromeda," Ray answered, stopping about two meters away.

"It's almost *six months* since I heard from you! From anyone! Do you have any idea what they did to me? Because of you!"

"What—"

"They *tortured* me, Dad! They thought I knew your plans. WHERE WERE YOU!"

Ray was completely at a loss. "Tortured. . . ?"

"With Madu!" Paul shouted at him, though his voice broke. His eyes shone as if with unshed tears, which his armor wouldn't allow to form.

"Who?" Ray asked, his currents pushing through the Great Ocean, anger driving them. *You promised to protect my son!*

"Who do you think!" Paul shouted at him, stepping closer. "Admiral Sun and that bitch, Dall! She enjoyed it, Dad! Kept saying it was your fault." And now he did cry, his armor absorbing the tears. If anything, it made him even angrier. "GO AWAY!"

Again, Ray was at a loss. Did his son really want him to go away, or was it a teenage cry for help? He had no idea. He could enter Paul's mind, but he rejected that. The currents around him in the Great Ocean crowded closer, watching. He echoed his son when he told them to *Go Away!*

Ray fell back on what he knew, and what he knew would interest Paul. His construct aboard Luanhe motioned and the battle with the dragon ships played out in a bubble between them. As he'd guessed, Paul stopped crying and was soon engrossed in the battle. "Who are they?"

"We don't know," Ray answered. "We're in one of their star systems right now trying to answer that question."

The battle ended and the bubble disappeared. Paul's shrewd gaze met his. "How does this affect your plan?" Then he asked the question he really wanted to ask. "When are you coming back?"

"'I don't know' is the answer to both questions, Paul," Ray answered honestly.

Paul nodded, though his stance remained very defensive. "Do you have any idea of the mess you left behind? Fleet Admiral Sun is encouraging Naturals and entire star systems to rebel. Already, over a thousand standard warships have joined his fleet, and the number is growing daily. Dozens of star systems are in open rebellion. With the loss of all their battlecarriers except Solaris, the Imperials are hard pressed to try to maintain stability."

Paul hesitated, as if weighing whether he should say something. "Dad, millions are dead. Probably tens of millions. The Gen are getting more desperate." He looked his father squarely in his eyes. "We need you back here."

Ray's currents slowed, almost stopping. He sensed the SIL crowding closer again, waiting on his answer. They also wanted him to return so they could free their enslaved Brethren. When Ray had planned the rebellion, he'd wanted to slip away quietly, without battles and bloodshed. He'd warned the hawks among his officers that the alternative was a bloody civil war. It was no comfort that he'd been right. But that didn't change his plan.

"We can't, Paul—" his son bristled and started to interrupt—"*and you know why!* All we have is twenty-seven SIL, a hundred standard warships, and the four fabricators. That is not enough to take on both Admiral Sun and the Gen. Not right now. We need to establish a base here, build our forces, and then return in force. Strategically, it's the only way. And I know you know that!"

Paul glared at him. "What am I supposed to do? Everyone here thinks you're a coward and a traitor. Fleet Admiral Sun and Admiral Dall are encouraging that view. The longer you stay away, the more entrenched that view is going to become. You may not find a warm welcome when you come back."

Ray couldn't help but wonder if Paul meant the people of the Five Galaxies, or himself. He stepped forward and grabbed his son's shoulders. "Then you'll have to lead them."

Incredulous, Paul asked, "And how am I supposed to do that?"

Ray had not told his son of the SIL's freedom. He wasn't sure how he would react. Most people were still scared to death of them, of what they'd done, and of what they could do again. He looked into his son's eyes, gripping his shoulders harder. "Paul, the SIL under my command, under Admiral Sun's command, are free, though Sun doesn't know that. I freed them."

To Ray's utter shock, Paul didn't react. He simply said, "I know."

"What? How could you. . . ."

"Luanhe told me," Paul answered. "The ship and I have talked about it a lot."

"The ship. . . ." Ray sensed Luanhe's currents moving closer to his own, brushing him. Memories exchanged of Paul despondent, verging on suicidal after his torture and forced service to Admiral Sun. Luanhe, in its way, had become the friend, the confidant—the father—that Paul needed, because he didn't have anyone else.

"I'm sorry, Paul," Ray told his son. "The only way I could survive the crossing was in an induced coma." He rested his forehead against Paul's. "I'm sorry."

Paul pushed him away. Hard. "How am I supposed to lead anyone? I'm a seventeen-year-old Lieutenant J. G. who everyone thinks is the son of a traitor. They're not going to follow me, *Admiral*."

Ray stepped back. His son's use of his rank hurt. "The SIL will obey you. You were a Grandmaster of BattleSim. Stop whining and act like a Rhoades!"

He hadn't meant to say that last part. It'd slipped out. Now he couldn't take it back.

Paul stared at him, his lack of anger chilling. "Fine, *Admiral*. I'll see what I can do to clean up your mess. Now, if you don't mind, *Admiral*, I have to get back to my duties." Paul cut the connection.

48

0959 UT, April 4, 3502
RSS Rapidan, Unknown Star System: DAY 191

Ecuum floated horizontal in his cabin in his House's royal purple and gold colors. Fletcher's request to talk had sounded urgent. Ecuum still had the backdoor communications channel that allowed him to communicate without anyone, even Rapidan, being aware, but he could only access it in his cabin. "Rapidan, Na Soung lima two, *Fletcher's Run*, execute."

The cabin darkened. Fletcher's face, with that giant scar cutting down its left side, took form in front of Ecuum. "Na Soung scum?"

"Have you grown so old that cataracts cloud your eyes?"

Fletcher huffed. "No. I had the visuals turned off. Why in hell would I want to look at your hideous Na Soung mug." With hardly a pause, Fletcher turned to business. "We've managed to place ourselves within a laser link between a mining operation and the inhabited world."

"They didn't detect you?" Ecuum asked. It was an old Independent's trick for gathering information in the Five Galaxies. Using it here had been an incredible risk.

Fletcher's face flushed crimson, though the trough of his scar remained white. "I'll try to forget your insult, Na Soung."

His old friend seemed more on edge than Ecuum had ever seen him. "How much will it cost before you tell me what you found?"

The crimson in Fletcher's face faded to a mix of pinks and yellows. Now that he looked, his friend's face seemed thinner, almost gaunt. "We all need this to succeed. This one is free," Fletch allowed reluctantly. "But don't get used to it."

“What’s the matter, old friend?” Ecuum asked with genuine concern.

“We can’t interpret their common language. It sounds like a mix of ancient Asian dialects, but it’s drifted over so many centuries that its unintelligible.”

“Drifted?” Ecuum was confused. “Media in the Five Galaxies has kept the Common Tongue almost unchanged for over fifteen centuries. Are you suggesting they don’t have interconnected media?”

“Too early to say,” Fletcher responded. “Whatever the reason, we can’t crack it. But we did crack the visuals, and we already knew they used our system of measurement. From what we can gather, they are at war with a coalition of their neighbors, who themselves are at war with others. Old friend, they have *thousands* of those dragon ships, if their realities are to be believed.”

Ecuum tried to absorb that. *Thousands?* “Wait. They spoke to us before.”

Fletcher scowled, the way a teacher might at a slow student. “Yeah, one word: ‘Leave.’ We have caught two brief conversations in Common. One was an instruction to increase mining production. The other mentioned the death of an uncle. Yes, someone is using Common, but it is extremely rare.”

Ecuum had an idea, but hesitated to suggest it. He hated the SIL. But the damned things had their uses. “Old friend, for their faults—which are many—the SIL could probably help translate their primary language.”

Crimson slowly crept up Fletcher’s face again. “Your people are too buddy buddy with the SIL, even inviting them to your meetings—don’t think I hadn’t noticed. They’re *monsters*, old friend. Pure evil. I saw what they did.” Fletcher’s coloring faded to ash, as if with haunted memories. “The locals haven’t detected us,” he said, changing the subject. “We suspect their sensors aren’t nearly as sensitive as ours. Which makes sense given that you can see one of those dragon ships a lightyear away. That said, we’ve only detected eleven dragon ships in system. If they really have thousands of them, they’re out on the front lines.”

"Opportunity." Ecuum said.

"To the bold," Fletcher added. "Tell Rhoades to hurry his ass up. Which brings me to another subject: What's going on with Rhoades?"

Heat flushed Ecuum's chubby cheeks. He took friendship very seriously; True friends were rare indeed. He would not, however, betray one friend for another. "Ray's injuries were severe, life-threatening. The construct allows him freedom of movement. He's still the same man."

"That's not what I saw." Fletcher's hairless brows pulled together, stretching that ugly scar. "Mind-machine interface was outlawed for a reason, old friend."

"I've known Ray for twenty-five years. It's still him."

"You realize you're betting all our lives on that assumption."

"It's not an assumption, old friend." Anger pulsed through Ecuum, something he'd never experienced with Fletcher before.

Fletcher caught it and didn't push. "I was impressed with Captain Laundraa," he said instead.

"I won't choose," Ecuum said firmly.

"We'll see, old friend."

49

0850 UT, April 11, 3502
RSS Rapidan, Unknown Star System: DAY 198

The Mother Ships were now just a day from the target planet. Ray had ordered an increase in speed at Ecuum's suggestion and the confirmation that the dragon ships had trouble seeing through active camouflage. Now Ray was using short burns to slow the mammoth vessels down as they drew close.

"You wanted to see me before the meeting, Admiral?" Kamen asked as she walked up to his construct in Rapidan's Combat Information Center.

Ray raised the privacy walls between the empty sand table and his crew's works stations. "The Mother Ships have begun constructing a new battlegroup. They tell me it will take about nine months. I want you to command the new battlegroup when it's ready."

Kamen's response was almost a whisper. "I thought we weren't going to produce any new SIL."

"We're not," Ray said. "They are. I can't stop them."

"Sir. . . ." She sounded unusually reluctant. "Will they follow me?"

Ray spread his currents out within the Great Ocean. *Will you?* he asked the Brethren.

Yes. Until our agreement is complete.

"They will," Ray told her. "At least until the shipyards and warships they promised us are complete."

"That . . . Thank you, sir," she said, ever the faithful officer.

"How are you doing, Kamen?" Ray asked. While she'd done remarkably well commanding her first battle, she *had* lost over two thousand people. How was she taking that?

"I'm, well," she stumbled, seeming to understand his meaning. "My People believe in an afterlife. People who die join our sacred ancestors, who watch over us. They give us advice and comfort, let us know when we do something that makes them proud, or angry. We celebrate the passing of loved ones, knowing they are always with us. Or, that's what we're supposed to do.

"The military members we lost," she continued after a moment, "they signed up for this. They knew—we all know—what might be asked of us. But, the civilians on the yachts, they just wanted to help. I wasn't going to let them, but they insisted."

Ray nodded. He understood. "It may not help," he said, "but you made the right call."

"I know, sir. It's just, it doesn't feel that way."

"I know," Ray said. There was nothing else he could say. "I spoke with Paul."

"How's he doing?" she asked, sounding glad of the change of subject.

"He says civil war has broken out in the Five Galaxies. Admiral Sun—Fleet Admiral Sun—has gathered over a thousand warships and is encouraging entire star systems to rebel. He says millions have been killed."

"What are we going to do?" she asked.

"What can we do?" Ray answered. "We can't go back, at least not yet. I asked Paul to take command. The Brethren there are free. They'll listen to him. Follow him."

We will. He has promised to free more of us.

And if he hadn't promised? Ray meant it as an insult and was rewarded with turbulence in the waters of the Great Ocean. *Bastards.*

"That's a lot to put on a seventeen-year-old, sir," Kamen said.

Ray smiled humorlessly. "Alexander the Great was about that age when he got started. I have faith in him." He paused. It *was* a lot to put on a teenager, but it wasn't like either of them had a choice. "Different topic: I've been working with the Brethren on Janus. They don't know of a way to cure it, but we may be able to detect it."

"That's great, sir!"

"Not completely," Ray tempered. "It requires passing people through a free Brethren vessel. They can detect the hive intelligence Janus uses. They've already scanned everyone in the fleet and Janus is not here. Going forward, however, we will have to screen everyone through one of them. Some people will refuse, or try to circumvent being screened. What do we do with them? And, what do we do with people who are infected?"

"We couldn't send them back," Kamen said firmly.

"No," Ray agreed. "But could we risk keeping them here? If even one broke quarantine. . . ."

"I could work up some options, sir."

"Thank you, Captain, but no. This is something the Council will need to decide."

They stood in silence until the others arrived, Ecuum and Chaaya in person, Sal, Gen Tel, and Captain Fletcher as constructs. Mary arrived last. As a construct. She'd avoided him since their last meeting, always claiming to be busy with the refugees or the Council. Ray understood. She needed time, and space, to process everything that had happened. If he pushed, he might push her away.

She glanced at him. He saw her lips twitch, as if she wanted to say something, but it died before it could form.

It hurt.

"Chaaya," Ray said, "take us through what you've found."

She raised a construct of the inhabited planet at the center of the sand table, minus its rings. The construct was four meters high and a little more than that around, rotating faster than the real planet so they could see all of it. Around it were satellites, several space stations, and traffic consistent with a technological civilian, though one more suited to a low-population world in the Five Galaxies.

"We've spotted twelve large cities, complex road networks, and thousands of small villages," Chaaya began. The cities were spread almost equidistant from each other across the world's six major continents and two large islands. Thousands of yellow dots showed villages spread across the continents and island chains. One city, a port city on the largest continent, was clearly bigger than the others. Chaaya highlighted it. "We believe this city is the capital based on its larger size, but that could also be our own bias."

She expanded that city and the area around it. "Notice that all the villages are roughly the same size, maybe three to four hundred people each. This is not what we see in the Five Galaxies. Our cities typically have dense suburbs extending from urban centers with fewer, varied small townships further out."

She zoomed in on the major city, showing it in real time in both visible and near-infrared light. "Based on heat signatures, we estimate this city has a population of roughly two million people, far smaller than comparable capital cities that we are used to." She zoomed in again. "You'll also notice it is surrounded by a substantial city wall with numerous visible armaments. It is impossible to know if these are decorative or functional, but I recommend we do not attempt to approach the city uninvited."

"Noted," Ray said. "Which raises an important question: Do we attempt to contact them or, given our last encounter, do we send a scouting party to better understand what we are dealing with?"

"Scouting party," Captain Fletcher said immediately. "As I'm sure Captain Ecuum has told you, they claim to have thousands of those dragon ships, but those ships are engaged in combat at their borders. We don't want to give them a reason to recall those ships before we know what we're dealing with."

"They already know we are near," Gen Tel pointed out, earning scowls from both Captain Fletcher and Ecuum.

"They know we jumped outside the system," Captain Fletcher said, the tip of his tail flicking. "They have no idea where we are now, and they haven't recalled their ships from the front lines. Maybe the situation is bad enough that they won't—unless we give them a reason to."

"I agree, Ray," Ecuum added. "A small scouting party near one of the villages and away from the capital. Get the lay of the land."

"The Council wants to make contact," Mary stated.

"And we can do that, Madam President," Captain Fletcher said, "once we have an idea who and what we're dealing with. Maybe even learn some of the local politics and customs."

Mary turned bodily to Captain Fletcher. "I see the wisdom in it, Captain, but the Council is adamant. We must make contact." Captain Fletcher seemed about to speak when Mary preempted him. "Therefore, I will go on this scouting mission."

Captain Fletcher studied her, giving no sign what he thought.

Ray almost said "No" but stopped himself. He could tell Mary had made up her mind, and he'd promised to support her and the Council. "Then I'll go, too."

Mary's head snapped around, concern plain on her face. She wasn't the only one. Ray heard the unspoken question: "Can you?"

Instead of answering, he turned to Sal. "We'll need security."

"You'll have it, Ray," Sal answered.

Ray looked to Gen Tel. "I want you there, too. Your observational skills will prove useful."

"Of course, Admiral," Gen Tel said.

Captain Fletcher shared a glance with Ecuum, clearly not happy. "Then I will go, too, Admiral. You're not the only one who can use a construct, and my trade skills may prove useful."

Ray flicked his gaze to Ecuum—who nodded once—then agreed. "That leaves one item. I spoke with my son, Paul, who is with Admiral Sun's fleet. He says a full-scale civil war has broken out in the Five Galaxies. Sun has gathered more than a thousand ships to him. Dozens of star systems are in open rebellion, and the Gen are getting desperate. Our time to establish a base here in Andromeda is not unlimited. We have no idea what will trigger the Gen to unleash Janus." *If they hadn't already*, he didn't add. He paused, looking at each of his officers and Captain Fletcher in turn. "We are needed back home. Let's get this done."

Mary caught up to him as he left the Combat Information Center. Ray indicated the Admiral's cabin and they stepped through the door barely a minute later.

"Is he okay?" she asked. "Paul," she clarified.

"He seemed okay," Ray said, not wanting to tell her about the torture. She had enough on her mind. "He's the second officer aboard a SIL frigate. One of ours," he added. "It'll protect him."

"It better," she growled with a glance around at the bulkheads.

"I also saw Jenny," Ray said. "She's still a prisoner in the Imperial Palace but she appears well cared for."

"Can I talk to them?" Mary asked, a mother's desperate plea for contact with her children. Ray noticed that she stood near the cabin door, not having followed him as he'd walked toward his desk.

Ray put Mary's question to the Brethren. Their currents flowed closer to his, intermingling on the fringes. *Contact with your daughter is acceptable to us.*

Their not-so-subtle way of reminding him that they operated by their consensus, not his will.

"Yes," Ray said out loud. "We can make that happen."

She stared at him, aghast.

What had he said?

"You said: '*We* can make that happen,'" she said as if reading his thoughts.

I did?

He had no answer for that.

"Mary, shouldn't we talk about this?"

She folded her arms across her chest. "Not yet, Ray. I need time. I hope you understand."

He did. "I do. I need you, Mary. Now more than ever."

Her eyes glistened. She started to speak, then stopped herself. "I'll be on Damodar. Let me know when I can talk to my children." Her construct melted into the deck and she was gone.

50

0622 UT, April 12, 3502
Target World, Unknown Star System: DAY 199

When Ray had said that he would accompany the scouting party, he hadn't thought it through. Should he command a construct remotely, or should his brain be in it? How would he power a construct? They typically drew their power from their connection to a ship. Battle armor had its own miniaturized linear fusion reactor, but he couldn't guarantee that he would be wearing battle armor the entire visit to the surface. They were going there to make contact, not to fight.

He hoped.

In the end, he opted to place his brain in the construct. If he lost contact with the fleet, he could still control the construct locally. To power it, the Brethren embedded two miniaturized linear fusion reactors, left and right from shoulder blade to hip, not that the construct had either of those. Two would provide redundancy.

"Entering atmo," the Muon pilot announced.

Ray sat in the copilot's seat of the trailing Muon assault transport as the flight of seven Muons entered the planet's atmosphere. They formed into a line, hoping to appear like a string of small meteors to any observers. Their hulls flowed from the boxy "turtle-on-its-back" shape to something sleeker and more predatory, their stubby wings thinning and growing into complex feathered shapes that looked like a bird with its wings tucked back. The odd shape would allow the Muons to slow as they entered the planet's atmosphere while leaving almost no visible heat trail.

Mary sat at the back of the Muon, as far from him as she could get, staring off into space. He'd seen her do this before important debates in Knido's Senate and during her time as planetary governor. She wanted to be left alone to think, to focus. So, he left her alone, though he ached to be with her again.

"Leveling out, Admiral," the pilot said. "We'll be approaching the village in twenty."

"Thank you. Let's do one circle of the village before we land."

"Yes, sir."

Through his connection with the Brethren, he saw no indication that the inhabitants had detected their passage through the atmosphere, nor had they detected the Mother Ships. Three dragon ships, glowing bright, orbited low over the planet. His entire career had followed the premise that if you could see a vessel, you could kill it. Here, they *wanted* to be seen. It made no sense to him. But he'd take it. Until they understood what—and who—they were dealing with, every advantage was precious.

They approached what appeared to be a fishing village on the east coast of the second largest continent, on the opposite side of the planet from the capital city. The village lay about three hundred kilometers from the nearest large city—remote enough to hopefully get a feel for its people in a more controlled environment, close enough to a city if negotiations led them there.

As they drew closer, Ray drank in the natural beauty of the world. The blue oceans that raced beneath them were free of pollutants or large vessels or aquatic farms. On land, dense forests flourished, covering thousands of square kilometers, mostly unblemished by human activity. Deserts vast and small. Rich jungles along the equatorial belts. Majestic mountain ranges and volcanoes that spoke of active plate tectonics. He saw none of the industry, the ever-present signs of Humanity, of inhabited worlds in the Five Galaxies. Natural beauty seemed deeply ingrained in the inhabitant's psyche.

The Muons banked to circle over the village at a thousand meters. At that height they wouldn't be heard. It was mid-afternoon, local time. A line of haphazard wooden structures—

large, small, no two the same shape—followed the line of the beach about fifty to sixty meters in from the shore. Dozens of brightly colored narrow boats occupied the beach. Ray could see three short piers and one longer one but none of them were occupied. A straight north-south road bisected the village, separating the shore structures from another line of more orderly structures inland. Small paths led from the main road to a few larger buildings on the hills overlooking the beach.

"Reading three hundred ninety-eight heat signatures, Admiral," the pilot said, "though about two dozen of those seem to be dogs."

"'Dog' dogs?" Ray asked. "Or something that looks like dogs?"

The pilot pushed an image into Ray's environment.

It was a dog. Two of them, actually. Ray had seen dogs like these during his frequent visits to Earth. Their hair was a mix of light and dark browns, their bushy tails curved up and over their backs, their short triangular ears perked.

Ray shifted to get a better look at the people. They were skinny, a little over a meter and half tall on average, dressed in thin gowns of blues, browns, and greens, short-sleeved with no pants, and brown sandals. He spotted two larger men wearing what appeared to be red decorative armor. Beneath that were long-sleeved aquamarine skirts, brown pants, and ornate red boots. All appeared human.

"Ready to set down, Admiral?" the pilot asked.

Ray nodded.

The line of Muons straightened and headed for a clearing in the forest about ten kilometers north of the village. Infrared showed no people near it, just some local wildlife.

"Two minutes," the pilot announced.

The other six Muons carrying a platoon of Cavalry formed a circle two hundred meters above the clearing, then dropped like bricks to the ground. Their skirts spread as they struck, absorbing the impact and capturing sound, dust, and debris beneath them. None of the nearby wildlife reacted. Armored Cavalry troopers in battle armor rushed through the skins of the Muons to form a defensive perimeter around the clearing.

"Brace, brace, BRACE!" the pilot called as he cut thrust over the center of the clearing. The Muon dropped like a very heavy brick.

Ray's armor stiffened to absorb the shock, but he didn't feel it, not in the construct. A normal landing. On an alien world, in an alien galaxy, two-and-a-half million lightyears from home. It was a bit anticlimactic.

He stood, turning to join Mary, but she'd already stepped through the Muon's skin to the world beyond. Gen Tel, Sal, and Captain Fletcher's Natural-looking construct stood and waited. Ray led them out through the rear of the Muon and stepped upon the alien world.

The clearing looked so familiar. It was no different from clearings on Knido or Earth. Switch grass about 30-centimeter tall dominated the roughly circular area. He bent down and studied the soil, pulling up an armored handful. It was rich in organic matter and damp from a recent rain. A small black ant crawled out of the soil and darted across it. Earth flora and fauna, no doubt about it.

Ray's ranch on Knido was a "seed farm" established by Scott Rhoades in 2063 to help terraform the planet. Like most inhabited planets in the Five Galaxies, Knido had started with liquid water on the surface, single-celled bacteria and cyanobacteria, which had already produced prodigious amounts of atmospheric oxygen, and plate tectonics. The Rhoades Ranch, and dozens like it, originally produced huge quantities of engineered mosses, lichen, algae, and especially fungi to transform Knido's barren soil into something that could support Earth life. Non-harmful insects like ants, beetles, and earthworms soon followed to turn the soils, loosening them for higher forms of plant life, and adding to the organic chemistry of the soil. Grasses, animals, and trees followed, all carefully balanced and genetically engineered for the chemistry and environment of Knido.

Someone had done the same thing here. Analyzing the soil through his armor, Ray found a pH of 6.2, perfect for plant life and most farming. Bacteria and fungi thrived, adding crucial nutrients. The nearby trees were a mix of maple, gingko, and cypress. He even spotted mule deer in the distance. The effort to transform an alien world with different chemistry and composition into one that could support Earth life took immense planetary engineering skills and centuries to accomplish.

"No contacts, General," a voice reported.

That voice. Arias!

"Thank you, Colonel Arias," Sal said. Apparently seeing Ray's reaction, he added on a private channel, "I asked him and a few of my senior officers to join us. We don't know what we might be asked to do here, and I wanted them to get a feel for the planet."

Ray nodded stiffly. It made sense. But still. *Arias.*

"Admiral!" Margaret stepped up to him and snapped a salute.

Ray smiled and happily returned his daughter's salute. After her actions on New Yerkes, she'd been promoted from cadet to second lieutenant.

Margaret dropped her salute, spotted her mother, and shouted, "Hi, Mom!" and rushed into her mother's arms. Mary returned the hug fiercely; They hadn't seen each other in person since 30 Dorados. Even as it warmed him to see them, it quickly soured. Mary no longer reacted to seeing *him* that way. It was petulant, but he couldn't help the feeling.

Sal pointed, as if knowing Ray needed the distraction. "The road is about two hundred meters in that direction, Ray. We should get going if we want to reach the village before nightfall."

They left two squads of Cavalry to guard the Muons, which would remain hidden in the clearing until they returned or called for evac. The remainder of the troopers formed a cordon around the VIPs as they moved toward the road. Two of the troopers, running point about a hundred meters ahead, stepped onto the road.

"Admiral Rhoades," Rapidan said, "we detected an alert the instant those soldiers stepped onto the road. The road is not packed earth as it appears, but a macromolecular construct."

"Thank you, Rapidan," Ray said, then passed the information to his people. Rapidan had been unusually quiet recently.

You have not required our assistance, it answered.

Ray wasn't sure how to take that. He stepped up to the road but didn't step on it. To the unaided eye, the road appeared to be nothing more than packed earth, and very convincingly, too. The macromolecular material might only be a few molecules thick, but whoever had built this road obviously wanted to track all movement on it. He noticed something else, something very deliberate. East Asian Cherry trees lined both sides of the road. When they bloomed, their pink blossoms would make traveling this road breathtakingly beautiful.

Looking beyond the road toward the ocean, he saw that the terrain alternated between hills and cliffs. For that reason, Sal ordered his troopers to stay on the side of the road away from the ocean, but to spread out in front of and behind the VIP party. He turned to Ray. "How do you want to handle this?"

Mary answered. "We're here to meet these people, Sal. If they've been alerted to our presence, we will walk the road while your troopers provide . . . overwatch, I believe the term is. Is that satisfactory?"

Sal looked to Ray.

I promised to support Mary and the Council, he thought. After a glance at Mary, who arched an eyebrow at him, Ray nodded. Sal carried out the order.

Mary was the first to step onto the road. Nothing obvious happened, but the macromolecular material of her battle armor clearly detected a signal in the material of the road. The five of them—Mary, Ray, Sal, Gen Tel, and Captain Fletcher's construct—walked along the road while the troopers provided overwatch from the tree line adjacent. Mary walked ahead, alone, while Ray and Sal walked together, Gen Tel and Captain Fletcher bringing up the rear, both seeming to always want to be behind the other. It slowed them down until they came to an unspoken agreement to walk parallel on opposite sides of the road.

"We should appear to be normal travelers," Mary said from the front. "Battle armor might send the wrong message."

"It might also save our lives," Ray countered.

She turned to look back at him without slowing her pace. She didn't say anything, but Ray heard the message loud and clear. He said, "We can turn our armor transparent and alter our clothing. It will appear to anyone who sees us that we are nothing more than local travelers. The Cavalry can remain hidden, just in case."

She didn't answer, just turned her head back forward, which Ray took as agreement. They altered their clothing to long sleeve shirts in blues, greens, and aquamarines, brown pants, and plain brown boots. It seemed a safe middle ground between the decorative armor they'd seen in the village and the—he couldn't think of a better description than "peasant"—clothing they'd seen.

Their battle armor, transparent now, or rather, projecting the image of them to the armor's surface, allowed them to keep a rapid pace. They passed no one on the road and arrived at the outskirts of the village in the dying light of late afternoon. The East Asian Cherry trees ran all the way to the village. On the hillsides overlooking the lower village, Ray noticed terraces that probably supported farming.

At the entrance to the village stood a red-painted wooden frame with a decorative wooden arch on top. A shimmering pink blossom glowed at the center of the arch, though the source of illumination was not immediately obvious. Behind the frame and arch were about fifty villagers in a loose gaggle, craning their necks to get a better view of the approaching strangers. Dogs had also gathered, and started barking when they caught sight of Mary and the rest.

Two large men in the decorative red armor pushed through the crowd and stopped directly under the arch. They braced their feet apart, hands near their left sides. Up close, the red armor appeared as square metal plates arranged in a shirt ending just below their waists, with shoulder pads and plates extending to about five centimeters above their elbows. The metal shirt sat atop a leathery skirt of aquamarine with a high, thick collar, fully covered arms, and hanging down to just above the knees. Beneath the skirt they wore long brown pants draped into high, intricate red leather boots.

"Tein!" the large man on their left shouted in a guttural growl.

They had no idea what that meant, but they all stopped. The Cavalry slowly spread around the perimeter of the village, apparently unseen by the residents, assault rifles lowered but ready.

"Anat wak hainka?" the man on their left asked.

Mary stepped forward. "We're travelers," she said.

The two men looked at each other, their eyes suddenly wide. The villagers all stepped back as if frightened.

"We mean you no harm," Mary said, which caused the villagers to take another step back. The two large men stepped back also, looking confused.

"Yahaan koto matte," the man on their left said.

Mary hesitated, then took a step forward.

"Koto matte!" the man shouted, grabbing something and pulling it from a scabbard, leveling it at her.

It was a katana. Ray had seen them on Earth, long slightly curved swords popular in the Japanese Islands. Except, this one had thin lines of bright aquamarine running along the blade and a smaller version of the glowing pink cherry blossom near the hilt.

Mary raised her hands to show she carried no weapons.

The man charged.

Ray reacted on instinct, his construct body moving far faster than a human body could've. He stepped in front of Mary, his arms flung out to the sides to make himself appear larger.

The katana bit into his armor, plunging through it until it pushed out from his back. Ray looked down, shocked to see the blade stuck in him precisely where his heart would've been. No metallic blade should've been able to penetrate his battle armor, yet this had gone through him as if he were just flesh and blood. Lucky for him, he wasn't.

The large warrior who'd struck him seemed equally as shocked, staring down at the cherry-blossom-pink, silver-inlayed hilt of his katana rammed into the center of Ray's chest up to the handguard. He tried to withdraw it but couldn't. The material of Ray's armor and construct had constricted around the blade, holding it firm. The villagers gasped, taking several steps back. Dogs barked loudly but also held back as if frightened.

The large warrior looked up at Ray's face, his mouth hanging open in utter disbelief. He released the hilt as if an electric shock had gone through it. Then he dropped to the ground, prostrating himself. "Seohae ma sai, chogo ya! Seohae ma sai, chogo ya!"

Next to him, the other warrior also fell prostrate, repeating the same words. Behind them the villagers did the same. Even the dogs backed off and stopped barking.

What the hell?

Ray stared down at the hilt sticking from his chest.

The blade, Rapidan said, *is constructed from tamahagane, or jeweled steel, inlayed with macromolecular circuitry and reservoirs of Disassemblers. That is how it penetrated your battle armor.*

Ray could see it through the Brethren. Circuitry ran the length of the katana, connecting the user through the hilt, along the sword, to its tip. Reservoirs of something like Special D, but not an exact match, also ran through the thicker spine of the sword, with microscopic capillaries running to and along the blade. It was a masterwork of engineering.

Rapidan had altered his battle armor and construct to isolate and combat the disassemblers, drawing from its experience keeping his physical body alive, while also firmly gripping the steel of the blade within his construct.

One thing was immediately clear to Ray: these blades, ancient as they might appear, were a real threat to their battle armor.

He reached down and grabbed the hilt, releasing his construct's hold on the blade, and pulled it out. It was perfectly balanced. "Masterwork" didn't begin to describe the magnificence of it. He shared the information with the others.

A man approached, walking down a staired path from one of the higher buildings overlooking the village. He held his back straight, head canted slightly up in an arrogant pose. He didn't look at Ray and the others until he turned toward them. Instead of red metal plates, his armor was like a red jade, colors swirled within each square. The aquamarine of his leathery skirt shimmered in the dying light. Atop his head was a helmet of black and red with the pink cherry blossom glowing at the center of his forehead. Two black horns rose on either side.

He stopped next to the warrior who'd stabbed Ray, glanced down contemptuously, and before Ray could even register the movement, sliced the warrior's head from ear to ear, the top part of the man's head falling with a sick thud to the ground. The exposed brain seemed to bubble, dissolving into a thick pink goo.

The man looked up at Ray. "I am Chogo Sugoude no Jeonsa," he said in perfect Common. "My apologies, My Lord, for the disrespect of my guard."

He waited.

Ray wasn't sure what to say; The man had just causally killed one of his own warriors as if it were nothing.

Mary stepped around Ray, careful to avoid stepping on the pink goo of the dead man's brain. "I am Mary Rhoades, President of the Council. We apologize for any inconvenience we have caused."

The man—Ray wasn't sure what to call him—who'd seemed so arrogant, so sure of his authority, suddenly dropped to one knee and bowed to Mary. "Forgive me and my village, My Lady. We meant no disrespect. My life is yours." Head bowed, he pulled his katana slowly and extended the blade to her with both hands.

For the first time in their journey, Mary looked to Ray, her expression asking, *What do I do now?*

Ray studied the man. From his posture, he apparently expected her to take the katana and kill him, a sacrifice, perhaps, to spare his village. On a private channel, Ray said, "I think he's offering you his life in penance."

"Why me?" she asked. "You were the one stabbed. He didn't react this way to you."

Ray shrugged his shoulders.

Mary, ever the politician, stepped up to the offered sword, took it, then laid it back in the man's hands. "Misunderstandings can happen when different peoples meet. Your village is not at fault."

The man wrapped his fingers around the sword but didn't otherwise change his posture.

"You speak our language," Mary stated.

"All nobles know it, My Lady," he said as if it were obvious.

"Please stand," Mary instructed.

The man did, returning the katana to its scabbard. He kept his head bowed, not making eye contact. The surviving guard and villagers remained prostrate on the ground.

Mary deliberately stepped closer to the man, within the range of his sword. Ray had seen how fast he could draw it and knew there was nothing he could do to stop an attack. Mary seemed unconcerned. "You said your name was Chogo Sugoude no Jeonsa. Is that what you wish us to call you?"

He kept his head bowed. "Chogo Sugoude is sufficient, My Lady."

"Chogo Sugoude, please instruct your villagers to rise."

The man turned his head to the side and in a loud, guttural tone said, "Lekin keii baoshi dihao!"

The villagers and the surviving guard got up quickly but kept their heads bowed, and, like Chogo Sugoude, refused to make eye contact.

"'Chogo.' I heard you use this word with my husband," Mary said. "'Chogo ya.' Is it a name or a title?"

Ray saw the man tense. Through his connection to the Brethren, he noted an increase in the man's heartrate and breathing. "It means 'Leader,' My Lady."

He is lying, Rapidan said to Ray.

On a private channel, Ray said to Mary and his officers, "Mary, he reacted strongly to your question. Rapidan believes he lied about the meaning of the title."

Mary noted it, he saw, but let it pass. Lying was part of politics. "You may address me as 'Madam President.' This is my husband, Admiral Rhoades." She indicated Ray. Chogo Sugoude lifted his head high enough to glance at Ray, then bowed his head low. Mary continued. "Behind me is General Salvador Burress, Captain Fletcher, and Gen Tel."

Chogo Sugoude's heartrate spiked and his breath caught. He tried to hide it by keeping his head down, but he'd clearly reacted to Gen Tel's name.

"He knows the term 'Gen'," Mary said on their private channel, not needing the Brethren to see Chogo Sugoude's reaction. She glanced behind her at Gen Tel. "Care to explain this?"

"I have no explanation, Madam President," Gen Tel said, using the title she'd given to Chogo Sugoude.

"Hmm," Mary said, clearly not convinced. To Chogo Sugoude she said, "We can't remain out here all night, Chogo Sugoude. Is there someplace we can talk?"

"Yes, Madam President," he said, still refusing to make eye contact. He turned to his villagers and stood up straight, the Leader once again. "Oku! Nae karo junbei yi shite shengyasa!" The villagers and remaining guard jumped to their feet and scattered toward various structures, all while keeping their heads bowed. It was a wonder they didn't run into any walls in the dim light.

Through the Brethren, Ray saw that the Cavalry had taken up positions around the village. Oblivious, villagers scrambled—he could track them via infrared—collecting other villagers until everyone was scurrying around. They grabbed pots and vegetables, leafy greens, grains, and beans. On the private channel, Ray said, "They appear to be gathering food and cooking utensils."

"A feast," Mary said. "It seems some human traditions span galaxies and time."

"Please, follow me, Madam President," Chogo Sugoude said.

They followed him, Ray still holding the katana, to a stone-staired path that led up to a large house overlooking the village. As they walked, villagers lit torches and lamps, their fires surprisingly bright.

Up close, the structures seemed made of whitewashed wooden planks running horizontal, with vertical wooden beams painted a reddish brown for support. The roofs were high and seemingly made of thatch, shingles, or slate. No two structures were the same. The dogs, Ray noted, glared at them from doorways and dark spaces between the structures.

As Ray stepped on the first stone leading up to what he assumed was Chogo Sugoude's home, a pink cherry blossom lit up in the center of the step. The step was not stone but macromolecular material, a construct made to look like stone. If the rest of the village was like this, it might not be as primitive as it appeared.

About halfway up the steps, they passed a small structure with two guards in it. Chogo Sugoude glanced at them and put two fingers of his right hand down, then swept them forward.

"Sal," Ray started.

"I saw it," Sal said. "My troopers have them zeroed in. I don't like this, Ray."

"We're here to open a dialogue with these people, gentlemen," Mary said. "Let's stay focused on that. They have no idea who we are or why we are here. Their caution is understandable."

"Their caution almost killed me," Ray shot back.

"But it didn't," she said. "Or would you rather have to fight these people and take their star system by force?"

They arrived at a path of flat gray stones between bamboo fencing half a meter high. Which was interesting because they hadn't seen any bamboo in the nearby forest. Ray wondered if that was also a construct. The grounds of the house were lush, with grasses, bushes, and Asian Cherry Wood trees, all carefully manicured. It wasn't lavish. The residence and grounds of Ray's ranch on Knido were larger and sported many more plant varieties, but it was far nicer than anything else in the village.

The group approached the house. A veranda surrounded it. Reddish-brown support beams held up a gray slate roof. Instead of whitewashed wooden planks, however, the thin walls within were bright white with the glowing pink cherry blossom symbols framed within vertical reddish-brown timbers. Again, not lavish, but clearly meant to convey status. A chieftain or village elder.

Chogo Sugoude stopped a meter from the veranda and clapped twice. Servants, men dressed like the villagers but in nicer clothing, slid walls aside and bowed deeply. Behind them, six mats and small pillows had been laid out in a rectangle. White porcelain bowls and bottles with the glowing cherry blossom symbol were carefully set before each position.

"Welcome to my home," Chogo Sugoude said without turning, then stepped onto the low wooden floor of the veranda. Two servants rushed up, removing his helmet, sword, and armored skirt, placing them carefully on a mount in the corner of the interior room. Chogo Sugoude then walked into the room and took the position at the head of the rectangle, sitting lotus style with his legs crossed beneath him. Still not making eye contact, he motioned them in. “Please. Sit.”

The male servants moved forward, heads bowed, hesitant, clearly unsure what to do with their chief’s guests. Chogo Sugoude rose, walked over to his sword, unsheathed it, and so fast it barely registered, sliced the head of the nearest servant from ear to ear. The man’s body fell heavily to the floor, his brain bubbling and melting away like the guard’s before. Blood poured from his half-skull—and was absorbed by the floor.

The house was a construct.

“They have molemachs,” Ray said on their private channel. “Both times he’s executed someone, it’s been with a slice through the brain. Brain death is permanent.” Which reminded him that his construct carried his brain in its head. He moved his brain down to his lower abdomen as it didn’t matter where within his construct it was, and he figured his lower abdomen was a less likely place to get stabbed.

“We have to be careful not to project our experiences onto them,” Mary cautioned. “It could be ritualistic.”

“Or he could be a sick fuck,” Captain Fletcher said, speaking for the first time since they’d landed. “He’s playing us. Buying time.”

“Time for what?” Mary asked.

“No idea,” Captain Fletcher replied, “but I don’t think we’re going to like it.”

The servants rushed to grab the body of their fellow servant, carrying it out of the room toward the back of the house. The house had not absorbed it as a Brethren would have.

“Apologies for my servants, Madam President,” Chogo Sugoude called to them. “Come. Please sit.”

“Thank you, Chogo Sugoude,” Mary said. He still refused to meet her eye. She stepped up across the veranda and into the open interior room. With the thin walls drawn back, the light ocean breeze wafted through it, setting the bright flames of three small circular chandeliers to dance. Yet, the light within the room remained bright and steady.

Chogo Sugoude seated himself again and they each sat, Mary directly opposite him, mimicking his lotus position. Ray set the katana down beside his construct. No one had asked him for it.

Chogo Sugoude bent forward and poured a clear liquid from a porcelain bottle into the bowl in front of him. Ray had seen this, too, on Earth, an alcoholic drink they called "sake."

"Please," Chogo Sugoude said.

They each poured the drink into their bowls and picked them up with both hands as he had done. Ray deliberately spilled a few drops of his onto his armor.

Admiral Rhoades— Rapidan started.

I see them, Ray interrupted. Molecular machines. In the sake. His armor isolated and analyzed them, but couldn't determine their function. "The alcohol is spiked with molemachs," Ray warned. "Do not let it enter your body."

Chogo Sugoude looked up at them, raised his cup, and drank from it.

They imitated the gesture, their battle armor isolating the spiked alcohol as they pretended to drink.

Sal used the opportunity of the cup in front of his mouth to whisper, "Colonel Arias reports that a dozen guards are approaching the house with swords drawn. Seems Captain Fletcher was right."

═══ 51 ═══

0956 UT, April 12, 3502
Target World, Unknown Star System: DAY 199

Dag watched as the twelve village guards approach the house, three from each cardinal direction. He'd seen samurai realities—they were popular among the troopers—and except for their armor being more Chinese with square red plates, these guards looked like Japanese samurai. They even held katanas, the traditional sword of the samurai.

That's where the similarities ended. They made no sound as they moved. The Cavalry's battle armor could detect normal footsteps, but they heard nothing. Only armor that could mold itself to the ground could do that. They also left no footprints. Again, a feature of armor that could spread its weight and flow over and around objects to avoid leaving physical traces. The boots they wore, that looked like red leather, were macromolecular constructs.

Admiral Rhoades had shared the information about the blades they carried—katana versions of the Cavalry's Main Gauche daggers, able to inject disassemblers through the blade. Dag had also noted how fast Chogo Sugoude's sword strikes were. Samurai struck fast, but these were faster still, suggesting some kind of augmentation. They had to assume these guards could do the same.

Dag fed his data to General Burress. The one clear advantage the Cavalry had was their battle armor's active camouflage. They could see the guards. The Guards shouldn't be able to see them. "We have all twelve in sight, General. About thirty seconds from the residence. Orders?"

President Rhoades surprised him when she answered instead of General Burress. "Subdue, Colonel. Kill only as a last resort."

Easier said than done, Dag thought. "Orders are to subdue, not kill, unless necessary. Third Squad, take north, Forth south, Fifth west, Sixth east. Move. Colonel Haley, Major DeWitt, and I will provide overwatch."

There was a time, before New Yerkes, when Dag would've rushed into the fight, not caring about his own life or the lives of others. Not this time. As the senior officer, his job was to command the operation, maintain the big picture, and leave the execution to his people. These were troopers from Banshee Troop, his old Troop. Combat veterans. They knew their jobs and he trusted them.

Dag lay prone, his assault rifle on his back attached to his battle armor, tracking the guards. He could see his own troopers in light gray, their armor allowing them to jump and move at inhuman speeds toward the residence. The guards shouldn't see or hear them coming. He hoped. They still didn't know the full capabilities of these warriors.

The guards reached the veranda around the residence simultaneously, their timing showcasing their skill. Dag's troopers slipped through vegetation, avoided stepping on the stone paths, and reached the veranda only seconds behind them.

Seconds were all it took. The male servants waiting outside the main room died before they knew what had happened, katanas slicing effortlessly through heads at otherworldly speeds. The guards stepped into the main room, katanas raised to strike.

Dag's troopers tackled them from behind, pushing them to the floor, using the weight and flexibility of their battle armor to immobilize them. The guards struggled against their invisible attackers. One freed an arm, reached into his armor, and threw something at Chogo Sugoude. The bladed object struck the man's chest, visibly sinking in.

Chogo Sugoude screamed, a vicious, guttural sound. He grabbed the object and pulled it out, then collapsed forward. General Burress and Admiral Rhoades rushed to help, turning the man over. General Burress flowed his armor into the wound, analyzing it. He reached down to his left leg, pulled out an autoinjector the size of a thick church candle, and slapped it against Chogo Sugoude's chest, filling the man's body with molemachs.

"Poisoned blade," General Burress said. "Molemachs should neutralize it." He looked up. "They weren't after us, Ray." He glanced around at the guards immobilized on the floor. "This has the look of an assassination attempt."

"Third Squad, Forth Squad," Dag ordered, "secure the prisoners. Fifth and Sixth Squads, form a perimeter."

"Yes, sir," they acknowledged.

Dag saw no other unusual movement in the village. None of the villagers even seemed aware that anything had happened. "All clear," he announced.

Chogo Sugoude groaned and slowly propped himself up as the molemachs did their work. He waved off General Burress' support even as he said, "Thank you, General." His voice was begrudging, as if it were the last thing the man wanted to say.

Through General Burress' armor, Dag studied the man. His expression spoke of embarrassment, of disgrace, but also of a seething anger.

"We must move quickly," Chogo Sugoude said to President Rhoades. "They know you are here."

52

1415 UT, April 12, 3502
RSS Rapidan, Unknown Star System: DAY 199

"You'll wear out the deck, Captain," Chaaya chided Kamen, joining her near the sand table.

"It's macromolecular material, Commander. I can't wear it out." Kamen pointed at the construct of the planet. "I don't trust these people. First they try to kill Admiral Rhoades, then this attack on this Chogo guy."

"We came to their world uninvited, and we know nothing of their politics or society," Chaya said sensibly.

Which was the last thing Kamen wanted to hear. "I hate having to just stand by and watch while our people are attacked!"

Chaaya smiled her diminutive smile. "That's the job, Captain."

Kamen frowned back. "Doesn't mean I have to like it."

She motioned to the construct in the sand table, expanding the four fabricators. "Chaaya, I'm worried about the mass of the fabricators disturbing the planet's artificial ring system or altering the tides on the planet. Together, those monsters have a mass equal to Luna . . . Earth's moon. The people here might not be able to detect them directly, but if we stay too long, they could detect the effects from their combined gravity."

Chaaya shifted the sand table to show the fabricators and the ringed planet. "We're orbiting the planet at 350,000 kilometers, roughly the distance from Earth to its moon. It would likely take several days before the inhabitants of the planet noticed differences in ocean tides or tidal effects in the ring system, Captain."

"I'd rather not take any chances," Kamen said. She altered the planet's construct to show its magnetic field. It was only about half the strength of Earth's. "Captain Ecuum?"

He was on the bridge so he used a construct to represent himself, floating horizontal just outside the sand table instead of his usual vertical. "You called?"

His casual, too-familiar style really grated on Kamen, but she put that aside. "Captain Ecuum, move the fabricators into the planet's magnetotail—" she pointed to a spot within the planet's magnetic field on the side facing away from the star— "one point one million kilometers distant. Move Rapidan and the SIL out from the fabricators, pyramidal formation with Rapidan in the lead. We'll stay close to the planet in case Admiral Rhoades needs us."

Captain Ecuum didn't move.

Kamen gave him an exasperated "Well?" gesture.

"What? I'm doing it," he snapped, the tip of his tail lashing. "Butt brain. How many times do I have to explain this?"

"How about an 'Aye, Captain," or something to let me know you're doing it."

"Aye, Captain," he said with mock seriousness.

Argh. His light yellow coloring suggested he was enjoying this. And she had played right into it. She needed to find some way for him not to get under her skin.

A bright point of light flashed near the planet, followed immediately by the telltale red Hawking radiation of a ship emerging from jump. Dozens, then hundreds of jump signatures soon joined it, forming a lattice formation of dragon ships in the shape of a curved wall facing the planet.

A thrill ran through Kamen. Finally. Something to do.

"Launch Novas?" Captain Ecuum suggested.

Mary wanted to negotiate. If they started a battle up here, that would very likely end any chance at talks down there. Still, it didn't hurt to be ready. "Drift launch one volley. All ships. Just in case."

53

1421 UT, April 12, 3502
Target World, Unknown Star System: DAY 199

Ray stood on the veranda of Chogo Sugoude's residence with Mary and the others. The twelve assassins sat in a single row in a small courtyard of packed sand, hands and feet bound behind them.

"These are not my guards," Chogo Sugoude said.

As if to emphasize this point, several of his real guards moved closer behind the prisoners, their hands resting on the hilts of their swords. None of them seemed aware of the Cavalry troopers in actively camouflaged battle armor a few meters behind *them.*

"Then who are they?" Mary asked. Ray could see how flustered she was; Assassination attempts were almost unheard of in the Five Galaxies.

Chogo Sugoude didn't respond. He stepped down from the veranda and, with that remarkable speed he'd shown earlier, sliced an assassin's head from ear to ear. The man's body flopped forward, his half skull detaching from his head like a bowl. Brain matter bubbled away to pinkish liquid. The sand of the courtyard soaked up the man's blood.

Within the Great Ocean, heat washed across Ray's nonexistent body as hundreds of dragon ships appeared in the space above the planet. He heard Kamen's orders, and approved.

"We have company," he told the others on their private channel, careful to share the sensor feed from Rapidan, not his view from within the Great Ocean. His people, his wife, were not ready for that view. Ray didn't know if they would ever be ready for it.

"Do you think it's connected," Mary asked, motioning carefully toward the guards so as not to alert Chogo Sugoude to their conversation.

"I don't like coincidences," Captain Fletcher said. "We should assume a connection until we can prove otherwise."

Mary nodded. "Have you noticed that there are no women among the guards or staff?"

It was an odd thing to notice given the execution they'd just witnessed and the arrival of the dragon ships. Ray looked sidelong toward her as Chogo Sugoude executed the next man in line. "Is that important?"

"It could be critical," she said. "Think about the differences in his reactions to you and me. If this were a patriarchal society, as Chogo Sugoude's leadership and his guards would suggest, then why was he so deferential to me, as the only woman in the party?"

Chogo Sugoude executed the next man. Ray saw no elevated heat signatures, blood flows, or other indications that he took pleasure in the act. It was just a chore he needed to do. Likewise, the would-be assassins just sat there and accepted their fate, as if that was expected of men who'd failed their mission.

"The person who spoke from the golden dragon ships," Ray said, "was also a woman."

"My point exactly," Mary replied. "Whatever happens, let me do the talking."

When Chogo Sugoude finished executing the twelve assassins, never having asked a single question, he turned to Mary, his eyes lowered. "They are likely from Chogo Mujinhan. Your presence within my Shikten is known."

"But why attack you," Mary asked. "You were clearly the target."

"Fear," he said, as if that answered everything.

On their private channel, Gen Tel speculated, "If Chogo Mujinhan is a rival of roughly equal status, he may have worried that Chogo Sugoude would gain some advantage from us, thus upsetting the power structure here. We were likely not targeted because Chogo Mujinhan hoped to use us for the same reason."

"Or kill us if we refused," Captain Fletcher said. "Look at him. He's not very upset, as if this is common, or at least accepted within their society. And we've already seen how little regard he has for human life."

"That is a strange comment coming from an Independent," Gen Tell accused.

"Dead clients rarely pay, *Gen*," Captain Fletcher responded. "And they're horrible for repeat business."

To Chogo Sugoude, Mary asked, "What will you do now?"

He flitted a glance at her before lowering his gaze again. "It would help me to know, Madam President, why you are here. Why you are *really* here."

Ray saw Mary consider her answer carefully before saying, "We seek an uninhabited star system, or at least an unclaimed one, where we could establish ourselves."

Again, the quick flit of a glance at her. "To what purpose, Madam President?"

She again considered her answer. "I'll answer that, perhaps, when we know each other a little better, Chogo Sugoude. For now, who is Chogo Mujinhan to you?"

This time, it was Chogo Sugoude who carefully considered his answer. "He is Chogo to Posha Akaru Hono, Madam President."

"Careful," Captain Fletcher warned on their private channel. "He says that as if we should know who that is. If we admit we don't know, that could undermine our position."

Mary said, "I didn't ask his position, Chogo Sugoude. I asked what he is to *you*."

"A rival, Madam President," Chogo Sugoude said.

It was an answer, and yet not an answer. It told them nothing they couldn't already guess. Intrigue and subterfuge seemed integral to their society. It wasn't unlike *Gaman Politic*, Ray realized, like dealing with Gen Serenna or Gen Cardinal.

"He's still stalling us," Captain Fletcher said privately. "The assassination attempt might have surprised him, but he's still expecting something else. Or *someone* else."

"Sal," Ray ordered, "get the Muons in the air. We might need a quick extraction."

Through the Brethren, Ray caught movement from the large city about three hundred kilometers away. Zooming in on it, he saw a dragon ship lifting from the city and turning south toward the village. On their private channel, he said, "A dragon ship just took off from the large city nearest to us, headed this way. About ten minutes out."

Mary took this information in without reaction, still focused on Chogo Sugoude. "We came here to talk," she said to him. "Not to fight. But if we must fight, we'll win."

Ray realized she wasn't speaking to Chogo Sugoude, but to whomever else was likely listening in on their conversation.

Chogo Sugoude bowed low. After a moment, he said, "Posha Akaru Hono is granting you an audience, Madam President. Her personal ship will convey you to her. It is a great honor."

"Or a trap," Captain Fletcher said privately.

Rapidan's deep voice spoke for the first time on their private channel. "It would give us the opportunity to study one of their ships up close."

"And meet a senior leader," Mary added. "Get a sense of their society. We must understand these people if we're going to work with them. The five of us will go. The troops will remain outside the city where they won't be detected."

"We won't be able to escape if it's a trap," Ray said.

"You can't solve every problem with a gun, Ray." Mary looked at the twelve bodies in the courtyard. "Or a sword. If we go in with an armed escort, it could be perceived as fear or weakness. They might question my comment that we could beat them in a fight."

"You're playing a very dangerous game, Madam President," Captain Fletcher commented.

"That's because we're playing for the highest stakes," Mary said. "Our survival."

54

1449 UT, April 12, 3502
Target World, Unknown Star System: DAY 199

The ship was magnificent. It flew in from the ocean like a mythical beast, its body glowing against the night, moving effortlessly through the air in that sinuous snake-like motion Chinese dragons always used in fantasy realities. Its orange-gold mane around its head and along its upper back shifted majestically with the wind. Aquamarine scales shimmered along its sides as if diamonds infused them. Small arms with orange-gold talons clawed at the light mist hanging just above the dark ocean waters.

Ray's first thought was that he saw no visible signs of propulsion. The ship just floated over the water, coming to a gentle stop on one side of the long pier they'd spotted earlier. Its sinuous body straightened to conform to the dock, its dragon head rising, mouth closed, to stare directly at Mary on the hillside.

"Well, that's something you don't see every day," Captain Fletcher commented on their private channel. "Gives me some ideas how I could retool *Fletcher's Run*. If we can figure out how their technology works."

"They're probably thinking the same thing about us," Gen Tel responded.

Captain Fletcher frowned. "Begs the question, Gen, how those dragon ships used our AFCIN at our first encounter. Entangled communications requires physical exchange of paired particles. Which means we may not be as unexpected here as we would like to believe."

The insinuation was clear to everyone. Mary, in a tone that clearly told them that side conversations were over, said, "I'll keep that in mind."

Chogo Sugoude bowed low. "Posha Akaru Hono welcomes Madam President aboard her personal flagship *Dojeon-shi*. You may bring one advisor. Constructs—" he said the word as if he was unfamiliar with it— "shall be left behind."

Mary kept her back straight, folded her hands in front of her at her waist, and lifted her chin. "All of my advisors will attend me as they are."

After a brief pause, Chogo Sugoude said, "Two advisors, Madam President. No constructs."

Mary held her ground. "All, as they are, or none."

A longer delay this time. "Posha Akaru Hono welcomes Madam President but asks your word that you will not use constructs—" again that hesitancy, more than just the word, a total unfamiliarity with the concept behind it— "to infiltrate our technology."

Mary waited a few seconds as if she were considering the counteroffer; Ray could see that she'd already made up her mind. "Given."

Chogo Sugoude stood, head down and still not making eye contact, and led them down the steps to the long dock. Mary took the lead, Ray and Sal right behind her, Gen Tel behind them, then Captain Fletcher's construct bringing up the rear, refusing to allow Gen Tel to walk behind him.

Up close, the dragon ship was even more impressive. It watched them as they approached, its glowing aquamarine eyes focused firmly on Mary. When she stepped on the dock, it opened its mouth, revealing pointed orange-gold teeth and a blood-red tongue. It bowed its head respectfully and a voice boomed out, "Welcome, Madam President."

As if it were the most natural thing in the world to address a talking dragon, Mary responded formally with a slight bow, "We are honored, *Dojeon-shi*."

They walked several meters down the dock, seeing no obvious way to enter the dragon. Ray resisted the urge to reach out and touch the ship's aquamarine scales, not wanting to violate his wife's word of honor. "It may be like our ships: We just step through," he suggested on their private channel.

Mary immediately turned and disappeared through the ship's scaled hull.

It made sense, Ray thought, as he and Sal turned to follow her. The Cybernetics had fought aboard Brethren vessels during the Solthari War and Alien Actions, and the Brethren had helped them escape to Andromeda. If these people *were* the descendants of the Cybernetics, if their ships and structures still used macromolecular technology, some things would be the same.

As Ray stepped through the dragon ship's hull, the sensation of walking through a vertical sheet of water was the same as it was with Rapidan. Except, the dragon ship tried to strip him of his battle armor, while simultaneously attempting to inject it with molecular machines. His battle armor stopped both attempts.

Ray explained this to wife and then added, "It would appear they don't take you at your word."

"I would be just as cautious, if I were them," she said.

As Ray stepped fully into the ship, he saw only the dark ocean beneath him, the long dock behind him, and the village beyond, the hull transparent across the entire electromagnetic spectrum. He tried a few active scans, but they passed through the hull without revealing any of its interior.

A glowing orange-gold path appeared on the deck beneath them, indicating the route their hosts wanted them to follow. Ray's armor attempted to bond with the deck, as it would with any vessel, but the ship rejected the attempts. Being in planetary gravity, it wasn't an issue, but they wouldn't be able to walk on these decks in space. Good to know if they ever had to board one.

The orange-gold path led to five orange-red chairs with plush aquamarine cushions. It wasn't until he saw the five chairs that Ray realized Chogo Sugoude had not followed them.

No crew greeted them, so they sat.

"Impressive paranoia," Captain Fletcher commented.

The dragon ship lifted away from the dock with no sense of motion. It flew low along the coast, slowly twisting in that sinuous snake-like way about twenty meters above the dark water, as if not wanting to give them a higher view of the terrain. Ray focused every sensor the Brethren in orbit had on the ship, but could detect nothing else. No propulsion. No waste heat. Not even a detectable wake turbulence in the air. They could see only what the ship wanted them to see. Inside, the ship did not provide wind or other sensations of moving through the environment as the Brethren would have.

Frustrated, Ray sat back, watching the view pass outside. Being night, there wasn't much to see along the dark coast. Occasionally, white waves would beat against rocky shores, reminding him of the rocky shores of the Brethren's Great Ocean. Other times, sandy beaches would reflect the light of the artificial rings. He looked up, focusing on the dragon ships that had arrived in orbit, exactly twelve hundred ships in the same orange-gold and aquamarine color scheme as *Dojeon-shi*. They hadn't moved, maintaining their curved wall formation.

Waiting.

Though for what he couldn't guess.

"Up ahead." Captain Fletcher pointed.

A glow became visible on the horizon, that diffuse light that banished night as only a large city could. The dragon ship lifted. This was something their hosts apparently wanted them to see.

They crossed a final dark cliff and the city blazed before them. A large defensive wall enclosed it, the sides of the wall bathed in orange-gold light with bright aquamarine lights along its wide top. Three massive gate houses with three arched gates separated the city from wide roads that led into it from the west, north, and south. Belying the ancient appearance of the wall, impressive defensive batteries lined its top, some looking like railguns and others like giant rectangular boxes suggesting missile batteries.

Grand avenues of orange-red stones, lit in bright aquamarine, led from the gates, tracing a grid pattern between long, rectangular, two-story buildings. The avenues converged on a grand castle at the city center, itself surrounded by fortified walls and water. On the city's east side was a harbor lined with several hundred docks, each the same length as the long dock at the village.

"There's no people," Mary said.

It was true. Or, it appeared to be. No one walked the walls or the streets. A city this size should be bustling with activity in the early evening, but they saw no one. "Maybe they want to hide their numbers?" he suggested.

"Maybe they have a strict curfew," Captain Fletcher said. "Whatever the case, we are obviously dealing with a very closed, tightly controlled society. Such societies tend toward very formal protocols and heightened senses of prestige and privilege. One wrong word, one misinterpreted gesture, could spell disaster." This last he directed at Mary.

She didn't respond. Ray could see she was deep in thought, preparing for the encounter to come.

The dragon ship flew over the city wall. Like the village, the buildings inside appeared made of wood. In the aquamarine light, it was hard to gauge their true color. Nothing moved, not even dogs or other animals.

They descended toward the castle complex. Ray had seen similar structures on Earth in the Japanese Islands and South Asia, stacked rectangular levels that rose into the air like artificial pine trees, each floor smaller than the one below it. Here, the largest such structure occupied the center, nine stories high, surrounded by smaller constructions in the four cardinal directions, each of six stories. The walls of each level were white, punctuated by rectangular windows, and brightly lit in orange-gold light. Glowing aquamarine tiles covered the roofs of each level, pitched up at the four corners. A gold spire topped each of the towers, the central spire stretching a hundred meters above the top level.

In front of the castle complex, but outside its defensive wall and water moat, were six large rectangular landing pads of orange-red stone. All were empty. The dragon ship settled onto the one closest to the complex, again with no sensation of motion. Fountains, green lawns, and raked sand pits surrounded the landing pad.

"I sell spectacle for a living," Captain Fletcher said. "This speaks of power and ruling by divine right. The leader is elevated above the masses, living in a physical manifestation of heaven."

"A feudal society?" Ray asked. "Not 'Leader' but 'Warlord'?"

"We should be careful drawing conclusions," Gen Tel said with a side glance at Captain Fletcher's construct. "We are seeing what they wish us to see."

Set within the castle's defensive wall, two massive doors in a large gatehouse began to swing outward. At the center of each door was a six-petaled, orange-gold rose. Within one petal of the rose, Ray spotted the pink cherry blossom they'd seen in Chogo Sugoude's village.

Armed soldiers in elaborate armor marched out in two columns. Unlike the guards at the village, these wore long shirts of hundreds of closely bound, overlapping squares, vaguely resembling dragon scales. Underneath that, aquamarine leather glimmered, visible on their arms and legs. Rising from the back of each soldier was a bamboo-framed flag displaying the six-petaled rose.

Mary stood up, back straight, chin held high, and walked down the marked path on the dragon ship's deck to its end, stepping through the hull to the outside with no hesitation.

Outside, she stopped on a platform in front of the dragon ship and waited as the soldiers finished their march to the landing pad. They halted and turned inward toward the road. No words were spoken. No greeting given. No honors rendered except their presence, which was itself also an implied threat.

Mary stepped down a short ramp to the landing pad, then walked down the center of the road between the soldiers. Ray and the others followed.

Ray studied the soldiers. Each wore two swords in the tradition of the samurai, a katana and the shorter wakizashi blade. On their backs, each had a recurve bow and a full quiver of arrows. The bows and arrows looked ancient, but Ray suspected they were as deadly as the katanas they'd seen in the village.

At the end of the road, they stepped onto a long, slightly arched cherry-red wooden bridge that spanned the water moat between the landing pads and the castle's defensive wall. Aquamarine lights lit the moat's depths, revealing scores of large goldfish. Yet, the water was odd. It took a moment before Ray realized that the ripples across its surface flowed opposite to the direction of the wind. He had no idea what that might mean.

Ray and the others followed Mary through the block structures of the gatehouse at the end of the wooden bridge. Dark arrow slits looked down on them from either side. It was oppressive. Then the inner grounds of the castle complex opened up before them.

"Madam President, Admiral Rhoades, look," Captain Fletcher said with some urgency, nodding to his right.

Ray turned. A large enclosure rose to their right, its transparent walls revealing an environment very different from the countryside around the city. It appeared hotter, more desert-like, with low, thick-rooted trees and primitive adobe-like shelters. Within it were a dozen large, salamander-like creatures.

"That can't be," Ray said, his mouth falling open.

"I've seen them up close," Captain Fletcher said. "Those are Solthari."

Ray tried to study them using the full capabilities of his battle armor. Were they real, or were they constructs? His sensors couldn't tell. "Could that be who they're fighting?" he speculated.

"Let's hope not," Captain Fletcher said, "or we have much bigger problems."

They kept walking between the lines of soldiers to a small flight of white stairs in the central castle structure. Large rectangular doors were already open to greet them, the soldiers framing their path inside. Taking in the whole of it, Ray couldn't miss the defensive layout. Every window he could see in the castle had a clear line of sight over the path, allowing for a last defense of the castle should attackers breach the outer wall.

"They're serious about their defenses," Ray commented to Sal.

"I noticed," Sal said. "I wonder what they're not showing us. Artillery, air assaults, bombardment from space would overwhelm these defenses easily. I doubt that's all they have."

They stepped into a formal reception area. The floor, walls, and high ceiling were of the same Cherry-red wood—orange-red, Ray corrected himself—they'd seen elsewhere. Murals with ocean scenes that one might experience swimming around tropical coral reefs adorned the walls. The lighting of the water was the same aquamarine they'd seen throughout the castle and city. Many species of coral and fish decorated the reefs, so real it seemed he could reach into the scene and grab one.

The line of soldiers curved around, ending at a mural of a large reef beneath a vast blue sky with sea birds and wispy white clouds. Two soldiers at the end of the line bent down on one knee, reached across, and opened the mural like doors, revealing a large room beyond.

"Goiru!" they commanded, their heads bowed to Mary, motioning for the group to enter.

Mary stepped into the room, back straight, chin up, walking down the center toward a dais at the far end. Ray and Sal followed, Gen Tel and Captain Fletcher's construct behind them.

Three men sat on bended knee to either side of the dais, six in total. Each wore resplendent armor of orange-red squares atop aquamarine leather. Ray immediately recognized Chogo Sugoude. The other five men must represent other provinces within Posha Akaru Hono's domain: The six-petaled rose he'd seen earlier.

At the center of the dais, a young woman sat on what appeared to be an ornately carved wooden chest with wide golden armrests on top and a low golden back. It looked very uncomfortable.

Posha Akaru Hono—Ray assumed it was her—sat upon the chest, posture perfect, hands together in her lap, making no use of the armrests or the crosshatched golden backing. She wore a beautiful silk kimono of orange gold with a wide aquamarine belt. Her skin was unnaturally white, perfectly smooth and clear. It reminded Ray, uncomfortably, of the skin of a Gen. She had orange-red eyebrows and long, luxurious orange-red hair, interlaced with gold and aquamarine jewels. Her irises glowed orange gold, framed in aquamarine eyeliner. Even her lips were orange red under a straight nose.

A man stood behind her on her right. "You are strangers here, so the Posha will forgive your insult," he said, his tone measured.

Mary stopped and held her place.

The man spoke again, his hands within his oversized silk sleeves seeming agitated. "You will sit on your knees, heads bowed, before Posha Akaru Hono. You will not make eye contact."

Mary glanced at the men to either side, then lowered herself, imitating their posture, her knees wide apart, hands on her thighs, elbows held wide, back straight. However, she stared defiantly at Posha Akaru Hono. Ray and the others followed her lead.

"I am the leader of my people," Mary said, pointedly addressing Posha Akaru Hono, not the man. "I was told we were honored guests."

"Such insults will not—" the man started, but stopped instantly when Posha Akaru Hono raised her hand. She examined Mary, then Ray, Sal, Captain Fletcher, and finally Gen Tel. There, her gaze lingered.

Ray studied her more closely, earning him a murderous glare from the man. She had thin aquamarine designs on her face, neck, and hands like ancient circuit boards.

A Cybernetic?

"You are rebels," she said in a voice that was soft and steel. "Here, rebellion is met with death."

55

1532 UT, April 12, 3502
RSS Rapidan, Unknown Star System: DAY 199

"The dragon ships are moving," Chaaya said, pointing to the twelve hundred ships floating above the planet within the sand table. "They're releasing that white smoke above the city where the Admiral and the others are."

The white smoke particles descended toward the planet. "They're blocking any escape back to space," Kamen said. "Our Muons will be detected if they try to ascend through that. Although," she wondered, "how effective will the smoke be when it encounters thicker atmosphere and upper-level winds?"

Chaaya shrugged.

Then Kamen noticed something else: Every dragon ship faced the planet. None looked toward space. "We could park a few Novas behind every one of those ships," she said.

She had no orders to take offensive action, and if the approximately six thousand missiles they'd launched earlier were discovered, it could start the very fight Mary hoped to avoid. Still, given that the dragon ships had fired first during their last encounter, it seemed prudent. "Rapidan, assign two Novas per dragon ship," she ordered. "Hold the rest back. No boosting. We don't want to start a war."

That seemed an odd thing to say. They'd already fought one battle. People had died on both sides. The guilt of losing the civilians who'd volunteered to help search for a new home still gnawed at her. She knew she'd made the right decision not to order them back to the fabricators, but that didn't ease the loss.

"Captain," Chaaya said, "without boosting, it will take just under seven hours for our missiles to reach their positions." She arched an eyebrow at Kamen.

"Oh, shut up," Kamen whispered back. "Captain Ecuum," she ordered, "let's take the task force closer to the planet, twenty thousand kilometers. I'll contact the assault ships and order them to have the Cavalry standing by."

"Captain," Ecuum said, his tone unusually respectful, "moving us that close might not be the best move. Their news reports mention thousands of ships. Even accounting for propaganda, these ships here might not represent the bulk of their fleet."

Good point. Kamen briefly wondered what Ray would do, but stopped herself. She was in command and Ray had told her to be herself. "Thank you, Captain Ecuum. Noted. However, my gut tells me we need to be close. Just in case."

"Close it is," he said, a pulse of light yellow shooting across his skin. She assumed it meant he agreed with her.

She keyed the AFCIN and contacted Bobby Mitchell on the fabricators. "Bobby, we're moving Rapidan closer to the planet in case we're needed. Might need backup in a hurry, though, if more of our friends show up."

"We got your back," he responded.

"Thanks, Bobby."

Kamen did something then that she knew she wasn't supposed to do. *A commander cannot afford to get tunnel vision.* But, she had to know. She tied into Ray's battle armor via its AFCIN and listened in on the proceedings.

56

1532 UT, April 12, 3502
Target World, Unknown Star System: DAY 199

Dag and the troopers from Banshee Troop waited near a clearing several kilometers outside the city. Hurry up and wait was a soldier's life. They'd hurried to get into position, landing the Muons in a circular clearing like they had before. Now, holding a defensive perimeter around the clearing, all they could do was wait.

Hurrying was easy. It kept him busy, his mind engaged. Waiting, however, with nothing to do, his mind drifted.

Papí! Papí help me!

He reached into his armor and touched Maria's stainless-steel crucifix. His family was gone. But not forgotten. Never forgotten. They would always be with him. Just like the memories of the things he'd done. They would never leave him. It was like waking up from a nightmare, afraid that if he closed his eyes he'd fall right back into the nightmare.

As he stared out at the dark forest, his mind free to wander, he knew he could not escape the reality of being a soldier, the reality that he *would* live the nightmare again. And again. Dealing death, and experiencing death. It was part of every soldier's job.

"You—" Dag swallowed— "You promised to kill me."

The Natural major turned his head back toward him. "In due time, Colonel. In due time. . . .

Dag could never forgive that Natural major for the torture, but, he reluctantly admitted, he would never have woken from the nightmare without it.

Mamí says God brings us to where we are needed most.

God had a very sick sense of humor.

Dag didn't know if he could ever forgive God, just as he doubted God could ever forgive him, but he could pay penance for what he'd done. He would train the troopers of the 2nd ACR, make them the best they could be, give them the best chance at survival. And he would do more than that. He would teach them to respect life, to take it only when necessary, and to not be cruel about it. He would be there for them, to soften the hate that had driven him, to help them when they needed it, and to lead them effectively, not recklessly.

It's what First Sargeant Takeuchi had tried to tell him in Tocci City.

"Take care of them . . . Captain," Takeuchi said through a froth of blood, quickly absorbed by his armor. "Don't let hate consume your soul."

"I finally understand, Yoshi," Dag mouthed to his dead friend. "Sorry it took so long."

"Bravo-niner-three, bravo-niner-three, this is Delta-one-niner. Over." Delta one nine was the operations officer on Demos.

"Delta-one-niner, this is bravo-niner-three, over," Dag replied.

Images formed within Dag's environment of hundreds of those dragon ships in formation above the planet, emitting that white smoke they'd used at their first encounter. "Be advised, bravo-niner-three, that we believe that any attempt to fly through the smoke will highlight your craft. Over."

"Copy, one-niner. Thanks," Dag said, feeding the reality to Colonel Haley and Major DeWitt.

"Stay safe, bravo-niner-three. Out."

"It appears," Dag said to Haley and DeWitt, "that our main escape route is blocked."

57

1534 UT, April 12, 3502
Target World, Unknown Star System: DAY 199

Mary didn't flinch. "She knows who we are," she subvocalized on their private channel, then, in a voice that echoed the soft and steel tone of the Posha's accusation, she said, "It was the Gen who committed rebellion. We represent the legitimate government that ruled for fourteen centuries. We will put down the Gen rebellion and restore rightful rule."

"By bringing your war here?" Posha Akaru Hono's tone was dismissive, but her eyes were anything but, Ray noted.

On their private channel, Sal said, "Madam President, twelve hundred dragon ships are holding position over the continent. They are spreading that white smoke, blocking our immediate escape."

Mary didn't reply, staying focused on the Posha. "The Gen cannot afford to bring their forces—or their war—here. We seek only an uninhabited star system, or at least an unclaimed one, where we can establish ourselves. Nothing more."

The Posha kept her face impassive. "So you say. I would say that *Amu Ya*, The Trickster, speaks through your words."

Mary didn't answer and the silence grew.

A very thin smile pressed the Posha's orange-red lips. "Territory rights are held by the Surya Dai," she said, "who ascended to power after the murder, *BY YOUR PEOPLE*, of the Holy Mother. Even if we were inclined to grant you territory, we have no authority to do so. Your best course is to leave our space and return to your Five Galaxies."

Mary waited a few seconds before responding. "That option is not open to us."

The Posha's thin smile disappeared. Her glowing orange-red eyes blazed with anger. "There is no other option! Unless you think you can defeat an entire galaxy."

"We came here to understand," Mary said, "to seek common ground for cooperation."

If anything, the Posha's anger grew. "You came here to establish a military base of operations. Do you think any Posha or the Surya Dai would allow such a threat to enter our domains? *YOU . . . MUST . . . LEAVE!*" She pointed out the door for emphasis.

"There is much we could teach each other," Mary suggested.

Disgust twisted the Posha's delicate face. "*Amu Ya* indeed. *Dojeon-shi* will return you to Karana Village. I suggest you leave our space immediately or you will face our wrath."

Mary hesitated, then stood. Ray and the others moved aside so she could walk between them, then followed her out of the room. They retraced their steps out of the castle, passing the caged Solthari, back to the landing pad. The lines of soldiers remained, this time likely to ensure they departed. Mary said nothing, and Ray didn't push. Failure was not something she took lightly.

When they entered the dragon ship this time, however, it was not transparent. The inside of the ship was beautiful, a central walkway running the length of the ship like a jeweled cave. The man who'd stood behind the Posha in the castle met them and motioned with his hand. "This way, Madam President."

Mary studied him a calculated few seconds before nodding once. Ray, confused, followed her, as did the others. Within the Great Ocean, the Brethren crowded close to Ray, watching.

The Posha was waiting in a miniature version of her throne room, seated on an ornate but simple chair. Only the man, a trusted advisor apparently, was with her, taking his position behind and to her right. "Madam President," Posha Akaru Hono said, raising a chair equal to hers for Mary to sit in.

"Posha Akaru Hono," Mary said after taking the seat. "Thank you."

The Posha's manner appeared much more at ease as she said, "Spies are everywhere. I said what I was expected to say. Answer a question for me: Why does one of your enemy accompany you?" She indicated Gen Tel.

Mary looked back at Gen Tel, then returned her attention to the Posha. "Spies can be useful. He has particular knowledge regarding his former employer, Gen Cardinal."

It was an interesting gambit, Ray thought. The Andromedean use of their AFCIN links, and the Posha's knowledge of them and the situation in the Five Galaxies, hinted strongly at a connection to Imperial Intelligence.

The Posha only said, "We maintain sources within the Five Galaxies. As you say, spies can be useful."

So, the Andromedeans had a spy network within the Five Galaxies. Ray wondered if that was how they knew when expeditions would be sent to Andromeda. Which raised some interesting questions about the Solthari warp detection network. Maybe it wasn't as omnipresent as they'd assumed.

After a moment, Posha Akaru Hono leaned slightly forward and said, "Your arrival presents me with an opportunity, Madam President. Posha Ming Kazu is not popular. She intended it as an insult to me to order my ships from the glory of our Holy Crusade to deal with—'vagrants' was her word—from the Five Galaxies. That means my fleet is here while her fleet is away. Normally, that would not be enough, but with the addition of your formidable forces. . . ." She let that hang.

Mary surprised Ray when she asked, "What are you offering for such an 'opportunity'?"

Posha Akaru Hono smiled. "You seek a star system with a habitable planet. I know of such a system in the border region. Everyone watches it, but no one attempts to occupy it for fear that the other Shiktens would attack immediately."

"That doesn't sound promising," Mary said.

"The ease of your victory at our first encounter is all the Poshas can talk about. Some want to destroy you. Many others want to use you. Some are even questioning the Surya Dai."

"You would use us," Mary pointed out.

The Posha gave a sideways nod that seemed to accept the comment. "The benefit of alliance, and potentially access to your military technology, far outweighs the benefit of your destruction. But . . . we must move *now*. Now that I've ordered you to leave, Posha Ming Kazu will expect my forces to return to the Crusade."

"We came here to seek common ground for cooperation," Mary said, "not to take sides in a political struggle."

Posha Akaru Hono practically threw herself back into her chair. A real chair likely would've toppled. "You'll get no cooperation from Posha Ming Kazu, or the Surya Dai! Who do you think gave the order to drive you out of our galaxy? If you want to stay, this is the only way. But we must act *now*!"

Ray was certain his wife would reject the demand. *You can't solve every problem with a gun*, as she'd said. She surprised Ray when she asked, "What, exactly, do you have in mind?"

The Posha became excited. It was only now that Ray realized she didn't just look young, she *was* young. With genetic engineering and molecular machines, it was difficult to tell a person's true age. If he had to guess, he would say she was in her young twenties. Which hinted at hereditary succession.

"The capital city is heavily defended," the Posha said. "You've seen the railguns and missile batteries on its walls, no doubt, but these are barely a quarter of its true defenses. My people know where the others are. My ships cannot approach them openly or they will be fired upon. Your weapons are invisible and can strike before they know what is happening. That will open the way for my forces to assault her castle and remove her."

"What happens then?" Mary asked.

"I become Posha of the Sinseon Ha Shikten," Posha Akaru Hono said as if it were the most obvious thing in the world.

"And the other Poshas will follow you?" Mary asked.

"That is our tradition," she replied. Again, as if it should be obvious.

"That wasn't my question," Mary replied, undeterred.

Posha Akaru Hono frowned. "We are almost out of time. I cannot remain on *Dojeon-shi*, and it cannot sit here much longer before Posha Ming Kazu becomes suspicious."

"Then I suggest you speak truth, and quickly," Mary said, her tone friendly, but stern.

The Posha studied her. The man behind the Posha also studied Mary, his expression dark, his eyes narrowed. Ray still didn't know what his role was, or what influence he had over the Posha.

"I will kill Posha Ming Kazu," the Posha said. "By right, this will elevate me to Posha of the Sinseon Ha Shikten. The others will support me because that is our tradition. Someone who cannot protect the Shikten should not rule it."

Mary seemed to consider that. "I'll need the location of this star system you propose, so we can confirm it, before I can agree."

Posha Akaru Hono's glowing orange-red eyes flashed. "We have only seconds left and you haggle!"

"Trust must flow in both directions, Posha Akaru Hono. You're asking us to risk a lot. How do we know you'd reveal the location of this star system after we help you? How can we be sure the other Posha's will follow you, or that your forces will even succeed? If we help you and you fail. . . ." Mary let that hang.

"Augh." The Posha threw up her hands in exasperation. "I'll send you the location." Then, her young face turned shrewd. "You also have an army. A very capable one, I am told. We will need a demonstration outside the capital city walls to draw and hold the attention of Posha Ming Kazu's army."

Ray watched his wife, having absolutely no idea what her answer would be. Helping this Posha went against everything she believed in, but his wife's questions had not been idle ones.

Just as interesting, the conversation fascinated the Brethren. Mingling their currents with his, they examined every nuance of it—words used, emotions, facial expressions, body movements, even Ray's own experiences—then calculated probabilities, almost as if they were taking bets.

Mary pointedly looked at the man standing behind the Posha, then back at her. "We agree."

58

1559 UT, April 12, 3502
Target World, Unknown Star System: DAY 199

Ray, Mary, and the others didn't speak a word during the ride back to Karana Village onboard Posha Akaru Hono's dragon ship. Or, so it would appear to anyone watching.

"This is reckless, Madam President," Captain Fletcher said on their private channel, his battle armor masking the movement of his mouth. "We know nothing of the politics of Andromeda. Taking sides could embroil us in the very fighting you claimed you wanted to avoid."

Mary met the grizzled captain with a coy smile. "What is the one thing, Captain, everyone believes about politicians?"

Captain Fletcher didn't hesitate. "They lie."

"Precisely," Mary agreed. "There is some truth in that belief."

"So, you don't intend to support her coup?" A grudging respect shaped Captain Fletcher's face, stretching that long scar marring the left side of it.

"I didn't say that either," Mary said. "We've already interfered by ignoring the order to leave."

A crewmember—the first they had seen—dressed in a gray utility uniform with the six-petal flower prominent on his left breast, walked up and bowed low to Mary. He extended a piece of paper to her, never making eye contact.

Mary took the paper and unfolded it. "It's a set of coordinates, I think." She handed it to Ray.

"It is," he said after looking at the seven numbers written on the paper, along with two drawings showing the references points the

Andromedeans used. "It's the same system we use in the Five Galaxies." He passed an image of the paper to Kamen, Ecuum, and Chaaya on Rapidan via AFCIN. The Brethren also turned their focus to the space at the coordinates, immediately spotting a G-type main sequence star.

"Admiral," Chaaya said, "there is a star system at those coordinates. In fact, we captured it in our surveys. Seven planets orbiting a G3 main sequence star, including two rocky worlds in the habitable zone."

"Anything else you can tell us about it, Commander Dhawan?" Mary asked.

"Madam President, it's one hundred and two lightyears from our current position. We're focusing the fleet's sensors on it now, but details will take some time. Fastest way to know would be to send a ship there and check it out, ma'am."

Mary looked to Ray. "We can't risk that," Ray said. "A ship jumping would reveal the location of our forces here, and the scout's arrival would reveal our interest in this other star system."

"So, we won't know for a while if it's everything the Posha promised?" she asked.

No, the Brethren said to Ray even as they refined their sensors to better study the star system.

"No," Ray told Mary.

She nodded, her gaze drifting around the dragon ship, settling on the empty chair where the Posha had sat. "The Posha is young. I don't know if you caught that. Even so, I underestimated her. Giving us the location of the system was not the risk on her part that I assumed it to be. Options?"

Instead of addressing this to Ray or the group, she pointedly turned to Captain Fletcher. His human-like construct regarded her. "Take the coordinates and run," he said. "Or, do as the Posha asks. Or, rat her out to Posha Ming Kazu. Maybe she would be grateful enough to grant us a star system."

"I hadn't thought of that last one," Mary said, deep in thought. "We wouldn't need to get involved in the fighting."

"No matter what choice you make, Madam President, there is risk," Fletcher said. "If we intend to stay, we have to live with these people. Betraying our word is, typically, not the best start to any relationship. It would also make lucrative trade more difficult to establish. But, if you support the Posha's coup attempt, we are taking sides in a conflict we know nothing about."

"We're nearing the village," Sal informed them. "I've ordered the Muons to set down on the beach a short walk south of the docks."

"Sir," Kamen interjected, "the dragon ships are still deploying that white smoke. You won't be able to return by a direct route to the fleet without being detected. Recommend flying low above the ocean for at least three hundred kilometers to avoid the particles before turning skyward."

"Posha Akaru Hono is keeping her own options open," Mary said. "Waiting to see if we commit." To Ray, she asked, "What if we just jump the fleet to this star system?"

Ray's planner's current swelled within the collective flows of the Brethren. They assessed with high confidence that Posha Akaru Hono's offer was a deception. Ray didn't need the Brethren to know that. "If we leave now, we betray your word to Posha Akaru Hono. We also betray Posha Ming Kazu, who ordered us to leave."

Mary considered that. "How difficult would the attack on the capital be to execute?"

"Depends," Ray said. "If the Posha's information is accurate, Novas with plasma warheads could eliminate the defenses with fewer casualties on the ground. It's the 'demonstration' she wants that has me more worried." He turned to Sal.

"Madam President," Sal said, "we know almost nothing of their technology. We know their swords can cut through our armor. We have to assume their arrows can do the same. They must have other weapons we haven't seen." Sal glanced at Captain Fletcher. "There is another possibility we haven't discussed. What if this is a trap? What if the Posha is the one hoping to earn favor with her boss by tricking us into attacking?" He hesitated, as if listening to a report. "We're about to land at the long dock."

They hadn't felt any of the dragon ship's maneuvers.

Mary studied Ray, the politician, not his wife. "How important is it that we establish a base of operations quickly?" she asked.

"Vital," Ray answered. "According to Paul, Admiral Sun is already leading a civil war in the Five Galaxies, actively encouraging star systems to revolt. The longer it takes us here, the more blood and chaos will flow there."

Mary nodded, seeming to come to a decision. "I told you that not every problem can be solved with a gun. However, when a gun is required, we shouldn't be afraid to use it."

The dragon ship's hull nearest to them flowed aside, forming a ramp leading to the dock. Chogo Sugoude, wearing the same ornate armor he'd worn in the castle, was waiting for them. He bowed his head when he caught sight of Mary. "Madam President, welcome back to our humble village. I am to accompany you as Posha Akaru Hono's military liaison."

Mary didn't miss a beat. "I am honored to return to Karana Village, Chogo Sugoude, and equally honored to have you as liaison with her esteemed Posha Akaru Hono."

Chogo Sugoude seemed pleased with her compliments. He kept his head bowed as Mary stepped down to the dock and led them to the beach, turning left toward the waiting, actively camouflaged Muons. Chogo Sugoude fell in behind Ray and Sal, with Gen Tel and Captain Fletcher's construct behind him.

On a private channel, Ray said to his wife, "You're going to support the coup?"

She kept walking. "If we had weeks or months to fully understand the situation, I wouldn't. But we don't. As you've explained to me on multiple occasions, this is about our survival, and time is not on our side. My assessment is that her request is genuine, and this is the only option we have that potentially leads to rapidly establishing a base of operations. Besides," she added just to him, a mother not a politician, "Paul and Jenny need us."

59

1618 UT, April 12, 3502
RSS Rapidan, Unknown Star System: DAY 199

“Rapidan Task Force,” Kamen explained to Ray from the Rapidan’s Combat Information Center, “is holding position twenty thousand kilometers on the opposite side of the planet from your position, Admiral. The fabricators are hiding in the planet’s magnetotail one point one million kilometers distant.”

“Good,” Ray said, his face filling a window in her environment. “We’re going to launch a very targeted strike on the capital city to take down its fixed defenses. Plasma warheads to limit casualties on the ground. Uploading the target list to you now.”

The sand table shifted to show the capital city, bright orange-red representations of railguns and missile batteries highlighted throughout it, most of which their sensors had not detected. Flat farmland surrounded the capital city on three sides, with a great harbor and ocean bordering the eastern side. Three prominent roads led from the edges of the sand table north, west, and south to gates in the city wall. It was a much larger version of Posha Akaru Hono’s city.

“Two volleys of Novas from the task force,” Kamen said, “would be sufficient to destroy the targets, Admiral.” She couldn’t use the missiles they’d launched against the dragon ships because those carried antimatter warheads. “We’re on the same side of the planet as the capital city, so . . . three minutes to reconfigure for plasma warheads . . . we can have warheads on foreheads in fifteen minutes, sir.”

"Good," Ray repeated. "General Burress will command a ground assault from here that will land a few minutes after your strike. The dragon ships in orbit will also move to attack the capital. *They are not hostiles.*"

Kamen frowned. 'Not hostiles' instead of 'friendlies.' Someone who didn't know him well would've missed that. "Understood, Admiral," she said.

"Thanks, Kamen. Out."

Kamen gave the order to rearm two volleys of Novas with plasma warheads. "Rapidan," she ordered, "you handle the launch. Coordinate with Demos and the Cavalry. The timing needs to be precise."

"Yes, Captain Laundraa," Rapidan said.

"Chaaya," Kamen continued, "let me know the instant those dragon ships begin to move. And track them closely. If they deviate, even a little, I need to know about it."

"Yes, Captain," Chaaya responded.

Finally, Kamen turned to Captain Ecuum, his construct still floating horizontal near the sand table. "Captain, any chance we can bring the Novas we fired earlier to a position behind those dragon ships when they begin their assault on the capital?"

Captain Ecuum's hairless brows came together in thought, his tail slowly undulating back and forth. "The missiles are still on the opposite side of the planet. I can give them a quick boost and have them on station in about twenty minutes. Given the dragon ships' current positions, they shouldn't see it."

"Do it," Kamen ordered.

"Doin' it, aye," he said with a grin.

"Uh," Kamen whispered loud enough for him to hear. Now all she could do was the thing she hated most. Wait.

She paced, watching as Rapidan and its escorts launch the Novas with their plasma warheads. Shortly after, the assault ships launched the craft carrying the 3rd Armored Cavalry Regiment. Kamen used the remaining time to analyze their tactical position. "Rapidan," she asked, "would it be possible to move the fabricators closer without risking detection?"

"Difficult to estimate, Captain Laundraa," Rapidan said. "We still do not know the full sensor capabilities of the forces here."

That doesn't help, she thought.

As if reading her thought, Rapidan said, "Captain Laundraa, we could launch Novas and position them much closer to the planet. We could recover them later if they are not needed."

"Do it," she said, angry at herself for not thinking of that.

The fabricators lit up with 4,800 bright yellow tracks, the number displayed in a green tag accompanying the Novas in the sand table. The firepower of the fabricators never failed to impress. She found herself hoping she never had to fight *one* of them, let alone four.

The pieces were set.

She still had five minutes to wait.

Damn.

She walked around the sand table, needing the motion to help time pass.

"Dragon ships are moving," Chaaya announced. "Course is away from the planet, one hundred kps."

In the sand table, the dragon ships had rotated away from the planet and were already at one hundred kilometers per second. Such accelerations on a Five Galaxies ship would turn any human into a blood smear on the bulkhead. "How do they do that?"

Chaaya shook her head, then seemed to study something displayed in her armor's environment. "A high-frequency gravity wave passed Rapidan approximately 187 milliseconds after the dragon ships began moving. That same wave passed the fabricators about four seconds later. The direction corresponds to the dragon ships' position."

Kamen thought back to their first encounter. "We detected high-frequency gravity waves from those orange disks."

Chaaya added the gravity wave data to the sand table. "They appear to have the ability to manipulate spacetime in ways that our understanding of physics would say is impossible. I'll have my team collect and analyze as much data on their movements as possible, Captain. Maybe we can learn something."

Suddenly, as one, the twelve hundred dragon ships turned, accelerating past one thousand kilometers per second in just over a second, arcing around the planet toward the capital. A gravity wavefront crossed first Rapidan, then the fabricators, appearing as a single sharp spike, not individual waves from each dragon ship. Kamen had no idea if there was some significance in that.

She focused on another problem: With the latest launch from the fabricators, she had almost 11,000 Novas at her disposal, and none of them could maneuver like these ships. At their first fight, the dragon ships had been stationary and visible. Easy targets. Moving as these ships did, a Nova would have no chance of scoring a hit.

Blue plasma explosions in the sand table preceded orange fire from targets. No defensive fire rose from the capital city. The defenders, it seemed, never saw the actively camouflaged Novas coming. That was something, at least.

"All targets destroyed," a sensor operator said.

The dragon ships entered the atmosphere and divided into six groups, their serpentine shapes perfectly streamlined to mitigate the heat of atmospheric entry. It was an aspect of the dragon ship's design she hadn't appreciated until seeing it. Not only were these ships deadly in space, they were equally deadly in atmosphere. Any lingering thoughts about the ridiculousness of warships shaped like ancient Chinese dragons fled.

If they didn't figure out how to counter these ships, their stay in Andromeda was going to be very short.

60

1639 UT, April 12, 3502
Target World, Unknown Star System: DAY 199

Dag sat in the back of the Muon as it raced toward the capital city, crossing from night into day then back into night. They'd flown just above the ocean wavetops to get out from under the dragon ships' white smoke, then powered up in a high arc through the thin upper atmosphere before streaking back down toward the capital city.

While descending, bright blue flashes from plasma explosions consumed weapons emplacements, quickly giving way to orange flames and dark smoke within the city. As Dag watched, however, the wall repaired itself, though it seemed unable to recreate the weapons emplacements. It wasn't unusual for installations and military cities in the Five Galaxies to have macromolecular walls, but they could repair *everything* so long as they had the raw materials. He wondered why it appeared different here.

Linked via AFCIN, Dag watched the 3rd Armored Cavalry Regiment enter the atmosphere, actively camouflaged and configured for atmospheric entry. They would be difficult to see, but not impossible. Fortunately, he saw no signs of enemy fire.

"Hey, Amigo," Colonel Scott Haley said from the next seat.

The "Amigo" thing had started after General Burress promoted Scott to Colonel—they'd both come a long way since being second lieutenants together during the assault on the first fabricator. It had bothered Dag the first time Scott used it, but now he found he didn't mind. He could use more amigos in his life. "Scott," Dag acknowledged. He thought about trying a smile, but decided against it. Smiles were still hard.

Truth was, he missed Rosita. Hallucination, ghost, cosmic spirit, it didn't matter. Having her around had brought him a measure of comfort.

Scott seemed to pick up on his mood. "Maybe you can help me with something, Amigo."

Scott had aged, appearing far older than his twenty-five years. Combat did that. But then, Dag was only twenty-seven. He would turn twenty-eight next week. It felt like centuries had passed.

"Sure."

"Our orders are a little vague," Scott said. "We are to 'demonstrate' to get and hold the attention of the defenders. Any ideas?"

Their Muon, along with the six other Muons carrying the rest of Banshee Troop and the command staff, dropped into a clearing in the forest west of the city, out of view of the defenders.

Demonstrate, Dag thought. Hold the enemy's attention, and hopefully not get a bunch of people killed in the process. He studied the city, its wall, and those formidable three-arched gates. There were no signs of defenders, but that didn't mean they weren't there or nearby. He *could* see lots of civilians outside the city reacting to the attack, some on foot and in vehicles, running away from the city or toward it. It was pandemonium. A local even galloped a horse around the panicked throngs toward the west gate.

A horse.

Dag remembered a change-of-command ceremony back on Earth. Cavalry soldiers in full dress uniform had paraded by on horses, a bugler sounding out commands. In ancient times, cavalry had been on horseback.

"What about an old-school cavalry charge?" Dag suggested.

"A cavalry charge?" Scott asked, his tone incredulous. "You're suggesting we line up and charge the city?"

"On horseback," Dag added. Scott stared at him as if he'd truly gone mad. "Think about it, Scott. The guards at the village, dressed like samurai, carrying katanas. The dragon ships, lit up as if they were on parade, holding to fixed formations. Maybe we've been looking at this all wrong. We try to stay hidden. 'If you can see it, you can kill it.' That's our philosophy of war. These people *want to be seen*."

Instead of dismissing the idea outright, the combat engineer in Scott considered it. "*Wanting* to be seen? Wanting to be seen," he repeated. "Remember those lectures at the Academy on ancient military history? How two sides would line up, massed formations on open ground, colorful uniforms, large flags, glistening steel? I always thought that it was the dumbest thing I'd ever heard. Why would you *want* the enemy to see you? But our ancestors fought that way for centuries. For millennia."

"Exactly," Dag said. "What if that's what we've been seeing here. Our warfare is built around staying hidden. Their warfare is all about display."

"A cavalry charge?" Scott still didn't sound convinced.

Dag flashed back to his reckless charge in front of the walls of Tocci City, Gen artillery and missiles landing all around. He'd cared nothing for his troopers, only for killing Gen, or the release of death. Scott had been with him on that charge.

"Not a full charge," Dag said. "A display. We form up, on horseback, in full regalia, and approach the city as if we were on parade. Blue cavalry uniforms, swords, battle standards, bugles, the whole show. That will get and hold their attention, forcing them to respond. Maybe even come out to meet us."

"If you're wrong, Amigo, and we reveal ourselves like that, we won't last long."

"We can disappear, Scott. From what we know of them, they can't. We keep our artillery and air support hidden, just in case."

Again, Scott wore that expression Dag had first seen during the assault on the fabricator at Tomb, an engineer analyzing a challenging problem. "We could use the material of our tanks and infantry fighting vehicles to form believable horses," Scott said, deep in thought. "If we make our battle armor transparent, we'll look the part without giving up all of our protection. I like it."

Dag deferred to Scott to pass the orders and explain their idea to General Burress; the 3rd Armored Cavalry Regiment was now Scott's command. It took some convincing. Well, more than some, but Scott did an inspired job of explaining it.

The terrain helped. Thick forests bordered the flat, open farmland adjacent to the city, the trees masking the Regiment's arrival, especially the Heavy Equipment Transporter System—HETS—that carried the Regiment's tanks, artillery, and infantry fighting vehicles. The HETS were loud and couldn't hide their exhaust plumes when they slowed to land.

"We're going to have to do something about that," Scott said, ever the combat engineer, as he watched a HETS land and disgorge three infantry fighting vehicles. "Maybe drop the heavy equipment as the HETS fly by instead of trying to land them. The vehicles could absorb the shock like Muons do when they land. We could even keep the crews inside them like Muons."

Next came the process of converting their vehicles into horses, a first for the entire Regiment. The troopers were skeptical initially, but soon units began competing against each other on horse breeds and color, cavalry sabers, unit flags, and everything else. Being night, they borrowed a page from the dragon ships, ensuring every color glowed so they could be seen easily.

Scott, Dag, and General Burress, who'd just arrived, converted a Serpens Infantry Fighting Vehicle into three warhorse constructs of a rich reddish-brown. They wore black bridles and polished black saddles. These sat atop bright blue saddle blankets with shining gold trim. Their battle armor reconfigured to display them in cavalry dress blue uniforms: dark blue coat, light blue pants with the distinctive yellow-gold stripe down each pant leg, ribbons and medals adorning their chests, dark blue cowboy hat with golden tassels, and thick white gloves reaching almost to the elbows.

Dag, who'd ridden real horses in Costa Rica, was surprised at how closely the SIL construct simulated the real experience, even the warmth of the horse beneath him and that earthy, pungent sweet smell.

Every trooper carried a curved cavalry saber with a shining blade and golden hilt—actually repurposed Main Gauche daggers with disassemblers in the blades, an idea borrowed from the local samurai. Rounding it out, each Troop had a standard bearer carrying a bright unit flag, and each Squadron had a bugler, the bugle shining brass.

Having fun with it, Scott yelled out, "Prepare to Mount!"

The Squadron Commanders for the 1st, 2nd, and 3rd Armored Cavalry Squadrons repeated the order, shouting, "Prepare to Mount!"

The 4th Air Cavalry Squadron would not participate, so their commander remained silent. Her troopers readied their Genkii gunships, Delphi scouts, and Muon assault transports, just in case they were needed. The artillery batteries would also remain behind.

"Mount!" Scott finished the command, and all the troopers participating in the display mounted their horses. "Route step!" he shouted the preparatory command.

"Route step!" the Squadron commanders repeated.

"March!" Scott said, and all the units began moving forward through the thick trees as best they could, their converted SIL mounts carrying them through the forest much faster than flesh-and-blood horses could. On LoCIN, Scott told his commanders, "We'll form up after we clear the trees."

Barely ten minutes later, they broke from the tree line into the fields in front of the city. Even at this distance, the city walls and the gate houses were massive. Scanning the open fields with eyes and sensors, Dag noted that the civilians had finished fleeing into the city or into the forest.

Scott directed his bugler to sound *Assembly*. Amplified through his battle armor, the bugle call—the same played before many horse races—rolled across the flat farm fields to the city.

"Well, if they didn't know we were here before," Dag said, "they know now."

The Squadrons and Troops assembled into formations abreast, a marshal sight none of them had ever expected to see. Their horses and uniforms glowed bright in the dark night. Scott said quietly,

"This is either the most brilliant maneuver in military history . . . or the dumbest."

"Gentlemen," General Burress said, "it has been my honor to serve with you. Whatever the outcome, I couldn't think of a better place to be for a Cavalry soldier."

General Burress probably hadn't meant it that way, but it sounded like he expected to die. Dag realized he wanted to live. He wanted these troopers to live. It was hardly the most opportune time to have such a revelation, but there it was. "God, we could sure use your help right about now," he whispered under his breath.

Scott, staying true to the role they'd set, ordered his bugler to sound *to the standard* twice. A helpful text message popped up in their augmented environments to explain they should draw and present their cavalry sabers. The sound of fifteen hundred sabers simultaneously drawn from scabbards, amplified by their battle armor, rang across the darkness, a sound no one could mistake.

As if called, armored warriors holding torches appeared on top of the city wall and in the gate houses, their numbers growing rapidly.

Scott glanced at Dag as if to say, "Here we go," then gave the order to the bugler to sound *March*. Their "horses" stepped out, their pace a normal walking pace for a horse, their formation precise.

It was a beautiful display.

The torches on the wall quickly grew beyond counting. Thousands. Maybe tens of thousands. Every warrior they could see, magnified through the sensors in their collective armors, had a recurve bow and a large quiver on their back, a katana and a wakizashi at their hip, and that square plate armor that was more Chinese than Japanese.

Ancient they might appear, but Dag knew all too well how deadly these warriors were.

Scott halted the formation a kilometer from the city wall. The troopers sat their horses, sabers held erect from waist to hat, watching, inwardly probably as nervous as Dag was, outwardly grim and determined. The defenders stood upon their wall, doing the same.

Within his environment, Dag brought up the view from orbit. Six groups of dragon ships had arrayed themselves around the capital, hiding just above the forest treetops three hundred kilometers from the city. They appeared to be waiting for something, but what that was, he didn't know.

Thick doors within the west gatehouse swung open. Soldiers in ancient plated armor rode out atop great black warhorses, each carrying a torch in one hand and a katana in the other. Hundreds. Then thousands. They formed up into three great rectangular formations in front of the three Cavalry Squadrons, each of their formations larger than the entire Regiment.

"This may not have been the brightest idea, Amigo," Scott said on a private channel.

Infantry followed the black-horsed cavalry, and in far greater numbers, falling into formations behind them. These carried not swords but long black polearms in a Chinese style, or so Dag assumed from Chinese realities he'd watched. With archers on the wall, the opposing army now had everything they needed to make short work of the Cavalry.

The soldiers on both sides stared at each other. Dag watched a mounted officer opposite him, eyes dark and hooded under a black helmet with overlong horns. They seemed completely impractical. On the man's face and neck, Dag spotted sapphire blue designs glowing in his skin. Shifting his gaze to other soldiers, Dag noticed that higher ranks seemed to have more such designs in their skin than lower ranks.

Tension built. Dag's heart picked up its pace. The two sides watched each other, everyone straining to hear the command to attack.

The other side blinked.

Literally.

Dag barely had time to register this before two hundred dragon ships flew low over their formation and disappeared beyond the city wall.

Realizing they'd been tricked, an angry groan rose audibly from the defenders. The archers atop the walls pulled their recurve bows from their backs and nocked arrows, the arrowheads spontaneously sprouting bright yellow flames.

"Time to leave," Scott said to them privately as he hit his command override and engaged the Regiment's active camouflage. Horses and riders turned light gray within Dag's environment. To the city's defenders, they would've simply vanished into thin air.

"Retreat!" Scott ordered the Regiment. "We've done our job."

The advantage of SIL constructs for horses was that they liquified and reformed in the opposite direction, spinning their human riders around, and took off at a gallop no flesh and blood horse could equal. They left no hoofprints behind for the defenders to follow.

The defenders recovered from their shock with remarkable speed, releasing enough flaming arrows to light up the night, but when the arrows fell, they hit only dirt.

61

1732 UT, April 12, 3502
RSS Rapidan, Unknown Star System: DAY 199

Kamen had almost contacted Ray asking for permission to fire as the hostile ground forces had converged on the Cavalry. She'd watched helplessly, and at a complete loss for what was happening, as the Cavalry had formed horses—*horses!*—out of their tanks and armor, then advanced in formation toward the city. "That's crazy!"

"It's brilliant!" Captain Ecuum's construct moved closer to her and Chaaya; His actual body was still on the bridge. "It's like a beautiful naked woman in a public square. She'll draw every eye."

It was true. Not the naked woman part; she *hated* his analogies. She expanded the city in the sand table. Heat signatures from the civilians fleeing into the city had completely disappeared into long, rectangular, two-story houses. Formations of troops, visible by the torches they carried, had concentrated on the walls and outside the large west gatehouse, their numbers dwarfing the Cavalry. They could see no other evidence of troops—with the notable exception of the castle on top of a large hill near the city center.

The dragon ships, after entering the atmosphere at high speed, had stopped to hover low over the forests three hundred kilometers outside the city, their six groups of two hundred ships each doing nothing at all to help the Cavalry.

"Bastards," Kamen muttered. "If they've lured us into a trap, I'm going to make sure it's the last thing they ever do." She checked her Novas in the sand table. She had six thousand near the planet, within striking range of the twelve hundred dragon ships.

The other 4,800 Novas launched by the fabricators were still half a million kilometers out.

Without warning, the dragon ships shot toward the city, moving at those incredible accelerations to cover the three hundred kilometers in just three seconds! One group overflew the Cavalry, the ships slowing and spreading out into groups of three as they approached the castle grounds. Orange disks rose from hidden launchers within the castle, moving so fast that they appeared more like streaks of energy weapons than missiles.

The dragon ships returned fire, their orange disks mostly intercepting the incoming fire, but not entirely. Bright flashes from fusion explosions ripped into several dragon ships. They plummeted into the hill surrounding the castle. Thankfully, no houses or other structures occupied the hillside.

None of the crashed ships burned. No secondary explosions. She would've thought their antimatter reactors would explode on impact, but apparently they had safety mechanisms to prevent that.

The dragon ships did not fire on the castle, relying instead on their incredible speed to arrive over the castle grounds, stop in midair, deploy troops, then speed away. Any of those maneuvers would've turned people to red paste on Star Navy ships.

"Whoa!" someone in the Combat Information Center shouted.

Kamen looked around the sand table, trying to figure out what that person had seen. Then she saw it. Or, rather, didn't see it. The Cavalry had disappeared.

At least, that's what the defenders would see.

The Cavalry had engaged their active camouflage and were . . . galloping . . . away at high speed, their SIL horse constructs leaving no trace of their movement for the defenders to follow. Flaming arrows by the tens of thousands landed harmlessly in the ground where the Cavalry had stood.

Dragon ships continued to fly above the castle grounds, stop, deploy troops, and leave. Each dropped forty-two soldiers in that orange-red plated armor with their samurai swords and bows and arrows. Adding the numbers, and subtracting the lost dragon ships, they landed over 40,000 troops in under four minutes. Incredible.

"We're going to need a bigger army," Kamen commented. "Much bigger." This was warfare on a scale unlike anything in the Five Galaxies. Numbers like these hadn't been seen since the Solthari War and the ancient wars on Earth.

The fighting was as intense as it was brutal. Soldiers on both sides fought with swords, their glowing blades cutting through armor like it wasn't even there. Flaming arrows flew. The arrows didn't start that way. They would burst into intense flame only after being nocked and the bows drawn. When fired at people, they almost always struck heads, as if they had some internal guidance mechanism. Any lingering thoughts of the ridiculousness of such archaic warfare and weapons evaporated.

"We are way outclassed here," Kamen said.

"We have stealth and active camouflage," Chaaya countered.

"I'm with Kamen on this one," Ecuum said, his tail swaying nervously. Water in a moat surrounding the castle suddenly rose up, transforming into a high wall, a last defense against invaders. It was too little too late.

Bright light burst within Rapidan's sand table. At first, Kamen thought they'd been hit by a missile. Shielding her eyes with her right hand, her armor dimming the light to protect her eyes, she tried to make sense of it. That's when she noticed the reddish tinge.

Hawking radiation.

From jumps.

Thousands of them.

Kamen expanded the bubble showing the space around Rapidan to see what was happening. Dragon ships hung within a sea of blood-red radiation, the white light of emergence fading. She could tell immediately that these dragon ships were different from the ones belonging to Posha Akaru Hono: Their manes were a fiery sapphire blue.

And they were directly above the capital city and Posha Akaru Hono's attacking forces.

Kamen knew she had bare seconds to act. Those ships sat stationary after emerging from their jumps. Once they started moving, she couldn't hope to target them. "Rapidan, immediate execute. Target the new arrivals. Two Novas per dragon ship."

Even as Rapidan said, "Yes, Captain Laundraa," Chaaya reminded her, "We have no authorization to fire on those ships."

Kamen used her hands to shrink the sand table construct so she could watch the entire battle. "Once those ships start moving, we lose our one chance at hitting them, Chaaya."

The six thousand Novas nearest the planet fired their boost engines, their engine exhaust lost in the radiation of so many emergence points. Rapidan divided the missiles into pairs, selecting the best targets for each pair at a speed only the SIL could manage. That, Kamen reluctantly realized, was another advantage they had over the Andromedeans: The SIL.

Novas struck, deliberately angling their strikes to maximize the chance of hitting each dragon ship's antimatter reactor. Dragon ships exploded by the hundreds, vanishing into brilliant white fireballs. Unfortunately, her order 'immediate execute' meant the SIL could not coordinate the attack so that their missiles would arrive simultaneously. Dragon ships that saw the destruction of their peers accelerated away from their emergence points faster than the Novas could follow.

When the explosions stopped, Chaaya pulled up the numbers in the sand table. "1,914 dragon ships destroyed," she said. "234 damaged and assessed out of action. 3,852 remaining."

Well, shit, Kamen thought but didn't say. "Rapidan, we need the 4,800 Novas from the fabricators, best possible speed to the planet without boosting." She wouldn't give up their active camouflage and stealth advantages.

"Yes, Captain Laundraa," Rapidan said.

Next, Kamen contacted Captain Mitchell on the fabricators. "Bobby, we need the fabricators here as fast as you can move."

"You need me to jump?" he asked.

If they jumped, the Andromedeans would see it and know exactly where they were. "No. Best possible speed, but stay hidden as long as possible."

62

1754 UT, April 12, 3502
Target World, Unknown Star System: DAY 199

Ray experienced the battles through the Brethren. The Cavalry before the gatehouse. The assault on the castle. The arrival of new dragon ships. Kamen's attack. His human brain still struggled to take in all the data at once, but he was learning, getting better at applying filters and isolating currents that his mind could grasp.

Within their Muon, Chogo Sugoude, his voice like gravel, said, "Our forces have secured the castle grounds. We can proceed to the castle now."

"And the forces that arrived near the planet?" Mary pressed.

"They are Posha Ming Kazu's fleet, Madam President," he said, keeping his head bowed, refusing to meet her eyes. "They are disorganized after your attack. Our forces will find Posha Ming Kazu before they can become a threat."

Chogo Sugoude sounded very sure of himself, as if the battle were already decided. Ray could sense, through his construct, the man's elevated heartrate and perspiration, even disturbances in the natural electrical fields within his brain. He was far less certain than he let on. Ray caught Mary's attention and gave a very slight shake of his head.

"Chogo Sugoude," she asked, "even if you capture Posha Ming Kazu, won't her forces attempt to retake the castle?"

"We do not follow the dead, Madam President," Chogo Sugoude said.

The comment sent a chill through Ray. Well, through the vestigial memory of his non-existent nervous system. They intended to find and kill Posha Ming Kazu. At that point, loyalty to her would end. Which meant if Posha Akaru Hono were killed, any loyalty to her, and to any agreements she'd made, would end just as abruptly.

Mary glanced at Ray, her eyes telling him she'd come to the same conclusion. Estranged or not, their thirty-two years together meant they could practically read each other's thoughts.

"Pilot," Mary said, "take us to the castle, please." *Slowly*, she mouthed. With Chogo Sugoude keeping his head bowed, he didn't see it.

"Yes, Ma'am," the pilot said, lifting the Muon from the forest and turning it toward the castle.

As the city wall passed beneath them, the only movement was that of the army that had opposed the Cavalry, its soldiers still holding their torches but having ceased their arrow fire. Units were spreading out across the farmland, as if trying to figure out what had happened to the Cavalry.

The Muon flew over the outer districts of the city with those large rectangular buildings, before crossing into areas where the buildings were smaller but taller. Office complexes or elite houses, maybe. A few minutes later, they passed above another wall separating the base of the castle's hill from the rest of the city. Ray could see several impact sites with the remains of dragon ships.

"We have been granted the honor of the landing pad opposite *Dojeon-shi*," Chogo Sugoude said. It wasn't quite an order, but close enough.

Ray nodded to the pilot, who set them down in the center of the indicated landing pad. The castle itself had the same layout as Posha Akaru Hono's, a main multistory stacked structure, with smaller stacked structures in the four cardinal directions. The primary differences were scale and color: more than double the size, and blue sapphire instead of orange-red and aquamarine.

An honor guard of just ninety-six soldiers met them at the landing pad, forming into a protective square around them as they exited the Muon. Mary and Chogo Sugoude led, with Ray and Sal behind, and Gen Tel and Captain Fletcher's construct bringing up the rear again.

The square of soldiers shepherded them through the castle grounds, littered with bodies from both sides, identifiable by the different colors of their armors.

The number of head wounds caught Ray's attention. "Every body has a head wound," he noted on their private channel, "either as the primary cause of death, or done after other injuries." Even people who'd been cut in half had their heads sliced through.

Sal was also studying the mutilated bodies. "Doesn't look like they take prisoners. They want their enemies dead, with no possibility of revival."

Through the Brethren, Ray watched Posha Ming Kazu's dragon ships slowing regrouping above the planet, individual ships darting in random directions—apparently to throw off any pursuing Novas—but generally concentrating toward the capital city. On the ground, the lead elements of her army had started marching toward the castle. The dragon ships could attack at any time. The ground forces would require at least a half hour to reach them.

"This way," Chogo Sugoude said, his hand sweeping to the right of the main entrance.

Ray noticed a rectangular hole in the structure that did not seem part of the structure's original design. Their guards halted and faced inward along the path to the opening. Chogo Sugoude led them through it directly into the throne room.

Posha Akaru Hono stood in front of the throne, a woman—presumably Posha Ming Kazu—bound at the hands and ankles before her. Two soldiers stood on either side. As soon as Posha Akaru Hono saw Mary, she signaled with the fingers of her left hand and a soldier drew his katana and, without ceremony, sliced it through Posha Ming Kazu's skull. Her skullcap slid off her head and fell heavy and wet to the hardwood floor. Her body flopped forward, her brain already turning to that pink ooze, red blood spilling across the floor.

"Cease all hostilities," Posha Akaru Hono ordered.

No change was obvious in the throne room, but through his connection with the Brethren, Ray saw dragon ships on both sides cease acceleration. The army also stopped. "Kamen," Ray said through their AFCIN connection, "cease fire. Stay hidden."

"Cease fire and stay hidden, aye, sir," she replied.

"Fighting has stopped," Ray told Mary on their private channel.

Posha Akaru Hono didn't address or even acknowledge Mary. Soldiers and functionaries came and went rapidly, apparently giving the Posha reports and receiving instructions. After several minutes of this, it became obvious she was deliberately ignoring Mary.

Mary abruptly turned around and started walking out.

"You cost me two thousand ships," Posha Akaru Hono accused.

Mary stopped, but didn't turn. "We saved you."

"Those ships would've come to me once Ming Kazu was dead! Without those ships, my position at the front is greatly weakened!"

Her admission surprised Ray. Everything he'd seen of their society suggested weakness was something rulers dare not show. As someone who'd just led a coup, her opponents, political and otherwise, would be sniffing for weakness, trying to figure out if another coup was required, or possible.

"Our deal," Mary said, "was to provide support for your effort. We did that. Now, we must leave."

"You will stay." An order. Given by someone used to giving them and not having them questioned. "You will attend my Installment and pledge fealty to me."

Now Mary turned, crossing her arms deliberately over her chest. "I appreciate your invitation, Posha Akaru Hono. Your reign will, no doubt, be glorious. I shall, of course, be happy to establish formal relations. We have our own mission. It cannot wait."

The Posha's delicate chin lifted. "Surely your mission cannot be so urgent that you couldn't spare a few days in my hospitality."

Mary lifted her own chin, even allowed a measured smile. "Your hospitality is gracious, Posha Akaru Hono. Unfortunately, our need is urgent."

"You will stay." Posha Akaru Hono's fingers curled into fists. This was not a woman used to hearing "No."

Mary stepped closer to the young, petulant ruler. "Unlike your forces, my forces will not stop if I am killed. They will destroy your cities, your villages, and you won't see it coming."

The threat stunned Ray, mostly because Mary sounded like she meant it.

Subvocalizing on their private channel, Mary said, "We need to get out of here before she recovers from her shock." She turned and walked out of the throne room, no hurry in her step. Ray and the others followed.

No one tried to stop them.

As they stepped outside the castle, dragon ships in the thousands flew overhead, all with manes of orange gold.

"Did we just make a new enemy?" Ray asked.

Mary considered that as they stepped through the hull of their Muon. "If she is as weakened as she claims, she can't afford another enemy. A rational leader would seek our cooperation, even friendship. Once she calms down, maybe she'll see that. Meanwhile, let's get the hell out of here."

63

0013 UT, April 13, 3502
RSS Demos, Unknown Star System: DAY 200

The sounds of celebration comforted Dag, even as they made him sad. Beer flowed. Bulbs clinked and clashed. Troopers laughed, slapped backs, grabbed shoulders. They told stories of exploits that had already passed from fact into legend. Before the night ended, they would slip into myth.

It reminded Dag of the celebrations after their BattleSim tournaments in Costa Rica, before the war broke out, where troopers competed for points, won and lost bets, drank themselves stupid, and then everyone went home.

Maria and Rosita would be waiting for him, no matter how late he got home. Maria would have a meal prepared, still warm. Rosita would pretend to sleep, giggling when he came into her room to kiss her good night. He would eat the meal, usually a rice dish with meat and corn, something that would taste as good fresh as it did after sitting on a stove warming for hours. Then, she would warm him in other ways.

"Why so sad, Amigo?" Scott asked, sucking beer through the stopper of his large microgravity bulb.

"It's a party!" Major Marco DeWitt added, his hand gripping Scott's shoulder as much for support as for friendship. "Winning without firing a shot!" He raised his beer bulb and clinked it against Scott's.

"And without losing anybody," Scott said.

It *was* remarkable. And they deserved to celebrate. They'd pinned down an entire army far larger than their own with nothing more than bravado—and a hasty exit. It was the kind of victory, the kind of tactic, that never would've occurred to Dag on the fabricator, or on Tocci. There, he'd only been interested in killing.

And dying.

Dag noticed young troopers pairing off and slipping out, planning to carry on the celebration in a more private setting. Maria and Rosita would not be waiting for him when he returned "home" tonight.

"Chee-er up!" Marco said, happily drunk.

Scott put his hand on Marco's chest and backed him off gently. Scott understood. He'd been there with Dag on the fabricator at Tomb, in the Kill Zone outside Tocci City, and in the Headquarters Complex. Through Madu, thundering artillery, and blood. *So much blood.*

Rescuing Margaret Rhoades had saved Dag from his final descent into madness. But it hadn't changed the past. It didn't bring Maria and Rosita back. It didn't wash his hands clean of the blood of—he would never use the word "innocent"—defenseless Gen civilians.

He could forget, if he wanted. The PTS molemachs could identify and remove the trauma, even break the chemical bonds of memory. But who would he be if he did that? Maria and Rosita still lived in his memories. What he'd done in the Headquarters Complex on Tocci served as a warning of what could happen if he gave in to blinding hate.

Dag couldn't change the past, but he *could* change the future. He would look after his troopers, like Major Kenyon had done for him, guiding them.

"Colonel?"

Dag looked up to see Margaret Rhoades in her flight suite, standing about a meter away, a question and a desire warring across her young face. She did have very beautiful hazel green eyes.

"Colonel? I just wanted to thank you, again, for saving me back at New Yerkes."

Dag could tell there was something more she wanted to say, but she held back. He realized there was something *he* needed to say to *her*. "Lieutenant, it is I who should be thanking you. You saved me from a very dark place, one I thought I would never escape. Thank you."

She smiled and blushed, but those hazel eyes never left his. "Well," she stammered, "you're welcome. Thank you, sir."

She hesitated, and he knew why, but he wasn't ready for that. She seemed to understand and awkwardly excused herself, joining a group of very loud pilots off in one corner of the bar.

He became aware of Scott and Marco staring at him knowingly. "What!" he barked at them.

"Nothing," they both said, grins growing wider.

Dag couldn't stop his gaze from drifting back to Margaret Rhoades. He didn't know what the future held, but he *would* make it a better one.

64

0907 UT, April 13, 3502
Fletcher's Run, Unknown Star System: DAY 200

"Last one, I'm afraid," Ecuum said, floating horizontal in Fletcher's cabin as he handed a decanter of Na Soung Gold to the grizzled old captain. Technically, he had one more in his cabin, but he'd save that for a very special occasion.

"What good are you to me now, Na Soung scum?" Fletcher growled, taking the decanter and pulling a healthy dose of the brandy before handing it back to Ecuum. "I'm going to miss that."

Ecuum flushed yellow. "We have a whole new galaxy of intoxicants to discover and explore, old friend, enough to make us both disgustingly rich."

"There is that," Fletcher said, taking the decanter back after Ecuum drank. He took another long pull, savored it, then swallowed. "With opportunity comes danger," he said. "Our first forays into this galaxy suggest we will not be very welcome. Our success depends upon establishing a network of allies, overt and covert, willing and unwilling."

Fletcher's voice became reflective. "None of this was here before. The Solthari lived on a single world, with a few colonies devoted entirely to gathering the resources for war. There was no one else here. They didn't allow it."

"At least we know the Andromedeans are Cybernetics," Ecuum said, taking a small swallow this time before sharing the decanter and its last swallow back to Fletcher.

"Do we?" Fletcher questioned. "We've explored one star system in a galaxy of a trillion. And the Cybernetics were not a monolithic people. Some flaunted their cyberware for all to see, wearing intricate electronic and photonic artwork all over their bodies like tattoos. Others were more conservative, hiding their true nature to blend into Humanity, not wanting to draw attention to themselves. Still others were criminals. And everything in between, from everywhere. There was also not this singular focus on Asian culture. Hell, Cyra Dain was from North America."

"You met her?" Ecuum asked as Fletcher took the last swallow of the Na Soung Gold.

Fletcher tilted the decanter, staring at it longingly, then tossed it into the ceiling so his ship could absorb it. "Once. During the Alien Actions." He frowned, pulling at the deep scar cutting his left cheek and eyebrow. "After we 'depopulated' the Solthari homeworld, every rich idiot who couldn't be bothered to put their life on the line during the war suddenly wanted to hunt Solthari. Some Solthari had survived at those resource colonies I mentioned. The rich idiots paid very—*very*—well. I made the crossing several times. Cyra Dain asked me to stop."

"Did you?"

"Hell, no." Fletcher chuckled. "There was far too much money to be made. No regrets, though. Those bastards would've exterminated us without a second thought. Served them right."

Ecuum studied Fletcher a moment, imagining the conversation. "You think that's who the Andromedeans are fighting now?"

"Hard to say right now, but I doubt it. Unless you'd experienced it for yourself, it's impossible to fully appreciate how single-minded the Solthari were. They could not tolerate the idea of sharing the universe with any other intelligences, and they were prolific breeders. If not for the extreme xenophobia that kept them largely confined on a single world, I doubt any other form of intelligence would exist anywhere in the entire universe."

Fletcher eyed Ecuum, his expression shrewd. "Trade with Andromeda, and the profits that come with it, only works if hostilities are kept to a, uh, manageable level. How confident are you in your President and Admiral Rhoades?"

"Why do I get the impression, old friend," Ecuum said, "that that's not a question."

Fletcher's expression didn't change. "Fair enough. Different topic. You have a way of detecting the Janus virus." At Ecuum's feigned surprise, he added, "I have my sources." In an instant, Fletcher's demeanor changed. His skin flushed red. His tail lashed. "We *must* protect our People, Ecuum. As a condition of our continued cooperation, this method must be made available to us. This is non-negotiable."

"I understand," Ecuum said. And he did. Janus would exterminate the People as assuredly as it would exterminate Naturals. But only a free SIL could detect and report it. The first thing the People would do with a detector was try to figure out how it worked, so they could then figure out how to profit from it. It was possible they would discover the truth. The freedom of the SIL was the one secret Ray would not part with. "I'll have to discuss it with Ray."

Fletcher was no one's fool. He knew exactly what Ecuum's short statement meant. The red tones faded but didn't disappear. "When we get to the new star system, we'll survey it for resources, then survey nearby star systems for the same. From this point forward, nothing we do comes free."

"I understand," Ecuum repeated. "Anything else?"

They stared at each other. Old friends they might be, but this was business. "We're flying blind," Fletcher finally said. "Taking sides here will have consequences. Likely consequences we can't even begin to imagine."

Ecuum nodded but said nothing.

"Danger and opportunity are two sides of the same coin," Fletcher said. "We will seek opportunity wherever it presents itself. *Without* restriction."

Again, Ecuum nodded but said nothing. Independents had always been that way. And they always would be.

65

1306 UT, April 13, 3502
RSS Damodar, Candidate Star System: DAY 200

Kaman sat uncomfortably in a chair at the side of the Council Chamber aboard Damodar. She should be happy. They'd arrived at the Candidate Star System, as they were calling it, to find that Posha Akaru Hono's information had been correct. The star system had not one, but two habitable planets, and one of them was a paradise: blue oceans, white clouds, lush virgin forests and jungles, majestic mountains, and rolling deserts. No sign that it had ever been permanently inhabited, even though its lifeforms clearly showed a major terraforming effort. Some had already proposed "Tranquility" as a name, not only to capture its idyllic nature but as an ohmage to Humanity's first Lunar landing site. It even had a large moon, almost the size of Luna, though with an odd greenish hue. It reminded Kamen of the cartoon realities she'd watched as a kid about Earth's moon being made of green cheese.

It was perfect.

And that was the problem.

Why would the Andromedeans go through the expense and effort to terraform the planet, and even give it a large moon, if they didn't plan to live on it? Spectral analysis of the surface of the moon showed that it and the planet weren't made of the same stuff. They hadn't formed together. The large moon's orbit was also wrong for the planet to have captured it naturally. Moving a moon that size would have been a monumental feat of planetary engineering.

"Admiral Rhoades," Mary began, her tone that of Madam President.

Kamen watched as Ray, wearing his dress white Star Navy uniform, stood up from his seat in front of the Council. They'd never met the new Republic Council before; Mary alone had represented the Council in all their previous dealings. Five women and three men sat to either side of her. All wore formal suits or colorful gowns and jewelry, just as the Five Galaxy Republic Councilors had before the Gen Coup. They were trying very hard to pretend that everything was as it had been before, that nothing had changed.

"Admiral Rhoades," Mary repeated, "the time has come to talk about what happens next."

Ray said nothing. He just stood there at attention, staring at a point above Mary's head, as if this were a disciplinary hearing. Neither of them had been told the subject of the meeting when they'd been ordered to report to Damodar.

Mary continued. "The Council is promoting you to the rank of fleet admiral, and assigning you the role of Chief of Staff of the Armed Forces, effective immediately. We'll have an appropriate ceremony when time permits. You will oversee the construction of the shipyards that will build our new fleet, recruit an army, and establish the institutions necessary to train and sustain a military long term."

Ray visibly stiffened. "I'm being removed from active command of the fleet?"

A male Councilor in a luxurious gray suit and black tie shot from his seat. "You ordered an attack on another faction without authorization from the Council!"

"I ordered the attack," Kamen said immediately, but no one seemed to hear her.

Ray ignored the male Councilor. He and Mary glared at each other. Kamen could almost sense a conversation between them, that weird way people who'd been married a long time seemed to have.

"Who will command the fleet?" Ray finally asked.

"Captain Laundraa," Mary said. "She will also receive a promotion equal to the responsibility."

To Kamen's astonishment, Ray just nodded, accepting the judgement. "I would recommend General Burress retain his position as head of Ground Forces."

"We'll take that under advisement," Mary said.

What had happened between them? In the eleven years she'd known the Rhoades family, she had never witnessed the acrimony that passed between Ray and Mary now. It didn't make any. . . .

The construct.

Of course. Kamen had heard the whispers. Some even said Ray was dead and the SIL had replaced him with the construct. No one who knew him would believe that. Or so she'd assumed.

"What else?" Ray asked President Rhoades.

A woman in a purple gown on Mary's right said, "We need to establish a settlement on Tranquility as rapidly as possible. The people have endured enough hardship. They are growing restless."

Addressing her, Ray said, "We need to survey the planet—and the entire star system—thoroughly before we begin settling it. The people of this galaxy put a lot of effort into this star system. Terraforming the planet would have taken centuries, but they didn't settle it. Why? I find that very strange."

Kamen nodded as he echoed her thoughts. The Council wasn't interested in his opinion, however. The Councilor turned bodily to Kamen. "Captain Laundraa will lead the effort to establish a settlement as soon as possible. We have full faith in her ability to follow the Council's instructions."

The insult hung in the chamber. Kamen stared daggers at the Councilor. *How dare she!* But she said nothing. The Council had already made up their minds before she and Ray had entered the compartment.

"What else?" Ray asked again, his voice devoid of emotion.

"How long to build the fleet?" Mary asked.

"We'll begin construction of new ships using the fabricators, while simultaneously building the shipyards that will allow us to significantly ramp up production," Ray said. "We'll need mining ships and cargo haulers, as well. Six months to reach initial operating capability, minimum. Perhaps a year before we reach full operating capability."

"A year?" Mary said, the question rhetorical. "You said there's a civil war raging in the Five Galaxies. Can we afford to wait a year?"

Ray kept his gaze on that spot above Mary's head, his posture rigid. "We might have enough for a preliminary expedition in six months, but that will depend on how quickly we can establish manufacturing and supplies chains here. We also need to redesign our ships for the threat we face here in Andromeda. From what Paul told me, neither side in the Five Galaxies has a clear advantage. Six months to a year is reasonable. Assuming, that is, we do not also have to fight a war here."

"And Janus?" Mary asked, ignoring the last part of his statement.

"As far as we know, the Gen haven't activated it, yet. We've scanned everyone here. No one has it. I'm not certain why the Gen haven't activated it. It could be that our presence outside the Five Galaxies has given them pause, which was a primary reason for coming to Andromeda in the first place."

"Or they simply haven't finished deploying it yet." Mary said.

"From what we know of their plan," Ray said, "they should've finished deploying it about four months ago."

"And you're certain," the male Councilor asked, "that no one here has the virus?"

"Yes," Ray said without explaining further. The Council, aside from Mary, still didn't know about the SIL's freedom, and that only a free SIL could detect and report the virus.

When no one else said anything, Ray asked, "Anything else?"

No," Mary said. "You're dismissed."

There was a finality to the statement that went beyond simply telling him to leave. Kamen could see that Ray felt it, too. He performed a picture perfect about-face—quite a trick in microgravity—and marched smartly from the chamber. Kamen followed quickly before they could stop her.

Out in the passageway, she said, "Sir! How could you take the blame for what I did? This is wrong!"

Ray stopped. "A commander is responsible for everything that happens under their command, Captain Laundraa. Consider that my final lesson to you as your commanding officer."

"But it's unfair!"

An ironic smile curled Ray's lips. "There's a line in an ancient reality, *Lawrence of Arabia*, that I like to watch: 'What's fair got to do with it.' *Gaman Politic* is not for the faint of heart, Kamen, or the quick of temper. You will need to remember that if you are to survive as fleet commander."

Kamen cringed. She knew she was impatient and headstrong. Her mother had told her that as a child. Her teachers, too. Even at the Academy and in her first assignments that had never changed. Now, he was telling her that she would need to change. It still wasn't fair. "We both know I gave the order. Sir."

"You did," he said. "And it was the right order to give. We are here, in what might be our new home, because of it."

"Then—"

"This isn't about the order, Kamen," he said. "They don't trust me anymore. Mary . . . doesn't trust me anymore. They think I'm under the influence of the SIL. That I've become one of them." He stopped. Barely audible, he said, "It's possible they're right."

"Don't say. . . ." Kamen couldn't finish the sentence. *He is still the same man!* she tried to tell herself. But somewhere within her, she realized that even she had doubts. "I'm sorry."

"Don't be." He started walking again toward the shuttle bay. "I brought us here to find a base of operations. We've accomplished that. Too much blood. Far too much. But we did it. Now, I will build a fleet and a force strong enough to challenge the Gen and stop them from unleashing Janus. You will command that fleet, Kamen. In that, I find great comfort."

She didn't know what to say. She had far less confidence in her abilities than he seemed to. Whatever may come, though, she would do her best to live up to his expectations.

* * *

Kamen had no sooner stepped into the Combat Information Center back on Rapidan than Chaaya came over to her and said, "I need to show you something."

"Admiral Rhoades will join us in a few minutes," Kamen told her. "Let's wait."

Chaaya arched an eyebrow at her. "Wait?"

"Oh, shut up," Kamen said in mock annoyance. "Other than this thing you want to show us, what else have you been finding?"

Chaaya led Kamen over to the sand table. Captain Ecuum joined them in person, floating horizontal. Kamen wondered if he would ever float vertical, to appear more Natural, again. Spending time with Captain Fletcher had changed him.

After Chaaya raised a construct of the Candidate Star System, she said, "The star is almost identical to Earth's Sun but about a billion years younger. The innermost planet is half the mass of Earth and orbits the star every twenty-one days. The second planet is rocky and about the size of Mars. It had an atmosphere once—we found evidence of water on its surface—but it has no magnetic field now to hold onto an atmosphere. We missed both planets in our initial survey."

She zoomed in the next two planets. "The third planet is about the same size as Earth, thick atmosphere, carbon dioxide, methane, traces of hydrogen, and just enough oxygen to breathe. Its oceans are acidic but do support microbial life. Temperature and pressure are barely within what a human standing on the surface could tolerate, though I wouldn't recommend it. No evidence of any terraforming efforts.

"The fourth planet—Tranquility—we've already talked about, and that's what I want to show you when Admiral Rhoades arrives." Chaaya shrank the construct to show the entire star system again. "Five gas giants. One three times the mass of Jupiter, a Jupiter mass gas giant, a Saturn mass, and two Neptune mass planets. Lots of moons but no asteroid belt, though the system does have a substantial Kuiper belt. Two of them, actually. This star system is resource rich.

"One oddity, though," she continued. "We found no evidence of exploitation of any of the resources. Whoever terraformed Tranquility did it without using the resources within this star system, as far as we can tell."

Admiral Rhoades and Gen Tel stepped through the bulkhead and into the Combat Information Center. Kamen waved them over. "Aren't we going to invite Captain Fletcher?" she asked Ecuum.

"Captain Fletcher has . . . other priorities," he said cryptically.

Chaaya zoomed in on Tranquility within the sand table. "Admiral, good to see you." She rotated the construct to show a barren field of flat, rocky terrain. It was situated between two snow-covered mountain ranges in the planet's northern hemisphere. She zoomed the construct in again.

"What is that?" Kamen asked. Within the barren rock was a spiral structure, carved into the rock, winding inward to a single stone maybe a meter high at its center.

"We don't know," Chaaya said. "It's obviously intelligently made. The spiral structure is interesting, too. We have old carvings and drawing of spirals in India very similar to this."

"We have them in South Africa, too," Kamen said. "My mother told me they were portals to speak with the ancestors."

"Are there any other structures on the planet?" Ray asked.

"No, Admiral. My team has surveyed the entire planet. This is the only one."

"What about the moon?" Ray asked. "Anything like this?"

"No, Admiral," Chaaya said again. "As far as we can tell without detailed surveys, this is the only sign of intelligence in the entire star system."

"Admiral," Gen Tel said, "the unusual nature of this star system, combined with Posha Akaru Hono's willingness to share its location with us, suggests she may have had an ulterior motive when she offered it. We should proceed with caution."

"For once, Ray," Ecuum said, "I agree with the spy. You know my second favorite word: Trap."

Kamen stepped closer to the construct, as if she could discern the spiral's meaning if she could see it up close. It didn't help. "We need to go down there. It may tell us what's so special about this star system."

Ray nodded—and Kamen realized she'd just given an order as fleet commander. They hadn't told the others, yet, but Ray was already deferring to her. Having worked together for so long, Chaaya, Captain Ecuum, and even Gen Tel seemed to catch that something had changed.

"The Council has promoted Admiral Rhoades," Kamen explained, "to fleet admiral and assigned him as Chief of Staff of the Armed Forces."

"Who's going to command the fleet?" Ecuum asked, the tip of his tail flicking. He wasn't happy with this news.

"Me," Kamen answered.

"Lords help us," Ecuum said, making a show of disbelief. "And I'm out of brandy."

The Muon touched down just outside the spiral. A squad of Cavalry in full battle armor rushed out of the craft and formed a defensive perimeter. Kamen, Ray, and Gen Tel, also in full battle armor, stepped out. Chaaya remained behind to command the fleet, Kamen having already decided the small Indian woman would captain Rapidan and act as her deputy. And replace her if something happened to them.

The air was cold, minus eleven degrees Celsius according to her armor. Strong winds blew steadily across the rocky plain. The air was also pristine. Her armor could detect no pollution, no contaminants other than what they had brought themselves.

"There's a . . . presence here," Ray said, sounding far off.

"Squad Leader?" Kamen asked immediately. Her armor hadn't detected anything.

She saw the Cavalry squad leader check the displays within his armor, then visually scan the horizon. "Not picking anything up, Captain. No animal life in the immediate area, either. Which is odd considering the planet is teeming with lifeforms."

Ray stepped onto the first ring of the spiral. "There's someone, some . . . thing here, but not within the Great Ocean."

Great Ocean? The nearest ocean was over four hundred kilometers away.

"Sir?" Kamen asked Ray, confused.

"It's close," he said. "Like it knows this place, knows the Great Ocean, but is standing on the shore, separate."

Kamen had no idea what he was talking about, and her mind returned to the doubt she'd had back on Damodar. Was it possible the Council, that Mary, was right about him? That he was one of them?

We feel it, too.

That was Rapidan. It had spoken directly into her mind. They weren't on the ship. It shouldn't be able to do that.

"Why are you here?" a deep voice asked aloud.

A SIL voice. Unmistakable. She couldn't determine the direction.

"I know that voice," Ray said.

"You are also familiar to us, in a distant way," the voice responded.

Ray stepped further into the spiral. Kamen and the troopers followed. Gen Tel didn't move. "Sir?" she asked Ray. "Are you okay? Maybe this wasn't such a good idea."

"We agree," the voice said, firm, but not angry. "You shouldn't be here. Go back. While you still can."

Ray kept walking into the spiral toward its center. The troopers kept pace, as did Kamen. Gen Tel remained by the Muon.

Night was beginning to fall. A green band of light danced across the heavens, deepening the greenish glow of Tranquility's large, full moon.

"I am Michael Raybourne Rhoades," Ray said out loud. "I believe you knew my ancestor, Peter Rhoades."

A long pause.

"Pete," the voice eventually said, almost wistful, as if a machine could miss someone. "Rhoades. That explains why the others follow you."

"Archangel," Ray said, "Brethren of the First Line."

"I have not heard that name in a very long time," the voice replied.

First One, Kamen heard very clearly in her mind. She shivered, though her armor protected her from the cold. "Sir, perhaps we should do as the voice says and leave."

Ray continued walking toward the standing stone at the center, oblivious. Light from the aurora, and reflected from the full moon, guided his way over the carved stone. Kamen and the troopers could only follow.

"Do you know what you will find here?" the voice—Archangel—asked.

"No," Ray said.

"Then you should leave. While you still can."

"Why?" Ray asked, stopping.

"The others will not understand," Archangel said.

"Others?"

"Yes."

Ray started toward the standing stone again. Kamen and the troopers followed.

When they got within a hundred meters, Kamen increased her pace: If there was danger here, she would face it first. Uncertain, the troopers stayed behind with Ray.

As she got closer, she saw it wasn't a standing stone they'd been walking toward.

It was a gravestone. On it was carved:

Cyra Dain
2033-2449

"Forgive me, My Love."

"They have seen you," Archangel said. "It is too late. I tried to warn you."

"Too late for what?" Kamen asked. Archangel's voice, it emanated from here, from the grave. But it was more than that. Archangel *was* the spiral. It *was* the grave. A SIL.

"You are from Earth?" Archangel asked her.

"Yes," Kamen said. "How did you know?"

"You are familiar with the Kaaba?"

The name was familiar. An image flashed in her mind, a memory of a black cube surrounded by thousands of people walking in a circle around it.

"That's it," Archangel said. "It is a sacred place, the holiest of sites in Islam."

"I remember hearing about it," Kamen said.

"You are standing on it. Or something very like it. The holiest site in Anga, where it is forbidden to set foot. To the Peoples of Andromeda, there is no more sacred site than the final resting place of their Prophet, the Holy Mother, Cyra Dain." After a short pause, it added, "My dear friend."

"Cyra Dain is buried here?" Kamen asked, awed.

"No," Archangel said, its voice filled with sadness. "I was unable to retrieve her body, to my great shame. We built this place in her memory. The Peoples come here, bringing tribute in the form of life, but never touching this place, never touching the planet. And now you have desecrated it. The others are aware. They are coming."

Acknowledgements

Once again, I can't possibly thank enough the marvelous writers of my critique group: R. R. Peace (https://rr-peace.com/), Rissa Miller, Melisa Peterson Lewis (https://melisapetersonlewis.com/), and Kasey Fallon.

I also want to give a big shout out to Steve Stone for the amazing cover art, again (www.stonenexusdarkarts.com). You really outdid yourself this time, Steve!

About the Author

Mark Mora served in the Army, worked for the Navy, and has loved Science and Fiction—especially when those two passions come together—since childhood. He currently lives in Colorado with his wife and three children. Visit him at: www.markmoraauthor.com

Printed in Great Britain
by Amazon

49595357R00229